"I'd like you to try my grandsons first."

"*Try* them? How?" said the bewildered Jenny.

"In bed. For sex. To help you know which is the right one for you to marry."

Jenny looked shocked. "Si, you don't just press a button!"

"You'll know, Jenny," he insisted. "You must make sure the sex part is right. And that there is love. And that, whoever he is, he is not after your money. Make certain of those three things. Before you marry."

"*Si!*"

"It'll work out. If you do as I advise. And don't waste time. You're a passionate creature, Jenny. Make love to one of my grandsons the day after I die, if you can! I want to leave you knowing that you have a program mapped out and will follow it."

"It sounds so——"

"Cold-blooded. Perhaps. But sensible, Jenny, my beloved. When the time comes, you'll fall in love. And the sooner the better."

There was such determination in his voice that she knew she must bow to his wishes. "Of course, Si. I will do as you say."

Also by
Francesca Greer

First Fire

Published by
WARNER BOOKS

THE
SECOND
SUNRISE

by Francesca Greer

WARNER BOOKS

A Warner Communications Company

WARNER BOOKS EDITION

Cover art by Elaine Duillo

Warner Books, Inc., 75 Rockefeller Plaza, New York, N.Y. 10019

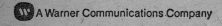 A Warner Communications Company

Printed in the United States of America

First Printing: February, 1981

10 9 8 7 6 5 4 3 2 1

For all my cousins

Contents

Part I
THE REQUEST

1

Jenny had never felt so miserable. Pale, tearless, wearing only a soft green robe, she wandered along the long wall of her dressing room, sliding open mirrored door after mirrored door, gazing within, drifting on to the next. Nothing. There seemed to be not one garment among the dozens that she could bring herself to put on for Si's funeral.

Si, darling husband Si. Sweet, old Si, who had just celebrated his eighty-seventh birthday. She felt that twist at her heart again, wished for tears, but there were none. There was only the sadness, the grief, the emptiness.

She slid open another door. Here hung dresses and silken suits in various shades of green—from the palest olive to the softest, coolest jade. And in the next section, hung every shade of gray. There were no bright colors. No black. Only green and gray.

She started down the line again, dimly aware of her reflection in the mirrors, her waist-length, burning-red hair brushing softly against her back. A lock had fallen across her cheek and she noted, not caring, that it looked like a brand of fire against the delicately tanned alabaster of her skin.

It was incredible to her that she was a widow at twenty. That, except for the maid Flo, Jenny Townsend was now alone in a splendid penthouse, from which she could gaze out across the endless blue of the Atlantic in one direction, and over the panorama of Hollywood, Florida in the other directions.

Her home had been heaven-on-earth, but now she had no joy in it. Without Si, she doubted she would ever feel joy again.

She moved to a closet filled with greens, remained there, gazed at them blindly, seeing only the past. Si, old enough to be her great-grandfather, was responsible for every good thing in her life. Had it not been for him, she could never have known all this wealth.

She had started out life as a homely, red-haired, newborn baby left, blanket-wrapped, in a church pew. The Sisters found her, and she was brought to Townsend Orphanage and put up for adoption.

She was so skinny and pale, her hair so shockingly red, her gray eyes so big and wanting in her very plain little face, that never did any of the ladies and gentlemen to whom she was offered take her home with them. Instead, they chose blond, blue-eyed boys and girls.

Thus Jenny grew, and no one noticed that she was changing, that her features had emerged and were perfect, that her lips had become vivid, and that when she smiled, which was as often as circumstances permitted, she was beautiful.

The change had begun when she was fourteen and by eighteen she was a striking young woman. It was then that Si Townsend first saw her.

For days the orphanage had been scrubbed, waxed, polished, in preparation for his visit. It wasn't needed, Jenny thought, as she rubbed brass and crept along corridors on hands and knees, carefully spreading wax. The orphanage always shone.

As she worked, she thought about leaving the orphanage. Now that she was a grown woman she'd be expected to go out into the world. The thought terrified her. What would she do? The orphanage was the only world she had ever known, and though the thought of having her freedom excited her, it scared her too.

She thought about Mr. Townsend, her benefactor. It was odd that she would finally meet him, just before leaving the orphanage forever.

She already knew a lot about him. From the Sisters, she had learned that he was the head of a great empire, the owner of farming lands and citrus groves, of grocery chains and banks and department stores and countless other enterprises. She imagined he must be a very great man indeed to donate so much of his money to orphaned children.

On the day he was scheduled to arrive the boys wore their gray suits and the girls their best gray dresses. Jenny's was of cotton and matched the gray of her eyes. Her hair, braided into a coronet, burned like fire and her lips, ready to quiver into a smile, glowed with natural color.

It was a glorious September morning, and the children, young and old, lined up in the front yard to greet him as he stepped from his silver limousine. To Jenny, he might have been a knight dismounting from his white horse. Her first sight of him took her breath away.

He was very tall and lithe with snow white hair and dazzling blue eyes. She'd never dreamed a man could be so old, yet so erect, so handsome. And with such a saintly look. His voice, as he spoke to Sister Marie Theresa and Sister Mary Martha, was smooth and pleasant.

"I commend you," he told the Sisters. "The children look so well tended."

As he spoke, he moved his gaze over the orphans, and Jenny noticed his eyes were kind, his thin, colorless lips gentle. Her heart warmed and ached. Why, oh why, hadn't she been fortunate enough to have been adopted by a man like this one?

Then his gaze met her own. To Jenny's embarrassment, he stared at her, locking her eyes with his for a long moment. A small, natural smile curved her lips, and it seemed to her that he tensed. Abruptly, he turned back to the Sisters and allowed them to lead him into the orphanage. After a tour of the childrens' quarters, and a quick luncheon, he departed.

Three days later, Jenny was told to go to Sister Marie Theresa's office, and she hastened there, her gray skirt swirling as she moved. She was curious about the reason for the summons, but not alarmed. She'd observed all rules, discharged all duties. Probably the good Sister wanted to discuss her upcoming job in the outside world, to give her some advice.

She tapped on the door.

"Come in," a man's voice called.

Puzzled, she entered. She closed the door, looked up.

Standing before her was Mr. Si Townsend. He was alone.

"Good afternoon, sir," Jenny murmured.

"Sit down, my dear. I have much to say."

She sat on the edge of a chair, conscious of the polished, bare look of the room, the desk with its many drawers, the table, which held a vase with one rose in it, the straight, leather-seated chairs. She waited, eyes lifted to him.

He sat in the desk chair, facing her.

"I've discussed this with the Sisters," he began. "They don't really approve, I must tell you that, but they don't forbid either." Jenny's hands twisted nervously in her lap as he paused, then continued.

"I've been a widower for many years, Jenny. I loved my wife and never wanted anyone in her place. But three days ago, when I came here and saw you—" He broke off, held her gaze, and she watched utter sadness come over him.

"I . . . don't understand, sir," she faltered.

"Please. Don't call me 'sir.' Si is my name. I'd be honored to hear it from your lips. Please. Now."

Dazed, she obliged him. "Very well. 'Si.' The honor is mine, too." She hadn't known she was going to say

14

more than his name, but, seeing his smile, was happy that she had. Besides, she'd meant it.

He was so very kind. And saintly. That word kept coming to her. He was an old man, grown in gentleness and goodness until surely he equaled even the holy Sisters.

"Jenny," he continued, "I'm eighty-four years old. I could be your great-grandfather. Yet the moment I saw you, I fell in love with you. As suddenly and thoroughly as a man of twenty-five."

Though she'd been trained never to do so, Jenny stared.

He gestured, let his hand fall. "I know, dear Jenny. You're shocked, and rightly so. It's impossible for you to respond to me in the same manner. But I have an honest proposition to make which could be to your benefit in every sense. Will you listen?"

Numbly, she inclined her head.

"I want to make you my wife, though I'm past the age when I can, physically, be a husband to you. For myself, I want the privilege of loving you, of having you bear my name. I desire your friendship and companionship until the day I die. I have a rare and terminal heart ailment which even the new methods—the time shouldn't be long. I want to fill it with you, your presence, your beauty. At the end, not so much as a reward, but as your just due, I will leave you ten million dollars."

Heart beating fast, she stared on.

"You don't refuse instantly, then."

She shook her head, mind in a whirl. She was so stunned she could hardly breathe. She liked him; she knew the liking could grow to friendship. But she had no idea how to respond.

Very gently he asked, "Are you a virgin, Jenny?"

She nodded.

"You'll remain one, married to me. Do you need time to think, to discuss it with the Sisters?"

Suddenly, for no reason except that she found herself trusting and wanting to please him, she made her decision. "You've offered me the world," she said, "and

15

I—I'm so dazzled I'll take it. And give you everything you want in return."

Then she stood up, reached across the big oak desk and lifted his hand in her small white one. Bending slightly, she brushed it with a kiss. She wanted only to reassure him, to seal their bargain, yet in that moment, with that kiss, affection was born in her.

The next two days were a blur of excitement and anticipation. Si took her to the best stores in Florida to furnish a new wardrobe. He loved watching her parade the clothes before him, giggling with girlish enthusiasm. He helped her with her choices and was quite insistent upon the colors.

"Your beauty is so blinding," he explained, "that you must only wear muted colors. Otherwise, you'd look garish. You'll wear only greens, some with degrees of gray to reflect your eyes, and you'll wear all shades of gray, which will do full credit to them. No jewelry except a platinum wedding band and watch."

"You sound like an artist," Jenny breathed with admiration.

"That's what I wanted to be. Then business intervened, money piled up, had to be invested, and here I am, too rich, too old, and so much in love it's both torture and peace."

They married quietly, Jenny in green so pale it was almost white, Si erect and handsome in a suit as white as his hair. They sailed on his yacht, *The Louisa,* to Nassau and Freeport for their honeymoon. At night he held her in his still strong arms, stroked her brow, her hair, her face, her neck, kissed her; and she, liking the tenderness, the gentle loving, kissed him in return. And stroked his hair and kissed it.

When they returned, he bought her the penthouse in Hollywood and had it decorated in muted greens, accented with off-white and touches of gray. He took her dining and to the races, and when she developed a passion for greyhound racing, tried to buy the Hollywood Greyhound Track for her. That failing, he had two kennels with runways built in the penthouse garden and bought her two greyhounds, which she kept there for a while, petting and playing with them, later taking them to a training kennel so they could learn to race.

A month after marriage, in bed with her in his arms, Si mentioned her future. "I want you to marry again, my darling," he said. "Within six months of my ... leaving you."

"Si! I never *want* to marry again! After you, after the wonderful life we have together, there will be no one else for me—"

"I know you have deep affection for me, sweetheart. But you're young; you'll still be young—later. It's vital that you fill your life with a young husband. And children. A man not after your fortune. One you already know, I hope."

"I don't know any men but your grandsons—"

"Precisely, my dear. When you choose a husband, I'd like for you to give first consideration to Simon III and Rolf and David."

"But I'm their stepgrandmother!"

"They're all half in love with you, Jenny."

"They're not! They disapproved our marriage! They think—"

"Think what, sweetheart?"

"That I'm a hussy! That I married you for your money!"

"So?"

"When they look at me they see a red-haired baby left in a blanket—"

"On a church pew, Jenny. Clean and warm."

"So ugly that nobody would adopt me—"

"Until I finally saw you, fell in love with you, no homely little girl then, and had to win you for my last days."

"Si! Oh Si, don't talk that way! It breaks my heart!"

"Then I'll say no more now. You've opened the gates of Heaven to me, Jenny."

But another night, after asking her permission, saying that he must speak of her future, he again broached the subject. "The reason I want you to consider my grandsons is sound, my darling. If one of them wins you, it won't be because he's after your money, don't you see, because he'll have ten million of his own."

She waited.

"There's good blood in them. My wife was a good, gentle woman, and she and I loved deeply. Our sons had much of our love in them, and it stands to reason that they passed it on to this new generation. I'd like you to try them first, Jenny."

" 'Try' them? How?"

At this, he stiffened slightly, but answered without hesitation. "In bed. For sex. To help you know which is the right one for you to marry."

Jenny looked shocked.

"Si, you don't just press a button!"

"You'll know, Jenny," he insisted. "You must make sure the sex part is right. And that there is love. And that, whoever he is, he is not after your money. Make certain of those three things. Before you marry."

"Si!"

"It'll work out. If you do as I advise. And don't waste time! You're a passionate creature, Jenny. Make love to one of my grandsons the day after I die, if you can! I want to leave you knowing that you have a program mapped out and will follow it."

"It sounds so—"

"Cold-blooded. Perhaps. But sensible, Jenny, my beloved. When the time comes, you'll fall in love. And the sooner the better."

There was such determination in his voice that she knew she must bow to his wishes. "Of course, Si. I will do as you say. I know you'd never guide me in the wrong direction."

"That I'd never do," he murmured. "I've given this a great deal of thought. Besides the reasons I've mentioned, there are others, from my own experience.

He fell silent and she knew that he was waiting, that he wished not to force information on her. But she wanted to hear; and she sensed that he had an urgent need to tell her something, something important.

18

So she whispered, "Yes, Si. Go on."

She felt his breath quiver. She stroked his chest, let her hair fall across his shoulders the way he loved. Then she lay back in his arms and listened to the story he had never uttered to another living soul.

2

"I married my first wife, Gladys, when I was twenty and she was eighteen," he began. "Both of us were virgins. I knew little about sex and being young and unable to wait, literally broke into her. I hurt her so then, and every time, that it made her frigid. In three months she filed for divorce, and I resorted to—women—and thought I was getting satisfaction for what I paid them."

"Only you weren't?"

"Far from it. It took Louisa to point the way."

He paused a moment and drew in a long breath. Then, cradling Jenny tighter to his chest, he continued with his story.

He was twenty-two when he met Louisa. He'd inherited money and bought his first citrus groves and now meant to make a substantial payment on a very large, luxurious yacht.

Louisa, the yacht's former owner, was sunbathing on deck, when he came to make his offer. She rose to meet him. The morning sun was in her eyes and shone on her black wavy hair.

"You're the man who's interested in *The Louisa?*" she asked. "Si Townsend?"

"Guilty," he smiled, and stopped. He could not get over the extraordinary beauty of the woman. She was black-eyed, deeply tanned, perfectly formed. There was the look of sadness about her, as if she'd been emotionally hurt.

"I'm Louisa Winterbury," she said. "Mrs. Lloyd Winterbury until a week ago. Divorced now, free as the sun."

"Would I—uh—need to see your ex-husband about arranging to buy the yacht? I'm *very* interested in her."

She smiled, a quick, hurting smile. "No. *The Louisa* is mine. In *my* name. I'm authorized to sell her. Anyway, Lloyd's flown off to London. Has an old love there." Again, that hurt look.

"I'm divorced too," he said, for no other reason except to tell her he understood.

Her eyes seemed to soften. Taking his arm, she offered to show him over the yacht, which he had already explored with his eyes. She pointed out things he'd not noticed, and he knew she loved the vessel.

She led him into the master suite. It was a large, airy stateroom, with an adjoining sitting room.

"I was planning to redecorate with burnt orange and silver," she told him. "That's why the cabinet work is blonde finish . . . to blend."

He nodded, frowning in spite of himself.

"Don't feel badly," Louisa said.

"What makes you think . . . ?"

"It's on your face, in your eyes. My divorce is new, but we had troubles for a long time. It's better that it's over. Really."

But the loneliness in those huge black eyes betrayed her. He wanted to reach out, take her in his arms, but he held himself back. Instead, he reverted to business.

"I would like very much to buy *The Louisa.*"

She smiled up at him in genuine pleasure. "Yes, I knew that you would. When I first saw you, I knew she was for you and you for her. If she cannot be mine, I am glad it is you who will have her."

They concluded their business arrangements over dinner that evening. He was glad to see that she was gayer, lighter than she had been that morning. But by the time dessert arrived, her mood had changed. Again, she seemed sad, withdrawn. Her beautiful eyes had a faraway look.

"Louisa," he said, placing his hand gently on hers, "tell me what is troubling you."

"I've no right, us being such new friends," she said, "loading my problems on you."

"It's only natural, Louisa. We were friends at first sight."

She caught her lower lip between her teeth, let it go. "I've a decision to make," she confessed. "And it isn't easy."

"Decision?"

"About one Winston Harris."

"The tobacco tycoon?"

"Him. He's in New York. I met him over a year ago when Lloyd had some business with him. We became friends. Now that Lloyd is out of the picture, he wants me to marry him. He loves me—I believe that—and he has a big, fine house and an ailing young daughter who needs a lively mother."

"He's got the reputation of being a solid man."

"And a generous and kind one."

They were silent.

"What do *you* think, Si?"

"Louisa, only *you* can make this decision."

"I'd still like your opinion."

"Well, he loves you. He can give you a fine life. Probably your love would grow. It boils down to whether you want to be a stepmother."

"That part's fine. It's—something else. Winston— he's very like you, Si. His warmth, tenderness. In the short time we've known each other, I've developed a strong feeling for you. I—want to be sure I'm not making a mistake. I—" She blushed, then met his eyes fully and came out with it. "Well, I think if you'd . . . if the two of

23

us could sleep together once . . . that might help me decide whether or not I'm truly in love with Winston. Or, whether there's a chance . . ."

Their eyes met and held. "Of course it's not that I don't want to sleep with you, Louisa. I've thought of nothing else since I first saw you. But—"

"No buts, then, darling," she whispered. She stroked his hand. "Please . . . Si?"

His loins were suddenly afire. Stunned, he looked into her face. It was blazing, but her eyes were steady. Now they leaned across the tiny table on which they'd dined, and their lips clung until hers parted, and the tip of his tongue caressed the inside of her mouth.

They went to his apartment. In the bedroom, she touched him and he hardened. And then, without his knowing exactly how they had done it, they'd undressed each other and were lying on the bed.

A lamp made a golden puddle of light on them.

He sat up for one encompassing look at her, nude. Her slim body was tanned all over. Her shoulders were perfect, her breasts a bit small but rounded and firm. The nipples were dark and tiny, but stiff.

Her body went far in at the waist, and her hips rounded and curved into shapely thighs. The heart of her womanhood was dainty, the black hair in soft ringlets.

She lay absorbing his gaze. She smiled, tenderness on her lips, which quickly turned to passion. She stroked down his sides with her palms, cupped him, pressed gently, let go.

"Now, Si," she whispered. "Right now!"

And with that whisper he caught the aura of gentleness about her. No other woman had shown him such gentleness; no other woman had inspired it in him.

Slowly, aflame with need though he was, he positioned himself and gradually, cautiously, entered. Her inner walls closed around him, warm, embracing. She moaned. They moved slowly and lingeringly, Si following her lead. They went into a circular rhythm and sighed together.

"Don't stop," she urged. "Slow . . . easy . . . gentle . . . yes . . . oh, yes . . ."

24

They reversed the cycle, reversed again, gasping softly, holding their breaths, gasping again, clinging to delight. He felt her small, warm hands on his shoulders, her face against his.

The instant came when they could contain themselves no longer, and they plunged vigorously and with joy. She was surprisingly strong, meeting his burning need, and he meeting hers as if there could never be enough.

When it was over, they lay apart, breathing so hard the sound was like the ocean tide. Then she rose slightly and kissed his body—on the shoulders, at the groin, his knee. He responded, kissing her breasts, outlining them with kisses. And then they came together again, and this time it was longer, slower, fiercer at the end, and again they met in glory.

He realized, now, what had been wrong between himself and Gladys. And then he forgot Gladys. Smiling, he stroked Louisa's hair.

"There is something . . . between us," he said, softly.

"Yes, Si," she breathed. "Something special."

"I . . . we . . . shouldn't have. I was easily persuaded."

"I hope to keep on persuading you."

He groaned. "What about Winston?"

"Let's wait and see. I have several days before I must give him my answer. Tonight and other nights are for us, you and me, and no other."

"And if you should decide to go to him?"

She pressed her fingers gently over his lips. "Let's just wait . . . and see . . ."

For the next week they were together constantly, reveling in their newfound passion. And by the time the week had ended Si knew he had fallen hopelessly in love with her. To celebrate their first week together, they planned a quiet evening aboard *The Louisa,* with a romantic candlelit dinner. Si intended to propose to her.

But before he had the chance to get the words out, Louisa interrupted him. "No, Si. It wouldn't work. I've decided to return to New York and marry Winston."

Si just sat and stared blankly. He could hardly speak. "But, why?—the sex—"

"Is glorious. But there's more to marriage, Si. There's love. What I feel for you is passion. Lust. But I'm afraid I'm not in love with you, Si."

"How do you know? How can you tell?"

"The way I'm drawn to Winston. As if satin ribbons are pulling me into his arms. I realize now that I must truly love him, if even our passionate lovemaking does not keep me from thinking of him. I only hope the sex between us is as good. Oh, Si, you have shown me so much. I am indebted to you always. I will never forget you."

His heart was in great pain, but he tried to keep his voice steady. "Nor I you, Louisa. Nor I you."

"I ask nothing, Si, but that we be together until I go to Winston. I hope to bring him great tenderness and love, much of which I have learned from you, Si."

Now, at this moment, hearing these words, Jenny felt her heart pound from the tenderness with which Si had told of his weeks with Louisa. "And *did* you love her, did you love Louisa?" she breathed, hoping that he had.

"In a way I did, Jenny darling. But not as I loved Blanche, my second wife. Not as I love you."

"You loved Blanche very much, didn't you?"

"She was a wonderful wife, gave me three fine sons. I was torn when the tragedy—when Blanche and all our sons and their wives were lost when the liner *Doria* sank."

Jenny shuddered. "At least your grandsons weren't on the ship."

"Thank God they were in school! For years I blamed myself for insisting that the others go on that voyage. But Blanche really wanted some Paris gowns, and I— No woman existed for me after that, not until I saw you, Jenny."

She snuggled to her husband. There was a warmth around her heart. If only Si were just a little younger, and he could make love to her as he had to Louisa and Blanche. How lucky they were, she thought, how blessed! And then she thought, How lucky I am to be here, now, in his arms, listening to his heart speak!

"You're not unhappy over my past?" he murmured.

"It was beautiful, Si! Louisa was fortunate. And Blanche had a treasure in your love and in bearing your sons."

"Jenny, beloved, precious." He drew her closer and caressed and kissed her. He ran his fingers slowly through her hair, along her cheeks. He lifted himself to one elbow and traced her eyebrows with a fingertip, following the line of her nose, her trembling lips, lightly touching her behind the lobe of one ear, then the other. His touch sent a tingle down her spine and up the back of her neck.

He kissed her earlobes, pressed his lips into the pulsing hollow of her throat, touched and stroked there with his tongue, kissed along the line of her collarbone. He lay back then, still caressing, and his hand, for the first time, came to her breast, held it lightly, reverently, with only the silk of her nightgown between. He moved the hand slowly, following the contour of her breast, and the tingle ran up her spine and she murmured contentedly, deep within her throat.

He kissed her again, holding her breast, and she cupped his shoulder in her hand, then moved it to rest in his hair. And the warmth and the tingle lasted until the kiss had clung for a long, long moment. He sighed then, drew away a trifle, and she moved so that he had more freedom of the bed.

Much as she'd liked his loving and petting, much as she'd longed to continue, she contented herself with what she'd had. He was old; he was tired; he was ill. She must take care of him, not be a drain on his strength.

But the next night he repeated the petting, and every night, until she looked forward to it. He went a bit further each time, until it seemed to be a thing she'd always kmown and looked forward to, until she longed, during the day, for his touch down the lines of her naked body, doing more, ever more, until he was doing all that he could do. And she was warmed and content with this old husband whom she liked so deeply, whom she almost loved.

One night, lying nude against her nude body, he

asked if he'd truly made her a bit content. "Not replete in the true sense, Jenny-love, but content."

She kissed him her answer.

"Do you understand now why you must make love with a man—one of my grandsons or some other—before you marry him? As Louisa made sure, so must you, Jenny-love."

In his arms, filled with his tenderness, she accepted this.

"You're right, Si," she whispered. "Before, I promised only because you asked. Now, since I've been with you like this, I'll never marry a man unless I love him—and have made love to him."

They fell asleep that night in each other's arms.

And now, this very moment, he slept in his bronze casket at the funeral home, and Jenny still couldn't decide which, of the garments he'd selected so carefully, to wear to his funeral.

Finally she took out a mint green dress that was one of Si's favorites. He had declared that it made her eyes the gray of rainfall. The dress was silk, fashioned in full, easy lines, striking her legs at midcalf. Under it she wore lingerie of a matching shade. Her sheer hose were so light a gray as to be almost invisible, and her high-heeled pumps, also a very light gray, were delicate and flattering.

She considered herself in the mirror. Yes, the dress was as lovely as Si had said. Without any contrasting color or touch of lace, it was stunningly simple. She wondered how she ought to do her hair. What would Si have suggested?

She regarded herself in the mirrored door for a long time—the outfit, the platinum gleam of her wedding band, the platinum watch Si had given her. Thus far she was on certain ground. She was dressed in his favorite gown, wearing his jewelry.

Soberly, she determined to go the full course. She moved to her dressing table, ran the silver-backed brush through her hair, drew it back so it covered the tips of her ears, gathered it at the nape of her neck and fastened it with a plain platinum clasp. When she'd finished, it flowed, waving and curling, down the back of her dress to her hips.

Standing again before the full-length mirror, she was fully satisfied. She knew some who attended the service today would be shocked to see a widow in green, hair tumbling down her back. But this was the way Si had liked her; he would have been proud to see his creation.

She patted her nose lightly with a powder puff, and was finished. She laid the puff down, smiling mentally at the bareness of the dressing table. There wasn't even one bottle of scent. That had been Si's taste too, and was now hers. The faint aroma of soap and cleanliness were enough.

Sudden tears stung her eyes, but she blinked them away. Without Si, she was on her own for the first time in her life. She had not even the nuns to protect her. She felt lost and lonely, yet at the same time something was tugging at her, calling for her to reach out toward some unknown destiny.

A tap sounded at the door. "Come in," Jenny called, knowing it would be Flo.

"I see you got dressed," Flo said, eyes going over Jenny.

Jenny looked up at the maid, a tall, stern woman of fifty. At first Jenny had feared her, but had come to rely on her as a trusted ally. "Yes . . . I'm ready. Thank you for not trying to help. What do you think? Did I choose right?"

Flo tipped her head with its perfectly dressed iron gray hair. Her eyes raked Jenny over; her plain, firm lips pressed together.

"Perfect, Mrs. Townsend. Exactly like Mr. Townsend himself would have got you up." She nodded briskly. "Hold your head high; you're being the widow he'd want."

Jenny's breath quivered in relief. Flo always spoke her mind. "Now there's nothing to do but wait," she said, glancing at her watch. It would be an hour and a half before Simon III would arrive to escort her to the funeral.

"There's a problem, Mrs. Townsend."

"A problem, Flo?"

"There's a man downstairs in the library. He wants to see you, says he won't leave until he does. I told him there's a death in the family, and he said he knows and is sorry about that, but he means to see you, just the same."

Jenny stared. "What does he want?"

"He won't say, ma'am. Just that it's urgent. 'Imperative' is the word he used. Do you want me to phone down and have them send someone to get him out?"

Jenny frowned. Of all things, there must be no commotion today. This was Si's day. All must go smoothly.

"I'll see him," she decided. "It's simpler."

Flo started to protest, but held back. "Just ring for me if there's trouble," she urged. "I'll get help."

Troubled, Jenny rode the penthouse elevator down to their lower floor, walked to the library, opened the door and entered, pulling it shut behind her. This had been Si's favorite room. Lined with rare books, furnished with leather, gleaming wood and a priceless antique carpet, it was everything he loved. She wished Flo hadn't brought a stranger here.

At first she didn't see him. Then, adjusting her eyes to the light that shone in from the louvered windows, she got the full impact of the man.

He was a couple of inches under six feet, large and muscled, big-boned, broad-shouldered, with a rugged look which displeased her. He was heavy-featured but handsome in a homely way, and looked to be all of thirty-six. He had black wavy hair and intelligent, probing, luminous black eyes which glowed in his deeply tanned face. He was casually dressed in brown pants and a work shirt. Jenny decided she didn't like him.

She firmed her chin. "What can I do for you?" she asked. "I'm Jenny Townsend."

She didn't offer her hand, nor did he offer his.

"Tom March is what I go by," he said in a voice like soft thunder.

She inclined her head.

"I know your situation today," he continued, "but I had to see you. I represent the migrant workers. And you, young lady, are about to be in a great deal of trouble!"

3

She stared at Tom March. Why, the audacity of him, to come here, on the day of Si's funeral, and talk to her that way. Who did he think he was? And the look of him, standing there with his bulging muscles, staring at her! He seemed so self-assured, and this, in addition to his gruff manner, irritated her.

She glanced at his hands. They were big and capable, she was sure, of the worst violence. A thrill of distaste ran down her spine.

What would be Si's opinion of this man? Noble, fatherly Si. What would he think of those muscles, that browned skin, the way those fierce black eyes caught her and wouldn't let go?

She wondered what he was thinking as he stared back at her. Probably he was shocked by her youth, the difference in age between herself and Si, whose picture had appeared in the morning paper.

Si had been right! Oh, yes! The sooner she remarried, the sooner she'd be safe from this kind of intrusion.

From having to face and deal with a ruffian such as this.

Tom March was no more enchanted with her, than she with him. Who did she think she was, standing there like some princess? She was too flamboyant, her hair too shockingly red. His fingers twitched with the impulse to dig into that shameless hair that reached her perfect hips, and damn it all, give it a good yank.

She was a gold digger on the hoof. She'd married old Townsend for his money and now that she was free didn't even have the decency to wear black to his funeral. A widow in icy green, with that fiery, curling, loose hair, and gray defiant eyes.

The two stood that way for some time, staring each other down. It was as if she were trying to drive him from the room with her eyes, as if he were defying her for the very attempt.

Finally his voice broke the silence. "I reckon you didn't hear," he said, in a low, menacing tone. "I represent the migrants. I'm not sure there ain't a powder keg in the making."

"That's no excuse!" she snapped, goaded by the thunder in his tone. "You had no right to come here on the day of my husband's funeral. Tomorrow would have done just as well! Then one of my husband's grandsons could have spoken with you. Why did you need to see *me?*"

"You're the great man's widow," he retorted. "And the papers are full of how much farming land, how many citrus groves, you now own. In the eyes of the workers already here to pick in late October, you represent the Townsend clan."

"That's not the way it is!" she cried. "It's a corporation, a conglomerate! I have nothing to do with the business!"

"They figure different."

" 'They?' Who is 'they?' "

"The migrant workers. They're from Texas mostly, and have come to Florida to pick your crops. They're furious over existing conditions and unless action is taken, they're going to make big trouble. They're going to eat into that ten million of yours."

What was he saying? She knew nothing of these matters. Oh, to get this over with, to send this unspeakable man packing! She had to discuss whatever he had on his stubborn mind, but was going to waste no time doing it!

"So?" she asked stiffly. "What am I supposed to do?"

"It's plain you're totally ignorant on the subject," he said. "It must be explained so it'll be clear in your head that's so full of other things."

The black eyes raked her from head to toe, recaptured her eyes, which she would not give him the satisfaction of averting. She stared steadily and furiously back at him and could see herself reflected in those bold, luminous eyes. She looked tiny there, like a speck of light. This increased her anger. If she were a man, she'd grip those powerful arms and march him out of the library, through the door, into the elevator and push the button and never have to see him again.

He was waiting for her to speak, so she spoke.

"Go ahead," she snapped. "Educate me."

Words came at her through his teeth; his fists hung at his sides. So. He was angry, was he? Good. Let him see how it felt!

"The migrants are people," he spat out at her. "They walk and talk and sleep and hurt just like you do. They don't look like you—they're of other bloods —Negroes, Chicanos, some poor whites. They're men and women and children who work the east coast of the United States and the length and breadth of Florida, picking crops for market. Apples, cotton, onions, tomatoes, squash, anything. They leave their home base, if they can be said to have one, and wander from June to December, picking. Have to, or starve."

"What do I do with them?" she demanded.

"Next to a soft-drink company that bought twenty thousand acres of orange groves, you're one of the biggest land owners in Florida. Your husband left you the land, the newspaper says. Is that correct?"

She nodded, angry.

"So you, personally, own groves and tomato fields from Orlando to down past Homestead. Right?"

"I don't know the exact locations."

"You own so much land you don't even know the extent of it. Fine for you. But for the migrants—"

"I don't see what the migrants know or care—"

"They know. And they know about the soft drink company. Here's what *that* outfit did, Mrs. Townsend. They built houses for their pickers, gave many of them year-round work, higher wages. For other companies, yours among them, the migrants slave for less than a living wage. They have swarms of kids to feed and clothe. Most of them go hungry. Some of them work in the fields as early as ten years old, to help feed the younger ones. They need food to eat, and decent housing."

"My husband used to provide housing," she told him. "He had most of it torn down, I believe."

"Ha!"

She wished to claw his eyes, those inexorable eyes. "Ha!" he said, just as though he'd caught her in some crime, such as murder."

"What does that mean?" she demanded.

"He tore the houses down. Why?"

"He said they were about to fall down."

"In other words, they'd been left to rot."

"That's what he said. That the pickers were very hard on them."

"Did he replace them, Mrs. Townsend? Remember, I know the answer."

So now he was calling her a liar. Her own fists clenched.

"No," she said. "he didn't replace them."

"Why not?"

"He said it was impractical for the short time they're used. And the workers wrecked them. I told you that."

He didn't speak for a moment. But he seemed to swell with anger, to grow bigger, wider, more filled with muscle. Her own anger grew, hummed in her ears, lodged in her throat, and she was so stunned by it that she almost forgot the horrible man who had provoked it.

Anger, real anger, was a new experience to her. At the Home, the Sisters maintained an atmosphere of love and peace; childish quarrels were quickly resolved and the ones involved were soon again on friendly terms. Being married to Si had been even more peaceful. Jenny had spent her twenty years in serenity. Until now. Until this man had charged in with his accusations. And demands. For there would be demands. They were in every line of his body, in his probing eyes, on his big, angry mouth. In those clenched fists.

"You don't provide living quarters," he said finally. "You don't provide bathhouses, and you don't pay a living wage. But you sell your crops at top price. And add the profit to your ten million."

He flashed a look around the room, across the great, tufted, leather sofa, along the wall of priceless books. "You have luxuries like these while migrant kids by the dozens try to find a place on the ground where they can spread a rag of blanket to sleep."

She felt a pang at that, but no, he was wrong. He must be wrong. "I'm sure we pay a living wage!" she cried. "As for houses, don't they have trailers?"

"A few," he admitted hotly. "Some live in tents or in rat-infested shacks! Animals have it better than these folks!"

"Why throw all this on me?" she demanded. "Why not at least go to the men?"

"I told you," he said from his teeth. "You own the land. Therefore, I reckon—"

"You're from Texas!" she accused. "The way you barged in, the way you speak!"

"Missoura."

"You said the migrants come from Texas!"

"They do, a lot of them. Some are from the Bahamas. Where they're from don't matter. It's what they can get to put into their bellies!"

"A migrant . . . from Missouri!"

Under his fury, he looked puzzled. "I ain't a migrant," he said. "I'm a friend to them, helping them. But there's one—Pablo Perez—that's a troublemaker. Even a killer, push him far enough. He's got a few on his side, and they're trying to get the rank and file from Davie to Homestead sore and ready to fight for decent conditions and decent pay. If they get worked up, they're apt to destroy crops, do anything!"

"Well, stop them, if you're their friend!"

"I've got to have Townsends to talk wages and living quarters with them," he growled. "There's got to be some action taken, or some promise that it will be. Else them rabble-rousers'll make trouble to get what they have a right to."

"Why don't they come and speak for themselves?" Jenny cried. "How come you're doing it for them?"

"I got acquainted with one fellow—Max Vernon, a smart and sensible black man, and he introduced me to others who agree with his thinking, which is to go slow. They're all scratching for a living but Vernon and his kind will negotiate. Perez and them'd as soon use force. Or organize, call a strike and let the crops rot in the fields and on the trees. Talking to Vernon and his pals, I offered to see what I could do."

"You offered to *interfere!*"

"Call it what you want. But being such a big grower, you owe it to these people to provide for them like that soft-drink company does. Vernon says the Perez faction is getting closer to making trouble evey week!"

"I can't do this myself!" she hissed. She glared, fingers arched at her sides. "I've never had anything to do with Si's business. It's all run by the corporation! You've come to the wrong person, at the wrong time. Now I must ask that you leave my house this instant!"

He slammed his fiercest look into her glare, and felt his lips draw back into a snarl. For the first time in his life, words failed him. Damn her! Damn that red mane of hair, which seemed to shout defiance of him and every word he'd spoken. She didn't give a damn about the migrants; she didn't give a damn that her old husband was dead. She was glad to be free. Now she could turn loose her selfish, greedy nature; she could spend a hundred thousand like it was only fifty bucks. She could go her un-feeling way, reward herself with untold luxuries.

God help any man fool enough to marry her, ten million or no ten million. Look at her—hair blazing, her shapely body shown off in that green dress, her face sparkling with anger, and beautiful beyond belief. And under it all, under that gorgeous facade, was an unfeeling, selfish bitch waiting for one thing and one thing only—to get her hands on ten million dollars! There was no way to deal with such a woman, no way at all. She was some kind of she-devil that had got loose and meant to mow people down like hay.

Jenny, fully aware of his fury and his hatred, unable to read the vast extent of it, stood rigid, eyes never leaving him, returning hatred for hatred. He said he wasn't a migrant, but he might as well be one. He looked the part, dark-skinned and muscular. The very stance of his body, the way his fist knuckles stood out, bespoke violence. He was the worst man she had ever met. An utter, insensible heel.

He'd proved that by barging into her home, ordering her to build houses from Orlando to Homestead and beyond, telling her the migrants must have more money. Expecting her, Jenny Townsend, to do all these wild things and do them now. Threatening her with violence from this Perez fellow and his cohorts.

Browbeater. That's what he was. Not man enough, with all his macho, to go to the Townsend grandsons. Instead, belaboring a woman, forcing her to his will, and on the day of her husband's funeral!

He was bringing out all the worst in her, stirring feelings she'd never experienced before. She had to get rid of him, fast, never see him again, get back into her own placid self.

She broke the silence. "I told you!" she whispered fiercely. "Get out of my house!"

"Not until you agree to move on this migrant issue!" he snarled.

He just stood there, eyes boring into her. He was like a boulder. She couldn't stand it another instant; she'd taken all she could.

"Temper," he growled, anticipating her. "Your red-headed temper is on the hoof!"

She flew at him, fingers arched, aiming for his face. He grabbed her, pinned back her arms, and held her fast. She struggled, but couldn't move an inch.

"I don't take that from no woman!" he growled. He began to shake her. Her head flopped and the tiny platinum clasp gave way, causing her hair to fly out in a fiery veil, slap against her back, fly out again.

She opened her lips to scream for Flo, but he slammed his hard, angry mouth over them and smothered the sound, which came out as a moan. Now the vise he held her in yanked and their bodies slapped together, and she felt the hardness of those muscles, and was unable even to squirm in the steel embrace.

His mouth was hot. He closed it until his lips pinned hers, and then he kissed—a vicious, grinding kiss that drew blood. Because it hurt, her lips parted and his tongue came between them, forcing its way past her teeth and into her mouth.

She tried to struggle, but he held her so she couldn't move. His tongue stroked the roof of her mouth, and a tingle went down her back. He withdrew his tongue and, still holding her, kissed her lips again, vigorously, and it hurt from where his teeth had cut the first time.

He kept kissing her, mouth hotter. She tried to bite his lips, and he shook her again, and while he was doing that, she managed to rake her nails down his cheeks. Then, as he caught her close to him, she seemed to ignite, to catch fire, and so did he. They kissed hard and long, lips clinging, and it didn't matter now that it hurt.

She could feel herself trembling. She didn't know what would come next, but she was too weak to struggle. She felt him take hold of the zipper at the back of her dress and pull. The dress slid down her body to the floor. He lifted her out of the puddle it made, swung her up into his arms, strode to the tufted couch, dropped her onto it and set about stripping off her bra and bikini.

She lay, eyes closed, and listened to him undress. She knew she should get off the couch and run, naked, for Flo. She should get into her suite and lock the doors.

But the world was standing still; she couldn't move. She could only wait, mind empty of thought, allowing this strange new sensation to wash over her body.

She glimpsed him as he came onto her. There was black hair on his chest, not much, and he was tan all over. He smelled of pine and the outdoors. A deep, woodsy smell.

She could hear him breathing; she could hear her own breath. She could feel her breasts tingling, and that was odd.

Then his hand came to the fork of her legs in a half caress, half slap and afterwards, maybe one second later, he tore into her, hurting, and she cried out softly. There was no stopping him, and she didn't want to stop him, now that the pain was over, now that he was giving her pleasure. It was wrong, all wrong . . . but she couldn't stop. When he moved, she moved instinctively, moved with him, as if they had been created to do this together.

His breath was hot on her face, as he plunged deep into her, driving her into the soft leather, releasing her, driving again. Every time he released, she followed, throwing her body helplessly against his, hating him, on fire from him, ready to explode from him. Every move he made she answered, until there was nothing but heat and motion and fire.

He flamed, felt her flame, knew when the two flames blended. That was the moment of bliss, of completion.

Slowly, he withdrew, sat back on his heels. He let her struggle to a sitting position. She covered her breasts awkwardly with crossed arms, held her legs to hold the spot which he'd only now freed.

Her face was wet with tears. "You raped me," she said simply.

"I'm—sorry. Really sorry. I had no idea you were a virgin—no idea. I wouldn't have done it if I'd known— No wonder you cried."

She had to be truthful even though she hated him. "I cried because . . . at the end . . ."

"You felt it too? That it was good?"

His voice was a whisper. All the anger had gone out of him and for a moment his gaze was tender.

She felt a blush take her whole body. She couldn't answer. The blush mixed him all up. She was a spoiled bitch, that he knew; one bedding and one blush, virgin or no virgin, weren't enough to change this little hellcat.

"Course, I ain't used to explaining," he growled, the anger back in his voice. "One thing, though. Mad as I was—still am—I apologize for not knowing you were a virgin. I assumed—"

"I *know* what you assumed!" Jenny snapped. "Drop the subject! It's over, and too late to remedy!"

She saw his smoldering eyes ignite, felt her own eyes take on heat from his. She resisted only weakly when he moved her arms away from her breasts, parted her legs. She didn't try to escape when he moved up over her.

As in a dream, she opened to him and this time, when he entered, there was no pain. This time, voice a bit hoarse and not angry, he instructed her, and they moved in a circular motion, then plunged, and near the end he rolled slightly to one side and like that, they fused. Her ears rang, and she touched the hem of heaven.

This time he helped her up, let her snatch her dress and clutch it to her. He dressed swiftly and she stood, waiting for him to finish, to go.

When he'd finished buttoning his shirt, he glanced at her. "Ain't you going to dress?"

"When you're gone," she said. Her ears were still ringing. There was no hurry. He'd seen her naked; he'd taken her, twice.

At the door, he turned. "Do some thinking about that migrant problem," he said, and there was the soft thunder in his voice again. "I'll be back in twenty-four hours."

He went out the door, closed it.

Trembling, ashamed, Jenny picked up her clothes and brought them into the bathroom which adjoind the library. She took a tub bath, sobbing dryly at what she'd done, how she'd felt, and Si not even buried. She tried to wash him from her, but no matter how she scrubbed, she did not feel clean. It would have to do. Simon would be calling for her in less than half an hour.

Dressing hurriedly, she slipped, unseen by Flo, to her suite and quickly brushed her hair, fastening it with the platinum clasp which she had retrieved from the library floor.

She took a long last look at herself in the mirror. What kind of a girl am I, she wondered? What would Si say, if he knew what I'd done? Shocked to numbness, she realized he would probably approve. She had, after all, taken the first step on the path which he himself had laid out for her.

She only hoped that Missouri migrant hadn't made her pregnant. Because now, she was determined to follow Si's plan to the letter. She was going to marry one of his three grandsons.

And as soon as possible.

4

Just as she finished her toilette, Flo tapped at the door. "Mr. Simon is here," she announced. "I brought him to the library, seeing that other man's gone. Miss Madeline's with him."

Jenny nodded, recognizing the disapproval in Flo's voice. Madeline was Simon's divorced wife. Flo was shocked.

On her way down in the elevator, Jenny forced herself to be calm. She'd not betray her shame, no matter how she felt. She reminded herself again that Si would approve the act, if not the man. She shuddered slightly as she thought again of the way the Missourian had made her feel. Si was right about one thing. He'd told her she wasn't frigid. She burned, but stepped calmly out of the elevator when the door slid open.

Simon met her in the corridor. He looked so much like his grandfather that it was a comfort for her to see him. He too was six feet, distinguished-looking, built with strong smoothness, and at thirty-five was already sporting wings of white at his temples. His clear blue eyes were dazzling.

"Jenny," he murmured in the voice so like Si's. He took both her hands. In his off-white suit, his fair skin lightly tanned, he looked handsomer than she'd ever seen him before.

It would be easy to love Simon, she thought. He looked so much like Si. But then the thought vanished, for Madeline appeared, ran to Jenny, held her close, murmured and wept.

"Don't get Jenny upset!" Simon exclaimed. "This is why I didn't want you at the service! To say nothing of the fact that we're divorced. It isn't suitable."

"I d-don't care!" sobbed Madeline, but she wiped away the tears from her soft blue eyes. "Divorce can't take away my right to sit with you and Jenny today! Besides, I'm the only other female Townsend and Jenny needs another woman with her!"

Holding to calmness, Jenny put her arms around Madeline. "You're right," she said. "I do need a woman with me, one my own age."

And she really did. Also, she was genuinely fond of Madeline. Si had thought her wayward, a spoiled, child-like woman not suited for his most serious grandson. But Jenny had always defended her. "She's just adventurous, Si. High-spirited."

"Let me look at you," she said now, to fill Simon's disapproving silence.

Madeline stepped back a pace and waited.

She was five feet, eight inches tall and proud of it. Her figure was lean, shapely, flowing. Her hair, worn in short ringlets, was such a tender red as to be a whisper compared to Jenny's. She had cameo features and a soft, bow-shaped mouth.

She indicated her white silk suit. "Will it do, Jenny? I know Si hated black."

"It's perfect," Jenny assured her. She looked at Simon, eyes pleading with him not to be difficult. "You look perfect too, Simon."

"Rolf and David are also wearing white," he told

her, and she was relieved. She'd wanted to ask that there be no black today, but hadn't dared.

"It's time to go," Simon said, placing his hand on Jenny's shoulder. "The limousine is waiting. So are Rolf and David."

They moved into the elevator, remained silent as it descended to the lobby. They crossed the marble foyer of the great Townsend Towers Condominium, passed the uniformed doormen, and went to the special gray limousine Simon had ordered. Billings, who had been Si's chauffeur for years, held open a door and Jenny got in, followed by Madeline and Simon.

Rolf and David, the other grandsons, rode the jump seats, designed so they could face the three in the back. Billings got behind the wheel, his door thunked richly shut, and they began to roll.

Rolf and David had flashed Jenny a warm smile. Now, as they rolled along the palm-lined streets toward the funeral home, no one spoke. There was nothing to say. Jenny gazed bleakly at Rolf, the middle grandson, who was staring out the window.

He was as handsome as Simon, almost as tall, but broader. His hair was blond, a shade darker than Simon's, and his features were softer, less classic. His eyes, light blue and wide-set, had a dreamy, faraway look. Jenny thought him sensitive looking, mysterious. No wonder there were so many beauties chasing him. But of the two most frequently with him, she doubted he'd marry either.

Then she studied David, the youngest of the three. He too had women on his trail. He was thirty-two, a year younger than Rolf, but looked younger still. Maybe it was the sunny blond of his hair, the devilish way his bright blue eyes danced. Lacking Simon's and Rolf's sophistication, David was nevertheless a charmer, and Jenny had always found him the easiest of all to talk to. He was so bright and sunny and warm.

Jenny sighed mentally. She fully appreciated Si's desire for her to marry one of these men. Outwardly they were all like him to some degree. Inwardly—that was what he'd requested she find out. She closed her eyes, kept them so until they arrived at the funeral home.

The chapel was large and filled with people there by invitation only. There were Townsend business associates, officers of the corporations and their wives, Si's friends, his doctors. Flo was in the gathering somewhere. Even Rolf and David's women friends were present, she knew. And Oliver Cranston, Si's securities analyst and trusted economic adviser, was there, along with a pretty young woman who was trying to lead him to the altar.

Jenny hardly looked at the sea of people. She knew who they were. She'd approved the list Simon had made up. She'd made only two requests, that the bronze casket remain closed, covered with a blanket of white roses, and that the immediate family ride in the gray family limousine Si had bought, and of which he was so proud.

The service was brief. When it was over, when Billings had deposited them at Townsend Towers, the three brothers and Madeline rode up to the penthouse with Jenny. She, who had sat with eyes closed through the entire sermon, who had heard not one word or note of music, wanted to lock herself in her suite, lie on the bed she'd shared with Si, and weep until she slept.

But she couldn't do that. The long funeral dinner was ahead of her. It was something Si had particularly wanted, so she knew she must go through with it.

She had fought him on the idea when he first mentioned it. She knew she would have preferred to spend the hours after his funeral privately, not at some lavish dinner party.

"You think so now, darling," he'd countered, "but really you'll be better off with people. It's an old country custom, the funeral feast. Give it for me, darling."

"Si," she'd gasped. "I'd want to show respect, not—"

"That *will* be respect, the kind I want. It needn't be a large gathering. Ask my grandsons, of course, and Madeline, and some of those young things who are after Rolf and David. Ask Oliver Cranston and that beauty who wants him so badly. Ask others, if you like, but have at least the ones I've named."

Now, as Jenny and the others stepped into the apartment, she saw that the catering service had done its work. Trained hands had transformed the vast living room, the dining room, the library, the big hallway.

As Jenny glanced into each room, her breath quivered with relief. No flowers. There'd been carloads of them at the funeral home and graveside. Here there was only the green of plants, with touches of fern.

She had Flo to thank for this.

Madeline insisted on helping her dress. The idea of changing hadn't occurred to Jenny, and she said so.

"I *knew* you'd not consider clothes!" Madeline exclaimed. "I brought some for myself—my new blue dinner gown, very simple, and nightclothes. I'm staying the night with you, darling! No matter what Simon has to say!"

For the first time Jenny's grief eased. She'd been dreading the night alone in the penthouse with only Flo. Madeline would be perfect company. They had no secrets from each other—well, none but Tom March. He was a secret, an awful secret.

She pushed him out of her mind and allowed Madeline to lead her to her bedroom suite. She'd let the girl select a gown for her. It had been a trying day and she longed for someone to take over, as Si had always done.

Madeline, happy to be of use, looked in closet after closet, awed by the variety and richness of Jenny's wardrobe. "Umm . . . what scads of clothes!" Madeline exclaimed. "You could open a boutique and run it for six months with all these things. I'll bet you haven't even worn all of them!"

"Nearly all. Si—had favorites—and I wore them often. He—that was one of them," she added, indicating a long silken gown of a green so pale it verged on white.

"Then you'll wear it now!" Madeline declared. "Strip, girl, I want to see it on you!"

With a half-smile, Jenny consented. Madeline was good for her. She was deliberately trying to cheer her out of her somber mood.

When Jenny had the gown on, Madeline stood back,

nodding her approval. It was a simple, graceful dress, with a high neckline, and smooth, full lines. But the back was plunging, and showed off Jenny's creamy tan. It was floor-length, even after Jenny put on the matching stilt-heeled slippers, which were bare-looking and tied with ribbons.

Madeline brushed Jenny's magnificent hair, talking the whole while. "I'm going to do your hair in my version of the French twist," she said. In no time she had the gleaming red hair piled up and fastened with cleverly concealed silver pins.

Jenny stood before the mirror and tried to see herself through Si's eyes. There wasn't a flaw, according to his standards. But was the gown a bit blatant for a funeral dinner? She was still trying to decide whether she was appropriately dressed, when Madeline distracted her, wanting to show off her own new gown.

She was softly beautiful in sapphire blue, the color of her eyes. "Simon won't be able to forgive himself for divorcing you," Jenny exclaimed. "Wait until he sees you tonight!"

Madeline's smile quivered. "I was a fool to play around with Oliver Cranston," she breathed. "To think I could get him to marry me! All I did was hurt Simon, and made him angry enough to divorce me!"

The first one they saw, when they approached the living room on the floor below, was Oliver Cranston. A handsome man, he looked five years younger than his age, which was forty. Jenny admired his six-foot-plus frame, the fine bones and slim build. She knew he ran several miles every day to keep in shape, and it showed. Jenny thought him a solid man, someone to be trusted. Perhaps she would get to know him better and he would become her friend, as he was Si's.

His attention was at this moment on Shirley Horne, the tall svelt, black-haired, black-eyed fashion and news photographer whom he had been dating. He was smiling down at her, murmuring a reply to whatever she had just said.

The instant he saw Jenny, he came to her, Shirley on his arm. He took her hands, causing Shirley to drop his arm, and just held them. No words were needed. His dark eyes conveyed to her his deep remorse over Si's death, and his concern for her. Jenny felt, at that moment, extremely close to him. She had the brief thought that Si would approve of her marrying this man, then suffered shame for entertaining the thought.

"Oliver," said Madeline. "Good evening."

He let go of Jenny's hands, touched Madeline's fingers briefly. "You know Shirley," he said easily.

The two women, the one with coal black hair and the one with tender red ringlets, nodded cooly.

Oliver moved the three of them smoothly into the living room. At the far end, gathered around the sound system choosing albums, were Rolf and David and four exceedingly pretty girls.

Simon, off to one side smoking his pipe, came to meet Jenny's group. "Jenny!" he exclaimed. "You're . . . exquisite! Sure you're up to all this?"

"Of course she is!" Madeline cried. "I'm watching every breath she takes! She's fine!" She half turned to draw Simon's attention. "Like my dress? It's new!"

"Nice," he answered cooly. "Watch out, everybody —here comes the tide!"

The other group was coming at them swiftly. Rolf had a woman clinging to each arm, as did David. They were a blur to Jenny, though she knew that Rolf's girls were Lila Stevens, nineteen, very petite and chiseled of feature, and Carol Lincoln, twenty-two, a sharp-tongued blond who was secretary to a famous attorney. Lila, on the other hand, didn't work, but had fun on her father's millions, exceedingly proud that he was a judge.

The girls dangling from David's arms were Sara Donahue, twenty, a rather striking brunette with green cat's eyes, and Ginny Dodds, twenty-three, a chestnut-haired beauty who often appeared on magazine covers with generous amounts of her lovely self showing.

Jenny had met all of them before. As always when she was with these women, she couldn't help feeling they were after the Townsend fortune as much as they were after the Townsend men.

She was glad when Flo announced dinner. They

moved to the dining room and seated themselves around the long oval table, which sparkled with crystal and silver and bone china. There were twelve of them, including Barbara Winters, a friend of Simon's who had come in late, having thought Simon was going to pick her up.

"Sorry, Barb," Simon apologized. "I thought you had an appointment with your attorney, and said you'd take a taxi."

"It doesn't matter, darling!" she said, smiling.

She was thirty, had shoulder-length, sunny brown hair and amber eyes. Despite being sharp-featured, she was beautiful, and gifted in handling men. She, too, was a young widow. Her husband, a wealthy investment broker, had fallen dead on the golf course and had left her a great deal of money. Yet she wanted Simon. Jenny noticed that she drew more than one smile from him, even tonight.

As dinner progressed, served by white-gloved caterer's men, Jenny half listened to the light chatter and the low, throbbing music. She was grateful that no one expected her to join in, though Madeline and Oliver shot her an occasional glance, just to be sure she was all right.

They had coffee in the living room, Rolf keeping the music playing Si's favorites, everything from Vivaldi and Bach to Chopin and Al Hirt. This wide taste led to Simon's telling a small joke about how old Si had almost punished him for scratching a valued disc. That reminded Rolf of a similar incident with their grandfather, and then David had a sad-humorous story to tell about himself and old Si aboard *The Louisa*.

Jenny listened sadly to the stories. They brought tears to her eyes, which she crushed back, but at the same time the stories were oddly comforting. She was taken by the feeling that Si wasn't gone at all, that he was right yonder, beyond an invisible wall, that he watched this dinner party and approved. It was then that she knew she'd never lose Si, that no matter what she did in life, regardless of whom she might marry, Si would know. It was almost as though she could reach out and touch him. And she was comforted.

She watched the women who surrounded the Townsend men. What chance have I? she wondered. And if I have the chance, can I keep my promise to Si? Will it be that any of them fits all three requirements?

The thought of Tom March crossed her mind, filling her with a mixture of fury and satisfaction. The satisfaction was in knowing, once and for all, that she was a passionate, responsive woman. The fury was in remembering the way he had barged in on Si's funeral day and raped her.

She had never known she could be so angry, had never before experienced that depth of emotion. He'd accused her of having a temper, and now, here she sat, realizing that, because of him, because of Tom March, she *did* have a temper. Already she had changed, and it was his fault. Well, at least she realized it.

And would put an end to it.

She abhorred him. He was the one person on earth she hated.

She looked again at the three Townsend men and thought how different they were from that Missouri ruffian, how much more gentle and polished. These were the kind of men she belonged with. But which one?

She watched David, saw how he flirted with Ginny and Sara, how he led them on. She almost smiled. They were so open about pleasing him that it was funny, but pitiful, too.

She watched Rolf and his women, saw the looks they stabbed at each other, the melting smiles and soft beauty they showered upon Rolf. And she knew it was wasted. Dreamy-eyed Rolf was far from ready to settle down.

She watched Simon. He didn't flirt with Barbara, but she never left his side. He looked across the room, caught Jenny's eye, inclined his head. She made a tiny nod. Barbara recaptured his attention.

Perhaps Barbara, of all the women, had a chance. She was older, more experienced. But no, Jenny thought. Simon was more worldly than Barbara, for all her pretense, and Jenny doubted if he was in love with her.

He looked Jenny's way again, inclined his head and

53

this time did not smile. She looked back at him, her head whirling: she'd come to a decision.

Simon. The name ran through her. She would try him first.

And probably need to try no other.

Part II
THE ADJUSTMENT

5

When all had left but Madeline, the two girls went to the luxurious guest suite, where Madeline was to sleep. Situated at the far end of the penthouse, it was some distance away from Jenny's quarters. Madeline flicked on a light and gaped at the splendor of the room, the rich olive green carpeting and drapes, the satin ivory-colored throw on the king-sized bed, the massive marble-topped dressing table. Madeline sat down on a plush chair and drank in the elegance.

"Si had wonderful taste!" she exclaimed. "And creative imagination, to decorate an entire penthouse to offset your beauty. *And* to dress you with the same ideas in mind!"

Tears stung Jenny's eyes. Madeline saw her blink them away, ran to her, enfolded her. "Jenny! Oh, darling, I shouldn't have spoken! I *know* how much you honored Si, respected him!"

"Loved him, Madeline," Jenny corrected gently. "I loved that dear man in a way it's impossible to describe.

As a friend, as a—" She paused, searching for the proper word.

"As a husband," Madeline supplied.

"Yes," Jenny whispered. "In that way too, in spite of his age and ill health. I loved him as a wonderful human being, knowing that it couldn't last, that this sad time would come."

Speaking thus, putting, however clumsily, her true feelings into words, Jenny felt better. She drew away, and Madeline let her go.

"Goodnight, darling," she murmured, and went swiftly from the room. She'd thought, before Madeline insisted on spending the night, that she herself would move into a guest suite, that she would find the master bedroom she had shared with Si too empty, too lonely.

But now, as she entered the familiar room, she knew she was in the right place. The very walls seemed to welcome her, to wrap her in the warm and tender love of Si, and again she had the feeling that he was with her, somewhere close-by.

But after she'd undressed, hung her gown in its closet and put her lingerie in the small basket of things for Flo to launder, after she'd taken the pins out of her hair and let it fall around her face and down her naked back, after she'd crept nude into the great bed, utter desolation swept over her. Here she lay, clothed only in her flaming red hair, the way Si had asked her to sleep, and he wasn't beside her.

Added to that, every time she closed her eyes, she saw the dark, angry face of Tom March. No matter how she tried, she could not seem to banish him from her mind. Nor could she forgive herself for her shameless behavior. He had excited her, awakened something in her, and she wanted to bury it forever.

Tears welled in her eyes, and this time she couldn't stop them from flowing. She wept on and on, uncontrollably, her heart, her very soul, drenched with tears, torn with regret.

At long last she lay tearless, her breath jerking. Her cheeks were wet, but she made no effort to dry them. She lay still and let herself recall that first wonderful night after she and Si had been married six weeks, and he'd caressed her in bed. That was when he'd first asked her to lie beside him nude; and he had joined her.

Puzzled but willing, she had laid aside her short night gown, and climbed into bed. Then she'd positioned herself close to him, not touching, as was their custom. He had turned to her, stroked his fingers through her hair. "Silk," he had murmured. "Silken hair . . . beautiful Jenny!"

After that, she had come to him nightly, naked and open to him. Each time, he went a bit further, first fondling her breasts, then letting his fingers wander to her navel, sending a tingle up her spine until she moaned.

One night, as he cupped her breasts, he spoke so low she had to strain to hear the words. "My wife," he breathed. "I want so much to make you happy—to show you, satisfy you—"

"Si, please—" she whispered. "It doesn't matter—"

"Yes, darling. It matters very much. Slowly, I have been readying you, leading you. Have you enjoyed what we have done?"

"Oh, yes, Si."

"You haven't disliked it. Am I right?"

"So right, darling."

"I've been teaching you, Jenny, guiding you into sex. Leading you along the paths of passion so that, in the future, you'll be ready for real lovemaking. So you'll be eager for it."

"Si! It isn't right, isn't fair to you!"

"It's joy to me. Tonight, with your loving cooperation, I mean to give you a taste of passion, of physical release. Are you ready, darling—are you willing?"

Instinctively she moved so that her breasts touched his naked chest. He lifted himself up on one elbow, kissed the nipple of one breast, then took it carefully into his mouth, stroking it with his tongue.

The tingles danced up and down her spine. She sighed with pleasure.

As if on signal, he freed the breast, stroked one hand

downward to her waist, along the curve of her hip, then across to that fiery patch in the center. Here it stopped, his fingers parted her and came to rest.

His touch was like electricity. She tensed, held her breath, waited for she knew not what. But for more; there must be more, had to be.

His fingers worked her, lightly at first, up and down. Her part grew warm, sprang to hotness. She felt herself move in rhythm with his fingers which went faster now. She moved faster too, and harder, the heat building faster and faster. That part of her was swelling, straining. Her heels dug into the mattress and her back arched, lifting her closer to the stroking. She was too swollen to endure; that spot, so new to her in this guise, burst, and when it did the tingles shot down her spine, then raced back up, reaching into the very center of her being.

His hand stilled, and so did she. She lay gasping, body dewed with sweat. Heart thundering, she moved her lips to his and they kissed.

"Was it good, really good?" he asked.

"It was wonderful! But not fair to you, Si! It must never . . . we must never . . ."

"But we must and we will, Jenny-love. It gives me joy and satisfaction that I can make you happy.

"Is it right, what we did, Si?"

"Any way in which a man and woman give each other joy is right," he told her. "Some people would argue otherwise, but you will always know differently. Now, shall we try again, another way?"

He instructed her to lie on her side, facing him. Then, he took her hand, guided it to his maleness.

"Just hold me," he said, "and do what feels natural."

He felt small and flaccid, but she held him, and with love. His fingers came to her and began to stroke, and she held him firmly while the hotness and bursting and tingles repeated themselves, better this time, richer, fuller.

She lay in his arms afterwards, and they slept.

The following night they repeated the act. And every night after that. Jenny looked forward to it, her one guilt being that Si couldn't enjoy it as she did, that he couldn't experience the bursting and the joy.

"If only I were younger," he told her one night, "we might have had a child. A homely little red-headed girl who would grow up to be as beautiful as her mother."

She felt a rush of affection, cradled him in her arms. "Si, dearest Si, it doesn't matter!" she cried softly. "It's you I want, only you!"

He stroked her fiery nest. "You always respond," he marveled. "Unless the wrong man beds you, you'll never be frigid."

Now, thoughts of the migrant came back to her. How right Si had been! She'd been shaken and seared to the roots by Tom March. But their wild and passionate lovemaking had proven her completeness as a woman.

In spite of the fact that Si was very weak, having suffered a series of mild strokes, he had continued to make his manner of love to her. When she protested, afraid he'd overdo, his answer was always the same. "It gives you pleasure which you need, Jenny. You're a woman who will shrivel and fade if you don't get love. Besides, it's what I want, too."

She ceased to protest, loved him tenderly, knew he adored her.

When Dr. Cline had insisted they have a full-time nurse, Si had refused.

"I have Jenny," he said. "She gives me youth and beauty and love. And Flo gives me my medicines, you know how capable she is. Why would I want a nurse? I'm not even in a wheelchair!"

"But Jenny needs freedom," protested the doctor. "So she can take proper care of you."

"I have it!" Jenny exclaimed. "Si forces me to go out!"

"I don't mean for just a breath of air."

"I exercise," Jenny explained. "The beach is our front yard, and every day I swim at least a mile. Si sometimes watches."

The doctor, a kindly, gray-haired man, smiled. "You should have some other outlet," he said.

"I have the penthouse pool, tennis sometimes, and two greyhounds training to race, Doctor. Si often comes with me, to watch them. So you see, he gets fresh air and outings, too. We don't *want* a nurse!"

Si chuckled. "This girl's so crazy about dog racing, Doc, that we're building up a string of racers that will be hers alone."

The doctor gave in, smiling. "You've got a strong will, Si Townsend. Always have had. Just don't overdo. Listen to this redhead of yours when she says to slow down."

When the big stroke came, the final one, he had just brought Jenny to climax. Suddenly she felt his arms loosen and fall away, felt all strength vanish from him. There was time only for her to hold him in her arms and whisper, "Si! Si, darling! I love you!" And then he was gone.

That was only two nights ago, and since then she had writhed in Tom March's arms.

A stranger's arms.

She began to weep again, in utter desolation.

6

Suddenly there was a tap at the door, and before Jenny could get control of her voice, a sweet-smelling figure had run lightly across the room and was getting into bed with her. It was Madeline, her touch on Jenny's shoulder a comfort.

"There, there, Jenny dear," Madeline said in a soothing voice. "You've cried enough, now. You've let the worst out, and that's good, for it makes it possible to face tomorrow. To look to the future."

Jenny burst into fresh tears, and Madeline held her, in her arms, rocking her gently. Jenny knew Madeline was right, That she would have to face the future, the one Si had laid out for her, and to which she'd given her promise. She would have to find another husband, keeping in mind the three requirements—he must love her, he must not be after her money, and he must satisfy her sexually.

But would she ever find such a man? She'd decided to begin with Simon. But after his disappointing first marriage to Madeline, would he ever consider remarrying? And if he did, would he choose her? He seemed interested, but perhaps he was just being kind to his grandfather's widow, helping her get over the first tough days.

No, if she wanted him as her lover, she would probably have to make the first move. Let him know, subtly, of her interest. It would not be easy for her—she had never approached a man before. But it was the only way. Of that she felt certain.

Madeline gave her a little shake, pushed tissues into her fingers. "Come now, Jenny," she prodded. "Blow your nose! Stop your crying. We *all* have problems, dear. You're not alone, believe me!"

Jenny stopped now, sat up. She'd detected hostility in Madeline's tone. Why, of course! She'd been thinking only of herself. But Madeline, recently divorced, had problems of her own.

Jenny leaned over and switched on the white hurricane lamp by her bed. She looked closely at her friend. Something was troubling her.

"What is it, Madeline?" she asked. "What's wrong?"

"It's Simon!" Madeline cried. "The way he treats me! I was his wife, his *wife,* mind you, for three years! You *saw* how he behaved toward me today, *heard* how he spoke! As if I had no right to sit with the family! As if I were a stranger!"

"Probably he thinks that's the way it should be, after a divorce," Jenny comforted.

"But I want him *ba-ack,* Jenny!"

It was as if she had dropped a bomb. Jenny's gray eyes went wide, her mouth opened in amazement. She'd never dreamed Madeline felt like this!

"You're sure, Madeline?" she asked, putting her own feelings aside.

"Quite sure. But, oh, what can I do about it? It's clear by the way he acted today, that he wants no part of me."

"This was a hard day for Simon," Jenny offered. "It's understandable that he'd not want any hint of . . . closeness . . . with anyone. But he loved you once or he wouldn't have married you. And you must still love him.

If you let him see it, as time passes, I think he's enough like Si to relent."

"He's not the least like Si! Only in looks! And I *don't* love him, never did! He was handsome, and there was all that money!"

"Madeline!" Jenny was shocked. "You don't mean that!"

"Oh yes I do," Madeline retorted. "A girl must look out for herself! You, of all people, know that, Jenny! You married Si, went from orphanage to penthouse, and with all that age difference."

"Yes," Jenny admitted. "Yes, I did. But I loved him. I still love him."

"Oh, I know that, dear. I know you were devoted to each other! It was beautiful. But it wasn't that way with Simon and me."

Jenny waited for her to go on. It was clear she had never confided this to anyone, and now had an urgent need to let the words pour from her heart.

Madeline drew in a breath and continued. "Our problems began right after we were married. From the day we got back from our honeymoon, Simon neglected me. The way he acted, you wouldn't even have known he was married!"

"Surely he didn't . . . so soon after . . ."

"Yes, he had a mistress: *business! That* was his mistress! He was fanatic about his work, was hardly ever home. And when he was, he busied himself in his study. I got so bored! I'd go shopping, buy the most fantastic gowns, put one on to dine with him at home—I could seldom drag him out—and he'd not even notice! At first I put up with it, because our sex life was good. Then even that became routine. He seemed to have his mind on business during what should have been our most tender . . . and I felt he was bored."

"Oh Madeline, poor dear!"

"And this was when I was still a bride! Then, fight against it though I did, I got bored! Bored with Simon. He was always deep in some facet of the conglomerate— farming land, factories, department stores, you name it!"

"Si gave me a list," Jenny said. "Endless."

"And needs endless attention! I understood that, but I needed attention, too! And didn't get it. Until Simon began inviting Oliver Cranston for dinner so they could discuss business." Madeline paused. "You're willing to listen to all this, Jenny? You'll keep it secret?"

She was so forlorn that now it was Jenny's turn to enfold and comfort. "Talk, darling," she urged. "Get it out!"

Madeline needed little encouragement. Her voice a half-whisper, she began to relate what had happened before the divorce.

At first, she told Jenny, she had resented having Oliver Cranston in their home. Not that there was anything wrong with him. He was pleasant and good-looking and entertaining. What bothered her was his manner toward her, which was, from the first, warm and seductive.

The first time he came to dinner, Madeline accepted this casually, knowing he had the reputation of being a womanizer. Besides, his attention was flattering, and did not seem to bother Simon.

But soon he began to focus on her. One evening, Simon was discussing a shopping mall he was interested in building. Oliver glanced at Madeline, eyes warm, lips smiling. "Simon," he chided in his pleasant voice, "not with a beautiful lady present! She's a vision; she commands our attention! Let's leave business until later!"

Simon's mouth tightened. But he was too courteous a host to contradict Oliver. He even displayed a bit of gallantry himself, warming to her, if only briefly. "She's a Townsend," he said. "Only a beauty qualifies to be a Townsend."

Oliver smiled. "Tell us, Madeline, what you do with your time. What people do you honor with your beauty and grace while Simon is off making millions?"

"I'm afraid you'll be disappointed," she replied. "I shop, lunch with girl friends, plan our meals, take piano lessons, spend hours practicing."

"I'm sure you're talented," admired Oliver.

"She is," Simon said. "She could have been a concert pianist. I'm pleased with her ability."

Madeline's breath snagged. That was the first complimentary thing Simon had ever said about her music! She looked at him. His eyes were like burning blue ice. He was furious that the conversation had turned to her; he wanted only to discuss his shopping mall.

"Perhaps you'll play for us after dinner," Oliver said. "I'm fond of Beethoven. Do you play his concertos?"

"She plays everything," Simon cut in, "but I'm afraid you'll have to hear her some other time. This mall—I have a stack of paperwork on it that will take us several hours to skim through. Madeline will undoubtedly be asleep before we finish."

She'd been so humiliated she wanted to vanish then and there. Instead, she moved her long eyelashes provocatively, holding back the tears. She forced her lips into a smile, which she bestowed first on her husband, then on Oliver. She hoped he would accept the smile as agreement with Simon; she daren't speak, not even to murmur, "That's all right, I'll play some other time," for she knew the tears would escape and he would see them. Simon would see, too, and be furious.

She sat through the rest of dinner, silently thinking up ways of getting even. No doubt he'd subject her to one of his tongue-lashings when they were alone. Though she didn't love him, those tirades cut to the heart. He never failed to tell her, among other things, that she was his showpiece, that her purpose in his life was to service him in bed, give him an heir, look beautiful at all times, entertain faultlessly and perform at the keyboard only when he requested it.

"Are you ashamed that I play?" she cried once.

"On the contrary. It's a definite plus to your image. But use your talent sparingly—familiarity breeds contempt. One selection infrequently, when we have an important affair in our home, two at most. Nothing elsewhere. Use only your own instrument."

Finally dinner was over. Simon and Oliver excused

themselves and went into the study. Madeline stared at the closed door, then went to the bedroom and cried until there wasn't a tear left.

By morning an idea had formed in her mind. Simon lived his own life. Well, she was going to live hers! She wasn't going to be his shadow!

At eleven o'clock, after she had showered and dressed, she went to the phone and called Oliver. Making some excuse about having a doctor's appointment near his office, she invited him to join her for lunch. He accepted without hesitation.

They met at her favorite lunch spot, a place where she'd be sure to run into people she knew. Her intention was to make Simon jealous, to pay him back for his selfishness. But, to her surprise, she found herself utterly captivated by Oliver Cranston. Not only was he witty and intelligent, holding her with tales of his sailing and hunting exploits, but he was also darkly handsome, like some beautiful Greek god.

That night, as she lay in bed with Simon, she could not get Oliver out of her mind. Feeling some pangs of guilt, she decided to tell Simon about her lunch date. "You'll never guess who I had lunch with today—"

"What does it matter?" he growled, cutting her off with his usual lack of interest. "I'm bushed. Go to sleep."

That was enough. She resolved she would see Oliver Cranston again, and perhaps this time . . ..

She did not have long to wait. The very next day, he called and invited her to lunch. They dined in a restaurant of his choice, an intimate spot in Fort Lauderdale. By dessert, they were holding hands and he had invited her back to his apartment.

This time, all the moves were his. He wasted no time. They were hardly in the door when he took her into his arms and kissed her passionately. She returned the kiss, parting her lips, hoping he'd slide his tongue between them, and he did.

He carried her to the bedroom and onto the king-sized bed. She lay on the maroon velvet spread, looking up at the oval mirror that was suspended from the ceiling.

"Take off that dress," he commanded.

Trembling, she moved her fingers to the zipper and slid out of her thin silk frock. He was smiling that handsome, exciting smile, as his dark eyes explored her body. "You're beautiful," he exclaimed. "Perfect."

He was out of his clothes in an instant. He moved on top of her, pulled away her bra, flung it aside. "I'm going to do all the things I've dreamed of doing to you since I first saw you," he muttered. His eyes were glowing, his mouth was passion incarnate.

"Do!" she cried. "Oh, do!"

He kissed her—slow, hot kisses which began at the soft ringlets on her head, traveled her face and lips, shoulders and breasts, all the way to the tiny red ringlets below. These he kissed with reverence, making her move and moan. And then he entered her smoothly and they moved together as though welded, and her heart seemed to pound in rhythm to their union. They flamed, long and sweetly.

Then they rested, each stroking the other. They lay quiet, his hand on her secret part, hers holding his slowly growing maleness.

They made love again, Faster. Sweeter. Longer.

"I love you," he said after the second time ended. "It's my rotten luck that you're another man's wife."

"I adore you," she whispered. "You're my real husband."

Now, telling Jenny, Madeline's voice rose.

"Try to be calm," Jenny urged. "What came next?"

"I acted the fool! Without a word to either Oliver or Simon, I flew to Mexico! I was so insane about Oliver, so mad at Simon, that I got one of those quick divorces. I came back thinking Oliver would be overjoyed!"

"And?"

"He let me down, Oliver let me down! He said he'd had no idea of marrying me! Said he loved me but loves lots of other women, and refused to lose the Townsend account by breaking up a Townsend marriage! I swore to him that I would never let Simon know the real reason for the divorce—and I never have."

"When did you tell Simon of the divorce?"

"The night before I told Oliver. It was foolish, I know. But I was so anxious to be finished with him, and to run to Oliver's arms. I told Simon it was because of his neglect that I had gotten the divorce. Oh, Jenny, I've *got* to get him back!"

"He's still as involved in the business as ever, darling. Perhaps it's just as well you did what you did. He'd still be no good for you."

"But I could handle it now, I'm sure I could. And there's no chance at all with Oliver! Oh, Jenny, you can't imagine how awful it was. First Oliver jilted me, then I begged Simon to marry me again, and he was like *stone!* He said he was through with me, didn't care what I did from now on. And all I got in settlement was half-a million dollars."

"That's a lot of money, Madeline."

"But nowhere near what he has! And I wouldn't have even got that much if he'd known I divorced him because of Oliver! Oh Jenny, I want him back. If I can't marry Oliver, I want to be Mrs. Simon Townsend III again!"

"You can't marry him just for the money."

"It isn't just that. I don't want to be alone, Jenny. I can't be alone!"

Jenny studied her friend thoughtfully. She sympathized with her, but doubted she had a chance to win Simon back. And Jenny had her own plan to set in motion. She was still convinced, in spite of what Madeline had said about him, that Simon might be the right man for her. She had to find out.

"There are other men," she soothed, as Madeline sobbed brokenheartedly. "Rich, handsome men, who will pay you all sorts of attention! And sit up and beg to marry you!"

"But I'm so alone in my apartment!" Abruptly the flow of tears lessened. Madeline grasped Jenny's arm. "Let me stay with you!" she exclaimed. "We'll be like sisters, be company for each other! I'd stay until I found a husband, or until you did!"

Jenny thought for a moment. She intended to pursue

Simon, and it might be awkward with Madeline living under her roof. But it would be good for her to have a roommate. And Madeline cheered her, made her laugh.

Her arms went around the other girl.

"It's a wonderful idea, darling," she said.

"You mean it? It's a deal?"

"It's a deal," Jenny promised.

They held each other, wept a bit more, then dried their tears. For good, they promised each other shakily. No more tears.

Madeline kissed Jenny good-night and returned to her own room. She fell into a contented sleep, dreaming that Simon held her in his arms.

Down the hall, Jenny was having the same dream.

Oliver Cranston, at forty, recognized and accepted the fact that he was woman-crazy. He had neither the desire nor the will to marry any of the nubile young beauties who came so readily to his bed. His appetite for lovely women—a variety of them—was as real and pressing as his hunger for fine food, which he consumed with unrestrained gusto.

He did think about marriage from time to time, but as of yet had found no woman he'd make his wife. His wife would have to be beautiful and intelligent, yet not clever enough to find out about the mistresses and one-night stands he'd have on the side. Madeline came close to what he was looking for. But a marriage to Simon Townsend's ex-wife was out of the question.

His thoughts turned to Jenny. Old Si had surprised everybody by marrying the flame-haired beauty. And from the moment Oliver had met her, he had been entranced by her. He knew that if he had Jenny, he would need no other woman in his life.

Well, he'd reasoned, Old Si wouldn't be around much longer. Oliver would get on friendly terms with Jenny. Then, after she became a widow, he would wait a respectable amount of time before making his move.

It was a masterful plan. And now, with Si dead, he'd be able to put it into action. Soon he'd have a diamond on her finger, and the redhead of all time in his arms every night.

Meanwhile, there was his work. He was as wild about that as he was about women. For now, he'd devote himself to it as much as possible, cutting down on his dates, so that Jenny would have the proper image of him.

For a moment, he thought again of Madeline. He still felt guilty about her. She didn't date, turned down every man who asked. He knew she was quietly working on Simon, to get him back, and on himself, to change his mind.

If he'd never seen Jenny, it was solidly possible he would have married Madeline. Chances are she might have caught him in a vulnerable moment.

Only things hadn't happened that way: the only woman he considered at all was Jenny.

And now she was a widow.

Soon, he could ask her out. Gradually, he could show growing warmth until the moment came in which he could declare himself. He half smiled, anticipating that moment.

7

When Jenny woke up it was still dark. She looked at the clock by her bed. Only three-fifteen. But she couldn't sleep anymore. It was so lonely in the bed without Si.

She tossed aside the satin coverlet, got up and stretched. If only she had a greyhound in the garden, she would go and pet it, put her arms around it, rest her cheek against its short, sleek hair. And it would lick her face, tail wagging, slim body wriggling. But both her dogs were at the training kennels.

On impulse, she called the downstairs garage and ordered her Lincoln-Continental brought to the front. Swiftly, she dressed in a pants outfit of pebbly gray crepe, pulled the brush through her hair, drew it to the nape of her neck, and tied it with a narrow gray ribbon. She tossed the wallet with her driver's license, two twenty-dollar bills, and some change into her purse, and was ready.

The elevator sank to the ground floor and she stepped outside. It was still dark and the fall air was cooler than usual. It gave her a little thrill to be up before dawn and out in the sheer darkness. She didn't know why, but it made her feel less lonely than she had in the penthouse.

"It's all right Mr. Woodstock," she told the uniformed man who had brought her car around. "I can't sleep and am going for a drive."

He looked concerned. "The keys are in the ignition. Is madam sure . . . it's, well, rather early . . ."

"Yes, Mr. Woodstock. Really, I'm fine. Don't worry." She flashed him a smile. "I won't be gone long."

She drove in her gleaming green car along Ocean Drive, heading for Miami Beach. She'd always loved that Gold Coast Drive, the beach road lined on both sides by great-glittering hotels. They'd be sparkling now like Christmas trees, throwing their shimmer against the night, penetrating darkness, outshining the stars.

She drove, not thinking at first, then trying not to think, and losing the battle. Si was no longer here to advise her; she was strictly on her own. She should have asked him how to get a man—any man—into her bed. She hadn't the least idea how to entice Simon Townsend.

Maybe he wouldn't want to go to bed with her. Not even if she gave him slow, warm smiles and spoke in an intimate tone. Maybe he'd see through such tricks and ignore her.

Then she recalled the gentle touch of his fingers on her arm at the funeral and thought, he will approach me, oh he will! He's so like Simon in appearance, he's bound to be a little like him inside, no matter what Madeline thinks.

She drove, the tropical breeze against her face, the smell of the Atlantic upon her. Tom March. Now that she knew from him what sex could be like, she was certain it would be even better with Simon. And if not, there was still Rolf or David. One of them would surely be right for her.

Her spirits grew a bit less heavy. As she came into Miami Beach and went skimming along Collins Avenue, she began admiring the hotels. The tourist season hadn't begun yet, but within a month, this stretch of beach would be packed with sun-worshipping vacationers. She came to the end of the strip and drove back to the Causeway, a lovely bridge connecting Miami Beach to the big city of Miami, and sped across.

She drove through the Cuban section, then beyond into the more affluent suburbs. There were streets of private homes, some of them estates, others smaller. All the houses had white-painted tile roofs, though she could see the white only as a glimmer.

Finally she entered Coral Gables, the exclusive area adjoining Miami, and cruised past estate after estate. All of them were dark except for night lights, and she pictured the occupants sleeping peacefully and wondered when she would sleep that well again.

She glided past the long campus of the University of Miami. Maybe she should enroll, get a degree in the English literature she loved. She'd read aloud to Si often; he had so enjoyed the English classics. They read poetry too, and listened to classical music. Rarely did they watch television, except for the news and an occasional program on the educational channel.

She wondered if her husband would mind her being a college student. Probably not. The kind of man she intended to marry would have no objections. He'd understand that she needed more in life than parties and a fancy wardrobe.

She was driving and dreaming thus, looking at the campus, noticing the lighted windows where students were studying, when she unconsciously drifted into the wrong traffic lane.

A police car sprang up from out of nowhere. Actually, he'd been behind her for some time, flashing his lights and blasting his siren, but Jenny had been too preoccupied to notice. He motioned her to the side of the road.

"Driver's license, please," he said in a gruff voice.

She fumbled through her purse, got the license from her wallet, handed it over. He had his traffic book out, and was copying into it.

"Please don't give me a delayed ticket, officer," she said. "It would be a real favor if I could just go to the police station and pay my fine now."

He studied her in the dim light. He looked, as nearly

75

as she could tell, to be in his early thirties. His face seemed to grow less hard.

"That's what I mean to do, ma'am," he said. "Your weaving all over the road—it may be that you need a drunkometer test."

She almost laughed; then tears threatened. "Whatever you say, officer," she replied. "You'll lead the way?"

The police station was brightly lit. It seemed to be filled with Chicanos, Negroes, white men so sunburned they were almost as dark as the others. They were sitting, standing, milling. They all looked surly; some had split lips and bruised eyes. Many wore torn, dirty clothes.

Jenny sat where the officer said, took the ticket he gave her. He muttered about getting back on duty and was gone, and she wondered how long it would be before he returned to appear against her. She hoped it was soon; the men in the station were staring at her, making her very uncomfortable.

They must be migrant workers. She gazed about, trying not to look at any of them directly. Tom March had said that their angry dissatisfaction might lead to an outbreak of violence. From the look of things, he'd been right.

Jenny sat back. She was in for a long wait. The police officers were busy dealing with the migrants, taking them one by one, question by question, then escorting each of them individually from the big room, probably to a jail cell.

Suddenly, out of the corner of her eye, she saw a man burst into the station. She looked at him and sucked in her breath.

It was Tom March!

The migrants—she knew now that they were indeed migrants—gathered around the Missouri ruffian, all talking at once. He waved them quiet, then went to the desk to speak to the officer in charge.

His voice, soft and commanding, filled the room. "What have these men done?" he asked.

"They've been fighting," the officer said. "Inciting to riot. Who are you, anyway?"

76

"Tom March, sir. I'm a friend to these men. One who was in the fight escaped your officers and he came to me. He'll be right in."

Tom's back was to Jenny. He didn't have the least idea she was there. She burned, watching how bold he was with the police. If he wasn't careful, he'd wind up in a jail cell himself.

They were still talking, voices lower, but by straining unashamedly she could hear. After what Tom March had done to her, she had a right to know what he was up to!

It evolved that the fight had erupted over a group of white pickers, new to Florida. It seems they were picking tomatoes cheaper than the Chicanos and Negroes. Several of the old-timers had gone to them, asked them to up their price to the going wage; the whites had refused, saying they had families to support and would work for pennies if they had to. Enraged, the others had fought back with their fists.

Tom argued with the lieutenant, trying to get all the men released, assuring him that he'd talk sense into them, but was turned down flatly. He came on stronger, but it was to no avail. The lieutenant, a surly older man, would not budge.

Only when he threatened to put Tom in, too, for disturbing the peace, did the Missourian turn away. It was then he spotted Jenny.

"What in hell are you doing here at four o'clock in the morning?" he demanded, his eyes wide with shock.

"I couldn't sleep," she said coolly. "I went for a drive and got a traffic ticket. I'm waiting to pay my fine."

His eyes narrowed. "The truth?" he asked.

"The truth."

His frown broadened into an ironic smile. "Well, aren't you the little devil! Still, that ain't no way for a lady to act, widow or not!"

"I've done worse!" she snapped, staring right into his hot black eyes.

Again, that mocking laughter. "So you have, so you

77

have." His voice deepened. "But now you've seen some of what I was talking about! This small fight is just a sample of what *could* happen!"

She looked away from him. His eyes, glowing like hot coals, made her uncomfortable, starting something up in her that she did not understand.

"I'll be late getting to your place today" he went on. "I've got to get to the bottom of this, find Max Vernon and see if Perez was behind tonight or not. Though I don't doubt he was."

Jenny said nothing. All this was so foreign to her experience that she didn't know how to respond. Besides, the sooner she could be rid of this man's company, the better. He only reminded her of what she wanted to forget.

"It'll take the whole day," he went on. "As soon as the banks open, I've got to bail all these men out. Then I've got some investigating to do. With two factions among the pickers, the trouble's got to be stopped. Else there's no tellin' where this'll all end up."

Before she could have replied even if she'd wanted to, he stormed away and out the door as though he, single-handed, was going to settle the whole mess.

Jenny sat back and breathed a little sigh of relief. Thank goodness he had gone. She would have to face him again later but this time, she told herself, it would be easier. She would be on her own ground and she'd make sure she had others around for support. She'd show that horrid man she could stand up to him!

She waited another whole hour while some drunks were brought in, then some longhairs high on grass. Finally her arresting officer appeared, brought her to the main desk, and she paid her fine.

It was six o'clock when she got into her car and drove away. At the first public phone she stopped and called the penthouse.

Madeline answered, her voice thin and anxious. "Where have you been?" she quavered. "Where are you now? I woke at five, and you were gone. Flo had no idea where you were. We've been frantic, ready to call the police!"

"If you had, you'd have found me!" Swiftly Jenny filled her in, including the traffic ticket and the long wait in the police station. She didn't mention Tom March.

"Thank goodness you're safe! Come on home, Jenny! Flo'll fix us a nice breakfast."

But Jenny couldn't face returning to the penthouse. Not yet, anyway. Seeing that odious Tom March had reminded her sharply of the rape, and of how she had liked it. She needed some more time away from home to collect her thoughts. She arranged for Madeline to meet her at a spot they both liked on the beach road.

As she drove toward Miami Beach, she tried to steady herself. So much had happened in the last few days, and she needed time to sort things out. She'd acted like a fool with Tom March. Both times she had seen him, she'd allowed him to bully her into submission. No more. She had to face life and she was going to face it. To start with, she was going to have this thing about Simon out with Madeline, clean and honest.

Dillingham's didn't have many cars parked in front at this hour. Jenny went through the door into the red-cedar interior. She loved the feel of this place, with its brass chandeliers, red-checked tablecloths, and heavy wood paneling. It was homey and inviting. A welcome change from the cool elegance of the Townsend penthouse. At the rear was a line of booths. Madeline was waiting in the most secluded one.

As Jenny slid onto her bench, Madeline drew the little checked curtains and they were enclosed, as if in a tiny room. "At last!" Madeline breathed. "I thought you'd never get here!"

"I had to drive all the way from Coral Gables."

"You're here, that's what matters! I've already ordered." She indicated the pewter pot of coffee, poured. "The waitress will be bringing toast and eggs in a few minutes."

They sipped hot, strong coffee, and Jenny again related the incident of her jailhouse visit.

"But, Jenny," Madeline said, turning serious, "you seemed calmer when we said good-night. What was it that upset you so, to make you wake in the middle of the night and drive all over Miami? Was it—anything to do with the things I told you about Simon and me?"

The waitress brought the food and Jenny had a chance to prepare her response. She wanted to be honest, but did not want to hurt Madeline's feelings. The girl had been so kind to her.

"Tell me," Madeline urged. "Please, Jenny."

Slowly, Jenny began to relate the story of Si's request. "He wanted me to remarry as quickly as possible after his death, and asked that I consider one of his grandsons first. And—well—before you told me you wanted him back—I had kind of set my sights on Simon . . ."

Madeline went white. It was clear that she had not expected this. "But why did you decide on *my* husband?" she demanded.

"Oh, Madeline. He *wasn't* your husband anymore. How was I to know you wanted him back?"

"Well, you know now! Why are you telling me all this, knowing how I feel?"

This was the hard part. "Well, you *are* impulsive, Madeline, running off for a divorce, wanting Oliver, wanting Simon! I needed to know you were sincere. That you wouldn't be changing your mind again."

Madeline was silent for a moment. When she spoke again, there was an edge to her voice. *"I'm* impulsive? You, only two days a widow, are talking of remarriage, and *I'm* impulsive? You know what, Jenny?" she said coldly. "They say a new widow goes a little crazy for awhile. I think you've gone a little crazy, I really do!"

"Madeline! It was Si's idea that I remarry so soon. Not mine!" But to herself she thought, maybe I am a little crazy. There'd been Tom March. And her driving all night and ending up in the police station. Now this.

"Why did you zero in on Simon?" Madeline asked.

"I'm not sure. Maybe because Simon is the eldest and looks so much like Si. I can almost picture him, as the years pass, becoming another Si. I loved him, Madeline . . . I loved Si."

"I know you did. But I told you before, they're not at all alike inside. Simon's sharp and single-minded. Si was . . . he took time with people. He was human. Simon is a money-machine, which is exactly what I want since I can't get Oliver."

Jenny listened sadly. Madeline was right. There could never be another Si.

"I'll help you snag Rolf or David," Madeline promised. "But if you go after Simon, you'll never be sure I won't tell him Si's scheme, and make you look the fool. Simon despises fools."

Jenny looked at her friend, smiled. What choice was there, really? If she went after Simon, there was no saying she'd get him. And then she'd have lost Madeline as a friend. It was possible she needed a friend even more than she needed a husband. "It's such an odd plan for getting a husband," Jenny declared, "Simon would think *you're* the fool!"

Madeline laughed and soon they were both laughing together.

Jenny had lost. She would not be able to pursue Simon.

But she'd have her chance with Rolf or David. There, the door was wide open.

8

It was later that morning when Jenny remembered. The quiet dinner party, the one Si had gently pleaded that she give the night following the funeral meal!

Dismayed, she told Madeline about it. "It meant so much to Si. And I completely forgot about it! Oh Madeline, what will I do?"

Madeline took charge immediately. "You just leave everything to me," she said. "I'll plan the dinner, with Flo's help. You go right to bed and sleep the rest of the day so you can be a proper hostess. Just tell me who's to be invited. Flo and I will do the rest."

"But you've had very little sleep yourself, Madeline," protested Jenny. "You can't—"

"Oh yes, I can! I'll take a long nap and be as good as new! Just tell me who's to come!"

Unable to resist her friend's generous offer, Jenny recited the list of nine—including the grandsons, their dates, Oliver Cranston, Madeline and herself—and headed for her quarters. No sooner had her head touched the pillow than she dropped off into a deep sleep such as she had not had in weeks.

When she awoke, she remembered a dream. She'd been stopped for a traffic violation, pulled over to the side of the road, and come face to face with a policeman who was none other than Tom March. He had laughed at her, baring his white teeth, until she could stand it no longer. She'd reached into the glove compartment, pulled out a gun, and shot him in the head. But he had not flinched. He'd just stood there, laughing down at her, his eyes black as the devil's.

Jenny shuddered. Now he was appearing in her dreams! She'd have to do something about this man. She wondered if he would keep his promise and appear early in the evening. She hoped so. Then Simon, David, Rolf, and Oliver would be here and would help her get rid of him once and for all.

She forced herself from the bed, drew a hot bath, and let herself soak for a long time. Then, noting that it was almost seven o'clock, she dressed hastily, putting on a floor-length, pearl gray gauze dress. Nodding her satisfaction to the mirror, she patted her hair in place and headed for the door.

In the upstairs hall, she ran into Madeline, a vision in a long, gold, sleeveless crepe dress, low-cut and slit up the sides. Her soft hair was more beautiful than usual, the ringlets loose and natural. Jenny gazed at her admiringly. "Don't *you* look ravishing!"

Madeline smiled. "And *you*, dear! When Rolf and David see you, they should get interesting ideas! If they don't, there's something wrong with them!"

Jenny blushed.

"And if they see you do *that*, they're lost! How often do you see a girl blush these days?" Madeline laughed and gave her friend an affectionate hug. "Just don't overwhelm Simon!" she warned. "I'm all set to do that myself!"

They paused for a last look into the antique hall mirror, then headed for the broad staircase which led downstairs. It was nearly eight o'clock, time for the guests to arrive.

As they reached the lower steps, they caught the

hum of the elevator. Flo, smart in her dark gray uniform and starched white apron and headpiece, stood to one side of the elevator to receive the guests.

The cage stopped silently and the door slid open. Simon was the only occupant. He stepped out, handsome beyond belief in an off-white silk suit. Presence, Jenny thought. He has presence.

His eyes blazed over her. Her heart went warm. "Jenny, lovely Jenny," he murmured, took her hands, kissed her cheek.

Jenny fought that warmness of heart, subdued it, as Simon turned properly to Madeline. He didn't take her hands and he didn't kiss her, but he did make a half-bow and spoke courteously. "Madeline. You've never looked lovelier."

"Thank you, Simon," whispered Madeline, proper and reserved. But those soft blue eyes betrayed her; they were pleading and shy.

It was hard to believe, as Simon and Madeline smiled and chatted about the weather and some hotel in Texas the Townsends were buying, that they didn't, in spite of all their differences, really love each other. Regardless of how Madeline professed to be after Simon's money and that alone, Jenny felt that she must have some affection for him.

As they moved toward the living room, the elevator opened again. This time, a party of four came out, the men in custom-made, off-white suits, their gay, clinging dates in pink and lilac.

Rolf, seeming more broad-shouldered than usual, looked especially handsome tonight. His pale blue eyes were shining and his cheeks had a healthy glow, as if he had just finished a set of tennis. He came directly to Jenny, the very blond, silvery-eyed Lila Stevens with him.

Gently, he disengaged Lila's fingers from his arm, put his hands on Jenny's shoulders, and lightly kissed her brow. As he stepped back, Lila immediately attached herself to him again.

David, prying himself loose from Sara Donahue, approached Jenny with the same enthusiasm. "You look good enough to eat," he teased, giving her a warm hug. Then he held her away and gazed into her eyes.

She gazed back, appreciating his rugged handsomeness. Both men were so attractive, in such different ways. Rolf was sensual, mysterious, harder to know. David had a boyish, rugged look and an easy disposition. Jenny couldn't decide which was more appealing.

Sara Donahue, David's striking brunette date, moved in and herself hugged Jenny. Then, not to be outdone, Lila Stevens, who affected a Southern accent, did the same.

"I was tellin' Rolf, dahlin'," she declared, "that we've all got to entertain you, Jenny-sweet! It'd be a *sin* to neglect you now, of all times. Why, if you'll let me, I'll be the same as a sistah to you, and so will Sara, won't you, deah?"

"Yes, indeed!" gushed Sara, looking not at Jenny, but at Rolf and David, who were greeting Madeline warmly and complimenting her appearance.

As they gathered in the living room for a predinner cocktail, Jenny was aware that all three Townsend men were eyeing her. That this disturbed Madeline and infuriated Lila and Sara made Jenny unhappy. Nevertheless, it did boost her spirits somewhat to think she might have a chance to carry out Si's plan. And then, remembering what that plan entailed, she felt that awful blush spread over her body, making her cheeks glow.

She was glad when the elevator opened and the last guests, Oliver Cranston and Shirley Horne, stepped out. They made a striking couple. He, with his dark Grecian good looks, in an elegant white suit; she, in a slinky beige evening dress, her shoulders tan and bare. Oliver's face lit up when he saw Jenny, and he glided toward her.

Gallantly, he lifted her hand, touched his lips to it. "A tribute to a valiant lady," he murmured. "I admire you deeply for this evening, and am grateful to be among your guests."

Jenny smiled graciously, leading the handsome couple toward the other guests. She noted that Oliver greeted Madeline with a mixture of warmth and reserve and that her friend seemed to take this in stride. How did she manage it, Jenny wondered? If only she could have such poise, such strength. Well, perhaps someday she would. Perhaps Madeline would teach her how to keep her emotions in check.

"Ah, here's our lovely hostess!" David exclaimed, noticing Jenny's return. "Tell us, Jenny, has that new greyhound, the one from Kansas, arrived yet?"

"Romantic Sally," Jenny responded, seizing on a topic for conversation. "She'll be here soon. I'm going to keep her in a kennel on the roof, try to gentle her."

"That shouldn't be hard," Rolf smiled. "You seem to have a way with those dogs. Charm every one of them."

"How *do* you *do* it, dahlin'?" drawled Lila. "Feed them steaks?"

Jenny laughed good-naturedly and pointed toward the kitchen. "No, but maybe Flo's been feeding them behind my back. She always did have a soft heart!"

"Well, and why not steaks," piped up Simon. "If that dog runs like its daddy, it'll deserve more than steak. Comes with quite a fancy pedigree, I'm told."

Jenny nodded proudly. She did indeed have high hopes for her new prized possession. She was about to speak again, extolling Romantic Sally's virtues, when Flo appeared in the archway.

"Mr. Thomas March!" she announced.

9

Tom March stood in the archway, wearing a modest dark brown suit. It made him look darker, his hair blacker, his eyes more intense as they bored past the guests and zeroed in on Jenny.

She was on fire, the boldness of his gaze turning her face scarlet.

"Mrs. Townsend," the Missouri ruffian said, the deep voice rumbling, "I apologize for interrupting your dinner. But, as I told you, I was busy all day. Unfortunately, the matter can't wait."

Furious, Jenny forced herself to remember her guests. She introduced him to each of them, then politely offered him a drink. He wasted no time in accepting. "I'd be honored." He smiled, bowing slightly.

Damn him, she thought with unaccustomed profanity, he's putting me on the spot! He has no compunction, no manners. Nothing matters to him except his precious cause.

She glanced around the room. The others seemed to be accepting him warmly. And why not? He was decently dressed, even handsome in a homely sort of way. No one could possibly suspect the animal things he had done to her only yesterday. The way he had taken her by force, tricked her into thinking she liked it.

It was because of her grief, because it had been her first time, she decided as she glared at him. She could never enjoy a real sexual encounter with this man, this beast who stood before her.

He was talking to Rolf now, a tall scotch in his hand. She couldn't help noticing the contrast in the two men. Rolf, with his clean, blond good looks and lean body; Tom March bulkier, squatter, like some bold, dark immovable force.

"I'm here about the pickers, the migrant workers," Jenny could hear the Missourian saying. "I'm trying to help them to better their lives by appealing to all the growers to pay higher wages and provide benefits."

"We pay the going rate," Rolf said, shrugging his shoulders.

"Granted. But what about the labor camps? They're deplorable; most don't even have usable bathhouses. How can the pickers keep clean under such conditions? There can be an epidemic at any time—typhoid, hepatitis—you name it."

"You certainly make it sound bad," Rolf admitted.

"That's not all," March went on, the others listening now. "The shacks some of the growers *do* provide aren't fit to live in, nor are the ramshackle trailers some pickers own, nor the tents some of them have for shelter."

"What do you suggest?" Jenny challenged, and all eyes turned to her at once. "That growers go to the expense of building houses that will be used only three or four months of the year? Anybody who did that would lose thousands."

"You mean their profit wouldn't be as big," the Missourian retorted.

"We don't make the profit you seem to think we do," Simon said. "Our crops are perishable. We lose money on spoiled vegetables every season. If we lose still more building—"

"Does that come before human rights? Have you toured your tomato fields, Mr. Townsend, or your groves? Have you seen the situation with your *own* eyes?"

Jenny knew he had Simon on that one. He had never, to her knowledge, toured the farmland, for Si had always encouraged others to do that kind of work. Had he been wrong, she wondered? She'd always sensed that Si, so gentle toward her, was ruthless when it came to business. And the three grandsons had learned from him.

"We're aware that there has been unrest among the pickers," answered Simon, his tone defensive. "We know that a few migrants have been arrested on various charges, but bailed out. Things always settle down."

"There's unrest *everywhere,*" David offered. "They *all* want to strike—factory workers, sanitation employees, bus drivers, schoolteachers. There's no end to it. Everyone wants something. Usually more money and shorter hours."

"Believe me," Simon said, "if we satisfied all the demands, we'd not operate very long."

The Missourian nodded. "I appreciate that. But I don't think you're aware of just how serious the situation is. The migrants, for one thing, are well organized. They've split into two factions—one willing to arbitrate, the other in favor of taking action—of any kind—to make their point. About thirty of them got into a scrape last night, one faction against the other. I spent the day bailing them out and trying to reason with them."

"What was the fight about?" asked Rolf.

"One group, led by a Chicano named Perez, wanted to uproot the tomato plants and crush the tomatoes. The others wanted to negotiate."

"Were you there, Mr. March?" Madeline asked.

"No, Mrs. Townsend," the Missourian replied politely. Jenny cringed. He never spoke to *her* that way. Obviously he thought Madeline a lady.

"Someone reported the fight to you?" Madeline pressed.

"A black worker, name of Vernon. He's levelheaded, represents the other faction, those who want a peaceful settlement.

"Exactly what is it you want, Mr. March?" Simon interrupted. Jenny noticed how he always seemed to get right to the point—so much like Si.

"Entrée to your corporate meetings. Serious discussion which will bring a change for the workers."

"But why us? There are other growers. Why pick on Townsend land?" Jenny cried, trying to hide the extent of her rage.

"As I told you yesterday, Mrs. Townsend, aside from that soft-drink company, you own more land than anyone else in Florida." He looked to Simon for an answer.

"All right," Simon said, "I'll agree to this much: we'll take a tour of the fields and groves. You can come with us, see what conditions exist. Then we'll take it from there."

Tom March smiled, extended his hand. "Fair enough, Mr. Townsend. You have yourself a deal." They shook hands cordially.

The Missourian stayed for dinner. Watching him, Jenny realized he had earned the others' respect, and she could not deny that he was a bright, witty dinner guest. But she didn't have to like him. She would *never* like him.

Madeline, on the other hand, seemed to hang on his every word. Jenny wondered if she really liked him, or was just trying to make Simon jealous. "David's just about to have us all aboard *The Louisa*," she was gushing. "Perhaps you'll come, too, Mr. March."

David had inherited the yacht and was in the process of having it refurbished. When it was ready, they were all slated for a short cruise to Freeport.

"Thanks, Mrs. Townsend," he said, black eyes twinkling mischievously. "But I'm afraid I'll be busy with the migrants. This situation's apt to spin out until they leave here to pick summer crops in northern states."

Jenny hoped he wouldn't stay long after dinner, but he took his place with the others in the living room, acting as if he'd been an intimate friend of the family for years. From time to time, Jenny could feel him gaze at her from the corner of his eye. He knows how uncomfortable he makes me feel, she thought. He knows and he stays just to torment me.

Rolf put a record on the stereo and asked Jenny for a dance. Happy for the diversion, she accepted, and was eased somewhat by the gentle feel of his arms about her. Perhaps Rolf, sensitive, sweet Rolf, was the man she ought to go after. Now that Simon was off limits, he was the next obvious choice.

She was startled, peering over Rolf's shoulder, to find herself face to face with Tom March. He was dancing with Madeline, but had obviously maneuvered himself to be up close to Jenny. He gave her a wink and she cringed slightly.

Rolf pulled back. "Are you all right, Jenny-love?" His voice sounded concerned.

"Yes, fine," Jenny whispered. "Just a bit tired, I guess."

He led her to the couch and they sat down together, her hand nestled comfortably in his larger one. It felt so good to be cared for, protected! She looked over at Tom and Madeline. Both were obviously enjoying themselves. If only she could relax, let loose a little. But not with that man in the room—yesterday's memory was too strong.

"You don't like him, do you?" Rolf was asking. The question startled her.

"Do you?"

"Oh, I don't know. He seems intelligent enough. A solid thinker. A bit rough around the edges, I grant you. But I'd say he's a man to be trusted."

Jenny stifled the urge to tell Rolf how she really felt. "Well, I'm not so sure about that. I wish he weren't accompaning us on this tour of the farmlands. Why can't it be strictly a Townsend affair? We can report back to him."

"I don't know, Jenny," Rolf replied. "Simon's Chairman of the Board, and he's already indicated that he wants March along. Besides, I doubt if he'd take kindly to being turned away at this point. I guess you'll have to just bear with him."

Probably right, thought Jenny. There was simply nothing else to do, at least not for the moment. She looked across the room and saw that the object of their discussion had changed partners. Now it was Oliver's date, Shirley Horne, whom he led gayly about the polished hardwood floor. She moved closer and he made no effort to hold her off. Suddenly he laughed, and threw back his head, showing the darkness of his skin. Every line of his hateful body exuded power.

He was an animal, a wicked animal. First he'd raped her before Si was even buried, then he'd crashed her party, taken charge of the dinner conversation, arranged an inspection tour of her farm property, and gotten himself included in the tour. Now he was dancing with women, *her* guests, as if he owned them! Oh, if only she could have the doormen come up and throw him out on the street, where he belonged!

At the end of the waltz, Rolf's date, who had been dancing with Oliver, came over to where they sat. Jenny immediately excused herself, saying she needed to talk to Flo in the kitchen.

Once outside, in the rich green foyer, she breathed a sigh of relief. If only she could head straight for her bedroom, escape under the covers. Life was so confusing without Si. Oh, Si, if only . . .

Suddenly she felt a strong hand on her shoulder, and, startled, turned to face Simon. He looked coldly handsome, coldly furious.

"What's wrong?" she asked, puzzled by his angry countenance.

"Tom March," he snapped. "I've been watching him —and you—ever since he came here. Jenny, I want you to know—we need him in this migrant situation. But as far as you're concerned, remember that he's a stranger, he's different. He's aroused emotion in you—dislike, yes —but emotion, nonetheless. You've been staring at him. You're on the verge of going overboard. Into a sudden, empty infatuation."

"I'm not!" she cried, her color rising. "I just resent his intrusion! Forcing his opinions on us, then staying to dinner! He's not our kind! He's—"

"I've seen the way you look at him, Jenny. The way you tremble. You're afraid of him."

"I'm not afraid! I just—"

Swiftly, he took her into his arms, laid his lips upon hers and kissed. She found herself kissing back, softly at first, then with more passion. His kiss was firm, gentle, not rough and hard like the Missourian's. He kissed her again and she let him. Then she thought of Madeline and the promise she had made. Regretfully, she pulled back from his embrace, and he let her go.

"That's how it is with me," he told her crisply. "I'm attracted to you, Jenny. But I'll give you time. What I won't do is stand aside and permit a vulnerable, beautiful woman to be swept off her feet by the first stranger who comes along. Or by some fortune hunter."

Then, not giving her a chance to respond, he walked back into the living room, shutting the door behind him.

Jenny just stood there, unable to move. Then her lips widened into a broad grin. She had thought it would be a problem to attract any of the grandsons, to get them to so much as look at her. Now it appeared she could have her choice!

If only she *were* free to marry Simon. He would protect her, stand up to the Missourian. He was probably one of the few men who could.

But of course, though he didn't know it, he hadn't a chance with her.

He belonged to Madeline.

Oliver and Madeline were sitting in a booth in a posh restaurant called Wolf's. The tables were covered with gold linen, set with crystal and bone china. Over the soft orchestra music, the diners spoke to each other in hushed tones.

Madeline had called Oliver early in the afternoon and asked him to bring her here. Now, facing him across the table, she asked why he'd been so easy to persuade.

"Frankly, Madeline," he said, "because it gives us an opportunity to talk."

"Do we have something to talk about, Oliver?" she asked sweetly.

"Not what *you* mean," he replied.

"What, then?"

"I'm fond of you, Madeline, always will be. That I didn't want to be tied down in marriage is beside the point. At dinner last night I observed you, saw that you're trying to win Simon back."

"Does that surprise you?"

"I suppose not. But you must know, my dear, that it's impossible. Lord knows I've seen how he is at board meetings. Implacable, immovable. Once he gets his mind set, there's nothing that will change it."

"You're assuming he's set it about me. Against me."

"I don't want to see you hurt, Madeline."

"That's a funny thing for *you* to say."

Oliver looked down. "I know I behaved badly. But I do care for you. And I know Simon. He's like Old Si. Never gives up on a decision. You must keep that in mind."

"Maybe he hasn't decided about me for sure."

"Don't bank on that, my dear. You hurt his pride divorcing him. It may have been better if you'd brought my name into it. What reason *did* you give him for the divorce?"

"Incompatibility. It was the *truth*, Oliver. It got so we had nothing in common, him always working, me stuck in a house run by servants. It was natural that I turned to you."

He nodded, remembering how she'd wept in his arms over Simon's neglect, how he'd comforted her with passion.

"After I fell in love with you," she continued, "nothing about him appealed to me. Not even his money."

"But you *love* money. You have an appetite for it. The more the better."

She nodded. "But you have money, Oliver. And you gave me tenderness and warmth, too." She blinked back a tear. "I wanted you so desperately I just took off for Mexico without asking if you wanted *me!*"

He put a hand on hers, pressed, withdrew it.

"But you're over that now," he said softly. "And you want Simon back."

She nodded. "I still love you, Oliver. Perhaps I always will. But it can never be for us. And I must be practical. I need Simon—and his money. I want you to help me get him back. That's why I asked you to dinner."

Oliver stirred his coffee thoughtfully. "All right, Madeline," he said finally. "I'll tell you what. I'll help you win Simon back, if you help me with my little dilemma."

"What's that?" Madeline brightened.

He smiled, looking into her lovely blue eyes. What a little devil she was! If he didn't have someone else in mind, he might be tempted to pick up where their affair left off, let it lead where it would. But no, he had bigger plans. "I aim to marry Jenny Townsend."

She stared. "You're joking."

"I assure you, I'm perfectly serious. I'm very much in love with her."

Madeline went very still. Her blue eyes stared off into space and she appeared to be lost in thought. Finally she spoke, her voice a whisper. "How long have you felt this way?"

"I've admired her from afar for some time, probably since the first moment I met her."

"Well, why don't you just tell her how you feel?"

"It isn't that easy. Jenny's been protected for a long time. She's suspicious of men. Doesn't trust them. I watched her last night around that stranger, that migrant fellow. She was terrified of him. I need to go slowly, not pressure her. Anyway, she hardly knows I'm alive—thinks of me as an uncle, not a lover."

"But how can *I* help?"

Oliver drew in a deep breath. "Pretend that we—you and I—are an item."

She stared. "What? Are you crazy? How would that possibly help?"

"If she sees me going out with you she may begin to think of me in a different way. She respects you, admires you. If we were together a lot, she might get to like me. Then we'd split up, and I'd try to change her liking to love."

Madeline's horrified expression had changed to one of amusement. She took a sip of coffee, mulling over the

97

proposition. The idea of deceiving Jenny was appalling. Still, if she were seen with Oliver, she'd be furthering her own cause as well. Undoubtedly, it would serve to make Simon jealous. It might not be a bad idea at that.

Oliver guessed what she was thinking. "It would help you, too, you know. Two birds with one stone."

Madeline smiled at the metaphor. "All right, Oliver. I'll agree to your little plan. One thing you should know, however. Jenny's not as easily influenced as you think. She's a mind of her own, and when she marries again, I know it will have to be for love."

"I *do* love her. Now all I have to do is get her used to the idea of loving me."

Madeline looked at the strikingly handsome man before her. Honestly, she didn't see why that should be so difficult. He was quite a catch.

Ah, well. If she played her cards right, this little scheme of his just might get Simon back for her. And if it didn't, she would at least have gotten to spend more time with Oliver.

Either way, she had nothing to lose.

10

Long before the evening ended, Jenny had made up her mind what to do about Tom March. She set her alarm for six, crept into the wide bed and was asleep almost at once.

When the alarm went off, she hurried into her clothes, tied back her hair with a gray ribbon, tucked a tiny change purse into her skirt pocket, and was ready.

She didn't take a car. She'd memorized the address March had given Simon. Since he was staying only a few blocks from Townsend Towers, she could walk it easily.

The palm-lined streets were quiet, only an occasional car passing. The air smelled fresh and clean. She walked briskly, enjoying the exercise. She saw a jogger on the other side of the street, and a white-haired man walking at a moderate rate a block ahead, apparently taking his morning constitutional.

At Indiana Street she turned left and walked toward the ocean to Surf Road. Tom March's house was the third in on the left-hand side of a narrow street. It was a neat two-story dwelling, with an adjoining garage and what appeared to be an efficiency above it.

Her heart thumping, Jenny went up the outside stairs to the front door and knocked. She intended to show him a different Jenny Townsend this time—one who wasn't such a pushover. She knocked again, boldly this time.

"Who is it?" His gruff voice sent a shiver up her spine.

"Jenny Townsend."

There was a brief silence, then the sound of the door opening. He stood before her, wrapped in a blue terry cloth robe, his dark eyes flashing. He feigned anger, but could not conceal his pleasure in finding her there. "Well, Mrs. Townsend—and to what do I owe this unexpected honor—at such an unexpected hour?"

Jenny started to answer, trying to ignore the fact that he was in his robe, his tanned chest partially exposed. "I have something important to discuss with you."

He opened the screen door. "Come in," he rumbled. "Or do you want to stand on my stoop for all the neighborhood to see?"

Instantly defiant, she refused to enter. "I can say what I have to say right here!" she snapped.

He joined her on the stoop. "Well?" he said, and waited.

She glanced away from him, out over the ocean, saw the incoming tide throw its great rollers at the beach and break in white spray. She looked at the houses that dotted the beach. They were small but lovely, uniformly painted in soft pastel colors.

"I'm surprised to find you living on the ocean," she said. "You're such a friend to the migrants who, you say, have no decent place to live. Yet you manage to get yourself a high-priced beach-front apartment."

"It's my own money, Jenny Townsend, put aside for my first trip to Florida. Anyway, this is hardly a luxury spot; the price is low enough. Being from Missoura, a land of prairies and hills, I wanted to swim in the ocean, have it at my door, sleep to the sound of it. Is that so strange?"

Who did he think he was fooling? The hypocrite!

Putting on a show of helping the underdog! She was fiercely glad she'd come, to see him in his true colors.

"Is that why you came?" he asked. "To criticize my apartment?"

"Not at all!" she cried. "I don't care how you live! It's nothing to me! But this tour—that's a Townsend affair, and I'm informing you that your presence on it is neither needed nor wanted!"

"Simon asked me to come."

"That doesn't matter! It's my land, and I—"

"It may be your land, but Townsend Corporation runs it, right? And he is Chairman of the Board."

"That's beside the point! I don't want you on the tour telling us what to do!"

Before she knew it, he lifted her up, propelled her inside and sat her down on the sofa. Indignant, she got up to leave, but he put one hand on her shoulder and pushed her back down.

He glared at her. "It's too bad you don't want me on the tour," he thundered in that deep voice. "But I'm going just the same."

"You—you savage!" she screamed at him, trying desperately to free herself. But his grip on her shoulder tightened. She was so close to his naked chest that she could smell his man-odor, a clean, salty smell, reminiscent of the ocean. She tried to get loose, but couldn't.

"Don't you dare!" she half whispered. "Don't you dare t-take advantage of me—"

"I'm not making a pass at you, damn it!" he growled. "But if I wanted to, I'd take you—anyway I pleased! All I'm trying to do now is to make you understand I've *got* to go on that tour. If you don't want to have to look at me, stay at home yourself."

"I won't!" she cried, struggling, but he still held her fast. "I won't turn you loose on my land! I'm going to be there every minute, to see what you're up to!"

He released her so abruptly she smacked against the sofa back.

"Good!" he exclaimed. "It's settled."

Jenny got up, headed for the door. She'd been defeated again and she felt like an utter fool. To have come here at this hour of the morning, only to be dragged down in the mud again by this—this animal!

He beat her to the door, opened it for her, and their eyes held for a moment.

Then she turned, walked briskly down the stairs and away from the house without once turning back.

There was more to say to Tom March.

But now was not the time.

At near midnight, Jenny lay in bed, unable to fall asleep. She was still simmering with anger at the Missourian, burning as with a fever. Madeline had shopped all day, then gone off to a late dinner. Jenny felt abandoned. There was no one to comfort her, no one she could confide in.

Feeling that only the ocean could calm her, she slipped on a suit and a beach coat and, telling the nightmen where she was going, ran across the sand to the water's edge.

She was alone in the night. There were only the brilliant stars above, the pound of the surf. On impulse, she stripped, folded her beach togs and left them in a pile well above the water line.

Then she raced to the ocean, ran into it until her feet no longer touched bottom, until the water enveloped her naked flesh. She swam until she was in deep water, swam hard, crosswise to the breakers, as she'd done for two years. She gloried in the watery battle, in the strength she'd developed.

She passed one block of shoreline, then two, three. She'd swim one block farther, then turn and fight her way back. She stroked steadily, enjoying the refreshing salt water, the hard, steady pull of her arms and the movement of her legs as she swam on across the breakers.

Suddenly she realized she must be about even with the Missourian's apartment. She thought of him, lying in his bed, sleeping peacefully to the music of the ocean. That he loved the ocean as much as she made her angry. She couldn't bear for him to like the things she liked.

It was right then that she collided with something hard. Panicking for a moment, she caught her breath and realized it was another swimmer. They bobbed up together, about ten feet apart, and the other swimmer started toward her. Frightened, Jenny started to swim in the other direction.

"Wait," the voice commanded, and Jenny recognized it instantly. She turned to see the Missourian, swimming toward her with bold strokes. It was no use trying to outrace him. She treaded water, allowing him to catch up with her.

"My, my," he sputtered. "Did you swim all the way from Townsend Towers?"

"So what?" she retorted, her arms and legs pumping to stay afloat.

"That's quite a distance—and at this late hour—and"—his eyes lowered seductively—"in a state not befitting a lady, especially one of your, uh, position—"

"It's none of your business how—or where—I choose to swim," she cried.

Suddenly a wave came from out of nowhere, knocking her down and dragging her beneath the surface. Tom March swam to her, wrapped his powerful arms around her struggling form. Both were coughing and spluttering, blinded by water, but he kept hold of her, his hands on her upper arms.

"Let go of me you . . . you beast!" she screamed frantically.

She pulled vigorously, and almost got away. But he caught hold of one arm and one leg and kept her. Then keeping her head above water, with one hand under her chin, he towed her toward the beach. Weary of struggling, she allowed him to pull her, naked, through the dark, rippling ocean.

When they got to where the water wasn't so deep, where they could stand, he held her tightly against him and she shivered to his touch. He pulled off his swim trunks and pressed his own naked body to hers. She tried to pull free, but dizziness swept over her, inundating her with weakness so that she had to give up for a moment.

They stood together, waves breaking over and around them. She realized, as he forced her legs apart, that she had a feverish hunger for this animal, this naked

103

brute. And it was all wrong, had gotten all mixed up. What she really wanted was a man like Simon or Rolf—a gentleman. She didn't want this beast, despite that wild fire between her thighs. She didn't want to stand naked in the ocean, water almost to her shoulders, and let him take her.

But she did it. Knees bent, she stood in the rolling waves and let him thrust himself into her fiery depths. Linked to him, she moved when he moved, dissolved into his arms, seemed to seep into his body and he into hers. They stood in the one spot. Wave after wave broke over them, and they moved faster with each wave until there was nothing but the ecstasy.

She was clinging to him now, pressing ever closer. He filled her with himself, with what she must have. The ocean laved them, and they moved, welded and melted, and then the joy they sought took them, pressed them in such delight that the ocean was nothing and the waves no longer existed.

They relaxed, still in each other's arms. Tom March felt, at that moment, that he was cradling all of heaven. There was so much he needed to say, but he was too shaken to utter a word. When he was finally ready to speak, she beat him to it.

"I hope you're satisfied!" she half screamed. "That's twice . . . three times!"

"Lower your voice," he ordered. "Folks can hear."

"Out of my way!" she cried, forgetting that the ocean was so big he couldn't block her by just standing still. "I'm swimming back home!"

"No, you're not," he announced. "You're walking, and I'm going with you."

"Oh, no you're not!" she cried and stared to swim away from him. She expected him to follow, to pull up alongside her and drag her to shore. But he didn't.

Tom March was damn mad. She had hell's own temper. Well, let her go if that was what she wanted. No point in chasing after her.

But by the time he'd returned to his apartment, he'd changed his mind. Jumping into his other swim trunks, he took out after her, running along the sand.

When he didn't see her anywhere in the water, he began to grow alarmed. Then he spotted her, just a half block or so from the Townsend beach. She was swimming gracefully, steadily, in the black ocean, bucking the waves. In spite of his anger, he was impressed with her strength.

He ran the rest of the way to the private beach, squatted in the shadow of some palm trees and waited. Eventually, she emerged from the water, and he saw her slender white body glistening in the moonlight. He watched as she located her swim togs, dressed, and hurried toward the beach entrance to Townsend Towers.

Slowly, he walked back to his apartment. He would sleep better knowing she was safe, that she hadn't drowned after he'd tired her with sex. The thought of their ecstasy came back to him, making him shiver with pleasure.

Then he pushed the memory from his mind.

Jenny nodded to the nightman, hurried into the elevator, went noiselessly into her rooms. Madeline was probably home by now and she didn't want her to suspect she'd been out.

She bathed, soaping herself twice to wash off all trace of him. Then she crept naked into bed, and pulled the satin comforter tightly around her.

She couldn't sleep. Her mind was racing. Damn that man, he was like a sickness growing inside her. Already, this soon, she wanted him again. And why, when he had treated her so badly? Missouri mule, she thought.

At last she made a decision. She would let him have sex with her one more time. She would prove to herself that he was a heel, a no-good brute. Then he'd be out of her system forever.

When she slept, she dreamed that several men were chasing her and she was trying to escape. When she woke she didn't know whether she'd broken free of them or settled on one to marry.

11

Jenny wasted no time in attempting to carry out her plan. She dressed quickly and hastened to Tom March's apartment. Trembling slightly at the thought of what she was about to do, she mounted the stairs and knocked softly.

She was shocked when the door was opened by a handsomely dressed Simon Townsend.

"Well, good morning Jenny! We were just having an early breakfast and were going to pick up you and Madeline—but I see you were as anxious about the tour as we were!"

She tried to hide her surprised look. "Oh, yes," she stammered. "I—uh—woke up early and just thought I'd come by to see if Mr. March was ready—"

But she could tell by Simon's stern expression that he didn't believe her. He seemed almost hurt.

The Missourian appeared now from the bedroom, gave her a knowing smile. "Why, how nice of you to come Mrs. Townsend—Jenny. Can I offer you some coffee?"

The cad, thought Jenny. He *knows* why I came here!

He *knows!* Silently, she accepted the coffee and sat down at the breakfast table to join them.

As they chatted about the upcoming tour, Jenny had her first real chance to look around the small living room. She was aware of scanty furnishings, rugged textures, several colorful prints adorning the walls. There were gleaming copper pots hanging above a small stove on the wall that made up the tiny kitchenette, and Jenny was surprised at the sense of order, the clean smell of soap and wax.

"Quite a view, isn't it?" Simon was asking her.

Her head turned toward the large picture window that she was seeing for the first time. The ocean was blue and calm. Jenny watched as a young boy threw a stick into the water and his dog went bounding after it. The dog retrieved the stick, brought it back to the shore and dropped it at the boy's feet. The boy picked up the stick, threw it back into the ocean, and the game began again.

She turned back to Simon. "Yes, it's lovely. A perfect day, too." Her eyes were still avoiding the Missourian's.

They were interrupted by a knock at the door. David and Rolf entered, both men looking cheerful and handsome in expensive white suits. They too were surprised to see Jenny there.

"Another early riser!" exclaimed Rolf. "We know Simon is all business, but you, too, Jenny-love?"

After David and Rolf joined them for a quick cup of coffee, the five of them left the tiny apartment, entered the chauffeured limousine in which Simon had arrived, and headed to Townsend Towers to pick up Madeline.

"So you were there all the time!" she scolded Jenny. "I was half out of my mind with worry that you'd miss the tour!"

David insisted that the six of them ride in his car. It was a new Cadillac and he was eager to show it off.

"It's got a jump seat, a tape deck, a telephone. And it's all white, inside and out, to match *The Louisa*."

They climbed into the luxurious car, Madeline scrambling to sit next to David in the front seat. "I get to ride next to the driver!" she declared. "I claim that honor!" She put both hands on David's arm when he slid behind the wheel. "Is that all right?"

He gave his sunny smile. "Fine, fine! Pile in, everybody!"

Jenny hurriedly took the remaining space in the front seat, beside Madeline. She wanted to avoid the embarrassment of being sandwiched in next to Tom March.

She caught a glimpse of Simon's face as he slid into the car. He seemed worried, anxious. Was it the tour, she wondered. Or was he still angry about her morning visit to Tom March? She looked over at Madeline, playing up to David for Simon's benefit. She might as well give up. From what Jenny could tell, Simon seemed oblivious to her.

As they rolled along, they talked about the migrant situation, Tom March mentioning that it had been briefly written up in the newspaper. There had also been a small piece on the evening news. But there had been no major coverage, at least not yet.

David drove first to a vast tomato field south of Miami. They walked to the edge of the field where the plants were heavy with fruit, some of it green, some growing red. Jenny thought the rows of tomatoes looked like jewels, glistening in the sun.

Off a distance, stooped over the rows of tomato plants, were the pickers. They were Chicano, Negro, deeply tanned whites—men and women both, and quite a few children. Their fingers were quick; Jenny was amazed at the speed with which they picked the tomatoes, dropping them into the baskets they pulled alongside them.

There was a big truck parked to one side of the field, where three white men were stationed. "The field boss is over there," Simon said. "Come on. We'll have a word with him."

They made their way through the rows of plants, careful not to disturb the pickers. They needn't have worried. None of them so much as looked up, but worked swiftly on.

Jenny stumbled once, and Tom caught her arm and

109

saved her from falling. "You all right?" he asked, steadying her.

She pulled away, saying that she was capable of walking by herself. She knew why he was playing the gallant gentleman. It was to aggravate her, to taunt her, to remind her of how wildly she had behaved with him. She glanced quickly at him and saw that he was scowling. Well, it was too bad!

As they walked toward the truck, they passed workers carrying their filled baskets to it, and those returning to the field with empty baskets. Jenny saw how they were sweating; most of them looked dirty, their clothes and even their cheeks and hair streaked with earth.

Simon led to the field boss, a broad, rough man in a blue work shirt and clean Levis. He wore a straw hat, tilted back, under which could be seen a shock of black hair. His eyes were hard and his whole appearance looked forbidding.

"You the Townsends?" he asked before Simon could speak. "I been wonderin' if you'd show up. Got a good crop this year, spite of the rains. Blessing's my name, Bud Blessing. I run the fields and these other two men keep a tally on ev'ry picker, how many baskets he picks a day."

Simon introduced their party. "Mrs. Townsend," he finished, "is the actual owner of this land."

"But it's part of the overall Townsend holdings, right?"

"That's correct."

"You see how the harvestin' goes," Blessing said, gesturing across the field. "The tally men inspect ev'ry basket, see," Blessing explained. "Then they mark it down to the picker's credit. At the end of the day they're added up and the picker knows what he's earned, and will be paid. He gets his money at the end of the week, or before, if he runs short. We don't like to pay daily— messes up the bookkeepin'—but we do it where it's needed."

"Is there a bathhouse here?" Jenny asked.

"Toilets. Up at the north end. In fair condition. Ain't no point you folks botherin' with them. They serve the purpose."

"That's one reason we're here," Simon told him. "To see if they serve the purpose."

Thus the party, including the disgruntled Blessing, trudged the distance to the toilets. Jenny couldn't believe her eyes when she saw there were only two small, unpainted shacks, each with one chipped, stained toilet.

She felt Tom's eyes on her, met them swiftly, looked away. There'd been what seemed to be a hint of sadness in them, but she told herself it was probably an "I-told-you-so" gleam.

"Where do your pickers live, Mr. Blessing?" Simon asked.

"Most of 'em live at the camp couple miles north," Blessing said.

"Is it a Townsend camp?" Jenny asked.

"No, ma'am. Fellow name of Clark runs it. He rents out cabins to them that hasn't got a trailer, rents use of the bathouse, even lets in them that pitches tents."

From the tomato field, they drove to the labor camp. Clark didn't greet them with pleasure. Nor did the name of Townsend change his attitude.

"What do you want?" he asked in a surly manner.

"Just a look at your facilities," Rolf assured him. "Then we're going to inspect our own facilities to see whether they fall short of what you offer."

"We-ell, seeing that you're owners, not do-gooders, take a look," Clark growled. "Don't be took back at what you see. These pickers is animals. Put 'em in a place, and first thing they do is tear it up. Help yourselves. I got a program to watch on TV."

He meandered to a fine-looking camper, disappeared into it.

The Townsend group started toward a row of ramshackle, unpainted shacks. There were eight of them; Jenny counted. Only one had an outside door; the others were wide open, announcing the contents of their shabby rooms to the world. Beside them were two old trailers and three ragged tents.

"This was your idea, March," Simon said, distaste in every word. "I suggest that you lead this part of the tour."

Tom nodded, strode to the nearest cabin, stood aside so they could enter. Then he came in. Jenny looked around wide-eyed, her hand going involuntarily to her nose. She drew a cautious breath; the stench was horrible.

She forced herself to look, to see. There was only one room. Pallets of ragged blankets and towels were rolled up and stacked against one wall. Against another leaned a wobbly little table with two unsteady chairs drawn up to it. A shelf with a hot plate and a small cabinet section above occupied the third wall.

That was it; except for a few battered utensils and some faded garments hung on wall hooks, there was nothing else in the room.

Jenny walked to the wall cabinet, opened it carefully; it leaned on one hinge. Roaches scuttled out and ran in every direction.

Jenny whirled, horrified. Her foot caught in a broken floorboard and she nearly tripped and fell as a rat shot past her ankle. She shuddered. People, human beings, lived, slept and ate in this pigsty.

Madeline was sobbing. She came to stand beside Jenny.

"Let's see the bathhouse," Jenny said to March.

It was worse than the toilets in the tomato field, worse than the shack. There was only one shower, its floor cracked and splintered, the shower head rusted. There were three toilets without seats or lids.

They went back to the car in silence. Jenny ached for the poor creatures who lived in such squalor. Much as she despised the Missourian, she had to admit he was right, at least about this one labor camp.

She was quiet on the way to the Townsend citrus grove they were to visit next.

At one point, David tried to reassure her.

"That was a labor camp, Jenny," he said. "Not on Townsend property."

"If *our* facilities look anything like that, we've got to do something!" She spoke with such resolve that no one tried to contradict her. And the Missourian, she noticed out of the corner of her eye, was grinning. Quickly, she faced the road ahead. She hated to give him the satisfaction of knowing he was right.

Orange Blossom Grove, Jenny discovered, as they glided to a stop at the manager's white-painted stucco house, was beautiful. Climbing vines covered with bright yellow flowers adorned the front of the house and dwarf palms outlined the manicured green lawn.

As they were getting out of the car, Woody Woodbury, the manager, appeared. He was a tall man, well built, with tough, weathered skin that made him look older than he was. He knew the Townsend men. After greeting them warmly, he shook hands with Jenny, Madeline and Tom.

"We're inspecting the living conditions of our pickers," Simon told him. "Where do your pickers live? Are there quarters in the grove?"

"No, sir. There's a passable labor camp two miles south. They live there. And I've kept up the toilet facilities here. We have three, in painted sheds, if you'd like to see them."

"We'd like that, sir," Jenny said quickly.

"Mrs. Townsend owns the grove," Rolf explained.

Woody Woodbury looked back at the striking redhead. Obviously he had not expected Si Townsend's widow to be so young.

"I was sorry to hear about your husband, Mrs. Townsend. He was a great man."

Jenny smiled her thanks, then followed as he led the way to the workers' facility.

She was relieved when she saw it. The toilets were clean, in good condition, and afforded privacy. She determined, on the spot, that every acre of her farmland would eventually be equipped in this way. If others did not agree, she would simply overrule them.

There were no pickers in the grove today, because the fruit wasn't quite ripe. "We start picking next week," Woodbury explained.

When they got into the car this time, Tom March suggested they take a look at the nearby labor camp that Woodbury had mentioned. All agreed, so David sent the car speeding toward it, driving over the limit.

113

Here, the manager's wife showed them around. The cabins were old and barely decent. But the bathhouse was fairly clean and everything seemed in working order. The manager's wife seemed to be under the impression that they were official inspectors and went out of her way to point out all the good aspects of the camp.

"You see the factory-built campers yonder?" she asked, motioning behind them. "No trash throwed on the ground outside. Same with the tents. My Jack, he sees to it that we run a decent camp. Some of 'em, a few years back, when the newspapers and TV raised such a stink, was really awful. But never ours."

It was nearly lunchtime when they headed back to Townsend Towers. Jenny had asked Flo to prepare a big meal for all of them, but now, thinking about what she had seen at the first camp, she felt far from hungry. She was half ill, remembering the cockroaches, the filth, the smell.

The others chatted among themselves, but neither she nor Tom March uttered a word as the car sped along the highway.

"Well, I just think it's awful, how those poor folks live," Madeline was saying. "It's inhuman, don't you think so, David?" She was still in the front seat, clutching David's arm.

"It looks bad, all right," David admitted. "But business is business, you know. There's a limit to how much we can spend on improvements."

Jenny continued to stare silently out the window. For the moment, she'd keep her opinions to herself.

She was still quiet when the six of them stepped out of the penthouse elevator. Flo greeted them, her voice unusually excited.

"Oh, Mrs. Townsend!" she exclaimed. "Your greyhound arrived. She's on the roof, in one of the kennels. And, oh, she's a beauty!"

12

The kennels were situated at the far side of the roof, so that the dogs could enjoy a view of the garden.

The slim greyhound which stared at them now, ears back, was pale silver in color. Not a mark of any kind marred her perfection.

Ears back, tail between her legs, she stared at the group of strangers and growled. Jenny moved slowly to the runway, sank to her knees and murmured.

"Sally," she said. "Romantic Sally. Pretty Romantic Sally. Pretty girl, nice girl!"

Still between her legs, Romantic Sally's tail moved. It fell short of being a wag, but the growling faded and the greyhound eyed the stranger kneeling before her with interest.

Simon advanced, and she began to growl again, this time baring her teeth.

"What is she, Jenny?" chuckled David. "Watchdog or racer?"

Jenny heaved a sigh. She stared at her beautiful new pet, wondering if she'd ever be able to race her.

"Boldness does it, Jenny," Simon said. "Show her who's boss. Don't let her get the upper hand."

Jenny knew he was right. Before she could lose her courage, she went to the gate, unlatched it, and entered the kennel. Romantic Sally shrank back into a corner, letting off a low whine. Steadily, Jenny advanced on the dog; when she reached her, she put out a hand to stroke and pat and soothe.

In a flash, Romantic Sally had Jenny's wrist in her mouth, and was biting down on the soft flesh. Simon was there in an instant, prying the dog's teeth loose, kicking her back to the corner, dragging Jenny out and to safety. David slammed the gate shut and locked it.

Madeline had her arm around Jenny, as Simon examined her wrist. Only a slight trickle of blood emanated from the tooth marks. "The emergency room," Simon declared. "That's got to be taken care of; you'll need a shot, too."

Jenny shook her head in protest. She'd been bitten before by a frightened dog. There was plenty of time, she knew, to get to the hospital. She let Simon bandage her wrist with a clean handkerchief, and thanked him for saving her from worse injury.

Then, from the corner of her eye, she saw Tom March approach the runway. He moved so noiselessly he seemed to drift rather than walk. Romantic Sally wheeled, eyes on him, growling. Tom continued his approach. Romantic Sally tensed herself to spring, but didn't. Instead, she stood like a beautiful silver carving and stared at Tom, who stopped near the runway and stood equally still.

The growl lowered, bubbled in the dog's throat.

"Sally . . . Sally . . . good girl," he half whispered, "Don't be scared . . . this is Tom . . . Tom . . . Sally . . . Sally . . . fine girl . . ."

The greyhound waited. Tom edged nearer, up to the tall gate, and still Romantic Sally didn't spring. Her ears twitched and her tail, pinned between her legs, was motionless. Everything about her showed that she was frightened, untrusting, waiting to fight for her life.

Tom continued to whisper softly. Finally Romantic

Sally took one frightened step toward the gate, then backed away. But her tail moved from between her legs and her ears lifted. Still, she was stalling.

Still whispering, Tom opened the gate, closed it gently behind him. His whispering never ceased. Romantic Sally, ever ready to spring, crouched like a vibrant statue. Cautiously he squatted, facing her.

"Sally . . ." he murmured, on and on. "Come to Tom . . . friends . . . Sally . . ." Inch by inch he extended his hand.

She whined, dropped belly-down to the grass.

"That's the girl! Come to Tom . . . come, girl!"

Whining, black nose glistening, the greyhound crept toward Tom. She was close now, and she stopped, sniffed his hand. She whined again and her tail began to wag. Then, suddenly, she jumped up and flung herself at him as if she'd found a long lost friend. Tom patted and stroked and hugged, repeating her name endlessly.

Jenny watched in a mixture of fury and relief. Relief that the frightened dog had lost her terror; fury that it had been the Missourian who accomplished the miracle. He turned now, Romantic Sally with her forepaws on his shoulders, licking his face.

"Jenny! Come on in! Let me introduce you and there'll be no more trouble. She's quieted down just like a new hunting hound would, back in Missoura."

Jenny forced herself to walk toward the runway. At her approach Romantic Sally stopped her cavorting; her ears snapped back, and she began to whine.

"It's all right, girl," Tom soothed. "It's fine . . . Jenny . . . nice Jenny." For the dog's benefit, he stroked Jenny's hair. Romantic Sally watched, tail beginning to wave slowly.

Jenny set her chin. His touch angered her, but she dared not jerk away because of the effect it might have on the dog. Finally, she extended her own hand to the greyhound and whispered softly.

"Nice girl . . . good Sally . . ."

Romantic Sally whined, smelled Jenny's fingers, gave them a lick. Carefully, Jenny stroked the sleek head, and gradually she was accepted. Not with the enthusiasm

117

shown to Tom March, but at least she was no longer rejected.

David had gone to fetch some raw beef, hoping to appease Romantic Sally with food. He returned now, and seeing her gentleness, approached the runway. Romantic Sally bared her teeth at him. "Doesn't look as if she wants any more friends," he said, backing away.

"Probably not," Tom agreed. "They're racing dogs. Working dogs, actually. Sally's done exceptionally well. She'll learn to work with her trainers and the handlers at the track, but that'll be about it."

Jenny gave the dog one last hug and she and Tom came out of the kennel. Madeline, wide-eyed, came running up to them.

"Tom, you were wonderful!" she cried. "You have a magic touch!"

"Oh, not really. Just learned how from handling hunting dogs," Tom said modestly.

Jenny looked at him. He'd put on quite a performance with Romantic Sally. Now he was pretending to be humble. Was there no end to the man's hypocrisy? Still, he *had* made Romantic Sally her friend, and she supposed she ought to show some gratitude.

"Yes, thank you, Mr. March. You do seem to have a way with dogs." And to herself added, *but not people!*

She allowed Simon to drive her to the emergency room, where she was given a shot and had her wrist dressed. They were back in a half hour, in time to join the others for lunch.

Sitting around the dining room table, they talked about Romantic Sally's future. All of them agreed that she had great potential as a racer. Rolf offered to drive Jenny and the dog to the training kennels outside Davie.

Jenny thanked him, but declined. "I'll keep Sally here for a while, make a pet of her," she said, "the way I did with the others."

"Seems to me," Tom March put in, "that'd affect her racing."

His daring to voice an opinion about her training method infuriated Jenny. "Tender loving care never hurt

118

anybody!" she snapped. "I want Romantic Sally to feel at ease when I take her to Davie, and then I'll go to see her every day until she's used to the kennels."

"You did that with the first two, and they adjusted," Madeline agreed. "Tom, I think Jenny's right."

Simon frowned, reached over and touched Jenny's bandaged wrist lightly. "Be careful, though," he warned. "Very careful. That dog has a wild streak. She's not like the others. And I won't always be around to save you."

Tom March's jaw muscles tightened visibly, but he said nothing. He watched as Jenny withdrew her arm from Simon's grasp.

"You're sweet to be concerned about me," she replied. "All of you. But, really, I can handle her just fine. Now, why don't we talk about this morning's tour; instead?"

But Simon overruled them. "I suggest we all think about it overnight. Sleep on it. Then have a meeting in my office at ten tomorrow."

All nodded, including the Missourian. Simon invited him to attend, and this made Jenny furious with Simon for the first time since she'd known him. To show that she wasn't going to spinelessly submit to their male whims, she invited Madeline to attend too, and the ex-Mrs. Townsend quickly accepted.

When everyone had left, Jenny asked Flo to serve her some tea on the patio. Madeline had gone shopping and Jenny was happy for the quiet moments alone. She needed time to think, to sort out the events of the day.

But all she could think of was Tom March. The look on his face when she had appeared at his apartment. The great show he had put on with Romantic Sally. The way he had forced himself into almost every facet of her life— telling her how to run her farmlands, how to manage her dog—

And yet, when he was around her, she burned with that unspeakable desire. She wanted him to touch her, to take her in his arms, to fill her with his maleness—

But, no! She had to stop herself. She had to wash all trace of him from her system, and fast. Then she'd marry a perfect man, a young Townsend, with Si's polish. A man who loved her and cared nothing about her money or what she did with it. A man who would also give her physical joy without degradation.

Tomorrow, after the meeting, she'd deal with Tom March. And when that was done, she'd be through with him forever.

13

Simon Townsend's office, on the eighteenth floor of the Townsend building, was luxurious. In front of a wall of floor-to-ceiling windows was a magnificent mahogany desk and a chair covered with rich brown suede. The walls, except for the glassed one, were lined with handsome bookshelves holding books pertaining to Townsend interests. A brown velvet rug covered the floor.

Jenny disliked the room. The only bright touch was the two tall umbrella plants that graced each side of the office. Otherwise, it lacked color and charm. Were it not for the windows, it would have been almost dreary.

Simon motioned for them to sit around the small glass conference table in one corner. Then he buzzed his secretary to bring them coffee, and joined them at the table.

"I preferred not calling a meeting of the entire board just yet," Simon began. "This problem has to do with Jenny's private holdings, which are apart from corporate control. Unless she so wishes to assign them."

"I'll not do so at present," Jenny said clearly. She

had anticipated this. "We're the ones who saw what conditions exist, and I'm the one, with your help, to decide what is to be done."

"Perhaps you'll reconsider," Simon replied. "You've not had any . . . er . . . experience with business matters. May I suggest that you consider taking a vote to include the corporation when the matter comes to decision?"

"Very well," Jenny murmured.

"Should such vote be tied," Simon continued, "we can lay the matter before Oliver Cranston and let his be the deciding vote."

"If I'm allowed to speak," Madeline said, "I think that's an inspired idea, Simon!"

He cast her a disapproving glance, then looked away.

"Now, what I'd like to do," he continued, his voice authoritative, "is to review some of the things we discovered on yesterday's tour."

He proceeded to give a résumé of what they'd learned, while the others listened intently.

"The labor camps are, on the whole, inadequate," Simon stated. "The Clark camp is the best in our immediate area, and we saw how poor it is. The bathhouses we saw were all below par and, except at Orange Blossom, the sanitary facilities are inadequate." He paused. "Have I missed anything?"

There was a silence, then Tom March spoke up. "Wages," he said. "At least ten cents more per basket for picking tomatoes, and a raise per box for citrus."

Simon frowned. So did Rolf and David. Jenny ached to cry out. Why not? Why not pay them more? But she wasn't going to uphold Tom March. Not in his presence. If they voted him down, she'd call another meeting with only Townsends, and maybe Oliver Cranston, present.

"Such an action needs consideration, March," Rolf said. "We'd have to talk it over with other growers. The Townsends can't give a big raise like that on their own, without possibly ruining the smaller growers."

"I can fully understand that," March nodded. "But you ought to have those talks soon."

"In due time," Simon replied. "This is a tremendous problem. Jenny's land holdings run from citrus groves near Orlando in the middle of the state to Homestead farmland, south of Miami. We had some trouble with pickers in Dade County last year; growers were forced to raise the picking price. We're aware of the problem, but we have to give it serious thought."

Tom March, however, was not to be quieted. "What's needed," he said, "is for plain, decent labor camps to be built."

"From Orlando to Homestead?" asked David, incredulous.

"Right. With good bathhouses."

Jenny, in a silent rage at the Missourian's interference, nonetheless had to smother a smile at the consternation on the faces of the Townsends. They just sat and stared, speechless for the moment.

She decided to speak up. "Bathhouses," she said. "I suggest that we start by building bathhouses so that every migrant who picks for me can, at the end of the day, take a good, soapy shower and wash his clothes. With toilet facilities in each bathhouse."

"What about shelter?" demanded Tom March.

"They do have shelter now, such as it is," she told him stiffly, hiding her real doubts. "My plan enables them to at least keep themselves clean. They can carry water from the bathhouses to the shacks, trailers and tents. Until we can do more." She hadn't wanted to make that last concession, but she'd had no choice. She didn't want Simon and the others to get the idea that a few bathhouses would solve the whole problem.

"Labor camps, bathhouses," Simon repeated tonelessly. "Have you stopped to consider how much it would cost to build them from Orlando to Homestead and beyond? You own acreage south of Homestead, too, Jenny. Labor camps are not a Townsend obligation."

"Nobody else will build them," said Tom. "It would be a losing proposition for an independent builder, because the pickers can't pay enough rent to make them do more than break even."

"Then they'd be a total loss for a grower!" Rolf exclaimed. "The rent would never repay the cost of construction, to say nothing of upkeep, insurance and taxes."

"The grower *would* benefit," persisted the Missourian. "The grower with decent camps, paying a fair wage, will draw the best pickers. His fields and groves will be picked clean, his fruit will be handled with care, and in the long run he'll make a better profit."

"But not enough to offset the original investment," Simon said flatly. "It could end up costing a million . . . more."

"The camps would offset the expense," Tom insisted. "Without them, pickers are going to make more and more trouble, and in the long run growers are going to lose money. And the Townsends will be the biggest losers, having the most to lose."

"We could build *some* bathhouses now, see how it goes," Rolf suggested.

"It's too late in the season," David objected. "It's November and the picking's underway."

"There'd be some advantage to starting now," Tom pointed out. "Even if they can't use them this season, it shows your goodwill and might help quiet their unrest."

They talked longer, and the more they talked, the more disgusted Jenny became. They were so stubborn! All of them! "We're losing sight of the problem," she said finally. "Which is that these people need decent facilities."

"We appreciate your womanly concern, Jenny," Simon explained. "We even share it. But we must be practical. Before we make a move, we must consult experts, find out what it will cost, whether Townsend farms and groves can absorb the cost without going bankrupt. For loss there will be, depend on that. Later, we'll decide what to do."

"Simon's right," agreed Rolf, and David nodded.

"We can't just jump into such a big undertaking. You do understand that, Jenny . . . March?"

She chewed the inside of her lips. Darn Rolf for making it seem she was in league with the Missourian! Couldn't he see, couldn't all of them see, that Tom March was purely and simply poking his nose into private business?

"I see your side of it," Tom replied. "You don't want to jump into a big construction program without thought. But you may be forced into it. One faction of pickers, the one led by Perez, will have no qualms whatsoever about striking, fighting, or doing whatever else they can think of to make things change."

There was silence.

"That," Simon said at last, slowly, "is a calculated risk we must take. If trouble comes, we'll deal with it. Meanwhile, we'll get our experts onto this building idea; and when all the facts are in, we'll study them. Then we'll take a final vote. I offer this as an informal motion. All in favor, raise your hand."

Simon's hand lifted. Rolf's. David's. Jenny clenched her hands in her lap. She was trapped. If she refrained from voting with the others, Tom March, conceited mule that he was, would think she was his friend on this project, that she was working with him.

She set her jaw. Kept her hand down. Let the Missourian think what he pleased; she'd soon rid herself of him forever!

That night she lay wakeful, naked, burning, impatient. Would the hours never pass? She'd determined to go to him tonight, to carry out her plan, come out of it freed from the hold he had on her. But she wanted to time it so the world would be asleep when she went to him.

She turned from side to side restlessly, both from the burning and from the anger. She turned again violently, because she hated Tom March. He had pounded this feeling into her, this compulsion to rid herself of passion.

Passion. That was the word. That was what he'd made her feel. And what she now needed to run from.

She lay quiet then, and longed for Si—his love, his gentle touch, his tenderness. Then memory of the Missourian's fiery passion crept over her, making her forget the other, and she was angrier still.

She was in this miserable state in the dark hour before dawn. Only then did she get into a bikini, throw on a light beach coat and steal out of the penthouse, toward the beach.

She left her beach coat on the sand, walked into the ocean to her shoulders, and began to swim south. The water was warmer than the air, but still felt cool and soothing, though she continued to burn at her core. She swam faster.

She ran across the sand, up the outside steps, knocked at his door. It opened right away and she could tell, in the first dawn light, that he was naked.

"What do you want?" he demanded.

"I came," she told him fiercely, stepping inside, "to inform you that I never want to see you again!"

He was silent. Then he closed the door, strode about the room closing the blinds, and snapped on a dim light.

"I know why you came," he said.

He took another stride and in one motion had her bikini top off. The next move stripped away the bottom, and he stood staring at her naked body.

"You beast!" she hissed. "You . . . animal!"

"You're the one who wants it," he said coolly. "Can you deny it?"

She stood glaring at him, unable to speak.

"We're all animals, Jenny," he went on. "The male is always ready. He has to wait for the female to come to him, in heat. Which you've done."

She flew at him, nails going for his face. He swooped her up under one arm, carried her, kicking and screaming, to the rumpled fold-out bed, and dumped her.

She sprang up, eyes wild. He put out one hand, pushed her back onto the bed, and ignoring her protest, mounted her still wet body.

He filled her, and the flame rose up to envelop him. She was so angry, in such a hurry to rid herself of this devastating hunger, that she began to move before he did.

At first he thought she was trying to get loose, so he bore down. Then her fingers were on his shoulders, the nails digging in as she pressed closer, moving as violently

126

as he himself did. So he'd been right. She did want him. She was ready for a man. And right this minute, just like the first day he saw her, and again in the ocean, he was sure as hell ready for her.

She took his thrusting, met it. His strokes quickened, and so did hers. She couldn't have stopped if she'd wanted to, and she didn't want to. She meant to get her fill, to be half drowned with sensation, never again to undergo his hot torture.

He felt his sap overflow and rush into her. She felt the strong pulse within, felt her own passion flash to every nerve ending and explode.

When it was over, she lay still, smiling. She'd done it. Gotten her fill of Tom March.

14

When she moved to leave the bed, he let her go. She went running to the bathroom, stepped into the tub, closed the drain, tuned on the faucet and sat down in the rising water.

He'd followed, for now he got into the tub, yanked the shower curtain shut, opened the drain, and turned on the shower full tilt. She shot up, grabbed at the shower control, and he brushed her fingers away as if they were cobwebs. The water thundered down, cascading over them.

"Get out of this tub!" she screamed. "This is *my* bath!"

"Seems it's my apartment," he rumbled. "And quit screeching. Want the landlord to find you stark naked, taking a bath with me?"

"I'm not taking a bath with you!" she hissed.

He'd taken hold of her arm, and she tried to yank free, and he held the other arm as well. Then he pressed her downward until she was sitting in the tub again.

"Don't try to get loose. Else you'll fall and break something."

"You . . . brute!" she hissed on. "Well, I'm going to take my bath! With you or without you!"

"Be my guest," he said, and handed her the soap.

Furiously, the shower cascading around her shoulders, she soaped herself all over, including her hair. While she was doing that, he stood over her, using another bar of soap on himself.

She had to half stand to soap her bottom and, just as she finished, her foot slipped and she fell backward. He managed to pick her up, his soapy hands sliding on her lathered skin, and then with a muttered curse he turned off the water.

"Turn it back on!" she cried. "I need to rinse!"

"Not yet, you don't," he ordered. He gave her a small push and, sitting as she was in the tub, her soapy body slid down and she was on her back. Before she could struggle back up, he was on top of her and, wet and slippery as they both were, he managed to enter her again.

She felt him bore in, press upward, harder and harder. The passion was rising again within her. She hadn't wanted this, had been finished with him. But she could not stop.

He thrust into her, felt her returning thrusts of pleasure. He was in ecstasy. Never had there been such a woman. He held out as long as he could and then he let go and was taken with such thunderous delight as he'd not dreamed possible.

Through her own flashing ecstasy, Jenny felt his deep satisfaction. She clung to his soapy arms, gave every bit of herself to sensation, cramming herself with it.

She was gasping for breath when it ended.

Tom got to his knees, to his feet. He turned on the shower and managed to help Jenny up. They stood together, sharing the pounding water as they'd shared each other's body. Even after they'd rinsed, they stayed there facing each other.

Then, tenderly, he took her chin in his hand, tilted her face up to his.

"Would you," he asked, "ever consider marrying a migrant?"

"You're not a migrant! You don't pick fruit!"

"Some. And I move as often as any. Makes them respect me."

"So that makes you one of them? You still live at the beach! Spend money like mad!"

"I've got enough to live on for a spell."

A strand of her wet hair fell across her cheek and she swiped at it impatiently. He had an answer for everything!

"I asked you a question" he said. "Would you give up your millions and live as a migrant's wife?"

She recognized that he was trying to trick her. If, in answer to his silly question, she said yes, he'd probably marry her and insist on keeping the money. He wasn't one to let ten million go, not him!

"I'll marry a gentleman or no one!" she cried. "Not a migrant, not a farmer, not a playboy, but a real gentleman!"

"Like you did the first time."

Choking with rage, trembling so hard that she couldn't get out of the shower, dry herself and leave, she nodded fiercely. She managed to swallow, and it made a sound he could hear.

"I get the drift," he said, bending to turn off the water. "I asked Madeline whether she thought you'd remarry soon. She seemed to feel you would—and that it would probably be to a Townsend. Which one do you lean to? Simon, because he's Chairman of the Board?"

Beside herself with rage, Jenny glared, wishing her eyes were daggers. She was furious, too, with Madeline, for having told him her secret. Well, she'd return the favor. "Not Simon!" she spat out. "Madeline's plotting to get him back—or did she forget to tell you that?"

A smile played at Tom March's lips. "No, she didn't tell me. But now I know, don't I?"

Tears sprang to her eyes, but she wouldn't let them fall. The brute! He had tricked her! Madeline had never said anything to him about her plan to marry one of the grandsons. He had figured that out on his own, then tested her to see if it was true.

"You know," he continued, "I'm beginning to understand you now. Beautiful, yes. But hot-tempered, greedy. Disloyal to your friends. Glad I found out in time. I was actually crazy enough to think that what happened between us meant something. I've felt an attraction to Madeline. Now I can pursue it. I can put Simon out of the running if I want to."

"You do that!" stormed Jenny. "It suits me fine!"

She got out of the tub, hastily dried herself, and pulled on her wet swimsuit. March didn't bother to dry off, just stepped out of the tub and watched her. He didn't say another word and neither did she, but ran out the door, across the beach and into the water, where she began to swim furiously homeward. Every stroke was a blow to Tom March's hated flesh; every kick was aimed at his vitals.

Back in the penthouse, she dressed in a light gray jump suit and came downstairs to the kitchen. It was just turning eight o'clock.

She poured herself a cup of coffee, sat down, and waited for Madeline to wake up so she could confess how she'd betrayed her.

She blurted it out after breakfast, telling the girl all about herself and Tom March. "He's evil, he is. He tricked me into giving away your secret. Can you ever forgive me?"

A brief smile tugged at Madeline's lips. Then she took Jenny's fist, straightened out the fingers, stroked them. "It doesn't matter, darling," she said. "It may even help. Perhaps Simon will be jealous of Tom. Even if he isn't, it's flattering to hear that a man admires you."

Gradually Jenny relaxed. Maybe things would be better now, with the Missourian shifting his attention to Madeline, who was less likely to be hurt by him. Her main interest was Simon.

"Jenny," Madeline suggested, "let's give a small dinner party tomorrow night. Invite Tom March. He'll have the opportunity to make a play for me if he wishes to—and, of course, Simon will have the opportunity to notice."

Jenny didn't like the idea. She didn't want to have to endure March's presence. But she agreed to it. She owed Madeline at least that much after what she'd done.

Madeline insisted on overseeing party preparations, and Jenny was glad. She was in no mood to discuss menus. She didn't give a hang what china and silver were used.

She had something else to think about, something real. It had been gnawing at the back of her mind, but so far she'd done nothing about it.

So right after lunch, she acted.

She went to the doctor for a pregnancy test, the newest, quickest kind. He wanted to use a twenty-four hour process and she wanted a twenty-four minute answer, which he assured her wasn't possible.

So it wasn't until the next day that she came for the result.

"The test was negative," he told her.

Jenny sank back in her chair and sighed. The doctor, a kind, elderly man, misread her reaction.

"I'm sorry Mrs. Townsend," he soothed. "You must have been hoping for a posthumous child."

"Thank you, Doctor," she said evenly, hoping he couldn't tell how her heart was leaping in relief. "Now," she continued, "I'd like a prescription for the birth control pill."

A hint of surprise showed on him, but he wrote the prescription. She took it to the pharmacy on the ground floor and had it filled.

At home, she went to her bathroom and swallowed one of the pills, tucked the box behind the aspirin in her medicine cabinet. Now she was safe. Now she could go to bed with Rolf or David.

Tom March was nothing but a bad taste in her mouth.

She was ready to make her first step toward getting a husband.

15

A new greyhound, Ebon Sue, the last one Si had ordered from Kansas, was delivered shortly after everyone had arrived for the dinner party. They were gathered on the patio—Jenny and Madeline; Simon; Roth with Lila Stevens; David with the bronze-haired Sara Donahue; and Oliver Cranston with Shirley Horne, looking chic in a shimmering gold pantsuit.

And Tom March.

Only he and Simon had no dates.

Which left Simon wide open to Madeline, and Jenny doomed to pair off with March. She was fuming over this when Flo came out on the patio, announcing the arrival of the new greyhound.

Jenny sprang up and followed the housekeeper to the roof garden, where Ebon Sue was being unloaded. A young handler was leading her down the runway, toward the door of the empty kennel.

Someone turned on the garden lights, and the area flared into brightness. Romantic Sally was on her hind legs at her gate, yapping excitedly. Ebon Sue, now at the edge of the runway, gave off a low growl and lunged at the bars that stood between herself and the other dog.

Suddenly the garden was filled with noise. The dogs lunged and keened at each other, Ebon Sue yanking the leash out of the trainer's hand. Jenny's guests, who had followed her to the garden, were shouting excitedly, the girls clinging to their men in fear. The dog, yellow eyes blazing, was heading straight for them.

Jenny sprang to grab the leash, but Tom March beat her to it. He got hold of it, wound it around his left hand, then pulled the dog to a stop.

Ebon Sue's head whirled, her teeth snapped together. Only the muzzle saved him from a bad bite. He reached forward cautiously, trying to place his right hand on the dog's back, between the shoulders. She backed away, hunkered, and growled viciously.

"Let go!" Jenny screamed. "She'll hurt you."

He ignored her. He bent slightly, tightening his hold, and began to croon at the frightened dog.

"Ebon . . ." he crooned repeatedly. "Good Ebon . . . it's all right, girl . . . we're friends . . ."

One of the girls giggled and Tom, never changing the tone or the rhythm of his voice said, "Go back inside . . . all of you . . . she's in a panic . . . needs peace . . ."

There was a general movement to the inside. Jenny stood her ground. It was her dog; she didn't have to leave.

"Mrs. Townsend?" The handler was approaching now, fear on his young face. His hands were dug deep in his jeans pockets. "I guess I did wrong, bringin' her to the other dog like that."

"It's all right," Jenny consoled him. "You had no way of knowing what would happen." She tipped him handsomely, and he hastened to the parked van and took off.

They were all gone now except for David, who had remained to watch Tom work with the greyhound. She seemed quieter now. Jenny tried to approach her, but this sent the dog into a new frenzy and she had to back away and leave her alone with March.

136

Bit by bit, he moved Ebon Sue away from the garden. Inch by inch he got her around the hibiscus planting, on the other side of which was the second kennel. Jenny, bent on helping, ran ahead and opened the gate and Tom half dragged, half coaxed Ebon Sue into it. Jenny followed, latching the gate behind her.

David stood outside, watching.

Tom managed to crouch beside the dog, get his arm around her. She trembling on her long, slim legs, and her tail was flat against her belly. Her ears were skinned back, and now she went into a whining howl. Tom still murmured, singsonging, saying her name, over and over.

Romantic Sally was still yipping. Every time she yipped, Ebon Sue cringed and whined.

"If you want to help," Tom said to Jenny in his singsong, "go quiet Sally. This one's terrified, thinks we're going to kill her . . . she's going through hell."

Jenny resented his ordering her around, but she knew he was right, and this made her even more angry. She took one last look at Ebon Sue and then she left, nodding when David said he'd latch the gate, and went to the other dog.

That one came straight into her arms, whining pitifully. Jenny crooned to her, even as March was crooning in the other kennel, and in moments Romantic Sally was licking her face and wagging her tail.

Still, every yelp that Ebon Sue let out set Sally to whining again. Jenny sat on the grass, her arms around the dog, soothing her.

David appeared at the gate. "March told me to get some red meat from the kitchen for the new dog," he said. "Want me to bring some for Sally?"

"Please do," Jenny replied gratefully. "She loves it. If her stomach's full enough, and Ebon Sue quiets with a full stomach, maybe they'll both go to sleep."

She continued to pet the greyhound. There was no sound now from the other side of the bushes, except for March's crooning. She knew she should be grateful to him, but the way he'd barged in again—after all that had taken place between them—rankled, and she didn't feel a bit grateful.

David was back in no time. She took part of the meat and fed it, bite by bite, to Sally, whose tail wagged as she ate. From the other kennel, she heard Tom tell Sue she was going to have a fine supper and then he was going to bring her a big dish of fresh water.

When Sally settled down, chin resting on her extended forelegs, Jenny ventured to leave the kennel. "I'll be back, girl," she promised. "Good Sally."

Sally whacked her tail on the grass, closed one eye. Jenny stifled the impulse to go back and pet her still more, and made her way to the other kennel.

Tom had taken Fbon Sue's muzzle off and was hand-feeding her. Sue's tail didn't wag, but it wasn't up under her belly, either, and her ears had lifted to a normal position. She ate eagerly.

David was there, right up to the cage. "March asked me to stand here," he remarked. "Get her used to more people than just himself."

Tom kept crooning as Sue ate. When she'd finished and had lapped up her water, he suggested that Jenny come into the runway.

"She's made friends with me," he said, "and tolerates David. She was just scared out of her skin, is all. That plane trip, a muzzle on her, and different folks yanking at her leash. She'd been through hell. But she's quieted; chances are she won't be afraid of you."

She wanted to scream at him, to give him her opinion of his taking charge. But she couldn't do that. She needed him now. Needed to make friends with the greyhound. She entered the runway.

"Ebon Sue," she murmured, and crouched some feet from the dog. Carefully, she held out one hand. "Fine girl, good girl. This is Jenny—Ebon Sue's Jenny."

Sue laid back her ears and whined, but Jenny kept talking. Finally the dog crept toward her, on her belly. When she was very close, she smelled Jenny's hand, then quickly gave it one lick of her tongue. Jenny ventured to stroke the sleek black head, and was allowed. As she talked and petted and stroked, Sue warmed to her, and soon was nuzzling up to her like an old friend.

138

At dinner, Tom March was the center of attention. The others were filled with praise for his handling of Ebon Sue. Even Simon, who wasn't free with compliments, patted Tom on the back.

"Got to hand it to you, March. That was something!"

Jenny burned. She hated to hear the Missourian praised. But she knew, once again, that she owed him a debt of gratitude. So she said coolly, "It was kind of you to work with her. It would have taken longer otherwise."

Which was true. She could have quieted Sue, she knew, but it would have taken her longer. Let him put any interpretation he chose on her remark. She couldn't care less.

"When are you taking Sally out to the training kennels?" Rolf asked. "Isn't she tame and workable now?"

"She's a darling," Jenny replied. "I may keep her here a bit, walk her for exercise."

"Seems to me," March put in, "that'd be bad for her. They need to have one main thing on their minds—that mechanical rabbit."

Again he was interfering. Jenny ached to inform him she'd do what she pleased with her own dog, that she didn't need his advice. But she couldn't. She wasn't going to give him the satisfaction of arguing with him in front of the others.

"You took Kolaka and Armand to the kennels quite soon," Rolf said.

"Yes," she agreed, relieved that Rolf's comment had shown March she made her own decisions. "As soon as Ebon Sue quiets, I'll take both of them to be trained."

When dinner was over, the dessert dishes cleared away, Jenny suggested they retire to the patio. It was a warm night, and the cool breeze that blew in off the Atlantic felt refreshing after the heavy meal.

Simon came over to sit by Jenny and she noticed Madeline scurry toward the Missourian. He made a space for her next to him on the lounge and bent toward her attentively. Well let him. It didn't mean a thing. She wondered, suddenly irritated, if he was complimenting the tender red of Madeline's hair and her beauty in the ivory lace dinner gown.

She turned away, looked at Simon. His eyes were soft and gentle in the glistening moonlight. He bent closer to her, seemed about to kiss her, and she pulled away.

She felt him stiffen, saw his lips compress. She felt sorry. Really, he was an attractive man—so handsome, so much like Si. But she had made a promise to Madeline and she must keep it.

She glimpsed a reflection of herself and Simon in one of the sliding glass patio doors. He was indeed striking. And she looked her best. Her tender green voile gown almost touched the floor, its gathered skirt snug at the waist, hanging in soft folds. The sleeves, fitted at the wrist, were split from shoulder to cuff the way Si had liked, and gave her, especially with her brilliant hair done in a long, loose knot from nape to top of head, a naked look. A look which Si had adored.

Simon got up, turned on the stereo and seductive music began to throb. He held out his arms. Jenny went into them, and they glided about the patio and around the shimmering pool.

But even as she danced with Simon, she was noticing Tom. He was dancing with Madeline on the far end of the patio. In his white dinner jacket, he looked as sleek and handsome as the other men. Yet underneath, she knew, lay the cruelty, the roughness. If Madeline knew the truth about him, she probably wouldn't dance with him, not even to make Simon jealous.

The number ended, and David requested a change in the music. "How about something with a beat?"

Simon went to change the record, leaving Jenny alone. But not for long. There was a tap on her shoulder and she turned to see the Missourian smiling down at her.

"May I have this dance?" he asked, and before she could refuse, he had taken her into his arms.

At first she held herself at a distance from him. But soon they were dancing in rhythm, moving together to the music, as perfectly matched on the dance floor as they

140

had been in bed. That awful flame was alive again in her, and she danced on, her body burning with desire.

She'd thought she was rid of him, rid of the terrible passion. But all he had done was dance with her, and it had come back! Her lips trembled. She pressed them together, and they were still. She knew what she must do about it. Concentrate on Rolf or David and will this animal away.

Suddenly the music stopped. So did the dancers, looking toward the stereo to find out why. It was Madeline who had turned the music off. She was standing beside the stereo, and next to her was the handsomest man Jenny had ever seen.

She got a full, flashing impression of him. He was maybe thirty-two, a couple of inches over six feet, a build as lithe and strong as that of a great jungle cat. He was wearing a rust-colored jacket, the exact shade of his hair, which was worn full but not long, and he had a full beard. He stood with his feet apart, like some feline king trying to decide which female to take. Jenny had the feeling of having seen him somewhere before, but could not remember where.

"Hey, everybody," Madeline cried. "See who I ran into on the beach today! He's in town, making a film. We'd met at a party some time ago, and he remembered! Everybody, meet Richard Snow. *The* Richard Snow!"

16

Jenny stood as if frozen. She could not believe it. Richard Snow in her home! The biggest personality in Hollywood—under her roof! And she had failed to recognize him! But it was understandable. He was even more gorgeous in person than on the screen!

Remembering her duty as hostess, she moved toward him and offered her hand.

"I'm Jenny Townsend. We're delighted to have you, Mr. Snow," she said, smiling graciously. "Please make yourself at home."

"The pleasure is mine, Mrs. Townsend—Jenny—" he said easily, his big bedroom eyes boring into her. "I think I may be very lucky to be here. Very lucky indeed."

Jenny felt a choking sensation, tried to swallow, to free her eyes from his, but could not. She was caught up in embarrassment and also in pride that he had singled her out. But then, maybe he hadn't, maybe this was the way he reacted to all his public. Lila Stevens was beside her in an instant. She deserted Rolf, linked her arm through Jenny's and smiled meltingly at the star. Jenny could feel the girl trembling with excitement.

"So good to meet ya, Mistah Snow" she drawled. "Why, Ah just can't believe it's you, in person. I've got to dance with you, simply got to!"

But Richard Snow had his own ideas. He bowed before Jenny. "You're my hostess?" he asked in an intimate tone.

"I . . . yes."

"Then I have the first dance with you," he said, putting his arms around her and drawing her close. "Music, Madeline-doll!"

The music started, and dancing was resumed. There was an excitement, an electricity in the room, which hadn't been there earlier.

"You're incredibly beautiful," Richard Snow murmured, holding Jenny close.

"You probably say that to all the girls," she said, and blushed.

"This time I mean it," he said, his voice tender.

"But you've been around so many beautiful women—starlets," she argued.

He gave a faint shrug. "Yes, I've met my share of beautiful women. But you're special. I couldn't wait to hold *you* in my arms. You feel exactly right!"

"But you must dance with Madeline—and the others," she protested. "It'd be . . . cruel otherwise!"

He laughed. "After this song. I'll dance with every girl. Then all of me is for you!"

He drew her tighter, and she felt him harden against her. Gently, he stroked her back. He moved his hand and suddenly, smoothly, touched the curve of her breast, caressed it, then returned his hand to her back. Her mind was in a whirl; she felt a bit dizzy. She was both disappointed and relieved when the music stopped.

After he'd fulfilled his promise, danced with the others, he got her into his arms again. He held her close and tight. Again she felt him harden. Dancing past the Missourian and Madeline, she saw the jut to that animal's jaw. So he was mad, was he? Because she was in Richard

Snow's arms, or because there was another man in the room who'd become the center of attention?

About then, Richard leaned into her, whispered softly in her ear. "Let's get out of here!" he said. "Let's go to my hotel." With her still in his arms, he cradled her breast for an instant.

Her pulse raced. She knew very well what he wanted. And he was the perfect male to rid her of the yen she had for Tom March. This superstar, this Adonis, could bed her once and blot out the other. He touched her breast again and warmth spread through her body.

Yet she couldn't just run off and leave her guests, could she? He moved his hand slowly down her body, caressing her, and she made up her mind. Following him into the penthouse, she strode to the hall closet, took a pale green velvet stole, and let him drape it around her.

They left the penthouse, got into Richard's rented white Cadillac. "Come over here," he ordered, and she scooted across so that she rode with his arm around her. Her heart was pounding with anticipation.

He sent the car smoothly out of the circular driveway and onto the street. On the beach highway he headed south toward Miami. There were other cars coming and going, but he was an expert driver; it was almost as if they had the road to themselves.

He drove fast, above the limit, but that didn't impede his right hand. He untied the little bow at her neck, unbuttoned the tiny, pearl buttons, thrust his hand inside and exposed her breast.

She gasped audibly.

But she didn't stop him, dared not. She had a purpose to accomplish and this was leading up to it. He caressed the tiny nipple until she felt it harden, and then all kinds of sensations flashed between her thighs, and she let him continue.

To her surprise, he didn't take her to one of the big hotels. Instead, reaching the edge of Miami Beach, he turned in at a motel, drove to the back, to the end cottage.

"Hideaway," he explained. "My agent rented it in

his name. I wanted a rest from the fans. I'm here early to make this film, and really need peace. Once this one's in the can, I start another right away. So I need some vacation time now."

"Indeed you must," Jenny murmured.

He stopped the car, removed his hand from her breast, then said, "Let's put this away for now," and covered it with her dress. "Don't button up," he warned, then came around to her door and helped her out of the car.

His cottage was a three-room marvel of ultra-modern furnishing, tropical plants and paintings. It had obviously been redecorated, especially for him.

Jenny followed him into the most incredible bed-room she had ever seen. The walls were painted a rich, deep brown—the same color as the mink bedspread adorning the circular bed. Over it, suspended from the ceiling, was a huge mirror.

Richard stripped back the fur spread, and began to undress. Jenny, despite her knowledge of why they were here, stiffened. Her hands went to the front of her dress, fell away.

"Come on, lovely one," he urged. "Undress with me. That's a real turn-on. To strip together, watching each other. A mutual unveiling!"

She unbuttoned the rest of her dress, let it slide. Suddenly she felt frightened, unsure. She was going to bed with America's sex symbol. She, Jenny Townsend. What would March say if he knew?

Angry for thinking of him, she pushed him from her mind. What did it matter what he thought? March was wrong, wrong, wrong for her. This beautiful man would take her into his arms and prove that.

They were naked.

She stared at his body, the tan flesh muscled and strong and smooth. His shoulders were broad, and they had a sparse line of brown, curling hair along the top. The hair around his smooth, tumescent organ was brown and curly too.

He stared back at her. It seemed he could scarcely wrench his gaze from her flaming, uptilted secret part. He

146

came to her, stood so that the tip of his manhood stroked above that spot.

"You're the most beautiful woman since Eve!" he murmured. He ran his palms lightly up her sides, followed the curve of her breasts, her neck, her cheeks, and put his fingers into her hair. One by one he pulled out the silver pins and let them fall. Her hair tumbled down, part of it on her back, curtains of it framing her face.

He stroked the hair that touched her cheeks, arranged it to fall over her breasts, making small openings for the nipples to show through. And then he took her into his arms, slowly drew her close, and kissed her, long and deeply. He didn't put his tongue inside her mouth, even when her lips parted and she found herself clinging to him, her innermost self on fire, wanting him, all of him. Instead, he encompassed her lips with his and kissed on.

"Ready?" he groaned at last.

Some faint, far instinct told her to run, to flee. But she didn't want to. Not now, not on the verge of some fabulous unknown. Not when this growing fire could be fed and put out, never to be felt again, except with the man she would marry.

He carried her to the bed and put her on it. She had one look at his face; it was filled with eagerness and passion. And then he entered her, went far in, slowly, and they sighed together.

He moved, gently at first, and she matched his gentleness. It was a delight. And beyond the delight lay the waiting for more. Now he went in a back and forth rhythm, easy to follow, soothing and stimulating. He went faster, and she watched him, moved with him, reaching for more. Lost in this new sensation, she had only one swift memory of how it had been with the Missourian.

Her arms and legs went around him, and they were a pounding, straining ball of flesh, bodies welded. Wave after wave of glory raced from her depths, bore her up on wings and, when she couldn't stand it another instant, released her in an ecstasy of sensation, and she lay quiet in his arms. As suddenly as glory had borne her aloft, she felt sated.

Good. Fine. That was what she'd been after. Richard-Snow sex was the best to be had. He'd cured her of Tom March.

Richard, elated, murmured love-words which filled her like balm. She absorbed them gratefully, thinking of how lucky she was to be with him.

"Did I make you deliriously happy?" he asked.

"Yes, Richard. Oh, yes!"

"I only wish I could have been the first."

"You were almost the first," she whispered.

"And was I the best?"

"Oh, yes," she told him. "You're the best."

"And you're a dream, Jenny. A dream come true. Jenny,"—his voice was a whisper—"I want to marry you."

Her breath caught. Just like that! America's heart-throb had bedded her once, and announced he was going to marry her!

"It's—too soon," she stammered.

"Wrong. It happens this way sometimes. You just know."

"But—I'd be afraid—A Hollywood marriage doesn't have a chance," she said, wondering if possibly it could have.

"Ours won't *be* a Hollywood marriage. We'll live wherever you say."

"But what about your career—you have to travel."

"Where I go, you go. Anyway, I've been planning to quit show business, maybe go into ranching. In a couple of years or so. How does that sound?"

"Tempting, Richard. It sounds—tempting."

"But—?"

"There are—problems."

"What problems? It can't be money. We both have more than enough!"

"No, it's not money."

"Then sex? Have you changed your mind about that?"

"The sex is perfect."

"What is it then? Love? I loved you the minute I

saw you. And the way you were in my arms, giving, even bold. I thought—I *knew* you were different from all the others! I knew you were feeling the same way about me that I was feeling about you!"

"That's the trouble—love," she confessed. "I feel tenderly for you. I believe that I can fall in love with you, given time. But for you to see me once, make love to me once, wonderful as it was—how can you *know* it's love?"

"I just do, Jenny. Oh, darling, let's not wait. Let's get a special license and marry tomorrow. Please, dearest, let's do it!"

Her thoughts were racing. Would Si approve? Richard filled the requirements, as far as money and sex were concerned. She found him terribly appealing—but then, who wouldn't? He was famous, a movie star. That didn't mean she loved him.

"Can you give me some time?" she whispered. "A month. Maybe less. I have to know—I have to be certain it's love I feel, not infatuation."

He nodded his agreement. Then he asked to make love to her again. "I'll not be in such a hurry this time," he murmured, "but make the sort of love your beauty commands. Lie very still, and I'll make your portrait in love."

Wondering what he meant, she did as he said, eyes on that beautiful, intense face. He sat beside her on his haunches, and smiled down at her.

Delicately, he placed his fingertips at the center of her brow then traced downward, right hand moving along her left cheek, left hand keeping pace with the other. His two hands traveled on downward. They outlined her neck, shoulders, breasts, the swell of her hips, the touch so sensual that darts of pleasure were released all over her body. Down her thighs, her legs, ankles, heels, and head they went, coming to rest in the center of each great toe.

Sensation lingered in every spot. Jenny shivered with delight, waiting for more, for all. She wished he would do it all over again, but knew she couldn't endure it unless, first, he fed her reaching, ravenous hunger.

"A love-portrait of Jenny, my wife," he whispered.

149

And then, blessedly, he entered her.

This time the throbbing glory lasted longer. She clung to him, would not let him go, and he quickened within her and she had her third period of bliss. Again she lay smiling, content, knowing herself free of the Missourian, knowing that Richard, beautiful Richard, could lift her to the very peak of bliss all her life.

"Still want to wait?" he asked.

She nodded. "Just to make certain, darling."

"I'll want more loving," he warned. "I put your love-portrait into my heart, you know."

She murmured, smiled.

They kissed, but with sweetness only.

17

It was nearly two in the morning when Jenny arrived home. She found Madeline drinking a cup of coffee in the kitchen. Her sweet face was frowning. "Jenny, we were all worried. You were gone with Richard for hours!"

Jenny nibbled the inside of her lip. She wasn't ready yet to confide in Madeline. "He was very—charming," she said.

"Which more than one girl has found out to her sorrow," Madeline said quietly. "You're different. Just take it slowly, darling. Richard Snow has a reputation for loving and leaving."

"I'm sure he has," Jenny agreed. "I'm being careful."

And she was.

Madeline looked doubtful.

"Don't worry, darling," Jenny pleaded. "I'll be very cautious." And she was being so, to the extent that she didn't tell Madeline that Richard wanted to marry her.

Madeline drifted away to her own suite, and Jenny went to bed nude. Not once since Si's death had she felt so free and relaxed, so ready for sleep. She knew the right marriage would give her this feeling every night. Very soon she was asleep.

Somewhere dogs were barking and yelping. Jenny pulled herself awake. It was no dream. The commotion was coming from the roof garden.

She threw on a robe and, naked except for that, rushed to the kennels, turning on the floodlight. Romantic Sally was jumping at the gate barking, but seemed to be all right. Most of the noise was coming from Ebon Sue's kennel, and Jenny hurried to her.

The greyhound was leaping at her gate, hitting the ground on all four feet, then limping about, on three legs, holding her right front paw aloft. When she saw Jenny, she went into a frenzy of yipping.

Jenny opened the gate, latched it, knelt, and the dog came whining and yelping to her. "You poor baby," Jenny comforted. "It's your foot, isn't it? Here, let Jenny see, let Jenny fix."

Ears back, whining, Ebon Sue permitted Jenny to examine the paw. It was swollen and very sore. When Jenny pressed it gently, the dog yelped and had to be comforted.

Finally Jenny found the cause of the problem. A big tack had gotten lodged in the soft padding. Taking firm hold, she withdrew it, and the dog yelped in pain.

"All right, girl . . . there, there. It will be much better now, much better," she crooned. But the dog continued to make pathetic whining sounds.

Jenny left her and ran into the house, to use the telephone. She dialed the veterinarian, let his phone ring, redialed, let it ring again. There was no answer.

If he'd gone on an emergency, goodness only knew when he'd be back. Meanwhile, both dogs were again barking furiously. The only way to quiet them was to ease Ebon Sue's pain.

Tom-bigmouth-March would know what to do. Frantic, she found his number. She was trembling when at last she heard his voice and spilled out her woes.

He was there in a flash.

Ebon Sue quieted the instant she saw him. She let him handle her paw, soak it in warm water, even let him cover it with some salve Jenny had found in her medicine cabinet and tape gauze on it. He fed her some steak, and gave some to Jenny for Romantic Sally.

When both dogs were quiet, he wiped his brow. "Sue's got an infection," he explained. "A couple more soakings and the salve will cure it. I'll be happy to tend her if you want. She seems to trust me."

Jenny was in a quandary. Of course, she should accept his offer of help. It was the only decent thing to do after he'd come running out in the middle of the night. Suitable words froze in her throat, and in their place she heard herself say, "I'll pay you, of course. Just as I would the vet. And if you treat Sue until she's healed, there'll be a bonus."

There looked to be actual fire in his black eyes. His face was like granite. The eyes probed her head to foot, and it was as if he knew she was naked under her robe, because the fire blazed.

His fury roused her own indignation. When he would have stalked past her, she grabbed his arm and, moved by impulse, hung on, holding him back.

Only then did he speak. First, he pried her fingers off his arm. "What's bothering you now? I'll be glad to help your dog, but I'm not your hired hand!"

"I didn't say you were! I—don't know what kind of creature you are! Manhandling me in the middle of the night—"

"*Manhandling*, is it?" he repeated. "We'll just have us a spot of *manhandling*, since you don't seem to know, yet, what it is!"

He made a grab for her, but she yanked free and ran, her robe flying open. She fled for her suite, him behind her. She ran faster, realizing that he could easily overtake her. If he chose. Instead, he just loped along, followed her into her rooms.

And locked the door and dropped the key into his shirt pocket. She darted at him, fingers arched. He trapped her in his arms.

She struggled, but he held her as if she were a doll.

She could smell that he'd been smoking a pipe; she got the man-odor of him she'd noted before and, furious though she was, found the odor not unpleasant.

She stopped struggling. "Let me go," she demanded, voice shaking with fury. "You don't need to show me anything about manhandling! You've already shown enough!"

He let go so abruptly she almost fell forward. That was when she realized she'd been leaning against him, and she became indignant. She clutched her robe together and stared at him defiantly, her chin quivering.

He didn't take his eyes off her as he stripped. He'd never meant to touch her again, her with that hell-fired temper, but she was bare under that robe and her defiant meanness had fired him up. He needed to have her now, now more than ever.

Let her stand like an abused angel, holding that robe shut. He had her number. She was no angel. She was, for sure, the hot-tempered wildcat he'd marked her down for, and he was going to make her understand, this time, that he was no country bumpkin to be messed with.

Jenny, too frozen with rage, too proud to scream for help even if she could be heard, stood her ground. He was like a maddened bull, yanking off his clothes and hurling them aside. If the fire in his hateful eyes got any hotter, it'd set the room on fire; if his mouth got any tighter, it would disappear.

He lunged at her, snatched off her robe. She went limp and would have crumpled, but he scooped her off her feet, strode to the bed, tossed her into the middle of it and bestraddled her.

She felt she was in a dream, a nightmare. But then she knew it was real, because he entered her with one angry thrust. Instantly her ears rang; instantly, as he moved, sparks flashed up her spine and into her head. She couldn't bear it. She had to thrust back, fury overcoming weakness, strength overcoming fear.

They melded. Her heels dug into the mattress, her body held his up, and they flamed and flooded. He shuddered and she clung, savoring her moment of ecstasy.

Then, replete, she dropped back to the mattress, and he rolled to one side and held her.

Tears were pouring from her eyes. He'd undone everything Richard had accomplished. He'd proven that he was able, one last time, to move her sexually.

And it was not over yet. He came on top of her again and they met, this time in a long, rolling flood of sensation. She let the flood carry her where it would, rode to its highest peak, and when she reached earth again, it was over. This time, she felt she was healed. She'd gotten her fill of him at last.

Drowsily, lying in his arms, her head on his bare chest, she hugged this knowledge of her new freedom, and then she slept.

When she woke, it was morning. Tom was gone. Fine. At least no one would find him here. Suddenly, a surge of panic ran through her. She scrambled into her robe and hurried to the garden. He wasn't at the kennels either. Good. She petted the dogs, went back inside to bathe and dress.

So he'd slunk away like a thief in the night. A sex-thief.

Scrubbing vigorously under the shower, washing her hair till it squeaked, she thought of Richard Snow. After last night, he seemed but a pleasant memory. His love-making had been delightful. Still, she knew now that she did not love him. Not if she could forget him so soon.

So she was no closer to finding a husband than she had been.

Besides that, she had to find a way of turning down the famous Richard Snow.

The breakfast room was filled with yellow roses. Madeline was finishing the last arrangement when Jenny entered.

She plucked a card from one bouquet and handed it to Jenny. "I'll bet a greyhound," she said, "that they're from America's heartthrob."

Jenny pulled out the little note.

"Sweetheart: I can't bear to be away from you. I

155

can't survive if I see you again before you say yes. My roses, every day, will remind you of the answer for which I'm pining. Your Richard."

Embarrassed, she tucked the note into the pocket of her blouse. She'd wait a day or so, then phone him and let him down easily. Perhaps tell him it was too soon for her to remarry. She was thankful that, in the meantime, he wouldn't attempt to see her.

After Flo had served them breakfast and left, Madeline, who had been unusually quiet, spoke. "I saw Tom March slip into the elevator this morning. He spent the night . . . didn't he, darling?"

"Ebon Sue—got something in her foot—" Jenny stammered. "I called him, and he stayed with her a long time."

"Sweetheart," Madeline warned gently, "you're getting off the track with both men."

"H-how do you mean?"

"They don't fit the requirements. Not for you. Tom has rugged appeal, but no money. Richard is rolling in it, but has no capacity for love. Just go easy. Put your attention on Rolf and David."

All day, and in the days that followed, Jenny thought about Madeline's words. She knew her friend was right. Neither man was the sort she should marry. Why was it so hard for her to keep on the right track?

Tom didn't come back to treat Ebon Sue, but Jenny called the veterinarian. After two days the swelling had gone down and the vet said she was ready to go to the training kennel, so that afternoon Jenny and Madeline drove them to Davie. She visited Kolaka and Armand, left all four there.

"I feel like a mother deserting her babies," she cried. "After the racing season, I'm going to keep two of them at a time at the penthouse and give them all the love they need!"

And Richard Snow? She still had done nothing about him. It was over two weeks since she'd seen him. His roses continued to arrive, but without further notes. Try as she might, Jenny couldn't bring herself to call him. The more time that passed, the less inclined she was to go to bed with him again. And still could think of no way to refuse marriage without hurting him.

She heard nothing from Tom March. That was just fine. Undoubtedly he was spending his time with the migrants. At least he wasn't forcing himself on her and she was perfectly content that he stayed away.

One Saturday morning, Jenny came down early to breakfast. Richard's roses had already arrived on schedule. The morning paper was on a side table, and Jenny picked it up, thumbed through it.

What she saw in the centerfold made her turn white with shock. There, plain as day, was a big picture of Richard, his arm around a beautiful blond girl. The caption read "SUPERSTAR WEDS DANCER!"

Dazed, Jenny skimmed through the story. "Richard Snow . . . Whirlwind romance . . . film locale switched to California . . . flew to romantic fate . . . love at first sight, stated America's idol . . . "

"What's so spellbinding?" Madeline asked, having entered the breakfast room.

Jenny handed her the paper, and the girl's eyes widened in amazement. "Oh, Jenny, I'm so sorry. Really I am. You're lucky you gave him only one date. I told you he wasn't to be trusted!"

It was then the telegram arrived. It was from Richard. "WHAT I SAID WAS TRUE WHEN I SAID IT," the wire read. "CHERRY SWEPT ME OFF MY FEET. FORGIVE. RICHARD."

Jenny showed this to Madeline. They smiled together and their smiles soon turned to laughter.

That solves one problem, thought Jenny, hugging her friend with relief.

One down, one to go.

Part III
THE TESTS

18

Simon, Rolf and David were lunching at David's yacht club. Their table had a view of the water, and in the distance, they could see *The Louisa* docked at her mooring. Her red and white flags flapped in the Gulf Coast breeze.

They were discussing the migrant situation and what to do about Tom March. Simon was speaking, in between forkfuls of cheesecake.

"My principal concern," he was saying, "is Jenny. She's reacting too emotionally."

"I've been noticing that," David said. "I think it's March. They look at each other, and sparks fly."

Rolf nodded. Himself attracted to Jenny, he'd wondered about this thing that seemed to exist between her and March. He eyed his cousins. They were both probably drawn to Jenny, too.

"Jenny needs another man in her life," he spoke up. "Someone to take her mind off Si. And it isn't Tom March."

The others nodded in agreement.

"I've been thinking of asking her out. Wanted to for some time, actually," Rolf continued. "What do you think?"

Simon stared at his remaining cheesecake. He wasn't going to let on to his cousin that he'd already tried with Jenny and been rebuffed. Actually, he doubted she'd take Rolf seriously, but maybe he would take her mind off Tom March.

"Good idea," he encouraged finally. "Don't you agree, David?"

David grinned. "Well, actually I'd considered the idea myself—but since you brought it up first, go right ahead, and good luck to you. I think she's quite a woman."

They finished their desserts, moving on to business matters. But the thought of Jenny lingered with each of them. Each thought himself, not the others, the proper husband for her. And each was determined to win.

The following day was Saturday, and Jenny had invited them over in the afternoon to swim. When he arrived, Rolf took her aside immediately and invited her to go dancing the following evening. To his delight, she accepted without hesitation.

But Madeline had overheard, and in a matter of moments, had turned the date into a social gathering, inviting herself and the others along.

"What fun!" she squealed. "We can go to that new disco in Coconut Grove. It's supposed to be fabulous!"

Rolf resigned himself to it, resolving to spend as much time alone with Jenny as he could.

They trooped from the penthouse—Jenny, Madeline, the three cousins, Oliver Cranston and Tom March. He had been invited along at the last minute, Jenny feeling she should show gratitude for his handling of the greyhounds.

They were surprised to find the water crowded with college students from the public beach next door. But Jenny didn't mind. She found herself responding to the overall air of excitement.

Pulling off her beach top she ran into the water, diving into the waves with confidence. No sooner had she swum out a distance, angling her way through the young strangers, than hands grabbed her ankles and suddenly she was underwater. She gave a vigorous twist, and the hands slid away from her. She surfaced, laughing, saw only wet, laughing faces everywhere, and the throng of youngsters getting wilder and wilder.

She noticed that Oliver and Madeline had swum out and were joining the students in their merriment. Oliver pushed Madeline under, then helped her, spluttering and laughing, to the surface. David and Simon were there too, frolicking with the others. Suddenly one of the college students grabbed Jenny and she was upside down again. She surfaced, breathless and laughing.

She was unaware of the underwater swimmer until hands took her right ankle in a vise, jerked her under, far under, and pulled her along. She twisted at first, thinking it part of the game, then, breath gone, she yanked harder, and was held, the hands like iron. She struggled and twisted, groping frantically for the surface, but there was no escaping. She began to panic.

Just then another swimmer came diving down, there was a scuffle, her ankle was released, and she shot to the surface, swallowing water, choking. Water was in her lungs. She tried to swim, but could not.

A strong arm came under her and she was towed, her rescuer swimming fast, to shallow water. Here he lifted her, and she knew it was Simon . . . Simon saving her again . . . and he dumped her on damp sand and began to work over her.

She knew David was there, and the others. She heard Tom March's voice sounding anxious, concerned. "We have to find out who did this—why she could be—"

"She's breathing," Simon interrupted, his voice a comfort to them all. "She's going to be all right!"

With Simon's help, Jenny managed to sit up. "Th-thank you—Simon!" she coughed. "You—saved my life. Whoever—it was—just wouldn't let go!"

"I broke his hold, all right," Simon growled. "Just look for a fellow—or a girl—with a sore wrist! Then we'll have our killer!"

Jenny gasped at the word. "Simon—they were all—playing!"

She flashed a glance at Tom March, then at Rolf and David. Their expressions were grim. They too thought a killer was on the loose.

But if there was such a monster afoot, it was impossible to locate him. The students were still playing in the water and just shrugged their shoulders at Simon's questions. They had seen nothing amiss.

Finally, the men gave up and returned with Madeline and Jenny to the penthouse. They made sure Jenny was all right, then departed, promising to be on time for tomorrow evening's group date.

It was a warm, beautiful Sunday evening. Jenny stared out her bedroom window at the pink and gold blaze of the setting sun.

She was looking forward to this evening. Rolf had asked her to join him as if it were a date. Perhaps she would finally get the chance to be alone with him, to find out if he was, after all, the man for her.

She came downstairs when she heard the men arrive, and was soon joined by Madeline, who looked seductive in a sheer violet dress.

"Ah, how lovely," Rolf said, complimenting both of them though his eyes were fixed on Jenny.

Jenny smiled, welcomed them. There were Simon and Rolf; David with Sara Donahue; Tom March; and Oliver Cranston: a party of eight.

Jenny came over by Rolf's side. He gave her hand a gentle squeeze. "Ready, love?"

"Ready."

Taking Jenny's arm, he led her to the door, the others following. "I'm so glad to have you by my side," he whispered, as they walked to his gray Mercedes.

In response, Jenny just smiled, hugging his arm tighter. A little shiver went up her spine as she thought of the evening that lay ahead. This was not Tom March. Or Richard Snow. This was a Townsend, and she felt right with him. They piled into two cars—Rolf's Mercedes and Tom's Buick—and headed for the new disco in the grove.

Madeline rode in Tom's car, her arms hooked into Simon's on the one side and Tom's on the other. She seemed the picture of happiness.

When they arrived at the disco, they were sure they'd made some mistake. Its outside appearance was surprisingly calm, AFTER HOURS printed in tiny white lettering on the outside of a drab storefront. If not for the sound of the music blaring its invitation, they would have left and gone someplace else.

Once they entered, they were glad they'd stayed. Inside the place was alive with flashing light and color. Everywhere were screens with projected images, pulsating in time to the music. Dancers lined the walls, gyrating to the heavy beat, caught up in the frenzy of their own movements.

Jenny just stared. Never had she felt so alive. The darkness, the flashing lights, the music, shot through her, got into her blood, and she found herself leading Rolf to the dance floor, letting the exciting rhythm take over.

The others followed and soon all were a part of the crowd, swept up by the same fever.

All except Tom March. He danced some with Madeline. And with Sara. But he didn't look happy. Several times he glanced over at Jenny and Rolf, a scowl on his face. Then he looked quickly away.

For her part, Jenny was wildly happy. During one slow dance Rolf held her close. He fondled her shoulder, let his hand slide down and across her breast, and she cuddled against him. For once, she felt no fear. This man was a Townsend. Si's grandson. He'd know how to treat a lady.

It was three o'clock in the morning when they decided to call it a night. Tom, Madeline, Simon, David, and Sara piled into Tom's Buick, and Rolf and Jenny got into the Mercedes.

When they came to the ramp leading onto the highway, Rolf's car was behind Tom's. Suddenly the Buick veered to the right and spun crazily off the road, into the soft shoulder of an embankment. When it landed, it was tilting drunkenly to the right.

Jenny was out of Rolf's car in a flash, running, Rolf

behind her, toward the disabled Buick. There'd been no crash, but Jenny thought someone might be hurt. Perhaps Tom, behind the wheel. Or Madeline, in the backseat. Or Simon.

They were all safely out of the crazily leaning car as she pounded up. Tom was kneeling at the right front wheel—or where the wheel should have been.

"It came off," he reported. "No damage."

"Just like that?" Jenny shouted. "It came off? Who ever heard of a wheel coming off?"

Tom glared at her. "The car was checked last week," he mumbled. "If anything had been wrong, they'd have spotted it. Lug must have come loose—or something."

Jenny winced at his carelessness. Why, if they'd been on the highway when it happened, they all might have been killed!

Tom got the jack out of the trunk and, with Simon's help, put the wheel back into place. Madeline and Sara sat on the ground, mulling over their good fortune in escaping a serious accident.

Jenny moved over to Rolf, sat by his side, his arm draped loosely around her shoulders. But it was not Rolf she was thinking about. She watched intently as Tom March did most of the work, helping to press the jack into place, then pumping it to lift the heavy car. Her eyes were fixed on him.

She could not get over the fact that he had come close to dying.

And she was astonished at how much she cared whether he lived or died.

19

On Tuesday of the following week the Townsends held another meeting with Tom March, at his request. This was the first time Jenny had seen him since the accident. She tried to avoid speaking to him, but he made that impossible.

"Good morning, Jenny," he said politely, taking a seat to her left. She nodded, motioning for Simon to sit on her other side.

The meeting took several hours. But when it ended it had been agreed to install new facilities for the farms south of Homestead, and a bathhouse at Orange Blossom Grove. Also to give the pickers a small raise.

"Are you pleased, March?" Simon asked, snapping his briefcase shut.

"Of course. But it's only a beginning, a show of cooperation on your part. It should be enough to stave off any immediate trouble; it gives the dissidents less to object to. Especially the five-cent raise per basket on tomatoes."

When the meeting broke up, Rolf came over to

Jenny, took her aside and whispered how beautiful she was today. She felt ashamed, for throughout the meeting her thoughts had been focused on Tom March.

She knew she must once again rid herself of that yen for him; the best way of doing that was to be with another man, preferably Rolf. So she smiled at him, thanked him, then left the office and headed for her chauffeur-driven limousine.

She arrived home to find Madeline excited and bright-eyed. "I've just had the most wonderful idea!" she cried. "You must throw a ball!"

Jenny stared. "But it's only been—Si—"

"Si would want it. It's been close to a month. You *must* do it, darling! Fill these rooms with people! I'll help; we can get caterers in, send invitations, have a really super orchestra! Invite all our society friends! It will be the social event of the season!

Madeline was so insistent, that Jenny hadn't the heart to refuse; her friend obviously needed an opportunity to bedazzle Simon. And she was right about Si. He would have wanted her to give the ball.

Consequently, after a trip to the Davie kennels to see her dogs train, after hugging and petting them, Jenny turned her attention to the ball. She and Madeline wrote the invitations on heavy, embossed paper, to be hand-delivered by Billings.

When she saw Madeline addressing one to Tom March, Jenny protested. "He's not in our social set!"

"But he's become one of us!" Madeline argued. She sealed the envelope. "Besides, darling, I need him here! He pays attention to me . . . Simon notices!"

"Just the same—"

"He's right at home with us, darling! Acts as civilized as anybody!"

Until he's alone with me, Jenny thought miserably. But she objected no more, and Tom March's invitation went out with the rest.

That night, as she lay in bed, Jenny thought, for the first time in a long while, about growing up at the orphanage. What would have happened had she stayed there, had Si not come, like a knight in shining armor, to rescue her? Would Tom March have seemed more respectable to her then? Would he have been a proper match for her?

But then, she would never have met him.

Unable to sleep, she tossed off the satin coverlet, got into her beach togs, and slipped out of the penthouse, heading for the ocean. The breeze blew through her long hair, which she'd forgotten to pin up, and for a moment she just stood at water's edge, looking out over the deep blackness. Then she removed her terry beach top and ran into the water, letting its soothing coolness wash over her.

She found herself swimming in the direction of Tom March's apartment. Well, why not, she thought. Perhaps if she saw him one last time, she would end this thing forever.

She emerged from the ocean dripping wet, and headed toward his beach front house. To her surprise, she found him sitting on the patio, wearing only his washed-out jeans, and looking sleek and tan in the moonlight. He seemed not at all displeased to see her.

"One-thirty," he scolded, looking at his watch. "Well, you're coming out earlier and earlier these days."

"I—couldn't sleep," she stammered, unsure of what else to say. "And as I told you, I like to swim in the late evening, when no one's around."

"Have a seat," he said, motioning for her to sit on the deck chair beside him. "I couldn't sleep either. Just came out here to look at the ocean. Sometimes that helps."

She came to his side, sat down. "I—uh—was glad that no one was hurt the other night. You were all pretty lucky."

"I reckon we were." He paused for a minute. "Were you worried?"

Her chin jutted in defiance. "Well, naturally—I mean, Simon, David, Madeline—it would have been awful."

"And *me?*" he asked, his smile teasing.

"Why don't you just find some nice woman, settle

down, get married!" she retorted, trying to change the subject completely.

"And stop bothering you?" he added.

Jenny said nothing.

"Well, Jenny, I would. Really I would. But girls these days don't want a dirt farmer," he said. "They want a man with a million bucks."

He looked at her beautiful face, her red hair glistening in the dim porch light. He ached to take her inside, and put her on the bed. He hurt with the need to make the flame rise within her, as he had done before. But he wouldn't. The game was over. Had to be.

Jenny, too, was burning with desire. Why, oh why, did she want to jump into bed with him every time they were alone? Well, at least he didn't know that was what she wanted. He didn't dream of the longing she had for him this instant. And he wasn't going to find out.

To prove that this was a normal conversation, she asked boldly about his background.

"Grew up on the farm in Missoura," he said. "Graduated from Texas A. & M., did some farming. Came down here on a trip, like. Wanted to see the Atlantic Ocean."

"And?"

"Met some pickers. Got interested in their problems. Decided to take time off from the farm to do what I could to help."

"No . . . women?" Her voice shook just a little.

"A few. Here and there."

He looked at her steadily; his lips moved, but said nothing. There was naked desire in his eyes.

Unable to stand it any longer, she cried, "Stop looking at me that way! It makes me—nervous!"

"Can't help it. Looking things over is a habit of mine. I'm one to make sure about a cow—or a female of any kind. Some are flighty, like Ebon Sue, some are spirited, some just naturally gentle. I'd rather find out about a woman ahead of time, know what I'm getting."

Shaken, she heard her own voice demand, "Have you ever been in love? Do you have the least concept of what love is?"

"I reckon I ain't been in love the way you mean," he said. "If I had been, I'd of been married by now."

"Maybe you're just stalling."

"What the hell do you mean by that?" he gritted. "I ain't afraid of settlin' down. But when I do pick a wife, it'll be the way I want to, on my own!"

"When it comes to women, you don't know anything!" she accused suddenly, unable to keep down her anger a moment longer. "You're been looking me over and— You *know* what you've done! And now you're trying to decide about Madeline! Next you'll get to wondering about Lila or Sara or one of the others, and then—"

"Be quiet!" he grated. He reached over and clamped her arm so hard it hurt. Then he pulled her to her feet and marched her into his apartment. The sofa-bed was open, the blanket in disarray, exactly as he'd left it.

He pushed her onto the bed, and she began to shake. She shook so badly she couldn't fight him as he pulled off her bikini. She lay on the bed quivering while he undressed.

And then he made love to her, hard and furiously at first, then with more ease, and she arched to him and clung and moaned and burned with joy and anger.

They came together again and again, until they were exhausted.

Until the fire had gone out.

20

The penthouse was alight on both floors. Flo, neat in a new black uniform and sheer white apron and headpiece, would be at the elevator to greet the guests as they arrived.

An orchestra dais had been placed against one wall with white roses all but surrounding it. White roses were banked in front of the mirrored panels which lined the room, and at the end, opposite the dais, roses balanced it and the orchestra members, who wore white satin, glittering with beads.

Jenny hadn't known the room could be so lovely. She and Madeline had planned it together. Now, with long tables of food and drink lining the lower hallway, attended by white-uniformed caterer's men, all was ready. In an hour the guests would arrive; already the orchestra members were assembling, arranging their instruments.

The two girls dressed together in Jenny's suite. They'd bought their gowns from an exclusive shop in Palm Beach, spending hundreds of dollars apiece.

Madeline's was deep rose crepe, the neckline plunging to the waist, the back plunging to match. Her breasts were visible; only the nipples were covered. The skirt was gathered and almost brushed the floor.

She'd insisted that Jenny break away from gray and green. "Just this once!" she'd pleaded. "Let people see what a sparkling beauty you are!"

Reluctantly, Jenny had agreed.

Now she stood dressed, gazing into a mirror, studying herself critically. The gown was of conservative cut, with a high neckline and long sleeves gathered into narrow cuffs. The skirt fell straight as a candle.

Candle, she thought unhappily. That's it, I look like a burning candle.

The fabric of the gown was brilliant gold silk which shimmered at her slightest move. Her flashing red hair was drawn to the top of her head, braided with a fire blue satin ribbon. She looked exactly like a candle flame. If she'd dreamed—but it was too late to change now.

Flo appeared to let her know the first of the guests were arriving. She headed downstairs with Madeline, feeling ill at ease in her flaming gown, despite Madeline's repeated assurances that she looked ravishing, more beautiful than ever.

Rapidly, the great oblong room filled with women in stunning gowns, with men in impeccable white for the mild November weather. Friends of Si's were there, pleased and happy to see Jenny again, not one failing to exclaim how beautiful she looked. Top executives of Townsend Corporation were there, with wives and daughters, all smiling and at ease.

Oliver Cranston, looking unusually handsome, came in with Shirley Horne. She was warm and gracious, her black hair halfway down her back, eyes sparkling. Rolf and David came alone, Lila and Sara appearing with a new date each. Carol Lincoln and Ginny Dodd, also with new dates, seemed happy and relaxed.

When the orchestra struck up, the dance floor came alive with grace and beauty, tiny dance cards dangling from the wrists of the women. David, who had filled Jenny's card with his name until she protested, danced with her the most. He raved about how she looked, warned her, laughing, against all the other men.

"Myself included!" he chuckled.

Simon, surprisingly, danced with a blissful Madeline a number of times, as did Oliver. Tom March danced with her too, Jenny noticed. Whirling her around the room, his smile flashing, he looked more handsome than ever.

Rolf had his name on Jenny's card a number of times. When he claimed his first dance, the orchestra swung into a waltz and he held her properly, yet quite close. She liked the feel of him. All over the room, feet were gliding, skirts swaying. The scent of roses filled the air.

Unexpectedly, Jenny was having fun.

"You're unbelievably beautiful tonight," Rolf murmured.

Her pulse quickened. She murmured in reply, closed her eyes and danced, wishing the number would never end.

But it did, of course.

Tom March stood before her. He'd scrawled his name on her card only once, and here he was to claim his dance. She wished he would go away. Seeing him made that passion rise in her again. The orchestra began to play. Another waltz. Madeline had pleaded for lots of waltzes, and it had made no difference to Jenny. Until now.

"Where did you get that dress?" March demanded without prelude. "It makes you look cheap!"

"I'll have you know," she flared, "there's nothing cheap about this dress! It was the most expensive—"

"I don't doubt that. It's not the money. It's the color with your hair, and that blue ribbon! You . . . *blaze* damnit, and no lady blazes! Look around and see for yourself. The other women have spent money too, but they look elegant, sedate. You look as if a man touched you, he'd get burnt!"

"Are *you* burning?"

He glared, yanked her closer, and they danced in icy silence until the number ended. Then he handed her over to Simon and made his way to Madeline.

Jenny was hurt but tried not to show it. Instead, she plunged herself into the dance, going from one pair of arms to another. She listened to compliments and smiled. What did *he* know, anyway! Surely the members of her society were better judges.

Each partner offered to bring her champagne, and much of the time she accepted it and drank thirstily. Soon she began to feel a little dizzy. Her partners blurred, as did the glasses of bubbly.

David had the last three dances. Seeing how high she was, he took her to one of the tables and she nibbled at the delicacies he piled on her plate. He didn't want to let her have more champagne, but she insisted. Tonight was, after all, a special occasion. Her very first ball, and it was a smashing success.

Dancing with David again, her head began to feel thick. She scarcely responded when he spoke, just laid her head on his shoulder and glided to the throbbing music.

"You asleep, little flame?" murmured David.

She looked up in sudden anger. "I'm *not* a 'little flame!'" she protested. "It's the color of my dress, and my ha-hair! And the ribbon! Colors of a flame."

"Well, what's wrong with that?" said David. "Flames burn! And I'm not afraid of being scorched!"

He held her closer, and she could feel his maleness harden against her and she liked that. He pressed against her, and she pressed back, meeting his desire. She did not know if it was the champagne or the music that was setting this new fire within her.

David kissed her lips. She kissed back. He held her closer. His maleness was harder. He rubbed against her in a half-circular fashion, and she returned the movement, heart racing at her own boldness.

She felt that inner heat.

"Know what you're doing, little firebrand?" David whispered.

"Yes—I know," she answered. She lay her head back on his shoulder and glanced out over the floor. There was the Missourian, Madeline held tightly in his arms, smiling as he danced. It didn't bother her, though she thought she'd love to tell that roustabout that Madeline was only using him to make Simon jealous.

"Will you, Jenny?" David was asking. "When the ball ends, will you go to my place?"

She thought for a moment, flashed another look at Tom March. He looked so smug, whirling around the floor with Madeline. Well, why *not* go with David! Hadn't she said he and Rolf were her two best choices? She'd expected to be with Rolf first, but what did it matter? As long as it wasn't the Missourian!

"Yes," she told him, as clearly as the champagne allowed. "I'll go."

His apartment was done in brown with splashes of burnt orange and yellow. In the living room the furniture was modern and comfortable looking, with a big over-stuffed couch the focal point of the room. The kitchen was sleek and compact, everything in its place. It looked familiar, and Jenny said so.

"It should," David laughed. "I copied it from *The Louisa*, right down to the pots and pans."

"You really love that boat, don't you, David?"

"Not as much as I love something else," he said and put his arms around her. "To the bedroom, flaming torch!"

She let him take her there. She saw the same comfortable decor, noted the giant bed. He snapped on soft lights, closed the drapes, and they were enclosed in a perfect, masculine nest.

"One more dance!" he whispered and drew her so close she could scarcely breathe. He began to hum a seductive tune, stepped back and forth to it, and she stepped with him. Her inner flame ignited.

She was going to let him do anything he wanted, absolutely anything. She had to know what sex would be like with a gentleman—a Townsend. She had to know how it would be different.

"Now," he murmured softly. "Turn around, darling."

She turned, putting her back to him. His fingers were quick as he opened the long zipper. He moved in front of her, grasped the gown at the shoulders, slid it off, dropped it, his gaze all over her in the scrap of bra and bikini, sheer hose and stilt-heels.

He helped her step out of the dress and laid it aside. Then gently, he removed her other things, palms sliding over her breasts, across and through the patch at her thighs, down legs and ankles. When she was completely naked, he kissed the tops of her feet, and a great tingle went down her spine.

He lifted her, carried her to the bed, placed her down gently. He smelled wonderful, of champagne, tobacco and shaving lotion.

He kissed her on the mouth, pulled back. "See! I didn't get burned!" he laughed. "Now, watch how fast I can get into the raw!"

He removed his clothes swiftly, eyes not leaving her. Never had he seen a more beautiful female. Her body was more sensuous than he had dreamed, her skin like ivory silk. Now that he'd gotten this far, he knew he wanted her for his wife and would have to fight Simon and Rolf to keep her.

It took only a couple of motions, it seemed to Jenny, and there he stood, naked. His very blond hair was a pale nimbus against the deep tan of his lean, muscular body, and the pubic hair, from which rose his magnificent manhood, was a second nimbus.

She stared at him, consumed by his beauty. She was astounded at how handsome he was. His build was splendid—from swimming, rowing, tennis—his belly flat and hard. Of course, she'd seen him in his swim trunks and noticed this. But naked! He should never wear clothes. It was a sin to cover that smooth, erect maleness, so perfect it made her ache with pleasure.

"David!" she whispered. "Oh, David!"

Promptly, he came to her, straddled her. He entered smoothly, firmly, confidently. He began to move with that same confidence. She moved with him, moaning with pleasure.

By the time he thrust deeper, she was ready. She gave him motion for motion, the hotness in her spreading, sending delicious tingles everywhere. She could go on like this endlessly, her pleasure growing.

178

Suddenly, simultaneously, they were in a whirl of movement. Faster and faster, and it wasn't fast enough. She felt the source of her pleasure swell, blossom, grow enormous, and she arched to him, arms and legs around him, and the unbearable tension burst and the flood of ecstasy took her. She felt David shudder once, twice, and still again, before they rolled apart, gasping.

"Know what we did?" he panted.

"No," she gasped.

"We practically burned each other up."

It was true.

He was getting control of his breath. Hers was still racing, but gradually quieted. Her whole being was at peace. She was satisfied and relaxed and content. She wouldn't mind lying right here, just like this, for a year.

"Darling, Jenny," he crooned softly, stroking her neck. "I've had many women—but it's never been better than this. Never come close."

She wanted to say the same thing to him. But she couldn't. It had been good, wonderful even. But there was still the memory of Tom March. That raw passion he brought out in her, of which she could not seem to get enough.

"I never knew I could feel the way I do this moment," she lied, not wishing to disappoint him.

This brought him to renewed passion. He drew her to her side, facing him. "Bend your right knee," he instructed, "and set your right foot on the mattress. Open your legs, and I'll show you some fun."

She did as he said.

He came into her from the side. At first she had only the sensation of being filled. Then, as he moved, she followed his lead. The heat arose, almost hurting, but then the tingles came and grew, more slowly this time, but to greater intensity. Each thrust went deeper, faster. They were wound together, arms and legs entwined.

The explosion came, shooting down to her toes and up to her head. He gave three final, long thrusts, and consumed with flame, she clung to him, willing it not to end. At the highest peak they cried out together.

After they rested, they explored each other. He

stroked her all over, let his fingers twine in the curls of her mound, and she did the same with him. The intimacy was delicious. She couldn't get enough of it.

Finally, he entered her from behind. She lay with one side of her face crushed against the sheet and held her breath under his pounding. He felt wonderful inside, but this time she didn't reach that exciting peak, though he stayed with her for a long time. At the end, he shouted his ecstasy.

He lay beside her, held her in his arms.

"How long do we have to wait?" he asked.

"Wait for what?"

"To get married."

Jenny tensed. She liked David a lot. And it was what Si had wanted. But now that the decision was upon her, she needed time to think. After all, Si's third qualification had been that she feel love—and love hadn't been mentioned.

"Jenny," he persisted. "How long?"

"David—I'm fond of you. But I have to be certain. About love."

He came up on his elbow, gazed, startled, into her eyes. "I *showed* my love, darling! I love you above anyone on earth, have been half in love with you since our first meeting! It's gone all the way now. I'm sunk in love, lost in it!"

She stroked his cheek, gazed into his blue, blue eyes. He would be easy to love. That sunny disposition, those rugged good looks. If they married, surely she'd come to love him.

"Don't you love me?" he asked.

"I may be on the way," she said, meaning it.

"Then there's nothing to hold us back. We can get married next week and let the gossip sheets scream!"

"Not next week, David."

"When?"

"When I'm sure I love you. Very, very sure."

Rolf. He'd been her first choice, after Simon. She had to consider Rolf.

"I'll see you every night— I'll—"

"No, please! We'll see each other, but in the group."

Though he argued, she remained firm. There was Rolf. There was also the need to prove that David's love making was strong enough to blot out the memory of Tom March.

And the fire he had started within her.

21

For the next two days, Jenny was at peace. Her liking for David grew. She remembered their lovemaking with pleasure and reveled in the release and freedom it had given her. David phoned, sent a bouquet of forget-me-nots, but didn't pressure her for a date; and since there was no gathering of their intimate group, she didn't even see him.

She spent more time swimming, heading north, away from the Missourian's apartment. Not that she had to avoid him; she could now think of him almost without feeling. She was free of him at last. And she had David to thank for it.

She went to the training kennels daily. All four of her dogs were becoming good runners. They greeted her happily, licking her, jumping about, but at a word from the kennel master loped away to chase the mechanical rabbit.

On the third morning she awoke feeling uneasy, wondering what was wrong. And then she remembered.

She had dreamed about the Missourian. Dreamed he was making love to her.

It can't be! she thought desperately. He's completely out of my system! I know he is! She tried to convince herself that it was David she wanted, but failed. The dream meant only one thing. The yen she had for the Missourian, that burning desire, had returned and was stronger than ever.

She flounced out of bed and into slacks and a halter. She braided her hair, wound it around her head, jabbed in the silver pins. Her lips were pressed firmly together. She'd spend the day at the kennels; later she'd swim until she couldn't lift a hand to take another stroke. She'd wear herself out, work off this unspeakable desire, leave not a tatter or thread of it!

Suddenly she was furious. Why should she exhaust herself? She hated the man, hated him more with every beat of her heart. Yet, as the hatred grew, so did the yen, going into a deep, pulsing ache.

Tiring herself until she fell into bed was no solution. The ache would still be there, tormenting her the more because she was too worn out to overcome it. The only way was to face him, to see him again, to shame herself so she'd turn from him in revulsion.

She ran the blocks to his apartment. She was out of breath as she trotted up the narrow stretch of beach and saw him ahead.

He was polishing his car, wearing only his blue swim trunks. His body, under the early morning sun, looked leaner, tanner than she'd remembered. He looked up, saw her coming, bent over his task as if she didn't exist. Her impulse was to go for home, but she trotted right up to him and stood glaring at his glistening back as he worked.

"I reckon you ain't had breakfast," he said, eyes on the fender he was rubbing.

She watched how those big hands treated the fender, with firm pressure, yet respect for the paint. Now he even paused, ran his bare fingers over the spot he'd been rubbing, stroked the cloth across it lightly. She could see how the fender glowed, how it responded to him. Her hatred worsened. He could be tender with a car, an inanimate, unfeeling car, while with her he was rough and overbearing and hateful.

"Breakfast," he repeated, lightly stroking the fender, never knowing or caring if he did know, the tingles his steady motions were sending over her. "Breakfast," he said again, as though he were talking to himself. Or to the damn car.

"You ain't eaten," he said. This time he shot a black-eyed look at her. "Neither have I. As long as you're here, I'll feed you."

He watched that hellcat anger which he'd felt simmering come to a boil in her eyes. Gray they were, but now they turned like the ocean in rough weather, a muddied gray, shot through with green. He wished to hell she'd stay in her penthouse, on her own part of the beach. It was bad enough seeing her in a group. That was unavoidable, because he was working to persuade the Townsend clan to help the migrants. But every time he had to be alone with her, her devilish temper riled him to the point where all he seemed to be able to do was fling her onto a bed. Which he sure as hell didn't want to do, no matter how terrific she was there.

She saw right away that he was mad, and that fed her anger. "Thanks!" she snapped. "It'll save Flo setting a place for me!"

His eyes turned furious.

Good, she thought, let him stew! She met his glare fiercely, and gritted her teeth to keep from screaming at him. Her glance happened to brush across the front of his swim trunks and the bulge there surprised her.

Good again! She hoped he'd hardly be able to sit still all through breakfast. Let him suffer. This time she felt less vulnerable, since she was fully clothed. This time she could keep her dignity, conceal her passion, and come out of this encounter the victor. The more times she won, the sooner she'd be rid of him for good.

Wordless, she followed him into the apartment, and sat at the table while he cooked, not offering to help. Mouth grim, he fried ham and eggs, browned some packaged biscuits, made coffee, thumped plates, mugs and silverware onto the table. He set down the platter of ham and eggs and the napkin-covered plate of biscuits, and took his place across from her.

"Some butter, please," she said icily. "And cream."

He looked at her through narrowed eyebrows, got the things out of the refrigerator, sat down again. "You don't take to kitchen duties," he stated.

"I can cook. Quite well, in fact. I learned at the orphanage!"

"What orphanage?" He glared.

"The one where I was raised. I can scrub floors, too, and wax them and polish furniture. I can iron anything, even shirts!"

His mouth was slightly open. Finally! At last she'd stopped him in his tracks.

"My husband married me straight out of the orphanage," she said with poison sweetness. "He said I was never to cook and clean again."

Mentally, he tried to throw off the shock she'd given him. Then he told himself she was lying, but that wouldn't stick. Terrible though her temper might be, she was no liar. He wanted to know how her husband had found her to start with, and she told him in one sentence.

"He financed the orphanage. Saw me when I was eighteen, asked me to marry him, and I did."

"I see."

"Not for his money, believe it or not."

He did believe her. But why, then, *had* she married him, a man four times her age? He decided not to pursue the subject, instead went on to another. "The migrants—the dissidents—ain't happy over the progress in building," he told her.

"Why not? They're already building the sanitary facilities below Homestead. Simon sent a man to check. What do they expect? For everything to spring up overnight?"

"The Homestead part is swell. It's the bathhouse at Orange Blossom Grove. They ain't even broken ground for that, and it's a mighty big project."

"They have too broken ground! Simon—"

"I was out there yesterday. It ain't been touched."

"I don't believe it! You're just trying to start—"

He was out of his chair, hands on her arms, lifting her. "You act like you're from Missoura!" he growled. "Well, I'm going to show you—Missourians have to be showed!"

Protesting and resisting, she was hustled to his car and inside. He struggled into a shirt he'd grabbed on the way out of the apartment, then got behind the wheel.

They didn't speak a word all the way to Davie.

He drove into Orange Blossom the back way, avoiding the manager's house. He spoke for the first time when he braked to a stop.

"Here," he said. "Right here is where the bathhouse should be under construction. It had top priority because there's a labor camp within a mile. The bathhouse there is unusable."

"There's been some mistake!" Jenny cried. "They're building it somewhere else in the grove!"

"Show me where!" said the Missourian.

They tramped the rows of citrus trees. She couldn't be wrong. When the Townsends said they'd do a thing, they did it. Any moment now they'd come to a clearing, and there would be the workmen, laying cement block.

Gazing ahead, she stumbled. He took her arm to steady her, and she yanked it away. They kept going. Nothing. Just acres of trees.

"There isn't any bathhouse!" she cried, stopping so abruptly he almost ran into her.

He caught his balance. "That's what I've been telling you," he said. "There ain't one."

"You're a big headache! Ever since you came, you've stuck your nose into our affairs! You've attacked me, raped me—"

"With all kinds of help from you!"

He was right, and that was what made her furious. He was always right. Because she herself was upset over the migrants, over no bathhouse, over the way he'd danced with Madeline, over the fact that she must choose a husband, she flew at him, fingernails poised to strike.

He grabbed her hands, crumpled the fingers, got

187

both of them into one big paw. She'd not feed his ego by yanking and kicking. Not this time. She stood her ground, stuck out her chin, glared at him murderously.

"Ain't but one way to deal with you!" he muttered. "Only way you understand—"

He gave her a yank. She came up against him so hard it knocked her breath away. Her lips opened to scream, and his mouth landed, open, over them, blocking sound. And then he was kissing her, lips grinding, teeth against teeth. Her lips moved to escape and ended in returning the kiss when what she wanted was to bite him. He rammed his tongue into her mouth, pushed her tongue to one side, and moved his around in her mouth like he owned it.

Somehow they were suddenly on the ground, hidden by trees. Her slacks were pulled down, his trunks were off, and he came into her the same way he'd pushed his tongue into her mouth. Next they were moving together, hurling themselves at each other, and she was aware of a stone which bore into her hip every time she struck the ground.

When he quit, she was crying—because it had hurt and been wonderful, because he'd overwhelmed her, subdued her. Again. But most of all because he'd brought her to breath-stopping ecstasy.

And because, in spite of her rage, she felt inner peace.

Her sobs built and her anger with them, but she knew now that she could control neither. Because that itch for him would come back; it simply would.

She gulped her tears away. Made herself glare at him. "I abhor you!" she whispered.

He stared back at her, eyes blazing. "Sure," he agreed. "I abhor you, too."

They left the grove in silence.

22

She called Simon the minute she got home. "What do you mean, they haven't started construction?" he raved. "That's impossible!"

"But true," Jenny stated. "I've just been there and seen for myself.

Simon hung up, promising to look into the matter. He would see to it that something was done immediately.

Satisfied, Jenny went to her suite, stepped into the bath Flo had prepared. As she let the perfumed warmth envelop her, thoughts whirled.

She had to take immediate action. She would seek out Rolf and go to bed with him. David had not taken her mind from the Missourian. Perhaps Rolf would.

When she was dressed, she called him, using the excuse that Tom March was unhappy over the lack of building progress.

"I know," Rolf said, sighing audibly. "March just phoned. I'd love to have your feminine view of the entire situation," he continued. "Will you have dinner with me tonight? In my home?"

She thought of his gorgeous, sprawling white villa in Golden Isles. It would be a welcome change of scene.

"W-e-l-l," she hesitated, not wanting to sound too eager.

"Please, Jenny? I've waited as long as I can."

"Waited for what?"

"To see you. Be with you. Alone. How long does a man have to wait before he can ask a new widow to see him privately, Jenny-dear?"

Her heart warmed. It was wonderful to be the recipient of tenderness. This was the first time she'd felt warmth from the men currently in her life. Richard had been exciting; David had provided pleasure and release. But she hadn't before experienced this glowing warmth.

"It's been long enough now," she assured Rolf. "I'll be happy to be your guest."

"Then you'll come!"

"Yes. It's no disrespect to—"

"Don't finish that sentence, Jenny. The future is all you need be concerned about."

She was silent, heart pounding.

He sounded so much like Si!

"Tonight, Jenny. At eight."

"Fine. Billings will drop me off. You can bring me home, if you will."

"Right. This way, I can open my door to you personally. And Jenny . . . wear the dress you wore to the ball . . . please?"

Reluctantly she agreed.

"One thing more, Jenny-dear. Your wedding band. Can you leave it at home?"

The request jolted her. The wedding ring seemed as much a part of herself as her hair. Yet she'd bedded three men with it on her finger, men she wasn't married to. Perhaps it *was* time to take it off.

Slowly, after she cradled the phone, she drew off the ring. This was the first time she'd removed it since Si had slipped it on her finger at their wedding. Sadly, she tucked it away in its box in the bottom of her jewelry chest.

Madeline caught her in the act. "That's the most sensible thing you've done yet!" she declared. "I've wanted to mention it, but didn't. A widow shouldn't go on wearing her dead husband's ring unless she intends never to marry again."

Jenny nodded. "I suppose you're right."

Then Madeline blurted out her news. "Jenny, you'll never guess!"

"Tell me before you burst," she urged, seeing the girl's excitement.

"Simon! I worked and worked on him, and finally! He's asked me to dinner tonight! And I'm going to get him into bed! That's all I need! Then he'll be putty in my hands!"

"Wonderful!" exclaimed Jenny, hoping Madeline was right. "I'm going out too. Rolf invited me for dinner."

"Ooh!" Madeline cried. "Maybe we'll both be engaged by the time we get home!"

Rolf, tense with anticipation, inspected the table. He was using the antique silver that his mother left him upon her death. He rarely used it, except on special occasions. The same was true for the Waterford crystal wineglasses. He knew Jenny would appreciate their beauty.

When he so much as thought her name—Jenny—he felt a glow of anticipation. He'd had to be ruthless with himself, when his grandfather married her, not to let on how he felt about her. But from the beginning, he'd been hopelessly in love.

The subdued clothes she wore helped him control his desire. Her beauty was displayed, yet toned down, to where he was just barely able to think of her as his grandfather's wife and not a love object for himself.

Every time he'd ever danced with her, he'd held himself strictly in check. Except the one time, when control had failed him and his recalcitrant hand had wandered. Apparently she hadn't noticed, and he'd removed it immediately. From then on, he'd stayed as far away from her as possible.

He was standing on the rear portico, looking out

over the water, when the limousine glided to a stop. He got to the car door while Billings was still braking.

He opened the rear door and held his hand out to Jenny. She placed hers in it, her small hand firm under the soft skin, and he helped her out. His pulse was drumming. She'd worn the flame-colored dress! And she'd taken off her ring!

Relief sliced through him. Hope. He sensed that both Simon and David wanted to marry this girl, that they were real competition. But now he believed he had the best chance of winning her.

"You've never been inside my home before," he said. "May I show it to you after dinner?"

"But of course, Rolf. I'd love to see it."

He took her arm as they moved up the walk to the front door. "Thank you," he said, "for wearing the dress. And for . . . the other."

"You noticed?" she asked in surprise.

"I notice everything about you, Jenny."

His deep, murmuring tone sent a thrill down her spine. Her pulse quickened. Her cheeks felt hot. It was as if he knew why she'd come here tonight. Yet, how *could* he know? She'd not given the slightest hint that she might be romantically interested in him.

They entered the house and Jenny gave a little gasp. The oval foyer, reaching back from the curved stairway, was breathtaking. It was tiled with white marble and its walls were lined with magnificent paintings. The ballroom-sized living room was equally beautiful, carpeted with a plush white rug and furnished expensively. The fireplace, a feature not often seen in South Florida homes, was white marble, the mantel centered by a glass and silver domed clock.

White roses in crystal vases stood on every table. Two large, tall, silver urns, filled with long-stemmed white roses, stood on either side of the hall entrance.

"You like it?" Rolf asked.

She realized she'd been holding her breath. She let it quiver out.

"It's the most beautiful room I've ever seen!" she exclaimed. "Is the whole house this lovely?"

"I think so. It's planned so that rooms just flow into each other. And there's not one chamber which wouldn't be a perfect frame for your beauty, Jenny-dear."

"Y-you shouldn't flatter me," she stammered.

"I never flatter, Jenny. I either speak the truth or remain silent."

Her face was really burning now. He noticed, smiled.

"You're a modest girl, raving beauty though you are, Jenny. I've always liked that in you. Now you're blushing—do you know that's almost a lost art since we have liberated womanhood? And you blush so delicately. It makes your cheeks glow."

"Oh, Rolf," she said helplessly. "You're so . . . sweet!"

"Just perceptive," he corrected. "Take this room for instance, and the dining room beyond. They could have been created for the flame of your beauty. And in that gown, with your hair, that touch of burning blue ribbon! My very dear, you're breathtaking! You overwhelm me; you're the heart of beauty."

"I've never heard you talk this way," she faltered. In his eyes she saw the same tenderness she had seen in Si's. It was like a homecoming.

Maybe I have come home, she thought. Maybe Rolf is the one, the perfect man. Her heart warmed, and she felt a tenderness for him, almost wished he would take her into his arms and tell her she was never to leave this house.

"You've seen the business side of my nature," he said. "And the respectful, social side. But you've never seen the private side. You don't know, for example, that I love to read poetry."

"Rolf!" she exclaimed. That he could be so much like Si and she hadn't known! Eyes locked, they gazed at each other. His arms moved and she believed he was going to embrace her, when the butler spoke from the archway, announcing dinner.

They went in to the dining room, which overlooked the water. But the view was wasted on Jenny. All she wanted was to gaze into Rolf's eyes, explore the new beauty she had found in them. They ate perfect French cuisine—Rolf said he'd managed to hire the best chef in Florida—and chatted of many things. They spoke of Jenny's greyhounds, of the upcoming racing season, of *The Louisa* and how David loved the yacht. When they spoke of David, Jenny's cheeks colored, remembering bed with him, and she hoped Rolf hadn't noticed.

After dinner, they danced on the Spanish-tiled floor of the patio, music emanating softly from a hidden speaker. Jenny felt comfortable and safe in Rolf's arms, and eventually laid her cheek on his shoulder, and they danced on.

Their steps slowed until they were standing in place, swaying gently to the rhythm. Rolf laid his cheek on her hair, drew her close, began to murmur.

"I'd meant to go slowly," he said. "To make myself indispensable to you, to work my way into your heart. Now, with all of beauty and all of love in my arms, my resistance has vanished. Jenny . . . !"

He stopped moving at all and they stood in an embrace, wrapped in the soft and sensuous rhythm of the music. Without realizing, she lifted her lips and his came to them with great gentleness and they kissed, a long, throbbing kiss, every line of his body following every curve and insweep of hers.

"Upstairs?" he whispered into her lips, which replied into his, "Yes . . . oh, yes!"

She was swept by warmth for him, by trust and eagerness. This was what she had come here for, to find out about Rolf, and he was showing her—oh how tenderly he was demonstrating affection and consideration and clean, manly urgency!

He took her to his bedchamber, which was palest blue. Inside the room, he stepped back and regarded her for seconds. Then he nodded. And she knew he was pleased with the way she looked against this pastel background.

"Jenny-dear," he whispered, "I can hardly wait. Will you take off the dress, while I—?" He indicated his suit, fingers on the buttons of the white jacket.

"You'll have to unzip me," she whispered back.

His hands weren't quite steady on the zipper, and she liked that. He was no David, practiced in the art of undressing girls, even if he was consistently chased by women.

They faced each other, nude.

He was handsomer this way. Almost six feet, broad-shouldered, flat-bellied, his body was leaner, less muscular than David's. He had Simon's coloring, but his features were a bit fuller, more sensual. His skin was tanned except for the part his swim trunks covered.

He was free of body hair except for the scatter of sun-bleached hair on his forearms and legs, and the golden patch at his groin. Her face burned as she gazed there, for he was ready, magnificently ready. The sight caused a stir in her own loins, and when he put his arms around her to move her to the bed, she went eagerly.

She was on the verge of solving all her problems. She was on the edge of her future, her bright, happy future.

He pulled back the pale blue spread and they lay down on the bed. She let him arrange her on her back, lay ready, let him kiss her—long, warm kisses on the lips, along the curve of her cheeks, on her chin.

He kissed her breasts, warmly and gently, and she felt the nipples harden. He kissed the throbbing hollow of her throat, her shoulders, her fingers. He kissed the nest at the fork of her legs, and she moaned.

As if the moan were a signal, he lifted himself, whispered, "Now, Jenny . . . now?"

Not knowing she was going to speak, she breathed, "Oh yes . . . yes!" She was so throbbing, so aching, so moist. To wait would be torture.

He came into her smoothly, pressed deep. "Move," he whispered. "It's a dance, remember, love is a dance, the true dance."

She followed his lead, as she had in the dance. Her head seemed to fill with throbbing music, or maybe it was the echo of the music to which they'd danced earlier, and she moved with grace, matching him. The dance quickened; the beat of that unheard music grew faster, harder, almost pounding. She was wild for it to grow, to carry them to the highest summit. She clung to him, quivering, never missing a beat.

When she could bear it no longer, the dance whirled into the stratosphere, Jenny with it, Rolf with her. The music attained unbelievable, breathless heights, then reached its limit, broke and burst and splintered, silver and lovely, and traveled the length of her body like quicksilver. Rolf gave two more hard beats, and then lay still, and the dance was ended.

He rolled to his side, kept her in his arms.

"Darling," he whispered, "Darling!"

She lay gasping. He kept murmuring "Darling!" She liked that. She liked his smell, too—a faint aroma of shaving lotion, a hint of tobacco, the clean man-scent of perspiration from lovemaking.

For a while, they lay still, cradled in each other's arms. Then he moved, and she saw that he was ready again.

"Jenny . . . ?"

"Oh . . . yes," she murmured.

This time they moved slowly and luxuriously. It wasn't a dance, but in a way it was better. It was soft, tender. At the end, a million silver darts shot through her, and he was crying out her name.

They rested, entwined.

"I want to marry you, Jenny," he whispered.

And again, she was surprised. First Richard, then David, and now Rolf. All had proposed after sex. And each time she had been confused, uncertain. As she was now.

"Jenny . . . ?"

"I . . . don't know," she whispered.

"I love you, Jenny-dear. I thought you loved me or you wouldn't— Was my lovemaking a disappointment?"

"No . . . oh, no!"

"Do you love me, Jenny? Think before you speak, darling. So you can give a true answer."

She tried wildly to consider. He was so much like Si—gentle, affectionate, tender. And his lovemaking had been wonderful. She was drawn to him, felt secure and beloved with him, was ready, at this moment, to lie in his arms forever. She hadn't felt that way with David. Or with Richard. Was this love . . . this tenderness and safety?

For no reason, just as she parted her lips to tell Rolf she'd be honored to marry him, she thought of Tom March, and could not. Because of that villain, she had to make Rolf, gentle Rolf, wait. She had first to be certain that Rolf's delicate, satisfying lovemaking had washed that miserable, recurring yen for the migrant out of her system.

Quietly, she told Rolf that she needed time. That she'd prefer not to see him alone, so she could assess her true feelings.

Like the gentleman he was, he accepted what she said. When he brought her home, he took her hand, kissed it, and then he left.

Sighing, she went to her suite.

23

Madeline was waiting up for her. When she heard Jenny come out of the elevator, she ran to her, flew sobbing into her arms. Her tears spilled onto Jenny's shoulder, and although she kept trying to speak, only choking sobs emerged.

Bewildered, Jenny held her, patted her back, made soothing sounds. She led her to the settee, sat her down onto it, sat beside her. She opened her tiny evening bag, drew out a dainty handkerchief, and pressed it into Madeline's fingers.

"Blow your nose, darling," she urged. "Wipe your eyes. You can't go on crying like this. You'll make yourself ill!"

Shoulders heaving, Madeline dabbed at her cheeks. Last, she blew her nose, then looked desperately at Jenny.

"H-he never wants to s-see me again!" she managed.

"Who, darling?"

"S-Simon!"

"What happened, darling? He *did* invite you out for dinner! What went wrong?"

"He d-didn't ask me to dinner of his own accord! I t-tricked him into it!" Madeline wailed.

"Even so, for him to put you in such a state as this! Something terrible must have—tell me what it was! Get rid of it!"

"I w-wish I could!" Madeline blew her nose again, drew a quivering breath, continued. "I w-wore my most revealing dress, the silver one, with the plunging neckline, knowing how passionate Simon is, h-how *inflamed* he gets! All through dinner I acted like a lady, but a very sexy lady, leading him on. And it worked! He became more and more passionate. I could see it in his eyes. And then—" She broke off, sobbing.

"Then what?" Jenny encouraged.

"After I'd waited and *waited* for him to make the first move and he didn't, even though I could tell he was bursting with desire, I made the move myself!"

"You mean," Jenny asked, dazed, "that you asked him to take you to bed?"

"Worse! I asked him to take me home with him to Golden Beach, where we lived when we were married. He said, 'Certainly, why not?' and we went."

Jenny waited while Madeline went into the bedroom and returned carrying a box of tissues. She sat beside Jenny again, dabbed at her face, blew her nose.

"There," she said, "that's better. Well, when we got to the house, I felt that was it. I had to make my play, all or nothing. So I ran upstairs into our old bedroom and he followed me. Looking right into those damn blue eyes of his, I stripped. To the skin. And then I lay on my back on the bed and held out my arms.

"He was too far gone—with alcohol and desire—to resist. He took off his clothes and came to me. We had sex twice. And it was great, really great . . . though very brief, as it always is with Simon."

"What went wrong?"

"I got in too big a hurry. I asked him, point-blank, to marry me again. He was furious! He swore, and said the only reason I wanted him was for his money! That I was tired of being poor!"

"Oh, dear," said Jenny, realizing Simon had guessed the truth.

"I told him divorce had made me realize how much I loved him! He *laughed!* I reminded him how much he used to love me, and he laughed again. Said it was only sex from the beginning. He s-said any time I want to have sex, he'll oblige unless he himself marries again, but that nothing will persuade him to marry me! He even suggested that, if I want a rich man, I try *Oliver!* Can you imagine? If he knew that I divorced him for Oliver and that Oliver turned me down, I don't know what he'd say!"

"You don't think you can change his mind? Talk to him when he's in a calmer mood?"

Madeline shook her head. "I doubt it. His mind's made up. He won't change it."

"I'm so sorry, Madeline."

"It's all right. I've had my cry. I'm disappointed, of course, but it's better that I found out now. You can have him, Jenny. If you want to enter him in your marriage tests, feel free."

"What will *you* do?" asked Jenny.

"I've been thinking of making another play for Oliver. I still find him terribly attractive."

Jenny nodded. "And if Oliver says no? Who then— Tom March?"

Madeline's eyes narrowed. "He's very macho," she replied, her tone careless. "But he hasn't got a dime. He's probably looking for someone with money himself."

Probably true, thought Jenny. Yet he had teased her, demanded to know if she'd marry a dirt farmer! Or words to that effect. He made her so angry she could scream!

She almost spilled all this out to Madeline, but then held her silence. She didn't want anybody, not even her dearest friend, to so much as dream that the Missourian upset her so!

For two days, she avoided men altogether. Both David and Rolf sent flowers; both called and asked for dates which they promised would be only friendly, with no demands on her. She refused both of them.

She spent hours swimming, free to pass Tom's apartment now because, Madeline had reported, he'd moved to a duplex in town. She also spent hours watching her dogs train, petting them. She learned from Simon that work on the Orange Blossom bathhouse was underway.

She couldn't, she knew, continue in this limbo. She had to put her mind on men, try to come to a decision. She felt shame over the number of men she'd already bedded and was unhappy for being unable to choose a husband.

Simon, she thought on the third day. Now that Madeline had given her permission to go after him, he was a possibility. Regardless of what Madeline said about his inner nature, she should find out for herself.

I'm going too fast, she fretted. Then: no, not fast enough. There's so much to accomplish in such a short time.

Consequently, learning that Madeline was going out shopping, Jenny phoned Simon at the office, invited him to drive to the training kennels with her and have lunch at the penthouse afterward. She held on while he consulted his calendar; then was pleased when he said he would cancel his appointments.

She told Madeline what she'd done.

"Good luck, darling," said the other girl, recovered from her despair. "Wear something seductive."

Jenny did. Dressed in a pale green jump suit that showed off her figure to advantage, she came down the stairs to the living room.

Simon had never looked handsomer. He wore a tan suit and pale blue shirt, the color of his eyes. His manner, even his voice, reminded her more than ever of Si. She found herself laughing and talking with him easily as they drove.

When they arrived at the kennels, Jenny was surprised to find Madeline there—with Tom March.

"We bumped into each other in town and decided to drive out for a look at the dogs."

The Missourian gave Jenny a cool nod, then turned his attention to Madeline.

Simon was clearly uncomfortable with Madeline's presence and tried his best to ignore her. He showered Jenny with attention, holding her arm gently and whispering softly in her ear.

He couldn't believe his good fortune in her having called him. He had bided his time, waited to make his move. Then, when he'd learned that she'd gone out with both Rolf and David, he'd begun to worry that maybe he'd waited too long. Evidently not. She seemed to want him as much as he wanted her.

Suddenly, Madeline was standing beside him. She was smiling, chatting about the dogs, and though he wanted to be rid of her, he responded in a courteous manner. He didn't want to make a scene in front of Jenny.

The shift in positions left the Missourian next to Jenny. He hardly looked at her, keeping his eyes fixed on the training oval. This infuriated her. Who did he think he was, to come watch *her* dogs train, even if Madeline had brought him? And then not have the decency to make conversation!

She remarked icily, "I hear you've moved away from the beach."

"That's right," he grunted.

"I thought you liked the sound of the ocean. Don't tell me that my swimming past chased you away!"

"Don't flatter yourself," he said. "I decided it'd make a better relationship with the pickers."

She fumed. If anyone could help his precious migrants, she could! How dare he move away from her! Furious, she leaned her elbows on the rail, watched the dogs run.

Madeline danced back to Tom, announcing they had to leave this minute if they were to lunch in Palm Beach. Jenny watched them go, still angry. Didn't he sense that he was being used? Did he actually believe that Madeline *wanted* to be alone with him?

After lunch back at the penthouse, Jenny and Simon went into the library and closed the door. Flo was busy stacking the dishwasher, after which she'd leave for her afternoon off. Which, with Madeline gone to Palm Beach, gave Jenny and Simon privacy.

They sat on the divan and chatted until Flo announced her departure. This put an unexpected lump into Jenny's throat and her pulse began to race.

She was alone with Simon. Now was the time to lure him to the bedroom. But she didn't know how to go about it. It was like trying to seduce Si himself, without the sanction of marriage.

"Why do you frown?" Simon asked. He moved close, put his arm around her, and she thought of moving away, but would not.

"I didn't realize I was frowning," she said.

"Have I displeased you, said something amiss?"

His arms tightened, and she really wished he'd take it away. But still she wouldn't free herself. She was going to see this through.

"No," she told him, "you've been perfect. You've been—"

"Like my grandfather? Is that what troubles you, Jenny, my sweet? For I am my grandfather, inside and out. And I love you as dearly as he did. Not in his aged manner, but in the way a vigorous man loves. Can you understand the difference, my sweet?"

I'm not your sweet! she ached to cry. But must not. Maybe the reason he was turning her off, his lips now against her hair, *was* that he reminded her so strongly of Si. Maybe that accounted for her aversion to his sexual overtures.

Go through with it, she told herself sternly. It's what Si wanted. You've started . . . now finish!

She let Simon kiss her. His lips were hot, not cool as Si's lips had been, but he was a young, hot-blooded man. And he was not Si. She must remember that. She returned his kiss, and when he continued the kissing, rested in his arms and let him do what he would.

She made no protest when he stretched her full length on the divan, unzipped her jump suit, opened his slacks. She let him remove her clothing, and as he did the same with his, she saw that he was fully roused.

He spread her legs and speared into her with no preliminary caress. It hurt, because she was dry, because she was far from being ready, but when he moved she responded, seeking whatever fulfillment she would find with him.

He plunged so fast she thought the speed equaled that of the greyhounds this morning, and she worked hard to match it. She reached for the little thrills, the darts, and they were not to be found. Abruptly, he quit moving, shuddered twice, then rolled off her.

He got up, smoothed back his hair, lifted her to a sitting position. He kept his arms around her; dazed, she remained in them. Is that all? she wondered.

"You see?" he said. "We're perfect together."

"You enjoyed it?" she whispered.

"To the hilt. You're the most beautiful, most sexually satisfying woman in the world, Jenny, my sweet."

He meant it, he really did. His desire had been sated with just one fast assault. Virtual rape. She recalled that Madeline had warned her about him. Well, now she had seen for herself and she would never repeat the act.

"We'll marry soon," he said.

"No, Simon. Never."

He stared, uncomprehending.

"But, Jenny, dear. Aside from being made for each other, there's the money. Together, we'll have twenty million dollars. You can't ignore that!"

For an hour he tried to persuade her, and she had to let her outrage show. But at last he took her refusal seriously, informed her that she would eventually reconsider, that marriage was inevitable for them. Finally, tight-lipped, he departed.

How had Madeline endured sex with him? No wonder she'd turned to Oliver, who was warm and considerate. Whose lovemaking was undoubtedly that way, too.

She began to roam the penthouse. Surely Madeline would be home soon. What were she and Tom doing so long, anyway? It was now nearly four o'clock. Miserably, her old yen for the Missourian flared. And he might be making love to Madeline this instant!

Well, she'd fix that. She'd rid herself of the yen—

Oliver. Madeline hadn't said he was off limits. True, she had said she was going to work on him herself, but that was probably only a reaction to Simon's behavior. And besides, at this very moment she was probably sleeping with Tom March!

So she phoned Oliver, asked to see him, and he told her to come to his office. "I've a bit of work to finish," he explained, "but I *am* looking forward to seeing you, Jenny."

She took a hot, cleansing shower, dressed swiftly, ran for her car.

The employees had all gone home by the time she got there. Oliver had to come and get her at the reception area, since there was no one to let her in. He came toward her, hands out, a smile on his gorgeous features. His deep brown eyes were tender. He was the complete opposite of Simon.

"I th-thought," Jenny stammered, still new to the seduction of men, "that we c-could talk about the migrant situation."

He drew her into his inner office, which was handsomely furnished. There was a great deal of dark, vibrant blue and black, including a soft black leather sofa.

"Don't sit down yet," he said quietly, and drew her into his arms. "I'm wasting no time on migrants today. I've stood back, forced myself to wait, to show respect, and I sense that the Townsend men are moving in on you."

She stared up at him. "H-how——?"

"They're all in love with you. Have been, ever since Si married you. But so am I. It's time I got my word in."

"Oliver!" she whispered. "I never dreamed——!"

"But you've liked me, been fond of me. Heaven knows I've been underfoot. You're used to me. I'm certain you have a fondness for me . . . is that right?"

"Y-yes," she admitted.

His arms felt so natural about her. She let him draw her closer. She was confused, anxious.

"I want you to be my wife," he murmured. "Will you marry me, Jenny?"

"I . . . don't know," she whispered.

"Is it the ten million?" he asked. "That's yours, Jenny. I have close to seven of my own. I don't want your money. Use it for a foundation, for the migrants, anything. I want just you, just lovely, lovable Jenny. I want you to give me sons, to make a home for us."

She trembled in his arms. He was persuasive. Oh, he was very persuasive, and she was tempted. But there was Madeline. And there was more she must know.

"Th-there's one element of marriage," she quavered, "that I have to . . . make certain of . . ."

"The part Si couldn't furnish, sweetheart? He spoke to me of it once. With regret."

He guided her to the sofa, sat her down gently. She watched him as he walked to the door and locked it. He was tall, dark, refined. He wasn't a Townsend, but he was the next best thing.

But when he returned, when he would have unfastened her dress, she couldn't go through with it. Because he loved her, or thought he did. And because of Madeline.

She'd come here to use him, to purge herself of the yen for the Missourian with warm, decent Oliver. Now that she knew how he felt about her, she couldn't stoop so low.

"What's wrong?" Oliver asked. "Would you rather wait until we're married?"

"The whole thing is wrong," she told him. "I want you for my dear friend, Oliver. But not for my husband, though I thank you for honoring me."

He didn't argue or plead. He took her word, assured her that his offer stood, that if ever she could find it in her heart to marry him, he was ready. And then he took her to the outer door of his office, gently kissed her on the cheek and let her go.

Miserable, she drove home. If this Tom-yen was the real thing—but it couldn't be, him so common and rough! There was only sex between them. Hate, not love. And he was probably after her money. No, Tom March was completely eliminated, had never been in the running.

Who, then?

Simon was out.

Oliver was out.

That left David and Rolf.

And she couldn't decide upon either of them. She knew why, too. She still wasn't over that yen for the Missourian.

Well, there was only one solution. She would have sex with him until she was so filled with it, so sated that she'd retch at the thought of sex with him. Then she'd be free. Free to choose a husband. And she would get married.

Actually, it was clear-cut and simple.

She had nothing to worry about.

She drove contentedly, a great load off her mind.

24

So liberated did she feel that she spent over an hour shopping for a dress. It was a perfect olive shade and she charged it, not even glancing at the price.

When she got home, Flo said Madeline had been in and gone out again. At least she was back from Palm Beach, not in the company of the Missourian.

She hung up her purchase, then wandered to her dressing table where she spied the note in Madeline's tiny scrawl. She picked it up, read it at a glance.

"Five p.m. Have driven to Tom's, 2400 Taft Street, to return his cigarette lighter. Back soon."

She crumpled the note, dropped it into the wastebasket. It was now five minutes of seven. Madeline should have been back an hour ago.

On impulse, she snatched up the phone, asked information for Tom's number, found that it wasn't listed. Within minutes, for no reason she could name, Jenny was at the wheel of her Firebird, heading for Taft Street. She was furious, though she had no idea why. But one thing she did know: Madeline should have been home by now.

She pulled up behind Tom's Buick. Madeline's car wasn't here. For no reason, she began to tremble with relief. Then she realized that anything, anything at all, could have happened while Madeline *was* here, and anger stilled the trembling.

She ran up the front walk, pushed the bell.

"Come in!" Tom called.

There—no manners, and no sense. For all he knew, she might be a thief, come to rob him. She'd not mention it to him, not give him the opportunity to say he was plenty able to take care of himself.

She found him in the living room staining bookshelves. He wore nothing but a pair of beige cutoffs. A lock of black hair lay across his brow almost in the shape of a question mark, and there was brown stain on his chin.

"Well," he drawled, "look who's here! How do you like my new pad?"

She had not even thought to look. She gazed around the small dark living room, peered into the sliver of kitchen. It was so bleek, it made her shiver.

"Where's Madeline?" she demanded.

"I have no notion," he said, and dipped his brush into the stain.

"How long did she stay?"

He stroked the brush along a shelf. "I don't see that's any of your affair."

"She only came to return your lighter!"

"So?"

"How long does that take?"

"I didn't time it."

She bit back words, glanced around. "Why are you staining bookshelves for a rented apartment?"

"I want the place to look decent."

"For the little time you'll live in it?"

"I aim to stay until the picking's done. Longer."

"Why longer?"

"To see that migrant conditions keep on the up-swing."

"What about your own farm work in Missouri?"

"There's somebody to see to plowing and planting."

She watched him stroke and stroke that shelf. A tingle went down her spine as she remembered how his fingers had felt stroking her skin. That inanimate wood, like the car fender, felt nothing; he could squat there forever and brush and it'd never feel a thing.

Staring at his broad, bare torso, watching him spread that stain on the wood, she longed for him to drop the brush and take her into his arms. But he wouldn't, of course. He'd been alone with Madeline long enough to quench his beastly passion.

She couldn't stand it another instant.

"You had sex with her today!" she accused.

He didn't miss a stroke with that damned brush.

"Who's 'her?' " he asked easily.

"Madeline! She was here, alone with you, and you can't keep your hands off a girl, any girl!"

"What makes you so sure?"

Now he'd gotten mad. He laid his brush down. Carefully. Put his big hands on his big knees, shot fire at her out of those black eyes.

"I'm sure because of the way you've treated me!" she cried. "You . . . you had sex with her two or three times! Deny it, if you can!"

"I don't feel like denying it," he said through his teeth. "It's easier to prove than to deny."

"What do you mean?" she demanded.

He stood rigid, face set in its meanest, homeliest lines.

"I'll *prove* that I couldn't have slept with Madeline," he growled. In one motion, he got up, swept her into his arms, and carried her to the bedroom. "You jealous, bullheaded, aggravating little jackass!" he growled on. "Don't you yell, don't you rouse the neighbors!"

He sat her down on the bed with a thump, but kept hold of her shoulders. He slammed his mouth onto hers, and that hurt, yet carried a fierce fire that danced along her spine. Her hands went up his arms and clung and they kissed harder.

He didn't bother to undress her. He only turned up

her skirt, pulled off her bikini, worked his shorts off, moved her so she lay flat. He hovered, still kissing, and like that, entered.

He went instantly into powerful thrusts such as she'd never experienced, even with him. She slammed herself up at him; their bodies slapped every time they met. And then the power bore deep, deep into her, and her innermost part gripped and climbed, and they ground together until she was overwhelmed with sensation which sprang through all her veins and into every pore of her body. She felt her nails dig into his arms, and still she pressed upward and upward, reaching for more, ever more. And it came, filled and eased her, then slowly dwindled.

They fell apart and rested. When she stirred, meaning to get off the bed and leave, he held her. She fought, but he entered her again, and again there was the motion, the pounding, the fury.

He felt right away that her inner embrace was greater this time. It was hotter, moister. He plunged and pounded, angry still, yet carried away by the passion that this female roused in him. Now they were in a deadly, endless bout, to see who was the better, and it was equal, their cleaving one to the other, moans blending in song. His delight went on and on, and he flooded her.

Panting, they rested again. And then they came together still another time, and he flooded her anew. He realized that she was trembling. Her breath was quivering mightily, and that almost moved him. But he caught himself in time, before he showed any tenderness. He could not, would not, trust her, not this redheaded wildcat.

"Tom," Jenny heard herself ask, "are you . . . in love with anybody?" Now why had she let that slip out? She knew he didn't even know the meaning of the word love.

"Why ask that fool question?" he growled. He knew what she was geting at, but he wouldn't give her the satisfaction of letting on that he knew.

"I asked because I want to know!" she cried.

"If you're asking am I in love with *Madeline*, the answer is no!"

"Ha! So! You're an animal! You prove it over and over again! T-to have sex without a drop of love, to—"

"I told you. I didn't have sex with Madeline. I thought I'd just proven that!"

"You like her though. I've seen the way you look at her."

"Sure I like her. But I ain't had sex with her."

Somehow, she believed him. He'd proven that he hadn't had sex with Madeline today. But she wanted to scratch his eyes out regardless.

"No one's good enough for you—the great Tom March!" she accused.

"I wouldn't jump to no such conclusions if I was you," he told her quietly. "I will say this much. If I ever settle on a woman for keeps, it'll be according to my own wishes. I'll know her when I see her. And whether or not I've seen her yet is none of your damn business!"

25

She got away from him without bursting into tears. At home, she couldn't find her elevator key in her purse and had to get a spare from one of the doormen.

Riding upward, she railed at herself. What kind of person was she? What had Tom March done to her? Why did she want to be in bed with him all the time? When was she going to get him out of her system?

She avoided Flo and Madeline and rushed to her suite, where she locked the door. Here she was safe; here, at least for a while, she wouldn't have to speak to anyone. Not until she got hold of herself.

She got right into the tub. She was always wanting to wash herself clean of him. He was a disease she'd caught, a plague that had taken control of her system. He had her so mixed up she couldn't remember if she'd taken her pill the last couple of days. He was ruining everything, her whole future.

She soaped until she worked up a furious lather, scrubbed until it hurt. She was going ahead with her plan.

She'd caught this sex-malady from him; she'd cure herself by using him; by having sex with him until she could stand him no longer. The day would come, it really would, when she'd be rid of this raging fever.

She'd dried, taken her pill, gotten into a robe and brushed her hair when a knock came at the door. It was Flo, with a dinner tray. Madeline was behind her, carrying her own tray.

When Flo had gone, Madeline expressed her concern. "Are you all right? You came in without a word—and Flo didn't know where you'd been—"

"I went shopping," Jenny said quickly. "Bought a dress. Drove over to Tom March's new place."

"I—see."

"And where were *you*? You said you'd just gone to drop off his lighter."

"Why, yes," answered Madeline, her voice carrying an edge to it. "But I went shopping afterward."

Something in Madeline's tone alerted Jenny. She wanted to know, so she asked, "Madeline, have you ever had sex with him . . . with Tom?"

"*Jenny!* Of course not!"

"I'm sorry," Jenny apologized. "I had no right—"

"You can ask me anything, darling! And anyway, I know why you asked. *You've* been sleeping with him, haven't you? Oh, Jenny, please don't. He doesn't fill the requirements; he's not the husband for you!"

"It's—I can't help myself," Jenny confessed.

Madeline smiled lovingly at her. "Well, I guess I know how you feel. Sometimes it's hard to resist."

Jenny nodded, happy Madeline understood.

"Oh, Jenny, I can't keep a secret from you!" Madeline blurted out. "Guess where I *really* went after I gave Tom his lighter. To Oliver's! I went to his office and we had a promising talk."

Oliver's! Jenny stiffened. Why she must have come right after Jenny left! Thank goodness she'd refused him. Now maybe he would go back to Madeline. She noted how her friend's eyes were shining.

"Is your talk a secret?" Jenny teased.

"Not from you! Oliver seemed unusually quiet at

first. Then, after one drink, he loosened up. We actually began to refer to . . . before. And he—well, I believe I may have a chance!"

Tears welled in Jenny's eyes. She was so happy for Madeline. "And oh, the best part," Madeline bubbled on, "is that I feel warm toward him, the kind of warmth that grows into real, satisfying love! Already the money isn't nearly as important as he is!"

They talked on, Madeline happy and hopeful, Jenny determined never to let her know of the advances Oliver had made.

Jenny was restless the next day. She drove to the kennels. She swam. She had lunch with Madeline, after which they played tennis, then showered and went for a dip in the penthouse pool.

Madeline had spoken to Oliver on the phone and was relaxed and happy. Rolf called and asked Jenny to have dinner with him, but she asked for a rain check. She and Madeline played backgammon and listened to the stereo all evening. They retired to their suites, Madeline happy, Jenny burning for the Missourian.

If this were really the plague, she'd be in the hospital, nurses tending her round the clock. She wondered if she'd turned into a sex maniac. Certainly she didn't seem to be able to get enough of it.

In bed, she tossed. That fire was deep. Painful. At midnight, she went naked into the pool, but the water was too warm. Maybe the ocean would be cooler. She slipped into a bathing suit, tucked some change into its zippered pocket, and headed for the beach. She kicked off her beach thongs and let the cool sand squish between her toes as she walked.

Then she broke into a run, heading into the froth of waves until the water buoyed her. She swam a distance more before she turned and slowly and strongly stroked southward. She passed a street intersection off to the right, passed another. Soon she was even with Tom's old apartment, and she swam a bit faster. She'd keep on until she was very tired, and then she'd walk back.

There were stars and a crescent moon. They glittered

on the water, shined down on the white, foaming waves. On she swam and on. Now to her right, rose a great building, once a hotel, now a small college. Beyond, near the old, inoperative bridge, a new one was under construction, a ferry service operating to the other side of the canal.

She was tired now. She slogged out of the water, crossed the beach, and trudged along the short street to the beach highway. The burning was still in her.

On impulse, she boarded the ferry, standing in the rear, away from the few cars that were on it, wondering if the idea of going to Tom had been in her subconscious when she slipped the change into her pocket. She got off the ferry on the far side and began to walk. There were no buses running this time of night.

She moved west on Hollywood Boulevard. Then north on Twenty-fourth Avenue to Taft Street. Barefoot, her suit wet, she went at a steady pace, hoping she wouldn't run into anyone.

At last she came to the small downtown business section. This was well lighted and a few cars passed. No one paid any attention to her. She didn't know whether some police car might stop her, but none came until she was on Twenty-fourth, and it padded on by.

All she wanted was to get there, to rid herself of this fever once and for all. Tonight had to cure her.

She punched his doorbell. There was no reaction, so she punched again. Now a light came on, the door opened, and she was face to face with him. He was naked, and staring as if he'd never seen her before.

So he was surprised. So what?

"What are you doing here?" he asked.

Didn't ask how far she'd swum, how many miles she'd walked, just what she was doing here.

"I swam and walked!" she snapped. "You might have the decency to let me in!"

He held the door open, still staring. She entered.

"You swam and walked," he said.

Just a flat statement. No appreciation of the effort it had taken. No recognition of how tired she must be.

Well, she wanted to be tired. That suited her purpose. She was so tired that a session in bed with him would completely drain her and work a cure.

Making no move to cover himself, he watched her through those black, damnable eyes. He looked as if he would kill her.

"Why'd you do such a damn-fool thing?" he demanded.

"Because I wanted to," she whispered fiercely. "I'm here," she whispered on, "to go to bed with you!"

He looked dumbfounded. His mouth turned angry. Damn her red hair, damn her stubbornness, damn her lack of shame! She was under his skin, keeping him so on edge that he could hardly concentrate on the migrants, they being all mixed up with her anyway.

"You've got the notion," he gritted, "that all you've got to do is come running and I'll crawl right into bed with you!"

Standing in front of him, defiant, she peeled off her swim suit, then flounced into the room where the light was on and the bed open. Flinging herself onto it, she lay with her arms out at her sides, legs slightly apart. He followed, stood glaring down at her. No matter how mad he was, his body was ready; he couldn't deny that.

Lured by her brazen beauty, sore as hell, he came onto the bed. He lost no time giving her what she'd come for. Their movements had never been as fierce, as deep, as long-lasting. It went on and on until both were sweating and panting, half delirious.

Furious as he was, he had new, tender thoughts of her. The long swim, that endless walk barefoot. The stubborn little mule! Filling her, meeting her thrusting body, he wondered how she'd look with a couple of Missoura toddlers calling her Mommy.

But he must not get carried away. She was trouble. A red-haired wildcat! No man with an ounce of sense would touch her with a ten-foot pole! Yet here he was, back in bed with her, and she was wound all around him, and he was growing inside her, bigger and bigger.

And now he was bursting. When he exploded, so did she, and his ears roared with the song of absolute fusion.

Part IV
THE CRASH

26

When she awakened the next morning she was in her own bed. For a moment, she didn't remember the long swim. The endless walk, the marathon love-session with the Missourian. Then the aches and pains all over her body reminded her.

Slowly, she got out of bed and headed for the tub. A nice hot bath would soothe her, ease some of the soreness.

She thought of Tom March. He had driven her home, wordlessly, neither of them acknowledging what had happened between them. And what exactly *had* happened? She tried to push it from her mind.

When she came down for breakfast, Flo handed her the morning mail. In it was a letter concerning a white greyhound Si had inquired about months ago. The owners had finally decided to accept his offer for the highly bred racer, Snow Blossom. They stipulated that someone must fly to St. Petersburg on the west coast of Florida, pick her up, and fly her back as a crated passenger.

"This dog is so high-strung it might end her racing days if she were shipped air freight," the letter concluded.

Excited, Jenny phoned St. Petersburg and arranged to pick up Snow Blossom the next day. That night, over after-dinner coffee, she told Madeline about the greyhound, relating her pedigree and the races she had already won. "She's just ready for her best racing," she concluded. "I'm lucky to get her."

"If she's to be a winner," Madeline asked, "why are they willing to sell her?"

"They're retiring," Jenny explained. "The man's arthritis has put him into a wheelchair and his wife has a full-time job taking care of him. They sound like nice people. You'll see for yourself, because I want you to go with me tomorrow."

"Oh, I'd love to, Jenny," Madeline enthused. "But you really ought to have the men along too—especially Tom March. He's so good with animals. If this dog is so high-strung you'll need him.

Jenny winced. She knew Madeline was right. She ought to have help with the dog. But she wouldn't have Tom alone. She decided to invite all the Townsend men— and Oliver, too. They could make it into an outing.

Madeline squealed with delight. "Great idea! We'll have such fun! I'll make all the phone calls to invite them!"

Later, alone in her suite, Jenny fumed. She didn't want Tom March along! Without him, the trip would have been pleasurable, helped to clear her mind. Now, she would have to face him, and they would undoubtedly quarrel again. Every time she saw him they quarreled. Even when they were in bed.

She'd just removed her slip when the door to her bedroom opened and Tom stepped in. Instinctively, she hugged the slip to her chest to cover her nakedness. "H-how did you—?"

He held up a key. "I stole it from your bag."

So that was where her elevator key had gone! He'd turned thief.

"Give me that!" she cried. "You have no right to sneak into my home!"

"As much as you have, busting into my apartment—"

"I rang the bell!"

"—making yourself at home in my bed. Madeline called, inviting me on your little excursion to St. Petersburg. I came to try to persuade you not to go. You ought to be here, devoting yourself to this migrant problem. Seems you can't get it through your head how serious things are. I've just learned there's been an outbreak of measles among the children, and it's spreading rapidly because of the way they have to live."

"I'm sorry to hear about it!" she retorted. "But I don't see how my little trip will make things worse! And another thing—the way you talk to me! You've never spoken a civil word, not one word of kindness, or . . . admiration or . . . liking. All you've done is grab all the sex you can get!"

"Because that's all you understand! What you've got to face, you ain't ready to face."

"Exactly what is that?"

"It's a problem every real woman deals with. That's to let go of her girlhood dreams—and face reality."

"I am facing reality! I'm—"

In one flowing motion, he scooped her into his arms and put her on the bed. She was still clutching the slip and he pulled it from her. Then he undressed and lay down on top of her, the lines of him following the swells and curves of her body.

"Get . . . off!" she whispered. "Don't . . . you . . . dare . . ."

But he did dare. First he stroked and petted her, barely touching, setting her afire. He kept that up until deep in her belly was such a knot of desire she knew she couldn't stand it another instant. But she had to, for those hands were still moving, touching, driving her wild. Her ears were roaring and into the roar came the sound of his moan.

Smoothly then, he took her. Instantly she got the

225

tightest inward grip on him yet. There was still the knot in her belly—low, very low—and when he moved she could hardly endure it. Everything was concentrated there, all her tension, all her hunger.

He moved with smooth, fast power, and she met this with her own. She arched to him, held her breath, felt sweat pour off her, and at the last nearly unbearable second, the knot broke and delight poured through her, even into her brain, and she savored the delight, the sound of his groans, until it was ended.

He sat up and she lay gazing at his face. It didn't look angry. Just . . . quiet. She waited. He'd say something now, something decent.

"That," he told her, "is reality. Think about it, Jenny. Learn from it."

And then he dressed and left. And she was right where she'd been with him. The plague was soothed, but for the moment only.

She was too depressed to get angry. Instead, she wept.

In the morning, she found her elevator key on the bedside table.

They gathered at the penthouse early the next morning—Jenny, Madeline, the three Townsends, Oliver, and Tom March. Billings drove them to the airport in the limousine.

Jenny tried to avoid looking at the Missourian. She did not want to let him spoil her day. But when they boarded the plane he was right behind her. And when she sat down in her window seat, he plunked himself down in the aisle seat next to her. This was maddening: she'd wanted to sit beside Rolf. Or David. But they had taken seats at the front. Other passengers boarded until the plane was filled.

"Better fasten your seat belt," March said, not even looking at her. He snapped his into place, then pulled a magazine from the pouch in front of him and began to read.

Furious, she locked her belt and stared out the

window. She watched the various airport employees, saw the steps rolled away, and the plane began to taxi. It moved into takeoff position, waited.

There was a continuous murmur as passengers talked to one another. She heard Madeline laugh, then Oliver. They were probably sitting together.

Finally, the plane began to move, gathered speed, and Jenny watched some tall grass along the edge of the runway bow to the ground from the wind their passage made. The plane lifted, and Jenny had that sensation in her stomach she always had at this moment, took a deep breath and waited for the craft to level off. Only it didn't level off, but made a gliding sort of forward dive, throwing Jenny forward, against her seat belt, then back.

Inside the plane there was instant bedlam. Women screamed, men shouted, a child shrieked. Jenny smelled fabric, realized she'd been thrown forward again and her face was rammed into the back of the seat in front of her. As she realized this, the plane crashed to a stop, standing on its nose, it seemed, and she was whipped back and sidewise into Tom, then forward again, her head thumping against the same seat.

The screaming was louder now; men were cursing. Jenny, aware that Tom too had been thrown back and forth, waited for him to do something. Only he didn't. Her neck hurt, but she managed to turn and look at him. The motion seemed to wrench her whole, sore body.

Tom wasn't moving. He was hanging forward, held by his seat belt, and there was blood on his face. She felt for her handbag, to get a handkerchief, couldn't find it. She placed her palm in Tom's blood, wiped it down his cheek, wiped again.

The pilot's voice came over the loud speaker; she caught only snatches of what it said. "Speed . . . unfasten seat belts . . . emergency exits . . . tanks . . . explode . . . be calm . . . orderly . . . stewardess . . ."

Again she wiped at Tom's blood. There was a gash at the side of his head. Her shoulder stabbed with pain and her back was stiff, making it impossible to move. But she had to move, had to pull Tom back and unfasten his seat belt, had to get him out before the gas tanks exploded.

She lunged to pull him back so she could reach the buckle of his seat belt. Pain shot through her. She tasted salt, felt blood in her mouth, knew she had bitten her tongue, swallowed blood. She got her hands onto Tom's left shoulder, heaved and pulled, letting pain knife her where it would.

He was too heavy; she couldn't budge him. Screaming at him, letting her own pain race over her, the screams and cries of others blending into it all, she pulled at him.

"Tom!" she shrieked, and blood filled her mouth and she swallowed again. She couldn't scream any more, but she had to. "Tom . . . open your eyes. Move, help me! Tom . . . we've got to get out of here!"

He hung inert, forehead against the seat in front, and she couldn't see any of his face now, only blood. Her own seat belt! If she could get it open, she might be able to manage better with Tom.

She found the buckle. It wouldn't open. She tore at it; it remained clamped. Instinct warned her to go slowly, to feel her way, so she did. Suddenly her belt opened, fell apart, and she whirled to Tom.

Tom heard a sharp, fine screaming. It was at his ear, piercing through his thick brain like a relentless needle. It kept on and on, and the more it came, the sharper it was. He had a throbbing pain in his head, and something kept clawing at him and tugging at his shoulder, when all he needed was a little peace.

Jenny, that's what it was. Jenny screaming his name, clawing at his waist, making it impossible for him to move. As usual, she was in the way; he could have no rest because of her.

The sound of his seat belt popping open cleared his head some. Then, little by little, he remembered what had happened, and he became conscious of the flurry of activity around him. Emergency slides were being lowered and people were sliding down them to safety.

Jenny. He turned and stared at her screaming face. There was blood on her chin. He'd lift her out of here, work them both into the aisle, which was filling up with crowding, frightened passengers, and get her onto a slide.

Jenny's heart leapt. He was conscious! He knew what was happening. He reached for her, she pushed his hands aside, staggered to her feet, put her arms under his arms and lifted.

He didn't stir. She lifted again, straining, blood from her tongue oozing out of her mouth. She had to get him onto a slide, then into an ambulance. She heaved again. It was no use. She couldn't budge him.

Someone was leaning in over them. Simon, and Rolf behind him. Simon dragged Tom up and into the aisle. Jenny followed, half falling, reaching to steady Tom, and then Rolf had her and they were all four of them in the aisle.

They made it to an emergency slide. Simon tried to get Tom onto it, but he turned and grabbed at Jenny, trying to put her ahead of him on the slide. She fought back, forced him to go first.

He hit the tarmac, waited for her, and, as she slid to the bottom, tried to yank her to her feet. She felt him stagger and flung both her arms around his waist, and he clutched her and they swayed, both about to fall, until Simon and Rolf parted them and moved them away from the plane.

Now they saw the others. Madeline was limping, and David had his arm around her, helping her to walk. Oliver was on her other side, ready to help.

Jenny looked around. They had landed, nearly nose-dived, into a rough field just west of the airport. From the position of the plane, it was clear that they had narrowly escaped a fatal crash.

Ambulances shrieked to a stop, out rushed ambulance men with cots. Those passengers from the wrecked plane who were unhurt parted to let them through.

Jenny saw that Tom was still bleeding. Panic seized her. If he was this badly bruised, what might be the extent of his internal injuries? She felt herself go dizzy. She hated him, but didn't want him dead. She tottered, felt arms grab her, steady her. They were Tom's arms.

But he shouldn't be helping her! He ought to be in

the hospital this instant. They had to get him there or he would bleed to death. Why didn't someone help them?

Simon was speaking, and she listened. Maybe he'd seen Tom's condition. "Driver!" he was saying. "Bring that first cot! For the young lady here!" He motioned toward Jenny.

The man put the cot down, moved toward her.

"Don't be fools!" she screamed, tried to scream, only it came out a squeak. "There's not a thing wrong with me!"

"Take her," Tom ordered.

She tried to pull away. This made her brain spin, but she drew a long, slow breath and overcame the dizziness. The men came at her again. "I will not go in that ambulance!" she cried. "If you force me, so much as touch me—"

She saw Tom's fist coming. Felt it jolt her chin. He grabbed her, and she could not fight back because he'd hit her and hurt her tongue again. She fell forward and he caught her and dumped her onto the cot.

When she would have sat up, he held her down with one hand. He kept hold of her while the ambulance men carried her and slid the cot into the ambulance.

She was half up when Tom took the seat beside the cot. He pushed her back firmly. "Stay put," he ordered.

"You're bleeding!" she screamed. "Go away . . . get into an ambulance. Do you want to die?"

"Usually takes a spell to bleed to death," he said. "Now lay back and be quiet."

"Give me your handkerchief," she demanded.

Bleeding, his movements stiff, he fished around, gave her the folded white square. She opened it and, before he knew what she was about, sat up and began to wipe at the blood flowing down his cheek.

He grabbed the handkerchief, pushed her down, held her. "You," he gritted, "ain't to move. Not until a doctor says you can."

"You beast . . . you unspeakable beast!" she cried. "You're the one supposed to be on this cot! You're the one who's hurt!"

He just held her.

Held so, she told herself that the reason she was concerned about his injuries was that she wanted him to live to see her walk out of his life.

For that occasion she wanted him alive and well.

27

· When they left the hospital, Tom had stitches over his left eye and tape wrapped around his sore shoulder. Jenny had been given medication for her tongue, but except for some strained muscles and the lump on her chin where Tom had slugged her, she was all right. Madeline had a slightly sprained ankle, but was able to walk. The others had come away shaken, but unhurt.

When Jenny saw Tom, she sucked in her breath. "Your head's bandaged!" she cried. "Did you lose a lot of blood?"

He shrugged, and she noticed how he favored his right shoulder. "Not so much they didn't let me walk out," he said.

"What's wrong with your shoulder?"

"A sprain. Nothing more. What about you? Are you all right?"

"Just this—" She stuck out her tongue, pulled it back. "Where I bit myself. And my chin where you struck me! And all I was doing was trying to help you!" She blazed a look at him.

A puzzled expression crossed his face. "I *hit* you?"

"You most certainly did!" Jenny cried. "I suppose you don't remember.

He shook his head. "Honest, I don't. But I was half knocked-out for a while," he said. "You must have got in my way."

"You punched me, then held me down on that cot all the way to the hospital! I guess when you're half-out your true nature shows itself! You'll even go so far as to hit a defenseless woman!"

The others converged on them, and Jenny hushed. So did Tom. She gave him a searching look. Maybe he *had* been groggy when he hit her, but he was his usual unbearable self now.

Back at Jenny's penthouse, they sat in the living room drinking strong coffee. Flo, shaken by the news of the crash, was hovering over them clucking like a mother hen. "You all better rest for a while. Especially you, Mr. March—and you girls."

"Maybe you'd better call the St. Pete kennel, Jenny," David suggested. "Let them know we're not coming."

"But we *are!*" Jenny protested. "At least I am! It's a short flight, and it's still early!"

Flo gave a disapproving look and was about to speak, when Simon beat her to it. "Flo's right, Jenny. You, Tom and Madeline should rest. But Rolf, David and I could go get Snow Blossom."

"No!" cried Jenny. "I must go! We all should!"

"Why?" growled Tom.

"We *need* to! If we let the crash keep us out of the air, we can easily be afraid to go up ever again! Don't you see?"

Tom looked thoughtful. So did the other men.

Madeline upheld Jenny. "I'm going!" she announced. "Jenny's right! The sooner we get on another plane, the better!"

In the end, all agreed to go. Simon phoned for reservations on an early afternoon flight to St. Petersburg and return reservations, including one for the greyhound, for that evening.

Snow Blossom exceeded Jenny's wildest hopes. She was white from tip to toe, and her coat glistened like satin. However, she was very high-strung, fled to the far end of her kennel when anyone other than Mrs. Davis, the stout, elderly owner, so much as spoke to her. With Mrs. Davis she was gentle and affectionate, though she kept watch, ready to dash away from these invaders who had come into her presence.

It was Madeline who suggested that Tom make friendly advances. "Remember the other dogs," she whispered. "You tamed them in a hurry. Didn't he, Jenny?"

Jenny, who had failed thus far to even come near Snow Blossom, nodded reluctantly. "Go ahead," she muttered. "See what you can do."

Tom thought it sounded more like a challenge than a request, but he agreed anyway. "Anything to be on our way," he said, almost under his breath, and began to move, ever so slowly, toward Snow Blossom's runway.

Jenny watched, angry that she couldn't manage her own dog, that she had to let Tom do it. It took forever—Snow Blossom was suspicious—but at long last she made friends with Tom. She even let him put her into her travel crate.

Mrs. Davis suggested that Tom keep her for a few days, and that Jenny and the others make gradual advances. "Then she can go to the training kennels," the woman said. "She's basically a gentle dog. When she gets to know you, she'll be easily handled."

"I'm afraid," said Tom, "I ain't equipped to keep a greyhound at my place."

Jenny fumed. She was always being caught in some impossible situation by this man. But at present, Snow Blossoms's welfare came before her own wishes.

"I'll keep her at the penthouse," she said. "And you," she continued, not looking at Tom, "can stay in the guest suite and keep an eye on her until she warms up to me. If you feel like it."

He shrugged his shoulders. "I'll divide my time between the beach and Taft Street. That's the best I can do."

Jenny seethed. Again, she knew she should show gratitude, but the words stuck in her throat. She breathed carefully, to hide her displeasure.

28

Tom and Rolf carried Snow Blossom, in her crate, onto the plane. Passengers stared and murmured.

The men slid the crate between the front seat and the inner wall of the plane. Tom sat in the aisle seat, stretched his legs along the top of the crate, and murmured to Snow Blossom, who was whining. She quieted.

Jenny and Rolf sat immediately behind Tom and the greyhound. The window seat next to Tom wouldn't be occupied; they'd paid full fare on that. It was Snow Blossom's seat, though of course she wouldn't be using it.

The rest of the party sat across the aisle, Oliver and Madeline together, Simon and David behind them. Jenny regarded each one briefly. None seemed nervous about flying. Nor was she. On the flight to St. Petersburg she'd been a bit uneasy until the plane was airborne, but now even that feeling was gone.

They landed at Miami International at 8:45. There was much activity at the great airport. Planes were landing and taking off; airport employees were pushing big, luggage-piled carts and empty carts; lines of passengers were streaming in and out.

Again Tom and Rolf carried the dog crate, weaving through masses of people in the terminal building, making for the proper exit. They'd driven to Miami in two cars—Jenny's Continental and Tom's Buick—because they'd have room that way for the crate.

They'd had trouble finding parking places, had been relieved to find a gap against the far fence, which would hold both cars. Thus they now had a long distance to walk. Once out of the terminal, they were able to go faster, but were still slowed down somewhat by the many pedestrians and moving cars.

They had barely departed the brightly lit terminal area when a burly, rough-dressed black man stepped around in front of Tom and Rolf, blocking them. They stopped, holding the crate.

"Max!" exclaimed Tom. "What are you doing here?"

The man was grim-faced. "Why didn't you say you was goin' 'round buyin' dogs?" he asked.

"I didn't see any point to it, Max. I'm trying to get the Townsends to do the migrants a big favor—"

"It ain't a favor, March."

"Sorry. Wrong word. I'm trying to persuade them to help the migrants. Folks," he said to the waiting group, "this is Max Vernon, the levelheaded man I told you about. Max, these are the Townsends and Oliver Cranston, though this is hardly the place for introductions."

Snow Blossom whined, yipped.

"Better let somebody else tote the dog," Max Vernon said. "Word of this—association of yours—leaked to Perez and his bunch, and he's been talkin' to them ever since, makin' threats. He even knows where you went today, and it ain't hard to find out where planes land. I been on the lookout, but ain't seen none of them. But I wouldn't be surprised if they paid you a little visit at your apartment tonight. They're fed up bein' put off, and figure you're playin' them against the Townsends to get somethin' for yourself."

"What am I supposed to be after?"

"Money. Payoff. You keep the pickers quiet and the Townsends don't never do nothin' for them."

"We have to get this dog into a car," Tom said, above Snow Blossom's barking. "Walk along with us, and when we get her settled, we'll talk."

Vernon agreed, and began to walk alongside them. They made better time now, because traffic had thinned considerably. There was only an occasional cruising car to avoid as they entered the far shadows.

Beyond the shadows lay darkness, where they were parked. Heaving and pushing, Rolf and Tom shoved the crate onto the back seat of the Continental. Rolf moved away and Tom stayed a minute with the frightened greyhound, talking softly to her. When she was settled, he closed the car door.

It was then that a hand from out of the darkness grabbed his sore shoulder, spun him about, and a fist crunched into his nose. Instinctively, he brought his own right fist up, delivering a solid punch to a jaw.

He took the next blow to the head, and returned a quick left to his assailant's belly, all power in the blow. The man staggered backward, landing on his rump and Tom was on him, fists working, beating him mercilessly.

They rolled, and a blow crashed into Tom's eye, another above his ear. He got his arms around the other man's neck, jerked his right arm so he had that neck in a vise, and began to press.

They rolled again, Tom using that choke-grip, taking whatever blows came, dimly aware that others around him were fighting, many others. Above the commotion, he heard the frightened cries of the women.

Suddenly the body under him went limp. He waited one second, maybe two; the fellow was out. Tom staggered to his feet and a pair of shadows detached themselves from the seeming horde of fighting shadows, and he knew, as he danced about, keeping out of reach, that this was the Perez gang.

This sent him into blind, raging fury. He dodged a blow, got one in the groin, returned it and saw the fellow double. Then another man jumped him from behind, and again he was down. This time he rolled, fought powerfully, doggedly, still sore from the plane crash and from the beating he'd taken from the first attacker.

He tried for a stranglehold, failed to get it. His assailant was pounding his neck, his face. He grabbed for the face above him, got a grip on each whiskered cheek, worked his thumbs into the eyes and gouged. The fellow screamed, flung his head back and forth, but Tom held fast, spurred on by the cries all around him. There was no way to guess how many Perez had brought, or how the Townsend men were holding up against them.

The whiskered one shrieked. Tom freed one eye, drove his right fist behind an ear. The body under him lay still.

Snow Blossom was yelping. Tom heard Jenny trying to quiet her. He dived toward a cluster of fighters, holding his punches, trying to make out which was enemy.

"Dios, airport cops!" hissed a voice, and suddenly the fighting was over. Tom made out shadowy figures helping others to their feet, then disappearing into the darkness.

"Into the cars!" Tom ordered. "Hurry!"

Jenny started to argue, but he pushed both herself and Madeline into the Continental. He tossed his own car keys to Rolf, then got behind the Continental's steering wheel.

Both cars started up simultaneously and roared out of the parking lot. Tom turned several times to see if the police were following, was relieved to find that they were not. He floored the accelerator, headed for the highway.

Jenny was trembling. She'd been frightened during the fight, but now she was mad. The way Tom had taken charge, appropriated her car even! She felt like a criminal, running from the police this way.

Snow Blossom was whining. She turned to the back seat and tried to calm her, but the whining just grew worse. Evidently the fighting had frightened her too.

"Those thugs!" wailed Madeline. "Who were they, Tom?"

"Mostly Chicanos. Led by Perez. Dissidents, every one. They're the ones I warned you about." He flashed a look at Jenny. "The ones we've got to watch."

"There were ten of them, *ten* against six! Jenny and I tried to fight too, but once I found out it was Oliver's hair I was pulling. He pushed me back and told me to stay out of it!"

They were on the highway now, and as they passed lighted areas, Jenny tried to see if Tom was badly hurt. She didn't think so, but it was really too dark to tell. When she asked him if he was all right, he snapped at her.

"Never mind about me. Try to quiet that dog! Way she's carrying on, some police car may take out after us!"

She tried again to calm Snow Blossom, turning in her seat and crooning softly to her. Finally Snow Blossom stopped howling and listened, her eyes still wide with fright.

Jenny kept it up, all the way into the garage at Townsend Towers. Tom's Buick, driven by Rolf, pulled in behind them.

They all piled out, Rolf once again helping Tom with Snow Blossom's crate. The doormen were both busy helping apartment dwellers into their cars, so by hurrying, they were able to get into the elevator without being seen.

Tom brought Snow Blossom to her waiting kennel. He removed her muzzle, then fed her some scraps of red meat. The rest of the group, dirty and bruised, but unhurt, drooped around, watching.

"She'll do until later," Tom said finally. "Now we'd best look after ourselves."

They gathered in the living room. Jenny studied each of them. What a sight they were! Their clothes were dirty, torn. Simon had an eye turning black; Tom was bleeding where his stitches had opened and had two black eyes; Vernon's face was lumpy and battered; Rolf kept dabbing at one ear which was bleeding slightly; Oliver had a swollen jaw.

"It was Perez, all right," Vernon said to Tom. "I heard him say they'll be back. And they will."

"Can't they be stopped?"

"Maybe. If they see the first houses goin' up for them. Then, maybe."

"But we need time, damn it," said Simon. "Don't they know that?"

"I don't know that it matters," replied Oliver. He had been unusually quiet all evening, and now his handsome face looked thoughtful. "I think we need to satisfy Perez and his group before they work up something really bad. The raise we gave them hasn't done it. And I have the feeling Perez, personally, wants a chunk of money, regardless of how he gets it."

"Why not have a meeting which includes both Perez and Vernon?" suggested Rolf. "Thrash out the whole problem."

Vernon was enthusiastic. "Good idea, if he goes for it. I'll help in any way I can."

Simon nodded. "Perhaps you could find Perez tonight. Persuade him to keep his group from talking to the press. Invite him to the meeting. Tell him that the two of you can both be present to represent the two factions."

Vernon agreed to try. "I think I know where to find him. I'll get right on it," he said. Then he picked up his jacket, thanked Jenny for her hospitality, and left the penthouse.

"We're up to our ears in it now," said Simon, after the door shut behind him.

"And for *all* our sakes," muttered Tom March, "we better not fail."

29

It was nearly midnight when the others left the penthouse. All except Tom March, who had agreed to stay behind to help care for Snow Blossom. Jenny retired to her suite; then, finding herself unable to sleep, went to the garden and sat on a bench watching Tom pet and soothe the new greyhound.

It amazed her how sensitive he could be with animals. If only he could be that way with people. But, no, he was a brute, a bully. Especially to her. For some reason they seemed to always rub each other the wrong way.

Tom looked up from Snow Blossom, noticed Jenny. He gave her a nod, then turned back to the dog. He was sitting next to her now, flat on the grass, fondling her ears. Tail waving, she licked his face. Jenny winced when that wet red tongue went across the stitches on his brow, but he let Snow Blossom lick again.

"That's dangerous!" Jenny warned. "You shouldn't let her lick your wound."

He ignored her, cradled Snow Blossom in both arms, put his face on her head. Snow Blossom's tail wagged, kept wagging. Jenny sat mute and glared.

Oh, he was doing a favor, no doubt about that! The thing was, he was supposed to be doing *her* a favor. Instead, everything was for Snow Blossom. He didn't care at all how achingly tired and sore Jenny was, sitting on this hard bench. He didn't come over to soothe *her,* to comfort *her*.

"Go to bed," he told her suddenly. "No need for you to sit up."

"She's quiet now!" Jenny retorted. "What do you intend to do, sit up with her all night?"

"Not unless I have to. Fact is, I'll try leaving her now. Leave on a dim light for her to see by."

After what seemed forever, he took his leave of Snow Blossom, and started back into the penthouse. Jenny followed.

He didn't wait for her to show him the way to the second guest suite, but stalked right into her bedroom and, after she was in, shut the door. She had her lips parted to order him out, when he turned on her.

"Now," he said, "I'll look *you* over. See where you're hurt. Take off your clothes."

"I will not! I'm not hurt! You're the one who's been in a fight! *You* take off your clothes!"

His face broke into a smile, the first she'd seen all evening. "Why don't we both do it?" he said. "See for ourselves. If you ain't bare by the time I am, I'll undress you myself."

He would, too. Now he was getting out of his clothes faster than ever before. Rather than submit to the indignity he proposed, she scrambled out of her own.

Nude, they looked each other over.

He had some severe bruises, and the bandaged shoulder made him look in even worse shape. She had only a couple of minor bruises, and the lump he himself had put on her chin.

"You see!" she cried. "I'm fine! But you—just look at you! You march straight to the bathroom! I'm going to wash that dry blood off your head and clean that cut on your knee and put rubbing alcohol on it!"

He glared, then walked to the bathroom, sat down on the lid of the commode. She followed him in and washed her hands thoroughly, disinfecting them with alcohol. Then, gently, she tended his wounds.

He watched her as she treated him. This was a side of her he had not seen. So she could be tender, caring. She had a heart after all.

When she was finished, she got up to go, but he swept her into his arms and carried her to the bed. Her impulse was to fight; then her better judgment prevailed. Hadn't she decided to have sex with him until she was cured of this passion? He came into her, and she didn't have another thought. Only sensation.

The moment they rolled apart, Snow Blossom began to howl. Muttering, Tom got into his clothes and left. He sat up the rest of the night with the greyhound; Jenny knew, because she went out there several times and he told her to sleep, that this would be Snow Blossom's worst night.

Finally, she went to bed and stayed there.

The next days crept.

Jenny and Madeline spent much time in the pool. Madeline's bruises faded and Jenny's tongue was healing; the lump on her chin had gone down. She'd expected Tom to object to their using the pool because it might upset Snow Blossom.

Instead, that first morning, before he returned to his own apartment, he practically ordered them to use the pool. "It'll get her used to seeing other people," he said in his high-handed manner. "Just don't go up to the runway."

By the end of two days, Snow Blossom had made friends with both Jenny and Madeline and tolerated Flo, who brought her meat. Each night she howled some, and Tom had to comfort her.

Each night, too, he came into Jenny's bed and she received him. The sex was so delightful she began to wonder how long it was going to take her to tire of it. She became thoroughly disturbed, the more sex she had with him the more she seemed to want. It wasn't supposed to work that way.

The third morning, Tom moved back to his duplex. He'd been spending his days in the groves, picking grapefruit, and was again on good terms with Vernon and most of the other pickers. Perez and his followers remained aloof.

That afternoon the Townsends, including Jenny and Oliver Cranston, met in Simon's office with Vernon and Perez. Tom, naturally, was also present. Perez demanded still higher pay and living quarters for the pickers, the pay to start pronto, the houses to be ready for next season. Tom suggested gradual building of houses; Vernon backed him up.

But Perez, who listened impatiently, would not back down; he wanted everything done immediately.

On the subject of raises, they were even less in agreement. Simon spoke for a raise of ten cents per basket. Perez just scowled, his face creased and ugly. But Simon stood firm.

Rolf suggested that Vernon and Perez discuss the proposals with the other pickers. "Maybe they'll approve. Ten cents a basket is really a decent raise."

Perez shot Simon a look, another at Jenny. "We take the raise," he said. "We talk of the other."

The Townsends voted for the raise to go into effect as of that day. Vernon and Perez promised to hold quiet discussions with the dissidents and to meet later for further negotiation. They all shook hands.

After the meeting, Madeline, who had waited in an outer office, came bubbling into the room. "I've a thrilling idea for tonight!" she announced. "I've discovered a new disco in Fort Lauderdale, and we're all going. My treat!"

The men looked at one another. They were all exhausted from the meeting with Vernon and Perez. It had been a long day. But not wanting to be rude, they agreed to go.

"Wonderful!" Madeline squealed with delight. "David, you can take Sara, and Rolf can bring Lila! Simon, you can ask Barbara! Oliver,"—she smiled dazzlingly—"I have dibs on you! And Tom—well, there's Jenny!"

"Well, you've got it all figured out," smiled David. "Who can argue?"

Jenny sat quietly. She didn't want to go, especially as Tom's date. "Snow Blossom," she said. "Who will baby-sit her?"

Unexpectedly, it was Tom who spoke up. "She's accepted Flo," he said. "No problem. And I'll look in on her before we leave and after we get back."

And so it was settled. They were going.

Because she had to be Tom's date—oh, how that sizzled through her—Jenny put on her gold silk gown, pulled her flaming hair to the top of her head, braided the blue ribbon through it. She didn't dust powder on her red lips to tame them. The more like a burning candle she looked, the better, because he hated her in this gown. He'd find out that she dressed to please herself.

Madeline wore a lavender dress Jenny hadn't seen. It was softly feminine, charmingly daring, with unexpected slits up the sides. It afforded glimpses of Madeline's shapely legs, and seemed ready to slide off her shoulders.

Jenny noticed, as they assembled in her living room, that Oliver gazed at Madeline admiringly. He gazed at Jenny, too, but being the perfect gentleman that he was, kept his regard merely admiring, not intimate, as David's for example, was.

Once, when no one was looking, he left Sara with Oliver and Madeline, came to Jenny's side. "You beauty!" he murmured. "How *long* must I wait? How can you be so cruel? To make me court you from afar, when I—"

Rolf, with Lila on his arm, interrupted smoothly at this point. "Jenny," he said, "delightful as ever!"

She blushed at the yearning in his sensitive eyes. She smiled, touched fingers with him, then turned to the pouting Lila. "Such a lovely gown!" she exclaimed honestly. "It's all white froth! Lila, you've never looked lovelier!"

Lila giggled, gave Jenny a vicious little hug, then linked both hands around Rolf's arm. Her fingers pressed into his sleeve, and she steered him away from Jenny.

Tom March was the last to arrive. He wore a new off-white linen suit and pale blue shirt. He was the only one without a tie, and his collar, open at the neck, exposed the top of his tanned chest. Jenny thought he had never looked handsomer—even with two slightly blackened eyes. He came directly to her, looked over her shimmering gown.

"Why don't you retire that thing?" he muttered.

"Because!" she retorted airily.

"I told you it makes you look cheap."

"I know. I suppose you'd rather I wore pale lavender, something soft like Madeline's wearing!"

He glanced about, located Madeline. "Color's fine, but that dress ain't for you. All them slits—seems you'd want a dress to cover you more."

She gave him a nasty-sweet smile. "It's time to go," she said. "You were the last one to get here."

But they didn't go immediately. First Tom stalked into the garden, petted Snow Blossom, made sure she was quieted down.

"Okay," announced Tom, returning in ten minutes. "She seems fine. Let's be off."

They sped to Fort Lauderdale in three cars, got to the disco in less than a half hour. There were lines outside, waiting to get in, but Madeline had evidently made some kind of advance arrangements, and they were able to enter immediately.

The discotheque was named, simply, "The Place." It was long and narrow inside and gave the impression of darkness, but was intermittently lit by long overhead lights of gold, silver, blue, and green. The music was very loud and the dance floor was alive with bright, whirling couples.

They were escorted to a rear table which held ten with some crowding, got themselves settled, ordered drinks. "It's my party, remember!" Madeline sang out. "I pay the tariff, and I make the rules!"

David laughed. "And what *are* the rules?"

"We dance only with our dates—no mixing! This is a *dated* party!"

Lila and Sara and Barbara squealed with delight. The men laughed; none protested. Jenny felt Tom, jammed in beside her, go stiff.

So! He knew he couldn't insult her by dancing with her just once! He was stuck with her. For once he would have to be a gentleman through an entire evening!

She knew why Madeline had made the rule. It was so she'd get to spend the whole evening with Oliver, be in his arms for every dance, the sensuous music binding them. She'd nestle in his arms when the number permitted, see to it that her perfumed hair brushed his cheek; she'd be her most delightful self. And maybe it would work.

They sipped drinks. The music grew louder, the light-flashing darkness dazzling Jenny. Watching March by the flashing lights, she longed for him to get up and pull her onto the dance floor.

She moved against him deliberately. He took the hint. Getting up from the table, he drew her roughly to her feet and led her to the dance.

"You don't have to *pull* me!" she flared.

"What do you mean?" he asked innocently.

"And the way you looked at me when the light flashed!"

"What of it?"

"You'll not get away with it! I've seen you look at Madeline the same way!"

"I won't deny that."

"Why? Tell me why!"

They were dancing now, standing apart, feet moving to the rhythm, hips grinding. They took hands and executed a double whirl before he answered.

"I've told you—I aim to make sure."

"About what?"

"Cattle . . . crops . . . dogs . . . women."

"Ooh!"

"Take your greyhounds. When you first get them,

they're high-strung. But they gentle down, if you handle them right. Some are slower than others, like Snow Blossom."

"Ha! You're comparing me to *her?* To a greyhound?"

The music sent her into his arms. He held her and danced, ignoring her question.

"And I suppose you're comparing Madeline to Romantic Sally, because she made friends right away!"

She felt him shrug.

"Lately I've been exposed to greyhounds. It ain't unnatural that I'd compare them to women."

"Which one, if you had your choice, would you take—Romantic Sally or Snow Blossom?"

"Can't say I'd take either one of them."

That shut her up. There was no way to get the truth out of him. He might be in love with Madeline, for all she knew. Certainly he never spoke against her. Always treated her like a lady. She wondered what he really thought of Madeline. And whether or not he'd taken her to bed.

"What do you think of a girl who isn't a virgin when she marries?" she half shouted into the blare of music.

"Ain't important. Man ought to bed a woman. Know what he's getting."

"Have you," she screamed against the music, "with Madeline, ever?"

"Shut up!" he said, his voice angry. "What if the music stops of a sudden, and you screeching all them things! Shut up and dance!"

She did what he said. She'd wait. Until she got him home.

It was 1:00 A.M. when they trooped into the penthouse for a nightcap. Apparently everybody but Jenny and Tom had had a wonderful time. They'd danced the rest of the evening without speaking, had driven home in silence.

David had just volunteered to fix drinks when the elevator door opened and four brown-skinned men, led by Perez, came charging into the living room. The other men looked at them in amazement; the girls shrank back.

At a gesture from Perez, his troupe surged to a halt. Simon stepped forward, Tom with him.

"What is it?" Simon asked.

"We wait while you drink!" Perez accused. "Our children starve while you dance! I, Pablo Perez, wait and mis amigos wait! We no talk no more, no more negotiate! We put on the speed! We start now!"

He dived at Tom, who was nearest. In the same instant, the others hurled themselves upon Simon, Rolf and Oliver. Suddenly the room was filled with sound; the thud of fist on flesh, the grunting of fighting men, the crashing of furniture.

Jenny and the other women stood in one corner of the room. Lila had her hands covering her eyes. Madeline was sobbing. Jenny thought for something to do.

Suddenly, she snatched a heavy bookend from the shelf beside her and ran over to where Tom had Perez pinned to the floor. But Perez rolled him off, sending him against Jenny's feet and toppling her over. She fell backward, but was up instantly. Still wielding the heavy bookend, she stood anxiously over Tom and Perez, who were wrestling furiously.

She was trying to hit Perez between the shoulders with the bookend. But everytime she lifted it to strike, Tom was on top, and she had to wait.

Simon, at a crouch, drove his fist into his assailant's neck. The fellow dropped, lay groaning. Then, before Jenny had a chance with her bookend, Simon yanked at Perez, pulling him off the Missourian. Instinctively, Tom reached for the man's neck, refusing to give up the fight. Simon pushed him down.

"March!" he shouted. "Let him alone!"

Puzzled, Tom got to his feet, but stood ready for Perez. Then he saw Simon mutter something in the rebel leader's ear, something which made Perez smile, nod and shake hands with him.

Then Perez shouted at his companions, "Stop the fight! El Señor, he has made it bueno! We go now!"

The fighting ceased. The five men, looking disheveled and bruised, disappeared into the elevator and were gone. The rest stared at one another, at Simon.

"What did you say to him?" Jenny asked.

"That I'll join March in his efforts to make life good for the migrants. That, given reasonable time, we'll fulfill all their demands."

Jenny stared. Simon, to change so suddenly! Simon, who had turned the deafest ear to their problems! To suddenly swing so completely in the other direction!

Tom also stared. "You've no notion," he said quietly, "how relieved I am that you've changed your thinking."

Now Jenny stared at Tom. For some reason, she didn't like the way he sounded. Was he doubting Simon's word? If he was, he had no right to do so. What Simon said, Simon meant. A Townsend's word was his bond. Still, he had changed his mind awfully fast. Jenny couldn't help wondering herself whether the eldest Townsend grandson didn't have something up his sleeve.

Well, she'd find out soon enough.

As the major shareholder in the Townsend Corporation, she had a right to know.

30

After the others left, Tom went to the roof garden to calm Snow Blossom. She was whining and howling, obviously disturbed by the fight.

This left Jenny and Madeline alone.

"I'm exhausted," said Madeline, the color drained from her face. "If you don't mind, darling, I'm going straight to bed."

"No, of course not," said Jenny, kissing her friend on the cheek.

When Madeline had gone up the stairs, Jenny hurried to the garden and Snow Blossom's kennel. The dog was lying quietly at Tom's feet.

"It was the ruckus that upset her," Tom said. "She's okay now . . . I can leave." He continued to stroke the greyhound.

Jenny almost shivered. The night had turned cold for November, and she'd left her stole inside. Crazily, she almost wished Snow Blossom would start to howl again so he'd have to stay. Then, for some reason she couldn't explain, she insisted on driving him to his duplex.

"Ain't no sense to that. I've got my car right out in front."

"Y-your head," she stammered. "It's bleeding again. Either you stay here and I'll treat it, or I'll drive you home and treat it! The blows you've taken on that wound—you're liable to get dizzy driving and have a wreck and end up in the hospital."

He scowled at her, but considered. His head did hurt. It hurt like hell. And he'd been dizzy ever since they'd left the disco. But Jenny had no business being out alone after she dropped him off; he wouldn't let her do it. A great, dark wave of vertigo came over him and it was all he could do to hide it.

Then, before he could protest, she had him in the Continental, and she was driving and talking to him. His head cleared briefly, and what she was saying penetrated.

"It's wonderful that Simon's come over to side with the migrants!" she was exclaiming.

He turned to face her. "How come *you* didn't come over to join them?" he demanded. "You never spoke up, though as the most important shareholder—and landowner—you could have. Want to know why you didn't? It's because you're on the fence! You can't make up your mind which way to jump!"

"Maybe so," Jenny defended, "but if it were *your* land, you might feel the same. If we actually go ahead with all that building from Orlando to past Homestead, the entire cost falls on me, not the Corporation! For all I know, such a sudden, tremendous expense would bankrupt the farming, and then I couldn't even pay wages!"

"I was right. You're money-hungry."

"It's not so! I want those people to have decent homes, but Si . . . he was my husband . . ."

"I'm aware of that!"

"*He* didn't spend enormous sums! I don't know that he'd want it done now!"

"You can't deal with this new situation in the old way. As I recall, you came right out and said once that you wanted these people to have decent housing!"

"I do—but I wanted it done slowly. Not all at once.

254

Bathhouses this year; then, over the next few years, housing."

"That might have worked years ago, but it won't now. They're too riled up. If you don't do as they ask, there'll be all kinds of bad publicity. Perhaps even riots will follow. At the very least. They'll strike and you won't be able to get any workers at all. Then where will you be?"

"You make it sound like it's all my fault!"

"It's your responsibility. It'd be your fault."

They'd crossed street after street and now she turned north on Highway One. "Hey!" he objected. "You turn south for my place!"

"I don't choose to go there this minute!" she flared. "I feel like driving a little, letting the wind clear your head! The way you're talking, it's certainly fuzzy!"

"My head's clear. Stop the car. I'll drive."

She stepped on the gas and the car lurched forward.

"You trying to get us killed?" Tom growled. "Mood you're in, we'll end up wrecked. Same way you caused that fight with Perez and his gang."

She gasped. Of all the unfair accusations! True, he was muleheaded enough to put the blame—any blame— on her. But how could he hold her responsible for Perez? Tears started; anger dried them and steadied her voice.

"Just how am I to blame for Perez?"

"Going dancing, dressing like a whore, living it up while he and his family wallow in filth."

"How could I have stopped him? Answer that!"

"By speaking up at the meeting for the migrants. But you didn't. You just sat there like a queen with her money—and Perez tried to do something about it."

She stepped on the gas. The speedometer went to seventy.

"Slow it," he ordered. "We can't afford to be taken in, way we look. Especially me."

She dropped speed, but didn't turn back. In frigid silence she drove through the canal section of Fort Lauderdale, even going onto some of the islands, turning at the end of them, driving back to the through street.

He didn't say another word. Just sat there staring

out the window. If she wanted to let off steam, fine. Let her. Maybe she'd come to her senses, admit that he was right.

Finally, she turned back for Hollywood, so tired she could hardly drive. Doggedly she piloted the car; stubbornly, he maintained silence. At last they rolled into Hollywood and streets ticked off behind them. She stopped by the curb in front of his duplex, cut the motor, sat with her hands still on the wheel. Her arms were trembling; she was trembling all over. She rested her head on the wheel, too exhausted to move.

The Missourian moved. Well, why not? He'd had a long, restful ride. He got out, came around, opened her door. He dragged her out and stood her on the grass.

"It's almost 4:00 A.M.," he informed her. "You're in no shape to drive back."

Her knees gave way, and he caught her. He marched her to the door, unlocked it, dumped her in a sitting position on his sofa.

She stayed there while he made instant coffee. She was so beaten from everything that had happened these past weeks that it was hard not to lie down and just give up. And on top of that, she was still burning with rage and passion. She still couldn't trust herself to be alone with him because of the feelings he aroused in her. This was what her life had come to!

He handed her coffee in a mug, sat beside her with his own. She took a gulp, swallowing fast, wincing. It burned her sore tongue, burned her mouth, and was rough tasting as whiskey. She took some more, needing the strength it would give her.

By the time they'd finished the coffee, she was able to look at him with a clear eye. There was blood around the edges of the gauze at the side of his forehead, dried blood and fresh blood. She reached up before he knew what she was doing, and yanked the dressing off.

The wound was discolored. One of the stitches was broken, and a fresh swelling had appeared. Both his eyes looked puffy and bruised again.

Her exhaustion vanished.

"That wound has to be restitched!" she cried.

He gaped at her. She could tell he'd turned groggy, because his eyes had lost their shine. "First thing in the morning, you go to the doctor!" she ordered. "Right now, to the bathroom!"

He sure enough was befuddled, because he didn't argue, didn't look angry, didn't hold back when she tugged at him. He wasn't exactly steady on his feet, either, as she steered him into the bathroom.

She sat him on the closed commode, ran warm water into the basin, took a clean washcloth out of the linen closet, unwrapped a fresh bar of white soap, and went to work. First she washed the open wound, then rinsed it thoroughly, drowning it with rubbing alcohol. Through all of this, he didn't make a sound.

It was while she was applying fresh gauze, that the real possibility struck her. "You get an X ray of your head, too!" she cried. "You may have a fractured skull!"

"Like hell," he muttered.

He was dizzy, sure, but that was her fault. Making him go to a disco, driving him all over Fort Lauderdale. No wonder his head was pounding so.

When he moved to get up, she pushed him back. "I'm going to wash your face. Then clean up those eyes and put ice packs on them."

When she finished, he wouldn't let her help him into the bedroom. He walked, sat on the bed; his head was letting up a bit, and now he wanted to sleep.

Jenny looked him over. He seemed a trifle better. Telling him she'd be right back, she ran to the kitchen, crushed up some ice cubes and wrapped them in two towels. He was still sitting up when she got back.

"Lie down," she ordered. She held up the ice packs impatiently.

"One condition. You stay here."

That stunned her. He must really be sick! "W-why?" she faltered.

"I don't want you driving. Either you stay here, or I drive you home."

She pushed him down. He sat right back up. She laid the ice pack on the bedside table, knelt, and began to take off his shoes.

"What the hell are you doing?" he growled.

"Hold still! I'm undressing you!"

"I'll undress myself when I get back from taking you home."

"I won't go! I won't let you drive in this condition. You'd kill us both!"

He started to argue, then didn't. He allowed her to pull off his shoes, his socks. He lay quiet as she took off his clothes. When she had him completely naked, she pulled the sheet and a cotton blanket over him, laid an ice pack over each eye. Then she turned on a soft lamp, snapped off the overhead light.

She sat watching. From the way he was breathing, she could tell he had fallen asleep. At first that pleased her, then it scared her. Was he all right? What if he really did have a fractured skull and had slipped off into a coma?

She sat right by him the rest of the night, never taking her eyes from him. The least change in his breathing, the first hint of fever, any strange mutterings or hallucinations, and she'd call the doctor immediately.

At nine o'clock he woke up. He looked at her as clear-eyed as any man with two shiners could look. He laid aside the ice packs.

"You really are as stubborn as a Missoura mule," he said. "You stayed. In spite of everything, you stayed all night."

She nodded firmly.

"Suppose they missed you at home? Called the police?"

"I forgot about them," she admitted. "I'll phone Madeline right now."

"Just get in your car and go home. Maybe they haven't missed you yet. You could just slip in quietly. No sense disturbing them."

He was right. Even beaten and cut and bruised, he was right. Trust him for that; trust him to make her feel stupid and inferior.

"Come here," he said softly. "To the bed. That's it. Now, lean over close to me."

Bewildered by her own obedience rather than by his

request, she did as he said. He put his hands on her shoulders and pulled her closer.

One of his big hands held the back of her head, pressed. Their lips met, lightly at first, then firmly and with sweetness. It lasted a while, grew sweeter. Almost . . . tender.

He spoke then. Asked—not ordered—her to go home. Volunteered that he would take a cab to a doctor, have his head restitched if need be, even have an X ray if it was deemed necessary.

By the time she got behind the wheel of her car, her head was reeling. Well, that was no surprise—first the plane crash, then the fights with Perez and his gang—and she'd been up all night worried over March. It had all got her into such a state that she was misinterpreting things, was unable to understand a simple kiss.

But darn it, that kiss really *had* been different. It had been tender! A *tender* kiss from Tom March! She couldn't believe it. Could a bump on the head really change someone's personality?

As she contemplated this, she almost laughed out loud. No, that was nonsense. But then, what *had* happened to make him change?

Turning into the Townsend Towers driveway, she was surprised to find herself humming.

Tired as she was, she hadn't felt so relaxed in weeks.

31

She hadn't been missed at home. Flo gave her breakfast in the kitchen, and Madeline came down twenty minutes later and joined her.

"Sleep well?" asked Madeline, yawning into her orange juice.

"Hmm" said Jenny, offering no information about her evening with March.

Simon phoned while they were finishing their coffee. "We're calling a special meeting at two on the migrant situation," he told Jenny. "Please be prompt. I'd like to get it over with by three o'clock."

"Are the migrants to be there?" she asked.

"No. The point is for us to decide what we're going to offer, what concessions we may have to make."

She wanted to ask if Tom March would be there, but didn't. Instead she told Simon she'd be on time, then went to her bedroom and tried to phone Tom. He didn't answer. It was nearly eleven-thirty. Hopefully, he was with a doctor.

She took a long, hot bath. This helped her soreness

but made her sleepier. Too bad she didn't have time for a nap, but this afternoon's meeting was too important.

She dressed. Gray. Dress, scarf, shoes, everything. The shade she chose made her eyes look almost charcoal in color.

She tried Tom again. And, in two minutes, again. She kept dialing until her finger was numb, but still there was no answer.

She began to panic. Why didn't he call her, tell her what the doctor had to say? Maybe he was in the hospital; maybe they'd knocked him out with some drug, and he wasn't able to call!

She looked at the clock. One fifteen. She had to leave now or be late for the meeting. She rushed downstairs, got into her car and sped to the Townsend office building. She was so upset that she had to be careful not to exceed the speed limit.

He was in the boardroom when she walked in. He looked straight at her and her knees buckled, but she stiffened them instantly. She breathed deeply and slowly.

He was standing by the window, looking at ease and perfectly strong. He had a fresh bandage on his head, and his eyes looked less swollen.

He was alone in the office. Evidently Simon had stepped out and the others had not yet arrived. She marched over to him.

"Why didn't you call?" she demanded fiercely.

"About what?"

"To tell me what the doctor said!"

"Wasn't much to say. He restitched my head, changed the bandage."

"What about the X ray?"

"All clear. My skull—and brain—are normal." There was a smirk on his face, which angered her further.

"Your brain has never been normal!" she flared.

He could have called her. He'd owed her a call.

He had time for one stabbing look, then Simon entered, followed by Rolf. He motioned for them to sit at the conference table. In a moment, David and Oliver entered and the meeting was underway.

It isn't fair, Jenny thought, then firmed herself. She'd wanted to have it out with him then and there. But this was big business and had to be dealt with as such. She'd have to shove aside her personal problems till later.

Simon called the meeting to order. "We have serious matters before us," he began. "This we all appreciate. Now, since I made Perez a promise last night, it's vital that we offer the pickers a solid plan. Something that will appease them. Keep them under control."

"The only way to keep them under control," Tom said, "is to give them exactly what they want. I thought that was what you intended to do."

"Not precisely," Simon replied. "Not what they *want*. What they can manage with, perhaps."

"What they want and what they can manage with are pretty much the same thing," Tom growled.

"Are they?" said Simon, his voice confident. "Look, March, in situations of this kind a compromise is always reached."

"The Perez gang ain't in a compromising frame of mind," Tom remarked. "They're . . . dangerous. They want the whole hog, and they want it yesterday."

"Which is out of the question," Simon replied. "What they want, amounts to Jenny's building whole villages which will be used, perhaps, three months of the year. The very idea is ludicrous."

"The very idea of your holding back on 'em again is ludicrous. If they think you're stalling, there's no telling what they'll do."

Rolf and David joined in the argument, backing Simon up. "We've got two factions we're dealing with, March. Don't forget that. Vernon's likely to be on our side, and if we can get him to accept a compromise proposal—well, we're likely to get Perez's backing too."

The meeting went on like that for another half hour, neither side backing down. Finally Simon raised his hand to quiet them. "Look," he said. "This isn't getting us anywhere. I've got a proposal drafted. March, why don't you just hear me out?"

Jenny looked at the Missourian. She had never seen him so beaten. "All right," he agreed. "Read it."

Simon held up a sheet of legal-sized paper and put on his reading glasses. "One, we raise wages the price we initially offered, ten cents a bushel. Two, we provide new toilet facilities and bathhouses, to be completed within one year of starting time. Three, we install two washers and two driers in each bathhouse. Four, we clear a campground at each bathhouse so the pickers with campers and tents and those who sleep in cars may also live in clean surroundings. That's it."

Tom looked thoughtful. It wasn't what they wanted. But it was a start. Perez just might go for it. Vernon definitely would.

He turned to face Simon. "Okay, I'll go along with it. It just might suit them for now. It's certainly your best offer yet."

Simon's smile was triumphant. "Great. Then it's settled. Let's just take a final vote."

"You have my vote," said Tom. "You continue amongst yourselves. I've got to go into the other office and make a phone call. To Missoura. If you don't mind."

"Go right ahead," said Simon, who would have agreed to anything at this moment.

Simon called for the vote as soon as March had left the room. Jenny voted in favor, as did the rest of them. She was actually unhappy over the proposal, felt the migrants were getting too little. But she understood that the alternative of building them a virtual city was prohibitive. Simon had made that perfectly clear.

Tom returned just as Simon was saying, "Vote carried. We will so report to the migrant representatives and wait for their decision."

"They'll probably accept" Tom said from the doorway. "Vernon'll slow Perez down, give the proposal time to be mulled over by all. But if they do accept, don't think that puts an end to the matter. They won't go long without some kind of decent housing. They may compromise this season, but next year's another story."

The group went quiet. Jenny realized that even Simon knew Tom was right. The day of the downtrodden was ending; workers were banding together all over the world to demand their human rights.

"We'll call a meeting with Vernon and Perez after Thanksgiving," Simon told Tom.

Tom nodded, sat down.

Thanksgiving! Jenny thought. Of course. November had been passing so swiftly, she hadn't realized the holiday was so near.

Simon was about to adjourn the meeting when Tom spoke. "Speaking of Thanksgiving—that Missoura call I made," he said, "was to my folks. I hope you'll accept their invitation for all of you to fly to Missoura to spend Thanksgiving weekend at their farm."

Jenny stared. Now what was he up to? The invitation sounded legitimate enough. But was there something else up his sleeve?

"That's awfully hospitable of your parents," Simon said. "What leads them to invite us—total strangers?"

And how, wondered Jenny crossly, could they entertain so many people? After all, Tom had made it clear that he was a dirt farmer; his parents would be the same. So for them to invite a whole crowd was preposterous!

"Actually, it was my idea, and they're with me," Tom said. "I thought it might be helpful for all of you to take a look at the old-fashioned farm tenant houses up there. Get a whiff of Missoura thinking. I told them the bind you're in with the migrants. They agreed that seeing Missoura might give you a new slant. Said to bring Vernon and Perez along too. Let them see how things look from the farmer's angle."

Simon and the others nodded their heads, open to the idea and the chance to get away from Florida for a few days. Jenny was the only one who didn't speak. She didn't want to meet Tom's folks, be trapped in Tom's territory. Weren't things complicated enough? But finally she agreed to go, proffering an invitation of her own.

"I thought you all might like to come watch the dogs run in the schooling races tonight at Hollywood Greyhound Track." These were trial races for young dogs; no betting allowed, but the public could watch.

"We can go in a group from the penthouse," she added. "Bring dates, too." She sent Tom a sharp look. "If you don't know a girl to ask, David can get you a date, or Rolf."

There. He was angry again.

"Sure thing," David agreed. "Who's your date, Jenny—me, I hope?"

She smiled. "Don't let Sara down," she chided. "You know she loves the track! I'm going alone—what the pioneers called a 'tar bucket,' I believe!"

She didn't glance at Tom. There! He wasn't the only one who could throw around those old farm expressions! She'd show him she hadn't lived in a penthouse *all* her life.

She shot him a quick glance.

He was smiling.

32

When Tom March showed up at the penthouse, he was alone.

"Where's your date?" sang out Lila, clinging to Rolf's arm.

"I reckon I'm a tar bucket," he replied, casting Jenny a glance.

"Which," declared Lila, "puts you and Jenny together! Now we're all paired off!"

Jenny reluctantly accepted his arm, got into the Buick with him. They quarreled all the way to the track.

"Why didn't you bring a date?" she asked.

"I ain't ever gone much for dates. You don't have to sit with me at the track."

"I don't sit! I stand, where I can see better!"

"I won't let you stand alone. Not in that crowd."

"I don't care what you do! All I'm interested in is watching my dogs!"

After they parked, they went in at the main entrance. Jenny didn't go to the kennels where the dogs were held, because she didn't want to overexcite them.

Instead, she headed for her favorite spot at the rail, well away from other people, almost even with the finish line. The rest of her party climbed to grandstand seats, which were more than half filled with spectators. Tom stayed with Jenny. She wished he would go away.

"Fine track," he commented.

Though she knew it well, she flashed a glance around the track. Behind them was the tall sweeping grandstand; to the right was the clubhouse, not open tonight; and before them the large oval track, newly dragged. It seemed to rear up at the middle of the far side by the toteboard on which, for official races, odds were posted along with the amount per ticket paid to those who had bet on the three winning dogs. There was quite a bit of movement, with people still arriving and milling about, and a constant buzzing of talk and laughter.

The first six dogs were put into the starting boxes. Jenny, forgetting Tom March, was so excited she almost jumped up and down. All five of her dogs were in this race! She didn't know why the trainer had agreed to it, but she was delighted.

"You're certainly excited enough," Tom commented wryly.

Even he didn't bother her. "You bet I am. I'm going to get to see how my dogs are matched!"

"You've seen that at the training track."

"This is different! The dogs know it's different!"

Music had been playing while the dogs were being put into the boxes. Now it stopped. The mechanical rabbit at the inner side of the oval began to move, bobbing up and down on the metal arm which held it, looking as though it were running on the turf inside.

The boxes flew open. The dogs shot out, making for the rail because that was closest to the rabbit, streaking after it. Snow Blossom and Romantic Sally and Ebon Sue stood out because of their colors. They were in the lead. Kolaka, a perfect brindle male, and Armand, a white male with tan spots, were neck and neck at the first turn, right on the leaders' heels.

At the far turn, Ebon Sue had the lead; Snow Blossom was at her shoulder, Armand at Snow Blossom's flank, and Romantic Sally was beginning to pull up on him; Kolaka's nose not an inch behind hers. Romantic Sally gained steadily on the back stretch, passed Snow Blossom; Kolaka's speed increased powerfully until, at the next turn, they were running in a clump.

Jenny was really jumping up and down now, shrieking their names, not knowing which dog to root for. As they sped around the final turn and flashed down the homestretch, Jenny had never seen anything so exciting. Kolaka, pouring on his magnificent strength, was now even with Romantic Sally.

They crossed the finish line nose to nose. Armand, Ebon Sue and Snow Blossom crossed the line nose to nose right behind them. The sixth dog, belonging to some other owner, trailed them by four lengths. The curtain beyond the finish line barred the oval, and the grooms came onto the track, snapped leads onto the muzzled, excited racers, and led them away.

"You ain't going to go and pet them now, are you?" Tom asked.

"Of course not! They need to be cooled down and taken to the kennels. They've had enough excitement!"

"Good thinking."

This irritated Jenny. Who was he to decide about her thinking?

"Snow Blossom ran fine, being so new," he commented. "It looked like she might be flighty, when you first got her."

"She isn't flighty. She proved that."

"You liked it when we took care of her, didn't you?"

"Of course. She's a wonderful dog."

"You didn't get bored those long nights?"

There was a quality to his voice she'd not heard before. It kept her from getting mad because it was ... well, tender.

Then she realized he was referring to the time they'd spent in bed those nights, and her face burned. What was he driving at? Just what was it he wanted her to say? Whatever it was, she wouldn't give him the satisfaction.

"I wasn't bored," she said. "I slept."

"How come?"

"I—Snow Blossom was quiet, and I . . . felt safe." She heard herself actually say that and, rocked by the knowledge, was further rocked by its truth.

Other dogs were racing now, but they were only blurred motion.

"Safer than you'd have felt with some other man?"

"Y-yes."

"Why?"

"No reason, none."

She shouldn't have felt safe with him. He'd been rough with her, treated her badly.

"How many men?" he demanded, of a sudden. "How many have you been to bed with?"

And now there was nothing tender about his voice. She had every reason to get mad, and she did better than that.

She turned on him and let her rage take over. "How many girls have *you* had?" she hissed.

"One here and there. That's beside the point. Answer my question."

"*Five!*" she threw at him, still hissing. "Counting you!"

He stared at her, shocked. "Why?" he roared, thunder in his voice. "There's got to be a reason, and I aim to find out what it is!"

Confused, furious, determined to end things with him once and for all, she heard herself blurting out Si's plan. The whole thing. The money, the love, the sex. Even to his desire that she try out the grandsons first.

His face took on a new expression, one of compassion. He looked sorry for her, and this made her even more furious.

"You've actually been *doing* it?" he asked. "Carrying out this—plan?"

"I *am!* Only you—"

"Only I what?"

"K-keep interfering!"

"Maybe I'm in the contest, too."

"You're *not* in it!"

"There's the sex part," he said wickedly. The fire

270

still hadn't left his eyes. "I sure as hell qualify there! It's best with me, that much I know!"

"What makes you so sure? Anyway, sex isn't everything. There are the other qualifications!"

"Just cool it. I've got things to say."

"Say them, then!"

"Well, if I was willing to overlook all these men, and if I was fool enough to accidentally fall in love with you—"

"Don't be ridiculous!"

"It ain't ridiculous. If I had me a big fortune, big as yours, and I was what you consider fit for you, measured up to this set of rules, would you marry me? *If* I wanted you, understand."

His blunders left her speechless at first. And then she found her voice, heard herself reply, "I might—consider you. But consider only."

"That is, if I had the money. And you were convinced I wasn't after your money?"

He was getting her all mixed-up. "Y-yes!"

"What about the love part?" he demanded. "Now you're ready to settle for sex and money! Where's love?"

"It never existed! Not with Simon, not with Richard, not with—"

"You don't have to recite the names of all the damned men you've had!"

"I'm not!"

"You are! Truth is, Jenny, you don't know what love is. That's your trouble."

I *want* to know! she ached to scream. I know what it should be, oh, I do! I had a taste of it, from Si! Gentleness and respect and consideration and warmth and tenderness, that's what love is!

"I'll tell you what love is," March ground out, "and you can put it in your craw and keep it there. Love is putting someone else first, yourself way down the line somewhere. It's taking someone as he is, no questions asked, knowing that someone's doing the same for you. It's actin' like a lady—not some spoiled princess!"

"Of all the—"

"Take you, now. So busy trying to follow a dead

271

man's plan, you can't see the truth! Wake up, Jenny. Come to! There ain't no perfect man! You ain't ever going to find him!"

Furious, she went to a hissing whisper. "You talk and talk about love. You have the actual gall to consider yourself in love with me . . . and you're jealous of the other men?"

"You're nothing more to me than a chigger," he grated. "An insect that gets under your skin and itches like hell until you claw it out. That's what you are, a damned chigger!"

"You—you animal . . . you beast . . ."

"You ain't done me so many favors, either. I came to Hollywood on a vacation, got interested in the migrants, tried to help them. Then I had the misfortune to lay eyes on you—"

"And raped me on sight!"

"I still apologize for that."

"Yet you repeat it, again and again!"

"With all kinds of cooperation from you."

"If you'd just go away!"

"I can't. Not while the migrants still need me."

"We can deal with them! I want you gone! I want you to stop interfering with my life!"

"Just what do you think you're doing with *mine?* Only I ain't going to sit still for it."

"What do you think you can do about it?" she snapped.

"I've got my ideas."

"Such as what?"

"That's my business."

"You're in love with Madeline! Now I see it all!"

And she did. He was always treating Madeline as if she were a fine lady and herself, Jenny, as a—a whore!

"Seeing I'm in love with her," he drawled, "how come I'm standing here with you?"

"That's what I'd like to know! To torture me, that's why! To confuse me! To keep me from carrying out Si's plan. Well, you won't succeed! I'll find my man, and I'll marry him"

"Swell!" he growled, and his voice was the angriest

yet. "You just go ahead with your manhunt. After you've slept with every candidate and are still looking, don't come running to me!"

He gave her a menacing look, then turned to watch the second race, already underway.

"Take me home!" she demanded. "This instant!"

"Won't that look odd to the others?"

"I'll tell them I'm tired. It so happens I didn't have a wink of sleep last night, though you couldn't be expected to remember it!"

He kept his eyes lowered, drove her home without uttering a word. At Townsend Towers, she got out of the car and ran inside, not saying good-night to him, even for the benefit of the doormen.

33

Because of the Thanksgiving trip, in which Vernon and Perez were to be included, Simon called a meeting for the next day, asking the two migrant leaders to be present. He read off the Townsend proposal, and Vernon and Perez listened closely. Vernon looked thoughtful, but Perez scowled, saying nothing.

Tom then explained the Missouri trip and its purpose, which was to stimulate both the Townsends' thinking and that of the migrants. Vernon and Perez reluctantly agreed to go to Missouri and to hold off any further unrest among the pickers until they returned.

"It does seem," Vernon said at one point, "to be a step in the right direction. Don't you agree, Perez?"

The Chicano grumbled, but nodded.

Throughout the meeting Jenny remained silent. She observed that the Townsends and Oliver Cranston, as well as the two migrant leaders, listened carefully whenever Tom spoke. And treated his ideas with respect. This irritated her deeply.

She got home from the meeting to find that Flo had

gone marketing and Madeline had left to go shopping in Miami Beach. She'd told Jenny that morning that she wanted some new things for the Missouri trip, and Jenny had laughed, teasing her about buying designer farm clothes. Jenny herself meant to take very little on the silly trip. Thank goodness they'd be gone only two or three days.

She was less than pleased when March showed up at the penthouse. One of the doormen phoned to say he was there, and not knowing how to get out of it, she gave permission for him to come up. He'd probably come up with some insane new idea and she might as well put it to rest immediately.

She met him at the elevator, led the way to her own sitting room. She had a stack of greyhound pedigrees on her desk that she'd been studying; let him see that he was interrupting her and maybe—just maybe—he'd have manners enough to make this short.

She motioned him to a chair, perched herself on the arm of the other chair. "What's your problem this time?" she asked snippily. There. That was the tone he deserved.

"It's about plane reservations," he said grimly. "I meant to speak to you after the meeting, but you took off so fast I didn't have the chance."

"What about the reservations? One of the men will see to them."

"No, I aim to tend to that myself. It's just—I know you'd normally go first class. But this time, with Vernon and Perez along, seems we should go tourist."

"Why? Since we're giving them a plane ride, why not first class?"

"Tourist will impress them enough. First class will just point up the difference between you. They'd resent it, that you fly like kings while—oh, hell, if you can't get the picture, then you haven't got any sense, for sure."

"So we go tourist. It won't make the difference you think—we'll still be flying off for Thanksgiving while the pickers—"

"Will know we're going in their behalf. I'm making the reservations for tomorrow, and I'm footing the bill."

She stared, surprised. Well, let him pay. If he wanted to squander his savings, it was no concern of hers.

"The trip is useless!" she declared. "You can't make Florida into another Missouri!"

"Like I said, what you Townsends need is a dose of Missoura thinking. That, mixed into your own business sense, will put an end to your trouble with the migrants. All you need is to think straight."

"If Missourians are so perfect," she demanded hotly, "how do you dare take me to visit your parents when you—when we— For all you know, I could be pregnant!"

He went blank-faced. "Well, ain't you pregnant?" he asked. "After all the times we've— Ain't you pregnant *yet?*"

"Certainly not!" she cried furiously, trying to remember if she'd really taken the pill every night without fail. If she hadn't, it was his fault for upsetting her all the time. "Do you think I'd run that risk?" she cried. "That I'd—"

He shot out of his chair, grabbed her shoulders, almost knocking her off the arm of her chair. He shook her hard.

"Damn your red hair!" he gritted. "Have you been on the pill all this time?"

"Why wouldn't I be? Do you think I'd—"

He shook her harder. "Where are they? Where are the damned things?"

"It's none of your business!"

"Oh, but it is. Now it is!"

He stomped into the bedroom, yanked open the drawers of her dressing table and chest, rummaged through them with her yelling at him the whole time. He went through her closets, muttering something about a king's ransom.

While he was doing that, his back to her, she tried to slip into the bathroom. He caught her at it. He pushed her out of his way, crossed the bathroom in a stride, jerked open the medicine cabinet.

He saw the flat blue box first thing, had it in his

paw. She dove at him, snatching and grabbing, wanting to at least see into the box, see if she'd forgotten a pill, but he held it so high she couldn't reach it.

He was bloodred mad. "No decency!" he accused. "Right out on your bathroom shelf for the world to see! No shame, no delicacy! I thought you'd at least hide the damn things!"

"This is my suite!" she flared. "I don't have to hide anything! *Give me those!*" She jumped, reaching, but he held the box too high.

Then, moving fast as a striking snake, he raised the lid of the commode, opened the little box, dumped the pills into the water, flushed the toilet. He closed the box, extended it to her.

She batted it out of his hand.

"You . . . *beast!*" she whimpered. "You madman! You—"

Still furious, he scooped her up and stalked into the bedroom. She quit talking and used her energy to kick and struggle and claw. He kept going, as if she were nothing more than a straw twisting in his grasp, a trifle he could control without effort.

He dropped her onto the bed, held her down with both hands. She got her elbows dug into the mattress, tried to push into a sitting position. He flattened her again.

"Off with them clothes," he ordered. "You know I'm used to you naked!"

"I won't!" she gasped. "Not this time, not after what you just d-did! And not ever again! Never!"

He laughed, a mad laugh. Held her fast.

She sizzled. Yet beneath her rage, hotter than fury, was that damnable itch. Worse than it had ever been.

She twisted and jerked. He held her, not even breathing hard, obviously enjoying himself. It was more than she could bear.

Suddenly she made up her mind. She relaxed so abruptly that he almost fell on top of her.

"Go on!" she hissed. "Do your worst!"

He had her stripped in seconds, lifting her with one hand as he would a doll, skinning off her clothes with the other. Then, not trusting her for a second, he held her down with one hand and somehow undressed himself quickly with the other.

He came onto the bed, and she saw that he was ready for her. She arched her body like a weapon, aiming for his maleness, not caring if she hurt the instrument of all her misery.

Instead of her hitting him, he entered her, swift as an arrow finding its target. With no preliminaries, he began to thrust and Jenny, in exquisite fury, struck upward with her body, meeting him again and again.

She tasted rage on her tongue, felt that taste fill her. His pounding increased, and so did hers. Consumed by rage and burning, she threw herself into their sex-battle, and met his mindless fury and gloried in it.

Her ears began to ring. The inner burning, knotted in her belly, slipped lower and set her afire. She slammed with all her strength, and he hammered back. She slammed again, on and on.

He didn't know how long he could hold out, but he sure as hell aimed to put the halter on her this time. She was a wildcat; she had the strength of a dozen wildcats. It took all his power and then some to keep from exploding inside her.

She kept throwing rage back at him furiously. She hated every horrible inch of him, yet this bed-battle was the fiercest, most stimulating they'd ever had. She couldn't stand it another instant. That knot was swelling, budding, blossoming. Her body arched again, held him in the air, and the knot burst. Scalding, delicious fire streaked through her and the knot was gone. He shuddered and groaned and, still arched, he jerked three times, and she cried out.

Her hips smacked the mattress. His weight rolled off, and he lay beside her. Out of the corner of her eye, she saw that he was breathing in great, audible gulps. She was damp with sweat, her breath stabbing.

Suddenly, uncontrollably, she began to cry. She couldn't help herself, couldn't stifle the sobs. Why would he do such a thing to her, throw away her pills, then attack her? What if she were pregnant?

Tremulous, she sat up. He raised to his elbows and,

like that, watched her cry. He didn't offer her any comfort, not even a handkerchief, just watched.

Suddenly she had the answer.

"T-trickery!" she whispered, enraged. "You tricked me!"

"I thought I was pretty damn open about everything I did," he said. "But you may have tricked yourself. According to the inside of that pill box you missed taking one or two pills. Reckon you didn't keep close enough track."

"You . . . were trying to get me pregnant!"

"Why would I do that?" he asked innocently.

"So I'll marry you and you can get control of my money," she said. "And spend it on the migrants and turn my land over to them!"

Now he was mad again—boiling mad.

"That ain't my reason," he told her. "Use that piece of brain. There's two ways of looking at what I just did. The way you accused me of. And . . . the correct way."

"Exactly what is the 'correct' way?" she snapped.

"That a man tarnation sure don't want to marry a woman that can't breed. He's better off knowing she can, even if the baby is a little quick on the trigger after the wedding."

She sucked in her breath. "I wouldn't marry you even if you did get me pregnant!"

She lunged at him, her aim being to scratch his eyes out, but he grabbed her wrists and held them in an iron grip. Then he got her flat on the bed again and held her there.

She hissed at him. "You can't fool me. I know you're trying to trap me into marrying you! And I won't do it! I'll raise my baby myself if I have to. And anyhow there won't be a baby, because I'll get more pills!"

"No, you won't," he said, his voice, surprisingly, a murmur. "You didn't miss taking a pill when you—with the other men, did you?"

"Certainly not!"

"You won't get more pills. You've already taken the chance . . . might as well go all the way."

She lay very still. He'd gathered her into his arms,

and she could feel the strong beat of his heart through her breast. He smelled of soap and shaving lotion and sweat and sex; he smelled male.

He kissed her. And she, in this strange lassitude of knowledge that she could possibly be pregnant with his child, kissed him back.

Then he rose from the bed, put on his clothes and departed.

Alone in her bed, she slept, exhausted by March, by her lack of sleep. She had no dreams, and when she woke no inner burning.

Only this time she wasn't deceived. It would take still more encounters with him to cure her of the plague with which he'd infected her, and she'd outwit him. She knew he would come to her room now, visit her regularly, his object being to get her pregnant. And he'd search for pills.

Well, there was the rhythm method. She'd use that. There were only about three days in the cycle when she could conceive; those days she'd avoid him. The rest of the time she'd use him, as he was using her.

34

A week later, on a warm November morning, they boarded the flight to Kansas City, nine of them in all. There were the three Townsend men, Oliver Cranston, Madeline, Jenny, Vernon and Perez. And Tom March, naturally. Neatly dressed, looking like butter wouldn't melt in his mouth, eyes black and shining.

Oliver and Madeline sat together, with Simon and David behind them. Vernon and Perez were across the aisle. Rolf sat with Jenny, much to her relief.

That left the Missourian by himself.

Except that he didn't stay put. He kept going from one pair of their party to another. In fact, he was on the move so much that some of the other passengers complained. Finally the stewardess had to ask him to please remain in his seat so they could serve breakfast.

Later, he was up again, perched on the arm of Rolf's aisle seat, talking about his parents. "I'm sort of warning everybody," he said, "about my folks. People claim that Missourians are chauvinists. We've got a different name for it—'old-fashioned, outspoken.' And my pa and ma are old-fashioned, even for Missoura. You might say they're a throwback."

"Is that why they're for helping the migrants?" asked Rolf.

"They believe a migrant's as good as a farmer, and a farmer's as good as a millionaire. They believe a human being is a human being, wherever he lives, however he makes his keep, so long as it ain't dishonest."

Rolf nodded.

"As far as Vernon and Perez go," March continued, "this trip'll point out to them that bosses ain't always dressed-up men in fine offices. Some of 'em are working farmers themselves. That may give them a better understanding of you Townsends."

"I don't see how," Jenny mocked, interrupting. "After all, we're hardly farmers."

"They'll see you in a new light," Tom maintained. "They're bound to."

Jenny turned her head, stared out the window at a formation of white, sun-streaked clouds in a very blue sky. Let him talk. Let him have his day. When she'd got her fill of him, she'd cast him aside with the same lack of compunction with which he'd flushed her pills away.

Out of the corner of her eye, she saw him move on, this time to Vernon and Perez. She'd been surprised when the migrant leaders had actually showed up at the terminal, surprised that they were neatly dressed in slacks and sport jackets, each carrying a topcoat for the colder Missouri weather. The clothes were new. So March had enough savings to dress up his pets!

She began to wonder what he thought he was going to get out of this grandstand play. Did he really want to help the migrants? Or were there other hidden motives? She leaned back into the seat and closed her eyes. She'd find out the truth soon enough.

The plane put down smoothly at the Kansas City terminal. Since they had flown tourist class, Jenny and the others were among the last to deplane. As they neared the door, she felt the cold bite of wind from the outside, and put on her lightweight coat.

March was the first off. His eyes searched the crowd. Suddenly, he hurled himself at a grinning man who spread his arms in welcome. They hugged and patted each other's shoulders, then stood back and regarded each other fondly.

From what Jenny could see of the other man, he was big—as tall as March, as broad and big-boned. His hair was black, but grizzled, and he had a big friendly face. Jenny liked him immediately.

"This is Pa," Tom announced, drawing the man forward.

Old Tom March greeted the men warmly, giving each of them his best Missouri handshake. Then he enveloped Madeline in a bear hug and did the same with Jenny, thundering his approval. "Shows you got a little sense, boy," he shouted at his son, "to fetch a couple of beauties along!"

Jenny smiled. It was odd to hear Tom being addressed as "boy." But he didn't seem to mind. Giving his father a gentle slap on the back, he stood grinning ear-to-ear.

Jenny noticed, too, how Tom let his father take charge. The elder March called for a Skycap to help with the luggage, then led them to, of all things, a pair of long, gleaming Cadillacs. Jenny was stunned. What were dirt farmers doing with such fine cars?

A tall, thin black man of around forty climbed out of one car. Pa March held up progress while he introduced the man to each of the arrivals.

"Hank Williams," he said repeatedly. "Hired man for Young Tom and me both. He lives in my tenant house. Tom's stands empty. Summers, we hire a couple of college boys for harvesting. Gives us five workers, and machinery does the rest."

As old Tom March spoke, Jenny noticed some movement in the backseat of one car. Suddenly a young woman opened the car door and came rushing toward them. Or, more properly, she rushed to Tom, flung herself at him, and he gave her a bear hug that matched the ones Old Tom had given Jenny and Madeline.

She reared back, still holding onto Tom, and stared

into his face. "Where'd you get those shiners?" she demanded gaily. "You been boxing again?"

He grinned. "You might call it that."

"Your ma ain't going to be pleased," Old Tom said. "Never was, even when you was little."

The girl kept hold of Tom. Jenny absorbed every inch of her. She was about twenty, had wide-set blue eyes and golden hair that hung down her back in loose waves. She wore no makeup, and her tight-fitting jeans hugged every line of her sensuous, little body; her least movement was seduction itself in a wide-open-country way. She was perfect, alive with energy, and Jenny knew, without any doubt whatsoever, that she was Tom's prototype of the perfect Missouri girl.

"This is Sally Meharg, folks!" thundered Pa March. "Our neighbor all her life!"

"That's right" squealed Sally, then stood on tiptoe and kissed the young Tom squarely on the mouth. Jenny winced slightly, wondering how many times he'd bedded the little Missouri flirt.

She got hold of herself by the time he introduced Sally to her directly. She smiled properly, responded properly, but it had no effect on Sally, who gave both Jenny and Madeline a hug, eyes cool as she drew away.

"Wait'll the fellows see you two at the pie supper tonight!" she declared. "There hasn't been a new girl in this neck of the woods for ages! The fellows will absolutely go crazy!"

Jenny managed a smile, wondering what on earth the girl was talking about. Pie supper? Men? She wouldn't ask; now wasn't the time.

Pa March herded them into the Cadillacs. Hank drove one car with Vernon and Perez with David and Rolf as passengers. The other six got into the second Cadillac, Sally nestled comfortably between young Tom at the wheel and old Tom at the window. Simon, Jenny and Madeline rode in the back.

Pa March—as Jenny kept thinking of him—gave out a constant stream of talk. "We've got about sixty miles to Butler," he said. "That's the county seat. Then it's twenty-odd to Appleton City, but we stop three miles

286

short of that. Our buildings begin at that point, though our land spreads out from there."

Jenny looked out the window, absorbed in the rolling countryside. There were farms everywhere, each with its cluster of buildings—tall farmhouse, great red barn, towering silo, outbuildings and garages—and removed from the big house, a tiny, white-painted cottage.

They drew up, at last, in the driveway of a plain, two-storied, white farmhouse. Well to the rear stood the inevitable red barn, the silo, the outbuildings, the cottage. Down the road to the west stood a similar cluster of buildings.

Tom saw Jenny gazing toward them. "That's my place," he told her. "We'll go there later, after you meet Ma."

She stared. At his house. At the tall, bare trees surrounding it. At him. "You didn't tell me you owned your own farm," she said.

"Didn't I?" he asked, wickedly innocent.

The others were out of the cars, surveying the lush farmland. Madeline pointed to two wooden doors, lying at a slant on the ground and asked what they were for. When she learned they were for outside access to the cellar, she squealed with delight. Then she spun around, gazing off into the distance as far as she could see.

"You must have *scads* of land!" she exclaimed, to Tom. "I don't see another house except these two!"

"We've got a couple of sections," Tom said modestly.

"Don't believe that!" laughed Sally Meharg, who was now hanging onto Tom's arm. "They own the whole county!"

Pa March's laugh boomed. "That ain't so, folks! We've got all the land we can handle—that's a better way of putting it."

Jenny walked with the others around the house to the back entrance. She was in a daze. She'd expected none of this. Not the pretty blond Sally Meharg, not Tom's farm, and certainly not the vast wealth of the March family.

They entered a big cozy kitchen that smelled of

fresh-baked bread. A rosy-faced woman came to greet them. "This is my wife, Bessie," Old Tom boomed, hugging the buxom woman to his side. "But you c'n call her Ma March."

Bessie greeted all of them in turn. When she came to Jenny, she held both her hands and marveled. "Such a beauty!" she murmured. "Most beautiful girl I ever saw!"

Flushing, Jenny smiled at Tom's mother. She looked into her deep brown eyes, noticed how much they were like Tom's. But gentler, Jenny thought, kinder.

Now Ma March gave her son a kiss, touched one blackened eye, then the other. She shook her head in despair, but made no comment.

Then she motioned forward a thin, horsey-faced young woman of perhaps twenty-five. She wore a starched cotton housedress not unlike the one which Tom's mother had on. Friendliness and goodwill seemed to flow from her.

"Hortense Flagg," Ma March announced. "Don't know what we'd do without her!"

Hortense accepted this praise as her due. "I'm the only girl in this part of Missoura," she confided, "that works as hired girl in two places. Here and at Young Tom's, both."

Tom gave her an affectionate hug. "And thank goodness for it!" he exclaimed.

After they had chatted a while longer, Ma March assigned the guests to their quarters. Jenny and Madeline were to have a room each in Tom's farmhouse; Simon and Rolf were to share a room; and Tom was to move into his attic room. David and Oliver would occupy the hired man's tenant house at the rear of Pa March's place, Hank moving into a room at one end of the barn. And Vernon and Perez were assigned to the tenant house off to the side of Tom's farmhouse.

It was nearly lunchtime, but Tom insisted on their all going to have a look at the tenant house Vernon and Perez were to share. "Both it and Pa's tenant house'll give you the feel of this kind of thing," he explained. "The houses speak for themselves."

They drove to Tom's place, passed his farmhouse,

which was a near replica of Old Tom's house, and parked in front of the tenant cottage.

Jenny caught her breath as she stepped into the small living room. It was plain, but sturdy and homelike. The wood floor was partially covered with a braided rug, and the furniture was old but comfortable-looking. The kitchen was cozy, warmth emanating from a polished iron heating stove in the corner. There was a small bedroom with a decent-sized bed and a roomy chest of drawers. The bathroom was small, but spotless.

"This is it," Tom said. "This is how us Missourians have always housed our hired hands."

It's like a home, a real home! Jenny thought.

"It's as nice as our farmhouses," Tom continued. "On a smaller scale, is all."

She wouldn't look at him, not with Sally Meharg hanging onto his arm and onto every word he favored them with. Instead, she eyed the two migrant leaders. Vernon had tears in his eyes as he looked around him. Perez just stared, openmouthed.

"It cost you plenty to build this house," Simon commented. "To provide a real—well, home—like this couldn't have come cheap."

"It's paid off, though," Tom countered. "With housing like this, we get ourselves reliable help."

Jenny glanced at the Townsend men, at Oliver. All were tight-lipped, and she knew they were mentally estimating the cost of duplicating these quarters in stuccoed cement block in Florida. The amount would be astronomical.

"For your workers," Tom continued, "the houses really ought to be larger. The migrant families are so big they need more sleeping space."

Simon frowned.

It was Oliver who spoke. "One point, March. Your hired hand lives, or used to live, in this house year-round, isn't that correct?"

"Right. But my thinking is that in time, given decent housing, the migrants will leave the road—settle down and be available for planting and cultivating and keeping the vegetable land and groves in apple-pie order. This would result in better crops and more profit for the growers."

"Perhaps," Jenny heard herself say cooly. "But if all the pickers settle in Florida, how are other parts of the country going to harvest their onions and apples?"

"All the pickers won't stay in Florida," Tom answered. "Growers in other states can follow the Florida example, and in the end the migrants will, as a whole, stay put and become, in effect, tenant farmers."

"That'd be heaven on earth!" cried Sally. "Trust Tom to come up with the perfect solution!"

He gave her an absentminded grin, put his attention on Vernon and Perez. "You men enjoy this house now," he told them. "Think of changes your wives might want. It ain't settled, understand, not by a long shot, but it ain't exactly an impossibility. Get the feel of the house and farm, then at future meetings maybe you can anyhow be met halfway."

Vernon muttered his understanding. Perez, still looking around the room wide-eyed, grunted his approval. The others looked at one another, shrugged their shoulders. But no one argued with what Tom had said. Not even Simon.

The four who were to stay in Tom's house accompanied him there and brought in their luggage. The house was much larger than the tenant's cottage, but had the same homey feeling. Tom showed them over the whole house, pointing with pride to his collection of wood sculpture that adorned the modest living room.

After lunch, which Hortense shared with them at the March's big round oak dining table, Jenny and Madeline returned to Tom's house while the men accompanied him on a tour of the farms.

It was Ma March who'd sent the girls back to Tom's. "We're all going to the pie supper at Comstock Consolidated School tonight," she said. "You girls'll have to make your own pies. Hortense'll join you, since she has to make hers in Tom's kitchen after the dishes are done. I'm going to be using my kitchen all afternoon, working on tomorrow's turkey dinner. I've already made my pie though—mince."

Madeline giggled all the way up the stairs. "I haven't the least idea how to make a pie. Do you, Jenny?"

"Hortense—we'll get her to show us how."

"What *is* a pie supper, anyway?"

"I don't know," Jenny laughed, "but I'm sure Hortense will tell us."

Alone in her room, changing into her gray cotton slacks, Jenny fumed. Damn Tom March and his secrets! Letting her think he was almost as poor as the lowliest picker, yet he had this big house and goodness only knew how much farmland! Her teeth clenched. *And* his yellow-haired country sweetheart!

She slammed around, unpacking. Yanking a comb through her hair, she tied it back with a narrow gray ribbon. Then she slipped downstairs to the kitchen.

Hortense was already there. On the big worktable in the center of the room was a lineup of mixing bowls, rolling pins and other utensils. Also, there was flour, shortening, baking powder, and assorted home-canned fruits in glass jars. At one side of the table was a stack of neatly folded aprons and two cookbooks, open to the center.

Jenny was confounded by the sight.

She'd never been taught to cook at the orphanage. Her duties had been scrubbing and waxing and ironing and bed-making. Actually, she'd welcomed the heavier work, had even volunteered for it. Now she was wishing she'd stayed in the kitchen.

Hortense was peeling apples. "I'm going to make an apple pie," she told them. "Men like apple pie. What you girls going to make?"

"We don't know how to make a pie," Madeline said, and waited.

"Cookbooks're open to pies—pastry and fillin'. Them's jars of cherry and rhubarb and gooseberries. Or you can make custard or choc'late—even lemon. Or you can make apple. Just look it up and do what the recipe says."

Jenny and Madeline stared at each other.

"Tell us," Jenny said. "Just what *is* a pie supper? What happens?"

"You don't know?" exclaimed Hortense, stopping work, an extremely long peel dangling from her apple.

They shook their heads.

"Well, I reckon it *is* old-fashioned," Hortense admitted. "It's a get-together for havin' a good time and raisin' money for a good cause. This one tonight's to buy books for the school library. All the girls and women, see, like us—we bake a pie. When it's cool, we put it in a box and wrap it purty, trim it up. Ribbons and bows. At the schoolhouse gym, there's music . . . singin' . . . sometimes a spellin' bee. Square dancin', too. At the end, the auctioneer—we always use Jake Roebuck because he can sing out words so fast—he takes up a pie box and auctions it off. Only the men bid. The winner pays for the pie, unwraps it, and inside finds the name of who made it, and then they pair off and eat the pie together."

"Oh," breathed Jenny with relief. That didn't sound so bad.

She met Madeline's look and said, "Gooseberry. I'll make a gooseberry pie."

"I'll make . . . uh . . . cherry," Madeline said weakly.

Hortense showed them where to find pie tins, then returned to her apples, letting them fend for themselves. They read the cookbooks carefully, watched how Hortense handled pie dough, listened to her excited flow of chatter as they struggled with their task.

"Old Tom and Young Tom is the richest farmers in two counties put together," she began. "Young Tom's the biggest catch in Missoura."

"Is that right?" murmured Madeline, carefully measuring her flour into the bowl. She spilled some on the table, ignored it.

"Young Tom's his pa's only heir," Hortense continued, "not havin' no brothers or sisters. Old Tom, he's got ten sections of good Missoura farmin' land, part of it wooded and with creeks, and he's got all kinds of investments. Only they're on paper. I don't trust money that ain't no place but on paper. It belongs in land. Young Tom, he's got five sections of land in his own right, and even more investment paper than his Pa."

Jenny's hand went unsteady and she spilled the salt. The conniving, deceiving heel! To masquerade in Florida as a common man trying to help the pickers, when all the time he had money coming out of his ears! No wonder that yellow-haired farm girl hung onto him! Couldn't he *see* that she was after his money?

"Surprised, ain't you?" Hortense asked.

"Indeed we are!" cried Madeline, kneading her dough, trying to make it stick together.

"The Marches could—either one of 'em—buy and sell all the rich farmers in this state. And a whole pack of them other farmers is millionaires, or close to it."

Jenny and Madeline looked at each other, resumed work clumsily on their pies. "You'd never know," Madeline said, "from the way they live that they are so—well, rich."

"That's a fact," Hortense babbled on. "But in Missoura it's what you are yourself that counts, not what money or even land you got. Ain't no one bothers to put on a show."

Stunned at the knowledge of the Marchs' vast wealth and the fact that it might even transcend the Townsend fortune, Jenny worked furiously. Having rolled out a halfway decent crust, she placed it into the pan, patching some holes with chunks of dough. She poured a jar of gooseberries into it, put on the top crust, made slits in it and pinched the edges tight as per the recipe, and slid it into the oven.

"Tens of millions," Hortense babbled, on and on. "Oh—oil wells! I forgot them. They're in Oklahoma. Old Tom cusses ever' time they have to make a trip there, wants to sell. But Young Tom, he says it's their duty to keep them, do their part in this here oil crisis. Supply our own country."

Dizzy from what she'd learned, dismayed over the cooking mess she and Madeline had to clean up, worried about her pie, Jenny simply wouldn't let herself think of Tom's fabulous wealth. It didn't change anything; he was still muleheaded and mean.

When she took her pie out of the oven, it didn't look right. Neither did Madeline's. Hortense glanced at the pies, but didn't comment. When she took her apple pie out of the oven, it was perfect.

When the pies had cooled, they put them in the boxes, each dropping in a slip of paper bearing her name. Then they wrapped them in the paper and gaily colored ribbons Hortense produced.

Jenny wrapped hers in gold foil with a blazing red ribbon bow. She braided a length of flame blue, narrow ribbon into the red. Madeline's package was beautiful, pristine white with a cornflower blue ribbon, the top covered with a great bow. Hortense wrapped her box in white too, and tied it with red satin.

"That's my trademark," she said. "Ever' man at the pie supper'll know this is one of my apple pies. You better tell your partners how yours is wrapped—that's how sweethearts pair off—the man knows which box to bid on."

When the men came for supper at Ma March's, Madeline sidled up to Oliver and whispered. He nodded, smiling. Jenny knew then that he'd bid on Madeline's pie.

After supper, when Jenny found herself alone with Tom, she heard herself babbling to him about how her box was wrapped. There. Now. She'd see whether he had the first drop of gentleman in his Missouri hide. Not that she cared. If he did eat her pie, it was all the same to her if he got a stomachache.

35

The pie supper was traditionally held at the Comstock schoolhouse, a small réd building just twenty minutes from the March farm. When they arrived, the place was brightly lit, the parking area already jammed with cars. As they approached the entrance, Jenny felt a wave of nervousness pass over her. Never ·had she seen so many strange faces. She was grateful when Simon came up beside her and·took her arm.

Inside, a burst of light and warmth and the sound of laughing voices enveloped them. Jenny found herself in the midst of chattering country folk of all ages. All wore "country" garb—the women in full, bright skirts or checked dresses, the men in blue jeans with colorful shirts and neckerchiefs. Jenny was relieved that she'd put on a bright green skirt and blouse, which, though not like the costume worn by the others, would pass.

Spotting the table piled with brightly colored pie boxes at the far end of the room, she got up her nerve, left Simon, and went to place her pie box among the others. Then she turned, let her eyes wander around the crowded, noisy gym.

She looked searchingly into the crowd for Tom. Surely he'd join her, introduce her. But she failed to single him out. Nor could she spot any of the others. The gym was alive with people and colors, and it was difficult to find anyone in the crowd.

Finally she spied the Townsend cousins and Madeline. They were in the thickest mass of people, centered around Pa March, who was booming away, gesturing widely, introducing them to the others. Jenny started toward them.

And then, in a momentary break in the crowd, she saw Tom. Sally Meharg was hugging his arm, standing on tiptoe, her blue, blue eyes admiring him, her blue-checked dress emphasizing her round bosom. She was laughing up at him, and he was grinning down at her as if he thought she was the cutest thing that ever came down the pike.

Jenny fumed. The least he could do was spend some time with his folks, even if he didn't have the decency to see to his guests.

Finally, weaving in and out, she reached the others. As she did, so did Tom and Sally. "We was wondering where you'd gone to!" scolded Ma March, giving her son a disapproving glance. "Thought you'd disappeared."

"Oh, don't blame Tommy, now!" Sally laughed. "It was my fault! I admit it! The minute I saw him step into the gym alone, I just cabbaged onto him!" She tossed her yellow head, tinkled out that laugh. "He's been gone from Missoura so *long* . . . I just can't keep my hands off him!"

Furious, Jenny put a careless smile on her own lips. March was mumbling something, and actually took a step in her direction, but Sally hung onto his arm, squealing with delight.

She was still holding on to him when the fiddlers lined up in back of the box-filled table and started to play. The floor cleared, and four sets of dancers took their places. Jake Roebuck, the auctioneer, got ready to call the turns for the dances.

Jenny assumed that March would claim her for the first set, but Sally tugged at him and whisked him off to the dance floor. David grabbed Jenny, and she let him lead her to join them. The four of them formed one set, Sally next to Jenny, March facing Sally from the men's line. March threw one look at Jenny, then turned his eyes to the front.

The tune was lively, and Jake Roebuck began to call the turns. Jenny, having done her share of square dancing, was quite adept at it. She threw back her head, and put herself into the lively music. Sally Meharg would find out that she had met her match!

The tempo quickened. The dancing feet beat out the time, the women's skirts whirling, folding back on themselves. Those sitting in the chairs clapped in time to the music. It soared and quickened as Jake Roebuck's voice kept an endless baritone running through it, holding it all together.

Set after set they danced. March partnered Jenny just one time, stiff as a board. Back to his old tricks. He danced with Hortense three times, with a black-haired, voluptuous female twice, with his ma often, and the rest of the time with Sally Meharg, who chased him shamelessly. Other girls tried to get him, but he stuck to Sally.

Jenny was never without a partner. She danced with the Townsend men, with Oliver, with Pa March, who boomed and thundered and claimed her three times, even with Vernon and Perez, once each. She also danced with a number of local men, both young and old. And enjoyed it.

Finally came the moment everyone had been waiting for. Jake Roebuck took his place at the long front table and began to auction off the pies. He singsonged fast, in his best auctioneer voice, selling pie box after pie box to the highest bidder.

"What'm I bid for this lovely pink box, covered with white ribbon . . . fifty cents . . . I got fifty, give me dollar . . . dollar . . . dollar and half . . . two . . . two dollars . . . give me three . . . three . . . three-fifty . . . give me four

. . . four . . . four . . . four . . . last chance . . . four once . . . four twice . . . four three times! *Sold* . . . to Old Tom March!"

Pa March strode up front and claimed his box. "Got his wife's pie!" yelled a man. "That ain't right . . . he eats Bessie's pie ever' day!"

A wave of laughter rippled over the gymnasium as Pa March joined his Bessie and sat down. With his face in a grin, he set the pie box on one knee, held it steady with a big hand. Ma was blushing.

Jenny saw the blush. How sweet! she thought. And then the auctioneer held up another box and went into his chant. This one sold for three dollars. Jenny could hardly breathe. She wanted her box to be next, and she didn't want it to be next. Surely Tom would buy it; of course he would.

But he didn't. He paid four dollars for a powder blue box covered with blue ribbons and Jenny knew, even before Sally Meharg squealed, whose pie it held. Her heart plunged, then burned. The cad. The absolute cad. He'd neglected her all evening and now, even after she'd described her box to him, he'd bought Sally's!

A raw-looking young farmer named Cecil Wright bought Jenny's pie for five dollars. They sat together in full view of Tom and Sally. The way the little flirt acted, it was obvious that she was in love with Tom. It was written all over her, shone from her bright as the strong gym lights above.

Oliver had bought Madeline's pie and they were eating it together, both of them looking highly amused. So. Oliver didn't mind that Madeline's pie wasn't a success.

Simon and David and Rolf were with local girls. Hortense, surprisingly, was with Max Vernon. Even Perez had a partner. So. March must have given the migrants pocket money!

She watched as her own partner unwrapped the gold box. She studied him nervously. She knew it couldn't be a very good pie; she hoped, fiercely, that Cecil would find it edible.

He gazed at it. "Umm," he said, tone implying that he was pleased. "Uh—what kind is it?"

"Gooseberry," she told him faintly.

Expressionless, he cut the pie with the knife she'd placed in the box as Hortense had said to do. She found herself assessing him, realized she'd been unaware of the farmers during both the dancing and the pie sale. They *were* different from Florida men. They were rugged, self-assured. Even bold. Like Tom. No wonder he was high-handed. Look how all the girls chased him; look at Sally Meharg, whose father was probably a millionaire. She just knew, suddenly, that nearly all these girls had big money behind them.

Tom March was money-hungry, that's what he was. He had all his own filthy wealth, but he wouldn't object to marrying more. To be fair, he could hardly avoid money, all these Missourians seeming to be so rich. Farm-land-rich maybe, but rich.

"Here's some pie," Cecil said now, handing her a wedge on a paper napkin. She took a cautious bite and went stiff. She'd never tasted anything so sour!

Before she could speak, her mouth being full, Cecil took a great bite of out of his own wedge, chewed. He blinked. Then he chewed some more.

She managed to swallow her own bite. "I don't know what makes it so sour!" she wailed. "I'm sorry, Cecil! You don't have to eat it!"

He chewed stoically on, swallowed. "Some women put too much sugar in a gooseberry pie anyhow," he said, and took another enormous bite.

Sugar! Had the recipe called for sugar? She couldn't remember.

Miserably, she watched Cecil eat, taking another bite herself. If he could stand it, so could she. Her whole mouth puckered, but she ate. They made it through the one wedge each except for the rim of the pastry, which was thick and doughy, scorched in places, pale in others.

"I never made a pie before," she confessed. "I apologize."

He laughed; then, saying her pie wasn't all that bad,

ate another wedge to prove it. She wondered whether Tom would have been a gentleman about her pie, doubted it.

After the pies had been eaten, the affair broke up. Jenny got into the car with Rolf, David, Vernon and Perez, and they drove to Old Tom's farmhouse because he insisted they end the evening with some of Bessie's coffee. Jenny didn't know whether Tom rode alone in the pickup or if Sally was with him.

He was already at his Pa's when they arrived. And by himself. Well, maybe he hadn't driven Sally home. That was one small victory—over what she didn't know. She couldn't care less where he went with that girl or what he did.

Pa March lit a fire and they gathered round the fireplace, taking the Missouri chill out of their bones. They talked ploughing and planting and sharecropping.

There was no hint of wealth in the talk. Jenny did, however, hear a snatch of conversation between Old Tom and Young Tom. From this she gathered that Pa didn't exactly approve of Tom's activity on behalf of the migrants. "Put your money where your mouth is," he muttered to his son. "Buy yourself a grove or two, build houses all you want. I know—these fellows came to you, or you more likely went to them—and they found a sympathetic ear. But I don't see no need for you to put the whole Townsend tribe in an uproar."

Jenny could have hugged the old man.

By listening keenly beneath the other chatter, she could just make out Tom's reply. "Can't . . . not now. It's the middle of the season . . . the trouble's now, not two years away."

They kept talking, but Jenny couldn't make out another word because Hortense was screaming with laughter over jokes she and Vernon were exchanging.

At last, much to Jenny's relief, the gathering broke up. Jenny and Madeline, Simon and Rolf, Tom and the migrant leaders drove one of the Cadillacs to the other farmhouse and scattered to their quarters.

Jenny put on a flannel nightgown because the night was cold and she wanted to keep a window open. Then she sat down in the rocking chair and relaxed, trying to calm herself so she'd be able to go to sleep. She kept only a soft lamp burning.

She must have dozed off, because Tom woke her up when he came in and closed the door quietly. She shot up out of the chair, stood behind it. How dare he invade her privacy! And her a guest in his home!

"What are you doing in here?" she whispered fiercely.

"Come to apologize," he whispered back. "Sally kinda took up my evenin'."

"Kinda, indeed," Jenny flamed. "You even bought her pie!"

"She makes good pumpkin—my favorite."

Jenny fumed. "And you danced with her all evening! And with me once, just once!"

"She stuck to me like a burr. Besides, every man there wanted to dance with you and Madeline. It was only fair to let them."

"I'm no Sally Meharg! I don't need to have men . . . fawning all over me!"

"Sounds like you're jealous."

"*Jealous!* You deserve each other, you and that . . . that predator! I suppose she's filthy rich, too!"

"I reckoned Hortense's been shooting off her mouth. Sally ain't *filthy* with money, no. Her Pa's got maybe a million easy enough."

"And you! You hid your money from me! You raped me! You lied to me! You're a—beast—a liar!"

She heard herself begin to cry softly.

To quiet her so she wouldn't wake everybody in the house, he clapped his arms around her and covered her salty lips with his mouth. Now she just made choking, muffled sounds, but cried harder.

He was so tarnation sick of fighting with this wildcat, was so sexually stimulated by everything about her, even her temper, that he backed her to the bed and pushed her down on it. He shrugged off his robe, mouth still on hers, and was naked. He pulled away her damnfool nightgown.

Entering her felt like a homecoming; so did her

301

instant, deep movements. She wrenched her lips free but arched her body up as though she wanted to hurt him with it. If she wanted another bed-fight, she sure as hell was going to get it.

He pounded. She slammed. Their panting filled the room. He gave her a mighty thrust for every vicious upward movement until, unexpectedly, they seemed to get stuck in midair and clung, and he exploded into her, and every inch of his furious body seemed to explode too. Sparkles filled his head, and he heard her crying out and sobbing for more.

Neither of them heard the knock. Only when Rolf opened the door and stepped inside, did they know anybody was near. They rolled apart.

Rolf froze. "I—thought you were in trouble, Jenny," he said. "I see you're in worse trouble than I imagined."

"*You*," Tom said, springing to his feet and grabbing his robe, "can go to hell!" Pushing Rolf aside, he went striding out, carrying the robe with him. Rolf, red-faced, backed silently out and closed the door.

Jenny began to sob.

Supplies being at hand, Vernon and Perez elected to cook and eat breakfast in the tenant house to get the feel of living there. The rest of them drove to Old Tom's in utter, cold silence. Madeline, not knowing what had happened, tried to start a conversation, then fell quiet, looking puzzled. Rolf and Simon were cold and aloof. Jenny was certain Rolf had told his cousin about last night.

At the table, their silence continued. Only Madeline chattered with Hortense and Ma March. Pa kept watching his mute son and Jenny and Rolf and Simon from under his bushy eyebrows.

Finally he asked what was eating them.

Simon replied, "Sir, if you don't mind, I'd like a private conversation with you. Rolf felt obliged to report a certain . . . er . . . event to me, which you have every right to know about."

"No time like right now," Pa said. "We'll go to the parlor."

When they returned, both men were grim-faced. They sat down in front of their plates. Ma waited openly for them to say something. When they remained silent, she took it upon herself to speak.

"What's wrong?" she demanded. "Out with it!"

"It's a private matter," Simon told her.

Tom scowled, started to speak, did not.

"No, by thunder, it ain't private!" exploded Old Tom. "It begun private, but it's past that!" He glared at Young Tom, at Jenny.

"Sir!" protested Simon. "This isn't the time—"

Old Tom waved the protest aside, bored his black eyes at Young Tom. "You bedded her," he accused, pointing at Jenny, "in your own house last night! She may be in the family-way right now—who knows how long this has been goin' on! You got to marry her today! My grandson, heir to all we got, is likely started! March men are potent!"

Cheeks burning, longing to sink through the floor, Jenny stared at her plate, trying to hold back the tears. Ma, shocked, was pale and gasped, "My boy . . . this lovely girl lost her virtue at my son's hands!"

Young Tom broke in. His eyes were deadly cold as he stared at Simon. "If you'd care to step outside," he hissed, "I'll give you something real to talk about."

He shoved his chair back, sprang to his feet. All the other men shot up. Old Tom lunged, grabbed his son's arm, pinned it back. Young Tom jerked free, took a swing at his Pa, who danced aside.

Ma jumped between them. "No fighting!" she ordered. "Not with fists and not with mouths! No more black eyes! Things are different today, Pa March, than they were when we was young! I don't like it, but they are! You don't *know* the girl's in the family-way!"

"I've got a gut feelin'!" thundered Pa. "Tom—you marry her today! I'll get Judge—"

"As head of this family," Simon interrupted, "I only want us to leave. And I demand, for Jenny's sake, that you never see her alone again, March," he said directly to Young Tom.

"That's for Jenny to say," Young Tom said, gritting.

Shamed, embarrassed, confused, and angry, Jenny snapped out the first thing that came to mind. "I'll do what I please!" she screamed at both of them.

"I'm callin' the Judge!" roared Old Tom.

"You'll call nobody!" roared Young Tom. "I ain't asked her to marry me, and—"

"And don't bother to!" Jenny screamed. "I wouldn't *permit* you to be the father of my child! *If* he is born!"

"What do you aim to do?" thundered Old Tom, turning on Jenny now.

"I'll find out whether I'm pregnant as soon as I get home. And then—*then* I'll decide what to do. What I won't do, Mr. March, sir, is marry your son! I despise the ground he walks on!"

She left the table, eyes blurred. All she wanted was to get away from this place. Far away. She'd get on a flight home. She'd find out if she *was* pregnant. And if she were, she'd make plans.

For herself and her baby.

Part V
THE GULF STREAM

36

Jenny had wanted to fly home herself. She'd even gone so far as to call a taxi to pick her up and take her to the airport. But Simon and the others had insisted and finally she'd agreed to fly home with them. They left that afternoon.

On board the 707, Jenny spoke to no one, not even Madeline, despite the girl's efforts to draw her out. She sat staring out the window, refusing the lunch tray brought by the stewardess.

When she arrived home, she went straight to her suite, barely greeting Flo, and made an immediate appointment with her doctor for the next morning. She'd find out once and for all if she was pregnant and make her plans accordingly. This was her life, and no one was going to tell her how to run it.

The report on her pregnancy test was ready the following day. As she'd suspected, it was positive. She left the doctor's office in a fog, two bottles of vitamins in her bag to cover the early months of pregnancy.

She drove straight to the duplex and walked in without ringing. Tom was in the kitchen, washing the coffeepot.

He turned, met her glance with one of his own.

"I hope you're satisfied," she snarled. "You *have* got me pregnant!"

His glare vanished. A grin split his face. "So!" he gloated. "I did right when I flushed away those damn pills!"

"It happened before that! You ... louse! Get a girl in trouble, then *laugh!*"

He sobered. "You don't want him. You don't want my kid."

"This is *my* baby!"

"One thing's sure. We're getting married."

"Oh, no, we're not!"

"That's my kid! He ain't going to be raised without his pa!"

"You can't force me!"

"You've got to marry somebody. You can't raise him alone. So who will it be? The Townsends? You cocky enough to try for one of them, after they know what happened? Maybe you think you can fool one of them into thinking it's his kid?"

"I'd never trick them! I'm not a liar!"

"I ain't having one of them pa to my kid!"

"Watch and see!"

"*You* do the watchin' and seein'!" he growled. "Why the hell did you come here anyway, if you don't want me to marry you?"

"So you'll know your plan backfired. Maybe you *did* get me pregnant, but you'll never take me to the altar!"

For an instant they stared at one another in silence. Then he grabbed her roughly, and pulled her down onto the bed. She struggled as he ripped off her clothes, but was unable to escape him.

Then, suddenly, she didn't want to. He was showing his macho, and it stirred the old itch and she wondered if being pregnant made her want him more. No. Sex with him was a drug; she was addicted to it.

He was on top of her, then deep inside her, and she

felt herself move with the rhythm of him. After all, it was only physical, a mere physical sensation, and this was the last time. So she drank of him, and he of her.

When it was over, they dressed, not speaking. She stood at the door, ready to leave.

"Whatever damn-fool thing you do," he said finally, "it'll make no difference. I've already won. The kid is mine."

But as she hurried away from the duplex, her sandals clapping smartly on the sidewalk, she knew that wasn't true. He still wouldn't admit it, but he'd met his match. Now she was free of him—free forever.

She found Richard Snow waiting in her living room. He sprang up from the plush sofa, and in one lithe movement, strode across the room, caught her hands, and drew her into his arms.

"Jenny, beloved!" he murmured in his charm-filled voice. "I've come to beg your forgiveness, to make you my wife!"

Dazed, she pulled back, stared into his handsome face, felt herself caught by those bedroom eyes. "You're already married," she reminded him. "How can you marry me?"

He tried to pull her back into his arms, but she held herself away from him. "The biggest mistake of my life!" he declared solemnly. "I must explain, beloved. When you told me you wanted to wait, my pride was hurt. I flew to Hollywood—and, well, there was Cherry. She swept me off my feet!"

"That's what I thought I'd done," Jenny said, bewildered.

"Cherry was—I'd never seen anything like her! I'd never seen anything like you! But she—the fascination! She's albino, Jenny! Her hair is pure white, her eyes so pale there's only a hint of color. And her skin! She was different, and she threw herself at me!"

"Doesn't every woman?"

"Every woman but you, Jenny. Anyway, my marriage is over. Cherry's hell to live with. We're getting a quickie divorce. And then I'll be free to marry you!"

"Are you crazy?" she whispered. "Do you think I would marry you now? You're no good, Richard."

"I admit it! But you can save me, Jenny!"

"I'm pregnant," she said flatly. "With another man's child."

"It makes no difference! I'll be a father to your baby, adopt it, love it as I love you!"

He seemed so sincere. For one instant, Jenny was tempted to say yes. Only she couldn't. She didn't love Richard Snow, America's sex symbol.

Odd. She wouldn't marry Tom for that identical reason. She didn't love him. Her feeling toward him was wild, angry—more like hatred than love.

It took an hour, but finally Richard accepted her refusal and left. Jenny didn't feel sorry for him. She knew the world was full of women who wanted a chance with Richard Snow. He'd fall in love again soon.

But there was no one for her. No one at all.

Jenny spent the evening alone, Madeline being out with Oliver. Actually, she was glad for the time alone. She needed to think, long and hard, about her situation, to decide between Rolf and David. If they'd have her, now that she was pregnant.

She felt, crazily, that she'd somehow be betraying Tom if she married either one of them. But that was ridiculous! Hadn't he tricked her, and then boasted over his victory? She owed him nothing! She went to bed, hugging that thought.

But she couldn't sleep. Her mind kept turning over the possibilities. Rolf. David. Could she find happiness with either of them? Did she feel the least vestige of love?

By morning, she had come to a decision. She had a quick breakfast, then headed downtown for a Townsend–migrant meeting that had been called by Simon. Tom March was there, sitting between Vernon and Perez. Oliver and the Townsend men were also there, and, Jenny observed, were rather cold toward Tom.

The meeting was brief. Vernon and Perez had relayed the latest Townsend offers to their co-workers, and had met with mixed reactions. One thing they were all enthusiastic about was the tenant houses.

Simon frowned. "Our Board hasn't yet discussed the building of houses at all," he said. "At the moment, the question is whether you people will accept the increase in wages—which you've already done—the toilet facilities and the bathhouses with washers and driers, and clean campgrounds."

"As final?" demanded Perez, instantly afire.

"Final for the present. We need time to consider the houses. We'll negotiate with you on them later."

"We need the houses *now,*" Perez maintained.

"Perhaps we should be more patient," Vernon urged. "They need time to make plans."

Tom nodded in agreement. "Yes, they do. *But*"—he turned toward Simon—"I hope you'll take this matter up *immediately.*"

By the time the meeting ended, Vernon and Perez agreed, as representatives of the pickers, to give the Townsends time to discuss the matter of houses. They'd wait a reasonable amount of time for an answer.

When Tom and the two migrant leaders had left, Jenny drew in a breath, asked the others to stay. Then, her eyes fixed on the table, she announced to them that she was pregnant, and that the father of her child was indeed Tom March. Then, chin out, she waited.

"We think none the less of you, Jenny," Rolf said. His face was very kind, his eyes gentle.

She looked at the others, and they were nodding in agreement. She suddenly heard herself spilling out the details of Si's plan for her to remarry. They were surprised, and for a moment sat in silence. Finally Oliver spoke up.

"You're a brave woman, Jenny," he said. "Not many women would even attempt to handle such a bizarre assignment."

"Of course," David smiled, "you could have had any of us. We've all been mooning over you from the first."

The others nodded.

"I—don't know yet what to do," Jenny stammered.

They closed in on her gently, but it was clear they

were eager for her decision. Jenny felt cornered, trapped. She had to get away.

Excusing herself, she left Simon's office and headed for her car. She took the long route home, rolled the windows down, and allowed the warm breeze to blow through her hair.

By the time she reached the penthouse, she had made a firm decision. The choice lay between Rolf and David. She would force herself to have sex one more time with each of them, if they were willing. Then she'd know if she could love one of them.

The next day, Wednesday, Jenny gave Flo the day off. Then she told a shocked but sympathetic Madeline what she proposed to do, and, after wishing her luck, Madeline departed for Palm Beach to shop and visit friends.

When she was alone, Jenny called Rolf and asked if he could get away from the office and come over. Eagerly, he said of course he could. After that, she phoned David and invited him for the afternoon, and he accepted.

She went to her closet and took out her sexiest, filmiest green robe. It was all she had on when she met Rolf at the elevator. Surprise, followed by instant desire, took his Townsend eyes, and she felt instantly guilty. She did like him so much; this was really a dirty trick, to test him this way.

"Jenny!" he whispered.

"Y-you know what I'm doing?" she asked faintly. "That I want to find out, to know—"

"I understand, love," he murmured, drawing her into his arms. He held her as if she were a treasure, held her reverently.

How kind he was! How sympathetic. No demands, no roughness, no high-handed statements. Just this holding her as if she might be a saint whom he worshiped.

He stroked her hair, kissed her, his lips tender, adoring. He demonstrated a clean and pure love. Which she needed.

But suddenly, when he would have taken her, transported her, she pulled away. She just couldn't go through with it. Reluctantly he let her go. She met his eyes, tried to speak, but found herself wordless. Contrite, she gazed at him beseechingly.

"It's all right, Jenny," he assured her. "You already know that love-making between us is wonderful. For me, anyway . . . and I hope for you. I'll not sully you with a further—trial. You've been through enough agony and degradation. I love you as fully as a man can love a woman. You'll know, in your own time, whether or not you love me, without what you now offer to do."

"And the b-baby?"

"Makes no difference."

Jenny's eyes clung to his. And slowly, despite the gentleness of him, the tenderness and honesty, she knew. She would always like Rolf, treasure him as a friend. But she would never love him.

Rolf held her once more. He kissed her briefly. "If you want me, dear heart," he whispered, "pick up the phone. That's all it will take. Meanwhile, I'll not burden you with my courtship."

He was gone. She began to tremble. There was no reason for her to feel that she'd almost betrayed Tom March. None at all.

She almost called to break her date with David. But no. She was going to go through with it. Seeing Rolf had helped her, had made things clear for her; perhaps seeing David would do the same.

She met him in the same filmy robe.

"You've decided on me!" he exulted instantly.

That turned her off, completely. She dreaded to disappoint David as she had Rolf, not because she loved him, but because she never could love him. She knew that firmly now, face to face with his eager confidence.

She explained honestly but, unlike Rolf, he protested, suing for his chance with his sunniest, most appealing air. So charming, so persuasive was the youngest cousin, that she almost wavered.

But, in the end, she stood firm.

"I can't, David. I apologize for dressing this way, for

leading you on so. But I thought—only now I can't. Or ever. I like you, but I'll never love you. I'm afraid Si was the only Townsend for me."

A fleeting look, almost surly, crossed his face, was gone. He left her with the same assurances Rolf had given. That all she had to do was call and he'd come running. That given time, he was sure she would come to him.

But she knew she would not.

After his prolonged leave-taking, Jenny paced the rooms of the big penthouse. At last, she settled in the kitchen. The late afternoon sun was streaming through the windows, and she looked to it, as if for the answer to her problem.

Suddenly the solution came to her. She recognized it as sound and resolved to follow it through.

She would give up all her money. She would keep only Orange Blossom Grove for herself. There, she would build some kennels and, with citrus to sell, greyhounds to breed, and absolute peace, she would make a life for herself and her baby.

37

Madeline came home at ten. She took one glance at Jenny and demanded to know what was wrong. Jenny told her, in detail, of her Orange Grove plan.

Madeline's lovely face registered shock. "It'll never do, darling!" she cried. "You need a man—Si recognized that!"

"I haven't found a man to love," Jenny said simply. "And now I'm pregnant. I have my child to think about."

"And what about *you*? Jenny, you owe it to yourself to think about this, give yourself time to consider! Please, oh please, give yourself time! Just until Christmas!"

"That's a whole month away."

"*Only* a month! It'll give you time to catch your breath, to think things over. Why don't you set a deadline —like Christmas, the day the dog track opens! You'll not be showing with the baby yet, and who knows what new solution, even what new man, will come to you by then!"

Jenny frowned thoughtfully. She really shouldn't act on impulse, and her decision to raise her child at Orange

Blossom Grove, though sound, was impulsive. Maybe she should give herself one month. To make certain.

So she promised Madeline.

"That's great!" she squealed. "But, Jenny-honey, promise me one more thing. Extend that Christmas deadline a tiny bit! Please. David's invited all of us to join him aboard *The Louisa* on a cruise to Freeport, right after Christmas. So let's have one last gay, happy time with our group before you announce this grove thing!"

Why not, thought Jenny. The way the Townsends felt about Tom, he certainly wouldn't be invited on the cruise.

She promised.

In the days that followed, she felt surprisingly relaxed. For the first time in weeks, she was free of that horrible pressure to find the right husband. Not that she didn't want to remarry. She did. But in her own time, and according to her own specifications.

She was even free of her passion for Tom March and wondered if that was due to the pregnancy or to her decision about the future. Whatever the reason, she was glad to be rid of him. Glad to be herself again.

She refused to attend further board meetings. Whatever the board decided, she told Simon, she'd go along with. That is, she thought privately, if she was still a member of the board when any decision about the migrants was reached.

At Madeline's insistence, she attended the social gatherings, even those that included Tom March. She was surprised to find the Townsends so willing to admit him back into their social circle; but as Madeline pointed out, they were probably maintaining the relationship for business reasons. After all, Tom was their only link to the migrant workers.

At first Jenny thought it was her imagination. Tom was treating her differently. Instead of picking fights with her, he was actually kind, almost gallant.

For some reason, this merely irritated her. It was easier to hate someone who was surly and mean. This new Tom was a puzzle to her and she almost longed for the old Tom's return. She found herself snubbing him as much as possible, keeping her mind on the future and the birth of her child.

As Christmas approached, she relaxed. The nights were again mild and she took comfort in late evening walks along the darkened beach.

They spent Christmas in a group, exchanged gifts. Jenny got a filmy green scarf from Simon, a tiny gold pin from Rolf, a beautiful nightgown from David. From Madeline she received a tiny friendship ring, of braided gold and silver. From Oliver, a bottle of perfume.

March gave her a bright red sweater in a large size. She put it on, wondering how he could have known she'd been craving the color red. You were supposed to crave foods in pregnancy. But colors? Yet for some reason she'd been longing for something red to wear.

As she hugged the soft sweater to her chest, she caught a fleeting grin on March's face. She turned away after he'd unwrapped the wallet she'd given him, and watched the other men unwrap their wallets. Madeline squealed over the gold link bracelet Jenny had purchased for her, and put it on instantly, holding out her arm for Oliver to admire it.

They turned on the news at five minutes of six. The weather forecast was for continued unseasonable cold. For three days now, they'd had an icy snap, unusual for Florida. Now the weatherman was predicting frost for early morning.

Simon snapped off the set and went grimly to the phone. They waited as he called every Townsend grove and farm manager in the area to make certain that all precautions would be taken for the crops as they had been for the past two nights. He offered to help with the actual work and relayed the eager offers of the other men in the room.

Jenny paid special attention to his last phone call. It was to Orange Blossom Grove. She was relieved when Simon reported back to them that the manager, Woody Woodbury, had things under control.

"They're all set," he told them. "They'll not need us."

That night they went to the track for Christmas opening night. They dressed up for the occasion, Jenny in a lime green frock of nubby wool, and over it a matching, satin-lined long coat; Madeline in a creamy white wool dress and coat edged with powder blue. With her pale red hair and fair skin, Jenny thought she looked like an angel.

The Townsend dates—Lila Stevens and Sara Donahue and Barbara Winters—arrived at the penthouse wearing Christmas colors. Their voices tinkled and their laughs rang out. They declared that Jenny's greyhounds would win every race and that tomorrow, when they all sailed for Freeport, the celebration would go on and on.

When they reached the racetrack, the air was so nippy that Jenny's cheeks were cold and the tip of her nose pink. She stepped out of the limousine and gazed out over the acres of parked cars. The cars far off looked dark, but those nearer shone of yellow, blue, green, and every other conceivable color beneath the strong lights. A breeze sprang up, bit at them, died down.

They always impressed Jenny, the hundreds of cars at the track, the throngs of people edging toward the turnstiles which would admit them to grandstand and clubhouse. She was so busy trying not to collide with anyone, that only now and then did she remember how cold it was. From beyond, inside the track, she could hear the hum of the crowd! She knew it was made up of avid racing fans who had arrived early.

Madeline caught up with her, and they had a moment alone. "Look, Jenny . . . look and believe!" she whispered, holding out her left hand.

On the engagement finger flashed a diamond which must have been at least four carats. "Oliver?" Jenny gasped, delighted.

Madeline giggled, let her hand drop. "Just before we got into the car!" she bubbled. "Ooh, Jenny, now I've got everything I want! Money—scads of money—but best of all, Oliver has fallen in love with me . . . he's wild about me . . . and I never *dreamed* I could love a man the way I love him!"

Jenny put her arm around Madeline briefly.

The other girl was instantly contrite. "Oh, I shouldn't have!" she wailed. "How could I, when you—"

"Don't be a goose," Jenny said. "I'm happy for you. And because of you, I have peace of mind."

The others caught up with them, and they moved on. They paused at a tall link fence and peered through. Beyond were the boxes which held the eight dogs running the first race. They were looking at the crowd and yelping excitedly. One dog was more excited than the others. This was Romantic Sally, and Jenny moved the others on so as not to upset the dog further. Between the caged dogs and their passageway to the racing oval was the big scale on which they were weighed before the race and where they were examined briefly by a veterinarian. This last was to make certain no stimulating drug had been administered to any dog to make it run faster.

They entered the track and went directly to the clubhouse, which was almost at the finish line and afforded the best view of the oval. Jenny wondered if all the hordes of racing fans were as excited as she was.

For her it was a special thrill, of course. Two of her own dogs were going to race tonight! Hopefully, one of them would win. She was going to bet only on her own—Romantic Sally in the first race, and Snow Blossom in the second.

They made their way through the crowd to seats in the heated clubhouse. The big race oval was like a stage of sorts—its sandy racing track smoothly dragged, brilliantly lighted; the toteboard cleared; the boxes in place at the starting line; the mechanical rabbit sparkling white, waiting.

The Townsend men sat with their dates, looking down on the track. Oliver and Madeline sat together, holding hands and whispering. This led to Tom's being paired off with Jenny.

"Mind?" he murmured, bending to her.

"No," she said uncomfortably, "not at all."

He sat down. "I hope you've noticed," he said in a low voice, "that I ain't pestered you this last month."

"I've noticed."

"Madeline said you would. Said I'd been coming on

too strong with you. That you needed time. I got pretty riled at first; then, more I thought of how many times we've—more sensible it was."

"I'd prefer," Jenny said, lips quivering slightly, "to drop the subject." She was all settled down now. She meant to run no risk of getting stirred up again.

"Right," he agreed, surprising her. "Suppose you explain all this racing business to me?"

"You were at the schooling races, remember?"

"I didn't ask questions then. Now I want to bet some."

"The smallest bet is two dollars," she told him. "You can buy a ticket for your dog to win, or to place—that means to come in second—or to show, which means to come in third. The win ticket pays the most usually, though the others pay more if the winning dog is popular and the betting on him is heavy."

"I see." He consulted the program he'd bought. "This Daily Double. What's that?"

"You can buy a two dollar ticket on it too. You pick the dog you think will win the first race, and the one you think will win the second race. They race under numbers. So you might choose number one in the first race and number eight in the second. You go to a seller's window and buy a ticket on one–eight . . . a Daily Double window, that is. And it doesn't have to be just one ticket. You can bet more."

Now music struck up, cutting through the noise of the crowd. It was time for the first race. The crowd only murmured now, all attention being on the track. A young, uniformed groom, brought out a muzzled dog wearing the number one blanket and paraded him back and forth on the track so the spectators could view him, then took him to the starting boxes and stood with him, leash in hand.

The process was repeated with each of the remaining seven dogs in the first race. Romantic Sally—number six, wearing the gold blanket—trotted smartly beside her groom, head up, her eye on the starting boxes. Jenny's spine tingled at her greyhound's perfect behavior.

Tom went to buy his tickets, and she gave him four

dollars. "Two tickets for the Daily Double," she said. "Six and Six. Romantic Sally and Snow Blossom."

He came back as the loud bell marking the end of ticket sales sounded. "Made it just in time," he said. "The place is jammed."

Now the grooms put the dogs into the starting boxes, unsnapping the leashes. The doors to the boxes slid shut at the same time. The music still played as the eight grooms trotted swiftly to the point of entry and left the track. The music stopped.

The track lights brightened. The racing odds glowed on the toteboard. The rabbit began to move, the boxes opened, and the greyhounds burst free, going for the rabbit.

Romantic Sally broke first, but was at a disadvantage, being number six and far from the rail. The number one dog got the rail and led the others. Romantic Sally cut through a gap, and fought to hold fourth place.

The crowds in both grandstand and clubhouse were on their feet, screaming their favorites on. At the first turn, Romantic Sally was edged to the outside by a big spotted dog, and began to run wide, now in fifth place.

She ran wide around the end curve; then, on the backstretch, shot through a momentary gap, taking fourth again. She poured on speed. At the next curve, she tried again for the inside and almost made it, gaining third place.

On the homestretch, she was neck and neck with a big black dog, but finally edged past him to take the lead. She was first across the finish line, stopped only by the dropping of the great curtain just beyond the passage way back to the kennels.

Jenny was so excited she was jumping up and down. Tom took gentle hold of her elbow and urged her to sit down, and she did, wondering if he was thinking about the baby.

The music started. The dogs for the second race were paraded. Snow Blossom too wore the number six blanket. Jenny looked at the tote board. The odds kept changing. Oh, Snow Blossom, you doll, Jenny thought fiercely. Win the race, win the Daily Double!

Snow Blossom literally romped around the track, leading all the way. She crossed the finish line three lengths ahead of the nearest greyhound.

The Daily Double paid winners two hundred dollars on a two-dollar ticket. Jenny, having bought two tickets, won four hundred dollars. There was also a purse to be divided between the owners of the winning dogs, all of which, in this case, would go to Jenny.

The Townsends, Oliver, Madeline and Tom were elated, all having bet on Jenny's dogs. They lost on some of the later races, but their spirits were still high when they left the track just after midnight.

Outside, they were shocked by the change in the weather. It had turned much colder. The air was very still. Simon said, uneasily, that it must be below freezing. Perhaps they should head for Orange Blossom Grove to see whether help was needed.

"We'll check on the temperature first," he said, "but that's Jenny's biggest grove and should be protected before the others if a choice must be made."

David and Rolf agreed. Their dates pouted a bit, but consented to let Billings drop them off at their homes. Jenny insisted on accompanying the men to the grove. She had more at stake than anyone but Madeline knew, and was intent upon protecting her future interests. Madeline too wanted to come along, and the men reluctantly agreed.

"But you'll have to stay out of the way," Simon warned.

As they made for the cars, Jenny spotted Perez and two other dark-skinned men in the crowd. Simon saw them too, for he nodded and kept going. They nodded back to him and continued on their way. Jenny wondered how they could afford to bet on the dogs, then decided they'd probably come for the excitement of the races.

Simon phoned the grove from Jenny's penthouse. Woody Woodbury reported that a freeze was now predicted and he'd appreciate all the help he could get.

That was all the men needed to hear. They were out the door in an instant, racing to their homes for warmer clothing—all except Simon, who'd had the foresight to bring a bulky sweater and his warmest topcoat.

Jenny hurried to her room and scrambled into wool slacks and shirt, warm socks and boots and caught up a short fleece-lined jacket. She offered to help Madeline, who had three outfits on her bed and was trying to decide which to wear, but the girl waved her on. "I'll be ready," she promised. "You go on downstairs."

Simon was alone in the living room. He looked his handsomest, held both arms out to Jenny and captured her hands in his. "You know what I long to say," he murmured. "Again."

Reluctantly, she nodded.

"I've waited, Jenny. Waited for you to gain some measure of composure. Now, in these moments alone, I ask you again to marry me. At once."

She breathed carefully. She didn't want to hear this, oh, she didn't! "If it's because of the baby," she faltered, "because you want to help me—"

"It's for myself. I am, in my own way, in love with you. I regret what happened between us that time—I had no right. I assure you that it doesn't detract from my love and respect. Nor does your child."

She didn't know which way to look, how to say what she must.

"I know you don't love me yet," he continued. "You even shrink from sex with me. I quite understand. But consider. Grandfather preferred that you marry a Townsend. As the eldest grandson, it should be my privilege to have you as my wife. I'm the most like Grandfather, the most experienced. The child will be a Townsend. I'll rear and treat it as well as I will our own children. We can start on that basis and build a marriage which will hold all the elements Grandfather specified."

Half convinced, but far from willing, she frowned. "It could happen that we could build a marriage the way you build a house, I suppose."

"Then you'll marry me?"

"No, Simon. I'm sorry."

"Is it March? Because he's the father of your child?"

"No."

It wasn't a real lie, not now. True, she had at one time been all mixed-up, trying out men the way you try on shoes. She'd been attracted to them all to some degree, and, at times, she still ached for the passion she felt with Tom.

"Think, Jenny," Simon urged. "Or don't think. Simply trust me. I'll make life right for you. I promise."

He watched her keenly. Though he tried to appear patient and reasonable, inside he was seething. He could think of no further pleas, no other way to win her. She'd captured him, body and soul. And he needed her. Together, with their fortunes combined, they would be rich beyond comprehension.

He tried again, told her how they would prosper if they combined their fortunes.

"And if I didn't have the money, Simon? Would you want to marry me then?"

"I'd want to," he said, and meant it.

She believed him, was truly sorry.

"Jenny?"

She shook her head. "No, Simon. I couldn't ever love you."

She saw his lips tighten, saw cold disappointment fill his Townsend eyes, "I'll not accept this as final," he told her. "I'll not give up."

Before she had time to say more, Madeline came rushing in. They waited for the others to arrive, then set out for Davie and the endangered grove.

38

They went in the limousine—Jenny and Madeline in front with Billings, Tom and Rolf on the jump seats, Simon, David and Oliver in the back.

Madeline was full of questions. "What's the temperature now?" she asked.

"Thirty degrees and falling," Simon replied.

"What does that mean? What will we do?"

"They've already got the central heating system going and radiant heaters along the north and west parts of the grove, with others at wider intervals."

"Why so many heaters on the northwest part?"

"This freeze comes from the northwest, from Texas," Rolf said. "Our job, as the temperature drops, is to see that every heater functions."

"Can they really *heat* the grove? I've heard they fire up during a cold spell, but just how much heat can they supply?"

"The heat can raise the temperature as much as eight degrees," David said. "The object is to get the grove temperature to above the freezing point of thirty-two degrees."

"Which means the groves are in danger, if the temperature is much below that," Oliver supplied.

"But Orange Blossom Grove has a windbreak of Australian pines on the north and west borders," Jenny put in, becoming increasingly alarmed for the safety of her fruit.

"That's to the good in this case," Simon said, "but no guarantee. According to Woodbury, the thermometers in the grove are dropping fast."

"All we can do," Rolf explained, "is keep that central system functioning and try to space the heaters through the grove so they'll keep the air above freezing. One thing in our favor is that we've already had some dry, cool weather."

"What does that mean?" asked Madeline.

"That the tree tissues may be well matured and can endure quite severe cold. However, a strike against us is the warm weather we've had just before this, and the lack of rain. That can make the trees water deficient and more susceptible to the cold."

They found Woody Woodbury at the heating shed. "Glad to see you!" he exclaimed. "Temperature's gone to twenty-eight outside the grove, but so far we've been able to maintain a pretty consistent temp of thirty-three inside. I've got six men out to see that the heaters function and to move them around where they're needed most."

"We can help with that," Simon offered. "There are seven of us—eight counting the chauffeur."

"Good! I'll take you to the spots where you're needed. All you do is patrol your section of trees and if a row or two feels colder, move heaters as far as the connecting hose allows, so the trees can 'see' the heat—feel it, in other words."

They'd brought several flashlights, but Woodbury furnished each with a lighted lantern. "Even the lanterns," he said, "set close to some tree isolated from decent heat, do some good."

Woodbury leading the way, they moved away from

the shed with its big heater, each carrying a lantern. The manager stationed Jenny first, in a pine-sheltered, less frigid section and indicated the area she was to patrol. Madeline he assigned to a nearby section, and to Tom he gave the next, central portion.

"It puts you into a cold area, where heaters'll need to be moved frequently," he told the Missourian, "but keeps you in fair reach of the shed. You remember how that central heater works, if anything goes wrong?"

"I remember," Tom assured him.

"Then I'll count on you to check it out. You other four," Woodbury continued, "will be in the coldest part of the grove and have even more heaters to shift. I'll patrol the entire grove, keeping an eye on the trees and the thermometers."

The others left, and Jenny was alone with her lantern. She was in a section of grapefruit trees, could glimpse the yellow fruit on the nearest ones. Beyond, in the moonless, almost starless night, the trees were rows of dark shadow. The night was so quiet that the silence hurt her ears. Her cheeks were icy, her toes cold. Even her fingers, in woolen gloves, were cold.

She moved to the nearest radiant heater and tried to warm herself. She could feel the heat floating out, but it seemed so weak compared to the frigid temperature, she wondered how it could possibly save the fruit. She held her lantern high, shone it on the branches of a grapefruit tree near the edge of her area, and the light glittered on ice which covered the twigs.

She wondered if a tree, once bitten by ice, could save its fruit. She wished she'd noticed the ice sooner, so she could have asked Woody about it.

She moved a heater closer, the gloves protecting her hands, so that it stood between two rows, nearer to the icy tree and others next it. She combed the area, shining her lantern along the rows of trees. Every time she saw ice, she moved a heater, wandered on.

After what seemed a long time, Woodbury shuffled in out of the darkness. There were two men with him Jenny recognized them, even in the dim lantern light. They were Max Vernon and Pablo Perez.

"These men say they know you, Mrs. Townsend," Woodbury said. "They want to help."

"Yes, I do know them," Jenny replied. "Do we need more help?"

"Need all we can get, 'specially on the far side, where the heaters have to be moved constantly. There's not much protection from the windbreak there."

"Then by all means, let them help," Jenny exclaimed. "And thank you, gentlemen. How did you find out?"

"From the weather, ma'am," Vernon replied. "And we aim to pick this grove next. Besides, we sort of agreed to be of whatever help we could in case of an emergency."

"We're grateful," Jenny said. "Put them where you need them, Mr. Woodbury."

When they were gone, she walked the aisle of trees, shining her lantern. The rich muck underfoot, which she recalled hearing made freezes worse, snapped sharply as she trod on it.

She kept moving heaters, worked out a pattern. She didn't let any heater stay in one spot a long time, but would shift them regularly, thus distributing their heat methodically.

Still, she couldn't help but wonder if it was doing any good. The temperature was dropping. She could feel the cold through her clothing; it even penetrated the knitted cap she wore and pierced her scalp. Her toes were numb, and her fingers, as she stooped to move a heater, felt like wooden sticks.

She put her gloved hands on still another heater, lifted. At first she didn't trust her own sense of touch. Then she flattened her palms against the heater, and she knew.

There was no heat coming from it. She could feel nothing, not even when she yanked off a glove with her teeth and slapped her bare hand against it. The heater had stopped functioning.

She went at a stumbling run up and down all her rows of trees. Every heater was stone cold.

Tom went through the grove, making for the shed to check the central, oil-fueled heater. Seemed to him the grove heaters weren't throwing off enough warmth; at any rate, he'd see if he couldn't step up that central system. The thermometer at the far side of the grove stood at twenty-eight, the one inside at thirty-one. The differential they were trying for was eight degrees, not three.

Somehow, it felt colder here at twenty-eight than it did in Missoura. Because of the normal warmth of Florida, the contrast was marked. In Missoura, twenty-eight was nothing; here, it was like the South Pole.

He broke into a run. The sooner he jazzed up that central system, the sooner more heat would radiate into the grove. It seemed like others were following him, but he didn't stop to find out.

Suddenly, he was flat on the ground. He'd stepped into an unexpected depression, his ankle had turned, and he'd been sent sprawling. While he was getting up, cussing and retrieving his lantern, he heard voices in the distance shouting something about no heat.

That meant the central system was on the blink, for sure. He ran again, ankle throbbing, as fast as he could go. There wasn't a moment to waste. If the fire had gone out, they'd lose all the fruit unless he could get it working immediately.

He pressed his body against the icy cold and pounded toward the shed. He ducked his head to avoid low branches, used his lantern, as best he could, to guide him. He passed a shadowy figure . . . Madeline . . . passed another . . . Jenny . . . and she was shouting at him, but he kept going.

His wrenched ankle gave way and damned if he didn't end up on his face again. Dirt got into his nose and he left it there, scrambled to his feet, went at a running hobble for the shed, forgetting about the ankle.

For some reason the shed was dark. Not even the outside light was burning. He hit the door broadside to get in faster. The impact sent him flying backward.

He steadied himself, went back to the door, shone his lantern on it. There was a wooden bar holding it shut.

In one swipe he had the bar up, the door came open under his mighty yank, and the smell of fresh oil struck him.

Leak! he thought. Clogged line. There was a sudden gust of smoke; it blew into his face and he choked and coughed, but kept going.

It was then that something hard came down on his head and he felt himself crash onto the wooden floor. Just before he blacked out, he heard a door slam, and saw a blinding flash of light. Then there was nothing.

A shadow, blacker than the night, raced away. It lost itself in the trees, moved on silent feet.

Far behind, flames ate into the shed.

39

Where was Tom going in such a hurry, Jenny wondered. Then, irritated at her half-frozen brain, she knew. All the heaters in the grove must be cold. Which meant something was wrong with the central system and Tom was on his way to fix it.

Her impulse was to follow him, then she remembered her assigned task. The instant Tom got the oil flowing, sending heated air through the pipes and hoses, she'd have a tremendous responsibility, moving her heaters wisely, fighting to save the trees.

She heard someone running toward her, raised the lantern, tried to make out who it was. It might be Woodbury, and she could tell him Tom had gone to the shed.

But the figure which panted up was Madeline. "Oh, Jenny!" she cried. "My heaters don't work!"

"I know," Jenny said. "Mine don't either. Tom just ran past, making for the shed!"

"Oh, *my!*" whispered Madeline.

The whispered words snapped Jenny's control. She couldn't bear this inactivity, this not-knowing, another minute. What did Tom March know, anyway, about oil-fueled heaters? He'd go bursting into that shed like a bull into pasture. He might get hurt if he tried to fix the main fuel line or the tank or whatever it was, and try he would, of that she was sure.

"I'm going to the shed!" she cried. "Something's wrong, I know it is!"

"You can't, Jenny! You're needed here! And I'm needed at my post. I'm going back in a minute; I only wanted to be near you a bit! I got s-scared, it's so dark and cold, and now this!"

Now this indeed. Jenny knew in a flash that she should have gone after Tom, right on his heels. He wouldn't have stopped her, couldn't have spared the time to haul her back here.

She tightened her grip on her lantern. "I'm going!" she declared, and ignoring Madeline's pleas, began to run.

The frightened girl, not wanting to be left behind, ran after her. "Wait for me, Jenny," she shrieked.

They ran headlong, stumbling, half falling, lanterns swinging wildly. Madeline trailed behind, unable to catch up.

Jenny's breath began to stab. First in her chest, then in her side, and still she ran. Every pain spurred her on. Once she tripped and went into a falling run, then somehow righted herself and sped on.

Her ears were roaring. Through the roar she heard Madeline, closer now, and maybe someone else, but she couldn't stop to find out.

It was then she saw the blaze.

"My God " shouted someone—Woodbury, she thought. "The shed's on fire!"

Jenny poured on speed, dropping the lantern, for it only hampered her now. The flames standing along the end of the shed were beacon enough. She kept running, pain everywhere, worse with every hurting step.

She staggered past that flaming end to the doorway. *"Tom!"* she screamed, making for the door. "Get out of there! *Tom!"*

The door was closed and barred. She pushed the bar up, yanked open the door. A cloud of smoke belched out, choking her, and she went into strangled coughing.

She choked away the cough, turned her head, gulped in a deep breath, dropped to her stomach and began to wriggle across the floor. She didn't know whether Tom was in there or not, but had to find out. Behind her, someone else was creeping along. And from the outside were many voices, grove workers come to see what was wrong.

She caught a glimpse of the blazing fuel tank; there was a jagged, fiery hole in it. A figure lay dangerously close to the tank, motionless. The heat was intense; her face felt so hot it seemed ready to explode into flame. Instinctively, she closed her eyes, wriggled on.

Now she came up against that inert figure. She let out a drop of breath, opened her eyes, and looked. It was Tom—unconscious! Fire was eating at his coat sleeves. She beat it out with her arms, her gloved hands, the skirt of her heavy coat, killing the flames which were trying to devour him.

Letting out her last drop of breath, she laid her cheek on the hot floor, carefully breathed in the scraps of air remaining. Then, holding her breath, she got to her knees, hooked her arms under Tom's arms, staggered to her feet, and tried to drag him.

He was so heavy she couldn't budge him.

Woodbury pushed her aside, took over. Another man—Simon—crawled in and helped.

Coughing, they carried Tom out of the shed and laid him on the ground. When Jenny tried to push in, to give him artificial respiration, Simon shoved her aside and did it himself.

The entire crew—Woodbury's men, the Townsend group, Billings, the two migrants—all were there and busy. Rolf raced to call an ambulance. The grove crew and the migrants played hoses on the burning shed, but it was too late. Already it was a charred, standing skeleton, ready to collapse.

Frantic, Jenny pushed in to see if Tom was alive.

She was relieved when she heard him cough, saw him sit up, rubbing his head. All of them were coughing, the smoke not yet out of their lungs.

Jenny and Madeline began to examine Tom, using someone's lantern for light. His wrists were burned, and they wrapped handkerchiefs around them. His ankle was swelling; they had to take off his boot, and Jenny wound her scarf tightly around the ankle. His hair was singed, and he had a small burn on his forehead.

Finally, coughing, he noticed Jenny. She'd just finished bandaging his ankle. "W-what the hell you doing?" he sputtered.

"She saved your life, is all!" Madeline cried before Jenny could speak.

"You lifted me out . . . ?" He looked at her, amazed. "You—shouldn't have——"

"Mr. Woodbury and Simon carried you out!" Jenny retorted. All of a sudden, she was deeply angry at him. He'd had no business barging into that shed, getting himself burned. Then pretending to be worried about her! Oh, he didn't fool her for a minute! He was thinking about the baby! He didn't give a damn about her, otherwise!

"No need for words," Woodbury put in. "What matters is that nobody got hurt any worse. What happened, March?"

"My heaters all went cold. I figured the fuel line was clogged, so I came up to see. I found the door to the shed barred, and as I went in something hit me over the head. I saw the tank go up in flames, then blacked out. That's all I remember."

"No idea what hit you?"

"Could have been a timber from over the door."

"Maybe," Woodbury agreed, "but I still don't understand that tank blowing."

"It did look strong," Tom agreed.

"It was practically brand new."

"When I got here," Jenny cried, "the door——" She felt David's hand on hers, pressing warningly, and said no more.

"No way to save the crop, I reckon?" Tom asked.

"We'll try," Woodbury answered. "We'll get out the old smudge pots and see what we can do."

"The Townsends," David said now, "shun adverse publicity. If you agree, March, this will be reported as accidental."

"You mean, not investigate?" Woodbury gasped.

"How do we know anybody did it?" Oliver asked reasonably. "The tank could have blown by itself. It *could* have been a falling timber that hit March on the head. There were no witnesses. Nothing could be proved. Simon . . . ?"

"I quite agree. It's Townsend policy, and if you, March—"

"I ain't keen for publicity, either," Tom said.

Jenny, bewildered, listened to it all. She didn't agree, but maybe they were right. And though it had been a close call, nobody had been seriously hurt. She bit back the impulse to speak of the barred door.

"Then it's settled," Simon was saying, "we'll keep the matter to ourselves. And when the ambulance arrives, we'll call it an accident."

Tom was taken to the hospital despite his protests. The attendants lifted him, laid him on a cot and slid it into the ambulance.

On sudden impulse, Jenny crawled in beside him and sat with him all the way to the hospital.

She'd make sure he was well. Well enough to walk away from her and out of her life for good!

40

The hospital kept Tom overnight.

Jenny went home but got very little sleep. She kept thinking of how he had barged into the shed without a thought for his own safety. She was convinced it had been no accident. Someone had tried to kill him. But who? And why?

He was just plain lucky. Smoke inhalation hadn't done him any real harm, and he had suffered only minor burns. A sprained ankle was the worst of his injuries and he could walk on that, properly bandaged.

She called the hospital at seven in the morning. Tom March, she was informed, had checked himself out at six. The voice of the nurse was icy. She would give no information as to the gentleman's condition; he was no longer a patient.

Crossly, Jenny put down the phone. She'd go straight to the duplex on Taft Street, make sure the big fool was all right. Then she remembered the promise she'd made to herself. To keep Tom March out of her life. No, she'd not go to him. He'd just have to manage for himself.

She looked into Madeline's suite. Madeline wasn't home yet. Probably still with the others, helping to battle the frost with the smudge pots. She roamed the penthouse.

By eight o'clock, she had changed her mind. She told Flo where she was going, got into her car and sped to Taft Street. She'd just check to make sure he was all right, then come straight home.

March was up and dressed and making coffee. He set a place at the table for her in magnificent silence; he didn't even say good morning, and she was blasted if she'd speak first. So she remained quiet, even though she was bursting with the need to tell him now he'd been locked into the burning shed.

They were eating breakfast that way when the Townsends, Oliver, and Madeline showed up. They swarmed in on a gust of talk—they'd been to the hospital and found Tom gone, and come to see if he was all right. As they chattered, they stripped off their coats and hats.

"What about the grove?" Jenny asked eagerly. "Were you able to save it or not?"

"Woodbury says the fruit is ruined and some of the trees," Simon answered. "He'll replant as soon as he can, nurse all the other trees along."

Tom got out another frying pan, filled it with bacon. He got out a dozen eggs and started a second pot of coffee. "Damn shame," he mumbled.

"Sure is," said Rolf, sinking into a dining room chair. "Now a new heating building has to be built while the work on the bathhouses and campgrounds is in progress. We've decided it's to be of cement block. The old one was sturdy enough, but should have been replaced before now."

"We're installing the best heating system on the market," David added, speaking both to Jenny and Tom.

"Woodbury recommends new piping to the grove, new hoses and radiant heaters—everything new," Oliver said.

"Good," Tom replied just as Jenny herself was going to say the same. She glared at him, poised over the stove, flipping the eggs over in the frying pan with a flick of his wrist.

In no time at all, they were crowded round the breakfast table eating bacon and eggs and English muffins. Jenny had to admit, March was an excellent cook. She ate as hungrily as the others, the blustery cold having worked up her appetite.

Over coffee, Oliver brought into the open what was on all their minds. "The fire was no accident," he exclaimed. "I can't account for it, but I feel it was set deliberately."

"I *know* it was!" Jenny cried. "When I got to the shed, the door was bolted from the outside, with Tom inside and the fire burning! Someone tried to kill him! I tried to say this last night, but the rest of you—"

"Had trouble enough without accusations," David interrupted. "And we'd got Tom out safe."

"Then you *knew* the door was bolted?" Jenny whispered.

David gazed at her soberly. "I sensed that you were going to *say* it was bolted. And knew it was a matter to be discussed later—not then and there, on the scene."

"But who would want to do that to Tom?" Madeline asked, bewildered. "Do you suppose the migrants—?" She looked around the table, wide-eyed.

"The migrants have no reason to harm Tom," Oliver said. "He's their friend, trying to help them. They'd be the last ones."

"Could be," Tom drawled, "whoever it was just wanted the crop ruined. And me barging in like that, they bolted the door on the spur of the moment like."

"Which does make it sound like the work of the migrants," Simon offered. "Some of them would take pleasure in seeing a Townsend grove ruined—or anybody's grove, for that matter."

"They aren't vicious people," Rolf commented.

"Agreed!" exclaimed David. "Why, Vernon and Perez fought all night to save the trees! They're certainly in the clear! Besides, they and their buddies have nothing against Tom. If they were going to kill someone, they'd pick a Townsend."

"Unless," Tom said slowly, "there's one bad apple who wants to speed things up—and doesn't give a hang who gets caught in the rush."

That made them all thoughtful.

"It doesn't add up," Oliver said presently. "At the meeting, we offered to experiment with the building program by putting up three cottages at Orange Blossom. Vernon and Perez were to report that to the pickers at once, making it a solid offer. Such word spreads among them like wildfire, meaning they all knew about it last night. They'd not respond with murder and mayhem."

"You're right," Tom agreed. "Perez is the worst of the hotheads, but he worked right along with us all night. I don't believe that either he or Vernon would have locked me into the shed."

"Then what *do* you think?" Jenny demanded.

"It ain't impossible that it was meant as only . . . a warning like . . . and whoever set the fire panicked and locked me in."

Rolf said quietly, "I think it was deliberate."

"A murder attempt," Simon added.

"But who?" David asked. "That's the question—who?"

"I don't recommend going to the police," Oliver advised.

"But if it was an actual murder attempt," Rolf offered, "we *should* go to them."

David immediately spoke of the unsavory publicity that would draw to the Townsends. "If law officers go snooping around looking for a culprit, the migrants will jump to the conclusion that they're suspect, and we'll have still more trouble from them.

Jenny disagreed. "Even if there were no publicity, Vernon and Perez and the others would think we suspected them! So even if they're innocent, some of them may start trouble! One of them may try again to kill Tom . . . or one of you!"

But the others outvoted her. It was agreed, at least for the time being, to keep the matter from the press. In the meantime, they would keep close watch over the migrant situation, take any necessary precautions.

When the others left, Jenny remained behind. They had hardly closed the door when Tom began lecturing her.

"Why in hell's name did you come into that burning shed?" he roared. "You might have died of smoke inhalation! You might have killed my kid!"

"I was trying to save your life!" she screamed.

"But you risked my kid's life!"

"Hush about that!" she shouted, so angry she hardly knew what she was saying. "I have news for you! I'm going to sign away my money and live at Orange Blossom Grove and raise dogs and my baby!"

His dark eyes narrowed. "That kid's a Missourian, and he'll grow up on a Missoura farm. As for your ten million, I don't care what the hell you do with it! In fact, I order you to get rid of it!"

"Order?"

"I've got plenty of money. You're marrying me, and we're going to do the proper thing for my kid right down the line!"

"Marry!" she shrieked. "I wouldn't marry you for *any* reason! I wouldn't subject my child to——"

"My child!" he thundered. "Don't you ever lose sight of that! He's my kid, and all hell ain't going to keep him away from me! The time has come for you to simmer down and start to act like a proper ma! The time has come——"

She lost her head momentarily. She was so mad she couldn't speak, so she just fisted her hands, closed her eyes and screamed.

When she stopped screaming, she opened her eyes and he was staring at her.

"You have them fits often?"

"I never did such a thing before! Never!" she hissed. "You made me do it! You brought it on with your—your——"

"Get undressed."

She sucked in her breath, bored her eyes at him murderously.

"Or I'll do it for you."

And he would. He was just mean enough, strong enough, crazy enough. Inwardly raving, and only to keep him from doing it himself, she yanked off her clothes, flinging them across the room.

Naked, she flew at him, began tearing at his clothes. He'd thought he was going to subdue her with sex, take her as he usually did. Then afterward, he'd be able to manage her, charm her so she'd do anything he ordered her to do. Well, he had a big surprise coming. She was going to bed *him* this time—have her way with *him*.

She jumped onto the bed before he could throw her there. He stood looking her over and she reached up and pulled him down beside her. She felt her body go hot, felt the old passion flame inside of her. She would have him one last time, and then she would say good-bye for good.

He rolled over, got up from the bed. Then he stood looking down at her.

"Here," he ordered, handing her the silk blouse she'd tossed aside. "Get dressed. I ain't touching you again until my kid's legitimate."

"He'll never be legitimate!" she hissed. "I'll never marry you! I'd rather—"

She didn't finish her sentence. Instead, she sprang out of the bed, and dressed hurriedly. He paid her no attention, but put on his own clothes.

When they were fully clad, they stood facing each other. Neither one of them spoke a word. Then Jenny broke the silence.

"I hope," she told him icily, "that things are clear in your mind. You've . . . taken me . . . over and over. But the end is here. I've won. I'll never be alone with you again."

"I get the message," he replied. "Only you've made a mistake."

She shot him an angry look. How cocksure he was! Ordering her around. Dress . . . undress . . . dress.

"You see," he continued, "you ain't the winner. I'm giving you one week to get that through your head. One week from today, we marry."

In a rage, she stormed out of the house, into her car, and roared away. One week, was it? Okay, that gave her time to keep her word to Madeline and go on the three-day cruise. They'd be leaving tomorrow as planned, for now that the sun was well up, the air was warm. Tomorrow was expected to be even warmer, and soon it would be as if the freeze had never clamped down on them.

After the cruise, she'd fly to Cap D'Antibes, in the south of France. Si, who'd owned a villa there, had told her it was the most beautiful place in the world.

She'd rent a villa there and stay until July when her baby would be born. Then, with Tom back in Missouri where he belonged, she'd go to Orange Blossom Grove to live.

It was as simple as that.

41

David put off the cruise one day, partly so the Townsends could meet with Vernon and Perez, partly to give the weather time to get back to normal. The meeting, which Tom March and his two representatives attended and Jenny did not, resulted in acceptance of the trial cottages. Perez, however, made it clear that they expected more definite action, and promptly. They promised to pick Townsend Groves and Louisa Groves, which had barely escaped ruin, at once.

"There are dozens of pickers," Vernon was reported to have said, "hungry and ready to work. They'll do a clean job, strip every tree, now that they feel something may be done for *them.*"

After the meeting, David phoned Jenny and asked if they could all meet that evening in the penthouse to discuss the cruise. She consented.

March was the first to arrive, leaving Jenny dumbfounded. She'd been certain David wouldn't invite him on the cruise. He'd probably felt sorry for him, after the grove incident. Well, this would be the last time she'd have to endure him. After the cruise, she'd be on her own.

They gathered in the living room, chattering excitedly, waiting for David to speak. Jenny sat next to him, as far from March as possible. She was glad she'd worn her brightest green dress, since she knew he preferred her in paler colors.

"There'll be ten of us on the cruise," David began. "The ten of us here. Is Freeport okay as our destination, or do you prefer Nassau?"

"David-honey," cooed Sara Donahue, cuddling closer to him, "you're the *host!* You've been talking all along of going to Freeport, so that's where we should go!"

"Sara's right!" squealed Lila Stevens, sitting on the carpet at Rolf's feet. "Who cares, anyhow? Just so we get to *sail!* Fine as *The Louisa* was to begin with, I'll bet now she's as luxurious as Jackie O's boat was when she was married!"

David laughed. "Well, not *that* fine," he said. "But she'll do—she's a beauty!"

They all agreed excitedly that Freeport must be their destination. Jenny said nothing. She'd been to both Nassau and Freeport with Si many times. It made no difference to her where they went. She just wanted to get the cruise behind her so she could fly to Europe.

"Seems like," March put in, "I'd best not go along. For several reasons."

"Not at all," David said, his voice sincere. "I really *want* you to come!"

"But the pickers—" Tom began.

"We'll only be gone two nights," David said. "The pickers will have their hands full with the two groves."

"David's right!" Madeline declared. "Tom, you *have* to come! After all, you were kind enough to have us to Missouri!"

"That's right," Rolf agreed. "We owe you hospitality."

Tom thought of Thanksgiving weekend, the abrupt way it had ended. He didn't want to go, didn't want them to feel obligated to him.

But in the end he agreed, mostly because he hoped

he might have more time to discuss the migrant situation with them. He might do the men more good by going, than by remaining behind.

David talked more about the cruise, told them what clothing to bring. "Remember soft-soled shoes are a must!" he cautioned.

When he had finished speaking, Madeline took the floor. "Oliver and I have an announcement to make," she cooed, holding up her diamond for all to see. "We're going to be married!"

All gathered round, the girls exclaiming over the size and brilliance of the diamond, the men congratulating Oliver. Simon offered his congratuations quietly and in a sincere tone.

Lila squealed in delight, urging Rolf to see how big the diamond was. "Let's call it an engagement cruise!" she chortled.

David agreed, and the others smiled and nodded.

Rolf turned on the stereo and Madeline went into Oliver's arms for the first dance. The others moved onto the parquet floor at the end of the room, while Jenny remained near the stereo.

She noted the wistful looks on the faces of Sara and Lila, wondered if David and Rolf would ever propose to them. Suddenly she was aware that Tom March was standing beside her.

"It'll look queer to them," he told her, "if we don't dance our one time."

"Your ankle—"

"I can manage. If we take it slow."

He opened his arms. Irritated, and only to keep him from making a spectacle, she went into them, and they began to dance slowly indeed. Fortunately the music was slow too. She could feel his body warmth, remember it from times in bed. There was a deep, faraway ache rising within her and she fought to ignore it.

He made a slow, sweeping turn, graceful despite his sore ankle, and she followed. It was as if their bodies were welded together. For one instant, replete with music and movement, a new, unsettling thought struck her.

She hated March, truly hated him. *But could hatred*

and love be one and the same? And if so, did that mean, was it possible, that she loved him? She thought of their battles, remembered the rough way he'd treated her, and realized immediately how foolish the question was.

She danced with him no more.

At dawn they drove to the Miami port and boarded *The Louisa*. The day promised to be warm and sunny, and all the girls were dressed in slacks and lightweight halter tops. Jenny's outfit was powder green; her hair, tied back with a matching green scarf, tumbled down her back. The men were all in white with brimmed yachtman's caps. The whole group was bright and cheery.

Except for Tom March. Unlike the others, he was quiet and sat apart from the rest of them. He nodded to Jenny once, then ignored her, his eyes on boats and water and sky.

The Louisa had been newly painted a beautiful, sparkling white, and trimmed with the indigo blue of the Gulf Stream. The deck furniture was also new and matched the blue trim. Even the swimming pool looked as if it had been painted to match the blue of the sky.

"My gracious!" exclaimed Lila, standing on the deck, gazing at everything. "How *big* she is, and so many crew membahs ev'rywhere! And all in white! This is practically an ocean linah! Tell us about her, David!"

David's face was at its sunniest. Jenny had never seen him look so happy.

"All you need to know," he answered, grinning, "is that she's 188 feet long, carries a crew of twelve, counting the chef, and has twelve double staterooms, each with bath."

"My goodness! A crew of twelve for ten people!"

"And a private suite for each guest," David said. "Later on, after the racing season, I'll take her on a real cruise—down to Aruba, on to South America . . . back among the islands."

"I hope we're all invited!" exclaimed Sara shamelessly.

"You be a good girl and not get seasick this time," David assured her, "and your chances will be good."

The bar pilot, who had come aboard, took the yacht out of the harbor to where she could sail on her own, then climbed down the nylon rope ladder into the small boat which had followed to take him back.

Jenny stood at the polished brass rail and let the breeze blow against her face. Her stomach felt a bit unsettled, and she knew it must be morning sickness. She'd cruised many times with Si, and had never been seasick. Si had been so proud of that.

She stroked the rail, thinking how much lovelier *The Louisa* looked now. She smiled. It wouldn't surprise her if David lived on board, at least part of the time, so crazy was he about the yacht.

She turned, looked back at the port. There were many crafts anchored there, some of them big yachts, some great, ocean-going freighters, others cruise ships. Steaming along the ocean were other vessels, many of them fishing boats, toys of the affluent.

She'd seen all this so many times. Now she gazed out to where the Gulf Stream, that great ocean river, ran its broad, deep blue ribbon through the lime green waters of the Atlantic.

David and Sara, Rolf and Lila, joined her.

"You're not at the wheel, David?" Jenny asked, surprised.

"Later. For now I just want to wander my boat and feel her move under my feet, with no responsibility. I have a captain . . . mustn't shove him aside too much."

"Tell about the Gulf Stream, David!" Lila urged.

"Well, it's the second largest ocean current in the world," David said. "It begins in the Gulf of Mexico, where the waters are warm, passes through the straits of Florida, and flows northeast across the Atlantic toward Europe."

"Ooh, it must be awfully big!"

"About fifty miles wide and three thousand feet deep in places. It's actually one of the wonders of the world. It flows as fast as 138 miles a day in spots, a thousand times faster than the Mississippi River. Four miles an hour in other spots."

"Where'd you learn all this?" asked Sara.

"From Grandfather. He knew all about these waters. Used to tell us how the Gulf Stream was an aid to shipping. Great oil tankers and ore carriers traveling from South American to Atlantic coastal harbors 'ride' the Stream north."

"Will *we* ride the Stream?" Sara asked.

"No. We cross it on the way to Freeport, cross it on the way back. It's only about a mile and a half from the Florida coast at this point. If you wish, we'll lower buckets and pull up some of the water so you can feel how much warmer it is than ocean water."

"Why not anchor and go swimming in it?" cried Lila.

"It's too deep to anchor in," David explained. "It takes an anchor line more than half a mile long and stout enough so it won't break, regardless of how hard the boat pulls as it climbs the crest of a wave and plunges down into the trough."

"Can't you lower the launches so we can be right in the Stream?" persisted Lila.

"Sorry."

"Not both of them, David! Just the little one?"

David grinned and shook his head. Lila pouted, then brightened again when he suggested they have a look at the staterooms to which they'd been assigned.

Jenny had been placed in the master suite, which she had always occupied with Si. She hardly recognized it. The teakwood walls and built-in furniture had been refinished, and gleamed more richly than even before. The twin beds were covered with scarlet quilted satin and there were scarlet satin curtains at the porthole windows.

The sitting room matched the stateroom. The teakwood walls gleamed, as did the built-in bookcases and tiny, rolltop desk. The same books filled the shelves. But the formerly pale green sofa was scarlet velvet, the curtains a scarlet and white floral print. The coffee table was glass-topped and had sparkling brass legs bolted to the deck floor. All ornaments, including two oversized reading lamps, were of brass.

The tiny adjoining bathroom was white with scarlet

accessories. Gold fittings glittered against the brilliant red of tub and wash basin. Even the towel rods were made of gold.

"Look at this big hook on the back of the door!" gasped Madeline, who had come along with Jenny. "It's gold, too!"

"The bathroom fittings have always been gold," Jenny replied. "They're about the only things that haven't been changed."

Together they went to Madeline's suite. It was similar to Jenny's, except the colors were Gulf Stream blue and white.

"David's really gone wild with color!" Madeline exclaimed. "But I don't mind—it's bright and cheerful! It can almost outdo the sea and sun and the Gulf Stream itself!"

Jenny smiled. She didn't mind the changes David had made. In fact, she was glad *The Louisa* had taken on a different look. Otherwise, there might have been too many reminders of the past.

And Si, too, would have approved of David's refurbishing of the *Louisa*. He loved change, believed it necessary. Hadn't he urged her to remarry as soon as possible? He'd wanted her to have a new life without him. He'd have felt the same about *The Louisa*.

But what about her, Jenny? Would Si have been disappointed in her? Certainly, she had not carried out the details of his plan. But the pregnancy hadn't been counted on. He would have wanted her to do the best for her child. And the best, she was convinced, was to get away, far away, until it was safe to return. Until Tom March was back in Missouri and she could resume her life at Orange Blossom Grove.

On sudden impulse she asked Madeline a question which had been nagging at her since this morning. "I wonder," she said, speaking slowly, "if any of the other girls suspect I'm pregnant?"

"Of course not!" Madeline declared. "You don't show yet—in fact, you've gotten a bit thin—and none of the men would tell!"

"I know," murmured Jenny thankfully. For they wouldn't. Not even Tom. He'd think it was none of their business. Just his own.

When they tied up at Freeport, they went through customs. Then, each carrying a small bag of evening wear, they taxied, driven by a black Bahamian, to King's Inn, the big hotel across the street from the beautiful casino and the International Bazaar. They each took a suite at King's Inn for the day and hung up the garments they would wear that evening. After gambling, they'd taxi back to *The Louisa* and sleep aboard.

They lunched beside the hotel pool and later went, all together, to explore the International Bazaar. This was a large area laid out in tiny streets lined with shops representing various countries. The French, English, Japanese, Norwegian and other sections were connected by narrow foot passages, some cobblestoned.

In and out of tiny shops, weaving through the sightseeing crowds, they went. The girls bought French perfume and, across from the perfumery, purchased frothy, exquisite French lingerie. They wandered through a fabulous china shop filled with tableware and art objects, into others, where they saw beautiful things made of polished wood—everything from bookends to inlaid cabinets and chests.

They lingered in a jewelry shop where Jenny, resistance a thing of the past, paid two thousand dollars for a triple strand of pearls with a pearl clasp. The jeweler remembered her from former trips to his shop with Si and was delighted to at last make a sale to her.

Oliver bought Madeline an emerald dinner ring; David bought Sara a heavy gold necklace, and Rolf waited patiently while Lila ohed and ahed and finally selected an ornate, eighteen-carat gold bangle bracelet.

Even Tom March bought a gold locket, saying it was for his ma. Jenny wondered fiercely if it was for Sally Meharg; then, remembering that she'd never caught Tom in a lie, believed him.

They wandered out of the Bazaar, the blue and white Bahama sky bathing them with sun and soft, warm breeze. They passed the fountain in front of the casino, strolled along plantings of flowering red hibiscus bushes, past hedges of Florida cherry, and back to King's Inn to dress for the evening.

Jenny wore her gold dress and the pearls. They glowed against her skin, lustrous against the flaming dress. Loving the pearls, loving the gown almost as well, she helped Madeline with the zipper of her brilliant silver gown, and they were ready.

When they came into the lobby, heads turned. They were by far the most elegant women there. Only Tom seemed disapproving. He gave Jenny one keen look, then turned away. That was all right with her. He didn't approve of anything but migrants, anyway.

They ate at the Japanese Steak House, sitting on low benches, a combination slab table and stove above their laps. Japanese girls, wearing native costume, broiled cubes of steak and exotic vegetables as they watched. They ate heartily and sipped sake, a heady rice wine.

Jenny was feeling a bit high when they left the restaurant, walked past the splashing fountain and into the great, plush casino.

The hum of hundreds of voices filled the gambling hall, and from everywhere came the sound of slot machines and the song of spinning roulette wheels.

The casino employees, men in proper black attire, were at their posts. There were shift bosses, pit bosses, floorwalkers, dealers, croupiers—all intent on the play. There were also cocktail waitresses bearing their small trays of drinks. And, on top of the employees, there were hundreds of gamblers, all richly dressed, the women on the arms of their men, who were hovering over the tables.

Players lined the dice tables, where the stickmen called out the numbers after the dice rolled. The blackjack tables were filled to capacity, the chuck-a-luck wheel was surrounded five deep, and every table in the roulette pit was filled, with players standing two deep behind the few who were seated.

Madeline went straight for the roulette tables, Oliver following. Jenny trailed them, aware that Tom was ambling along after her. The others split off to the dice tables.

The four at roulette bought chips. Jenny got one hundred dollars worth, a dollar per chip, meaning to hold herself to that amount. Oliver bought two hundred dollars worth and divided with Madeline. Tom bought twenty-five dollars worth. Jenny was surprised he bought any chips at all, since she didn't think him the gambling type.

The wheel clicked to a stop. "Seven!" called out the croupier, and began to rake in all the chips on the table that weren't on the number seven. A second croupier stacked the chips, fingers like lightning, as the other one swiftly pushed extra chips toward the winners.

Recklessly, Jenny stacked five chips on the number six. Then she split the zero–double–zero at the top of the table by placing another five chips on the line which divided them. All the players were setting out their chips fast, leaning across the table to reach a number, or having the croupier place the chips for them.

Now the croupier spun the wheel. It went fast, the little ivory ball jumping and dancing from number to number until it stopped. The ball lay in the number seventeen slot.

Again Jenny played the six. She'd won the Daily Double with six and six. This was her lucky number. She noticed that Tom was conservative, playing one chip at a time. He'd not win much that way, she thought to herself, but hadn't the desire to tell him.

When Jenny was down to her last ten chips, the wheel finally stopped on six. She had five one-dollar chips on the number, which paid thirty-five dollars for each dollar bet. Glowing, she collected one hundred seventy-five dollars. March, who had been increasing his bet, had ventured his last chip on this spin.

"I'm wiped out," he said.

"Buy more chips!" Madeline urged.

"No sense to it," he replied.

"Here come the others," said Oliver. "Let's see what they want to do next."

"The floor show!" Lila bubbled as they came up.

"It's time for it to begin! I lost two hundred dollars, and Rolf won't buy me any more chips!"

"I lost too," Rolf grinned. "David and Sara won ten dollars each. We'd better watch the show, then call it a night. We can play again tomorrow before we sail. The casino opens at seven in the morning."

They went to a cashier's window, where Jenny, David and Sara cashed in their chips. Then they walked through the slim metal strands that formed a curtain between showroom and casino and sat at tiny cocktail tables, waiting for the show to begin.

It was the midnight show, featuring topless dancers, and it held them in rapt attention. The final number, the one just before the grand finale, involved a slight, fair man, nude except for a tight clout, and an almost completely nude girl who was so thin every rib stood out. Neither was particularly attractive, but their act was sensational, consisting of various poses in which the man held the girl aloft, handling her as if she were light as a feather. Every time they achieved a new pose, they held it for a moment, resembling a work of sculpture.

"No wonder she's so thin," Madeline whispered. "If she weighed another ounce, he'd never be able to hold her!"

The show ended. They went back to the casino, which was somewhat less crowded, played the slot machines, which Tom called one-armed bandits and refused to play, and then returned to King's Inn to pick up their luggage.

Jenny's head had cleared, the effects of the sake gone, and she was both aggravated and mollified that Tom walked beside her. He spoke not a word to her, just walked in silence, all the way to the hotel.

He remained moodily silent in the taxi that brought them back to *The Louisa*.

And after they'd boarded, he walked to his stateroom without so much as saying good night.

42

The next morning they taxied in and played tennis on the hotel courts. Jenny was surprised that Tom was such a good player. She'd always thought of him as a muscular outdoorsman, and was surprised he'd taken the time to master what was essentially an upper-class sport. Sitting alongside the courts, she watched him play, noting that his serve was stronger, more accurate that Simon's.

In the afternoon they gambled, and this time, every one of them lost. They ate dinner in the Rib Room at King's Inn, savoring the incomparable onion soup and Caesar salad. It was ten o'clock when they returned to *The Louisa.*

They sailed at once. There was a three-quarter moon, a sky filled with stars. Jenny walked the deck, feeling the gentle motion of the boat. It was like something alive under her feet.

The others sat on deck, gazing at the moon shining on the water, loath to go to bed and leave the beauty of the ocean. Lila, Sara and Barbara lamented that they had to go home so soon, and badgered David to promise them a cruise to Nassau next month without fail.

Jenny rejoined the others, sat with them for awhile, then excused herself and went to her stateroom. It had been a lovely cruise, but she was glad they were returning tomorrow. She was anxious to get home and make arrangements to fly to Europe. She'd leave America in three days, at the most. She'd have gone sooner, were it not for her greyhounds. Kolaka was running in a stakes race tomorrow night and Ebon Sue and Armand were running in the first and second races the following night. They'd done so well in their schooling, that it was just possible she'd bring in another Daily Double.

Lying nude in bed, she considered staying in Florida until the racing season ended. But that would be too late. No, she was going to put herself out of March's reach. For good. Besides, by the time the racing season ended, she'd be showing, and though she wasn't really ashamed of her condition, she didn't want to flaunt it either.

She tried to sleep, but couldn't. She heard the others call good-nights. After that, the yacht grew very quiet. There was only the rush of water against the hull, the slide and dip of the vessel as it climbed a wave, plunged down into the trough, glided, climbed another wave.

She switched on the lamp by her bed and looked at her watch. Nearly 2:00 A.M. Maybe a bath would make her sleepy—better yet, a dip in the pool. She'd exercise until she was tired, then go right off to sleep.

She got into her bikini, and beach coat and towel in hand, made her way silently along the corridor, up the companionway, and across the lower deck to the pool. The lights had been turned off, leaving it shimmering darkly under the night sky.

She went toward the pool feeling blessedly alone in the world. And at peace. Then she glimpsed movement between herself and the wheelhouse and stood for a moment, breathless. It could have been the captain leaving the wheel to check on something. Or one of the men, who, discovering Jenny up and about, would no doubt join her, perhaps waking the others for a late swim.

She waited. The movement wasn't repeated. Still she

watched. If someone was spying on her——! There! It came again, and she saw what it was. A shadow cast by the light of the moon, a shadow which moved because the yacht was moving. She breathed a sigh of relief.

Walking to the pool, she dropped coat and towel on a deck chair, then went down the small ladder into the dark, cool water. She didn't dive in as she would have liked to do, because she wanted to make no sound.

She swam the length of the pool as silently, as effortlessly, as a fish. She swam back and forth several times, enjoying the feel of the cool water. Then, silently, she dived to the bottom, moved the length of the pool underwater. She came up smoothly, water streaming off her hair, down her face and shoulders and back.

She wasn't tired yet, so she kept on. The wind grew stronger. She held her face to it, enjoyed its definite nip, felt her worries fade with every stroke.

She swam and swam. At last, short of breath, she climbed out of the pool, feeling heavily and blessedly weary. She dried herself, then wrapped herself in the beach coat, shivering slightly in the chill of the night air.

Then, feeling utterly peaceful, she lay on the chaise lounge, face to the sky, and drank in the night. She swept her gaze across the stars, making out the constellations, the piece of yellow moon. Once she sat up and looked out at the shimmering, black ocean. They were crossing the Gulf Stream about now, she estimated. She determined to stay up all night, watch *The Louisa* go into her berth, then get into bed and sleep.

She lay flat again, searched the stars. She listened to the ocean river surge along the hull. She let the peace and the wind, filled with salt smell, drift over her. She thought sleepily of the Gulf Stream all around her, and how its waters were warmer and saltier than those of the Atlantic and, by day, bluer.

She grew sleepier, heavier, knew she should go to her stateroom, but did not. She drifted into sleep the way the boat slid along the waves, and let herself go.

It was then that out of nowhere hands lifted her, carried her—two pairs of hands—and sent her flying through the wind. And then, suddenly, she was falling, forever falling, smacking the water below so hard it knocked her breath away and she sank.

She swallowed salt water. Instinctively, she held what breath she had, kicking fast, making for the surface. Something hindered her—the coat, the beach coat, sodden and dragging. She kicked on, arms above her head, hands together, forming an arrow.

She broke surface, gulped air. She was in a long trough of water. Behind her a wave was cresting; any second it would crash down on her. She gulped air again, treading water frantically, working to rid herself of the heavy coat.

The wave came hurtling at her. Just in time, she abandoned the struggle with the coat, threw herself face down, and let the wave take her, bear her swiftly to its crest, then into the next trough. Treading water, remembering that the water was more than three hundred feet deep here, she worked doggedly to rid herself of the coat.

One arm was free when the next wave grabbed her, and in the next trough, gasping aloud as she gulped in air and let it out, she rid herself of the other sleeve. She watched, thankful, as the Gulf Stream swept the garment away.

Another wave was upon her. This time, she hadn't been able to draw in any reserve air. The water struck broadside when her lungs were empty, and she was borne to the top, rolled into the next trough.

Her lungs were bursting. When she opened her mouth for air, the coldness made her lungs worse. And the water was so warm, too warm. Now she felt the tug of the current, pulling her northward.

She began to swim, trying to buck the current. But it was no use. Wave after wave helped the Gulf Stream, forced her to swim crosswise when she could swim at all. Another wave inundated her, took her where it pleased, and she fought against it, struggling to stay afloat.

She was under again, the water surged, but she clawed to the surface, gulping for air. She didn't know where the yacht was, but she tried now to pursue it, knowing its course angled across the Gulf Stream ... or did its course let it ride the current north until at a certain point the captain steered directly west to land? Was she in the yacht's wake, or was that it over yonder? Could she catch up with it, even keep behind it until she was missed?

But she wouldn't be missed. They were all asleep.

Except the ones who had thrown her overboard.

She swam powerfully now, between waves, keeping, as best she could, on course. In this manner she might, just might, catch up to *The Louisa*.

Fighting the waves, swimming against the current, battling for every drop of air, a thought pierced her mind.

Once she was out of the Gulf Stream she'd be only a mile and a half out from the Miami port. She could swim that far. Of course she could! She had to!

Unless the captain had seen her thrown overboard. But then they would have already lowered a launch to come after her. And they hadn't.

She was on her own.

The only thing she could do was swim.

43

Tom hadn't slept a damn wink, and it was after three-thirty in the morning. He lay on his bed until he couldn't stand it another minute. Then he got up, slung an oversized bath towel over one of the green velvet chairs in his sitting room, and plopped onto it, stark naked.

That damned, stubborn little wildcat! What kind of power did she have over him, anyhow? He'd bedded her he didn't know how many times, had got her pregnant with his kid, and still, this minute, he was ready—burning —to bed her again.

He'd tried to stay away from her. Having given her the one-week deadline, he'd tried to let her alone so she could come to her senses.

Why he was so set on marrying her when she riled him so, he couldn't quite figure out. She needed a pa for his kid. That was one fact. She needed taming, that was another fact. She sure wasn't a lallygagger like the girls back home, Sally Meharg, for instance; though which was worse, a lallygagger or a wildcat, he didn't know.

Anyhow, she wasn't so sugar-sweet she made a man sick to his stomach. She was also smart, maybe too smart. No, that couldn't be. If she was born smart, she had a right to it, like she had a right to that red hair.

He lit up a cigarette, biting off puffs of smoke. If she was so smart, she didn't need a week. He wasn't going to give it to her, either. On this whole voyage, he'd stayed away from her, let her have her way.

Now he was going to change all that.

He stubbed out his cigarette, struggled into swim trunks. They'd hardly go on, he was so ready. After he had her this time, he'd somehow get a promise out of her to marry him.

Barefoot, he padded out of his stateroom, noiselessly closed the door, and soft-footed down the aisle to her suite. He didn't knock. Pushing the door open, he went right in.

But she wasn't there. A lamp was on in the state-room, and the bedcovers had been turned back. The bathroom door was open, swinging freely with the motion of the boat, so he flicked on the light and looked in. She wasn't in there, either.

He sat down in the darkened sitting room and thought for a minute. Where could she be at this hour of the night? The answer dawned on him like lightning—the swimming pool! She was just wild enough to get out of bed and go swimming by herself in the middle of the night.

He moved swiftly to the companionway, walked as quietly as possible toward the pool. He didn't want to be heard, though she was sure to raise hell when he tried to get her to go back to her stateroom with him.

He'd try to surprise her. On tiptoe, he moved toward the pool. The water was still. Not a sign of her anywhere.

Moving fast now, he made the rounds of both decks. Perhaps she was lounging in a deck chair, looking out at the ocean. It would be just like her to do a fool thing like that at this time of night.

She wasn't on the deck.

He was growing alarmed. And angry. He'd give her hell when he found her! Then he thought of Madeline. Sure. She'd probably decided to spend the night in Madeline's stateroom.

He knocked twice on Madeline's door before she answered, sleepy-eyed in a lacy white nightgown.

"Tom! What is it?" she asked. "Is it morning?"

"Jenny in here?" he demanded.

She shook her head.

"She with one of the other girls?"

"Not that I know of."

"We'll check them, check every suite!" He turned, hurried to the next stateroom.

"Why?" Madeline called after him. "What's wrong?"

"She's missing!" he threw back. "We've got to find her!"

She wasn't in Lila's room, or Sara's or Barbara's. The Townsends and Oliver, roused by the hammering on doors, the loud voices, all appeared. None of them had seen Jenny.

"Rouse the crew!" Tom yelled at David. "Search the ship!"

In five minutes, *The Louisa* was alive with movement. The passengers, the crew of twelve, including the captain and the chef, searched everywhere. Every suite, the lounge, the galley, the decks, belowdecks.

A crewman found the ship's ladder dangling at the stern, disappearing into the water. "Maybe she went into the Stream for a swim!" he said wonderingly.

"She wouldn't!" Madeline cried.

"Man overboard!" shouted David. "Lower the launches!"

"Drop anchor!" roared Tom.

"Water's too deep!" David yelled. "Captain, cut the motors! Let her ride with the current!"

"That'll take us away from her!" yelled Tom. "God knows where she is!"

"Depends on where she went in," David said. "We have a chance, with the launches!"

Tom, in swim shorts, the others in their bed clothes,

took their places in the boats. Rolf took charge of the small boat, two of the crew with him. "We'll head south, back toward Freeport!" he shouted.

David commanded the big launch. Tom and Simon and a crewman piled in with him. "We'll go toward land!" David yelled. "If she tries to swim, the current'll carry her that way, and also north!"

"She'll swim!" Tom bellowed. "She'll swim with all her might!"

The launches bobbed in the rough water. The big one, which Tom was in, might have been a cork, the way it was buffeted about. David turned on the powerful searchlights, roared the motor, and moved away from the yacht into the watery, perilous blackness where a girl, alone and at the mercy of the Gulf Stream, was fighting desperately for her life.

Tom searched the billows, prayed that she would have the strength to fight them.

44

She had to rest. Had to. The water was tiring her out, sapping her energy. Her arms, heavier than lead, would not, could not move again. Or her legs. Not now. They must rest for a few strokes, only she couldn't rest.

Sucking in air, hoarding it, letting it out sparingly, she relaxed her body as a wave seized it, bore it up, rolled it down the other side into the trough.

Then she stroked again with her dragging arms, kept her legs going, struggled crosswise of the tide, arms reaching out in front of her, never to the side, conserving effort, making all possible use of the comparative smoothness before the next wall of water grabbed her. She had to get out of this Stream, had to get her baby out, guard his sweet, unborn little self, battle for his right to be born, to live.

She had to get out, for his sake.

But all she had to battle this awful power of nature was her body. And it was unprepared for the challenge. Even her long nighttime swims from her beach to Tom's had not prepared her for the churning waters of the Gulf Stream.

But she had one thing that was stronger than any ocean—the will to live.

She kept on—swimming, lifting an arm laboriously, pulling it forcefully back through the water of the trough, lifting the other arm. Pulling, always pulling, legs working, progressing, inch by inch.

Another towering wave. She'd let it take her. Then, the next trough, she'd rest, not swim at all, only tread water, arms outstretched from her sides. And she'd breathe, draw in one blessed lungful of air after another until she was filled with air, saturated with it.

While doing this, she would let the Stream carry her north, not even think about sharks. She needed to go slightly north anyway, to bring her on a parallel with Miami or Hollywood.

She'd rest just the width of one smooth trough, however wide that was. Then she'd give herself to the oncoming wave, and when it let go and she was in another trough, she'd swim. She'd have the strength, then, for deliberate, powerful strokes, proving to the current that she would, after all, make headway toward land.

She grabbed a deep breath, held it. If only she could keep her eyes open! But it was no use trying; the salt got into them and stung and then she couldn't see anyway.

The wave had her now. It submerged her, swept her northward, spun her down its far side into the trough.

She did what she'd planned. There was so little time, but she tread water, gulped breath after refreshing breath, the current sweeping her along. She was riding it now, deliberately, the way heavy-laden ships rode it.

Too soon, she was in the boisterous arms of another wave, holding her breath, letting it out in drops. This time, she was flung underwater in the trough and had to fight her way to the surface.

Swim! panic shouted. Rest! her body demanded. Breathe. Wait for the next trough, rest again.

Doggedly, because it was all she could do, she tread water. This time she breathed slowly and calmly, sending air all through her body and it seemed, almost, to buoy her up.

Like this, she waited for the next wave, relaxed into it and at its bottom drew in one quick, deep breath and swam, pulling strongly to the left, toward land.

Methodically, endlessly, she followed her pattern. Swim. Ride. Rest. Pain shot through her tired body, but she carried on, determined to reach land. She had no way of telling whether she was making progress. All she could do was endure the waves, the pain, stroke on.

She had no moment for prayer, but was herself a struggling, wave-tossed, frantically swimming prayer.

The water seemed thicker now. Stroking hard to the left, she tried again to think. Surely she was making progress and would eventually be out of the Stream. From there she'd have only the mile and a half to shore. She could swim that, oh, she could! But first she had to get out of the Stream.

Oh, why hadn't she married Tom? She loved him so. She was sure of that now. She loved him and she wanted him. She'd found the right man, the perfect man, and hadn't had the sense to know until now, when she knew she might never see him again.

But she had to see him. She must, if only to tell him that she loved him. Loved him with all her heart and soul. Loved his bossiness, his strength—his gentleness, for he was, at the core, soft and gentle. She knew that now. Just as she knew he was her man, her mate, and she was going to get herself and their baby out of this treacherous Gulf Stream, and tell him so!

She swam harder—surely it was harder, because it hurt more, deep in her loins, all through her body.

She was tired, too tired. And the pain gripped her. But that didn't matter.

All that mattered was that she reach Tom—and declare her love.

45

The launch crested a wave and rode into the trough. Tom peered keenly where the searchlight reached, strained to see beyond.

"Faster!" he yelled at David, who was steering.

"Not in this sea!" Simon yelled.

"Too much speed is bad," the crewman said. "We might miss her."

"What about the course?" Tom asked for what seemed the tenth time. "Seems we're going north, not east!"

"The current, you fool!" David shouted. "It'll carry her north! Rolf's the one who'll probably find her! Going south, against the current, he'll find her behind *The Louisa* somewhere, being swept north!"

"No, damn it all!" Tom yelled hoarsely. "She'll make for land! She's a good swimmer! She'll make for Miami or Hollywood!"

"If that's what she's doing, she's not doing much thinking!" shouted Simon. He held onto the launch as it rode another wave.

Tom searched into the lighted distance, the darkness beyond. He heard the sound of the water, the crash and surge of the waves against the launch.

Jenny was somewhere out there. He was going to find her, get her into the boat, never let her out of his sight again.

"This course is taking us too far north!" he bellowed. "We're north of the yacht now!"

"So is she!" Simon yelled. "This is fast water!"

"She's making for land, damn you! Change course, damn it to hell, and change now!"

"That means we turn, go south against the current!" screamed David. "Rolf's doing that!"

"We're north of Rolf!" bellowed Tom. "Do it, damn you! It's our only chance of finding her!"

"Do what he says!" Simon shouted. "Let him have his way!"

Slowly, the launch began to fight its way to port. Tom pierced the leaping waters as far as the searchlight reached, strained, as always, to see beyond. All it would take was a white flash of arm, and he'd know. He'd have his darling, pull her onto the launch, take her to safety.

"Jenny!" he thundered into the night. *"Jenny!"*

There was only the rush of water, the leap and dip and roll of the launch. The beam from the searchlight bobbed over the waves. Tom's eyeballs ached and he scarcely felt it, stared harder into the lighted, watery expanse, into the unlighted unknown.

Jenny was the only girl in the world who'd ever meant anything to him. She was fire and pride and guts in one beautiful package. She was passionate, proud. And, oh, how he loved her. Ached for her. She *had* to be alive.

He yelled her name. The others yelled. They listened. The four of them together bellowed her name. David steered, played the searchlight.

There was nothing. Only the searchlight, and that showed nothing but dark, churning water. And the blackness beyond.

Tom gritted his teeth. Pain shot through his jaw, into his neck. His idea to get Jenny pregnant so she'd marry him hadn't worked. He'd find her and explain, had to.

Had to confess how he'd loved her on sight, loved her from the very beginning. It had taken him awhile, but finally he could admit that it was love that had pushed him into everything he'd done, every fight he'd picked with her. But first he had to find his girl and his kid and pull them out of the water.

"We're on course!" David called. "South by southeast! You've got your way, March!"

Simon, on the port side, Tom at starboard, the crewman in the stern, combed the water with their eyes, yelled Jenny's name, listened, yelled again. Without letup. Until all of them were hoarse.

"She'll fight that current a long time!" Simon shouted once. "She's got stamina, that girl does!"

Pride for his beloved flared in Tom. Then a fist seemed to crash into his gut. And he knew: Jenny, his Jenny, hadn't lowered herself into the warm Gulf Stream for a dip as that dangling ship's ladder suggested. She'd been thrown overboard to die.

There was no time now to figure out who had done it or why. Time existed only to be used to find her. To find her alive and swimming.

The launch bobbed on and on, the searchlight beam dancing on the rough water. The men peered in every direction, calling Jenny's name. David wanted to change course again, but Tom protested, and they held their course.

No matter what these amateur seamen claimed, Tom had a gut feeling that Jenny was right out there somewhere, that they'd get to her.

Time—that was the important thing. If he had all he needed, he'd search every moving inch of this crazy Gulf Stream. But he had only a measure of time. And if there were sharks— He yanked his mind off that thought, leaned out, probed the waters again with his aching eyes.

"Jenny!" he cried. *"Jenny!"*

All of a sudden, in the darkness at the end of the searchlight's beam, Tom saw a flash of what might be an arm. "Keep going!" he bellowed. "Dead ahead!"

He saw the flash again. *As in a dream—a miracle.* His heart leaped.

The searchlight beam was closer now, and he saw a hand at the end of the arm. The launch speeded closer, and he caught a glimpse of face.

"There she is!" he yelled. "Cut your speed! Ease up to her!"

He dove into the water, swam powerfully to her, got one arm under her, bearing her up. She tried to pull away, tried to swim. He opened his mouth to yell at her, and a wave came and he swallowed salt water. He hung onto her, and when they were in the trough, began pulling her with him, toward the launch.

She was still struggling to swim alone, not knowing what she was doing. He couldn't see her; the searchlight blinded him. But if he hadn't know it was Jenny, he'd know now. Who else would be fighting him off, even when she was at the point of drowning!

"It's me!" he choked. "Tom! We've got a boat!"

Immediately she stopped resisting, let him tow her to the launch, kicking her feet in the water to help.

He hoisted her, and the crewman pulled, landing her in the stern. Tom scrambled in, the crewman giving him a hand.

Jenny was lying, spent, chest heaving. He lifted her into his arms. She was shaking. He held her tighter, wrapped his strong arms protectively about her. Drenched, they clung together, letting the cold morning breeze envelop them.

"Back to the yacht, David," Tom ordered. "She's got to get into a hot bath, have some soup——"

"There'll be no need for any of that," said Simon. "She's not going aboard *The Louisa* again. Nor are you, March, or you, Crewman Turcotte."

Tom jerked to face Simon.

Simon had a small handgun trained on them.

He was braced against the side of the rolling boat, both hands steadying the weapon, its ugly little muzzle never wavering.

David, at the wheel, was grinning.

46

Even in her semiconscious state, Jenny recognized Simon's voice, felt Tom go rigid, ready to attack.

"I'd not recommend it!" Simon snapped. "This may look like a toy, but believe me, it isn't!"

Jenny was coming to fast, coughing. Tom's arms were still about her but she felt them stiffen. His eyes were on that gun. He was going to hurl himself across the boat, and if he did that—

"No!" she gasped. "Oh please, no!"

She felt some of the tension go out of him, struggled to sit up, and he helped her, but never took his eyes off Simon. The launch rocked and pitched, but Simon held the gun steady on them. David cut the motor. A wave rolled at them, under them, bearing them up, and still Simon had control.

Jenny, sitting against Tom, managed to keep her balance. She was bleeding. Her bikini was soaked with blood, and there was pain, but she realized these things only faraway in her mind. It was Tom she had to think of now. Tom and that wild lunge he planned to make. She stared at the pistol, so steady in Simon's hand, and wondered that he could keep it so with the boat pitching and dipping.

"Keep your arms around her, March," David ordered.

Tom sat very still.

Simon laughed. "That's it! Hold her! When you go overboard, you'll be together. But not alone. Turcotte will join you."

The crewman's face was a blur of fear.

"You're insane," Tom gritted, his eyes still on the gun.

"Like geniuses we're insane!" David snapped in a new, hard voice.

"Turcotte," Simon ordered. "Get closer to them!"

The crewman moved closer. He, like Tom, was tense, ready to spring. But the murderous little mouth of the gun pointed at them, Simon's finger on the trigger, and they waited.

Another wave rolled under them. The launch, wheel unmanned, spun in the current, and was swept northward along the wide trough. The revolver kept pointing at them.

"You pull a stunt like this," Tom shouted over the roar of the water, "and want us to believe you're not crazy?"

"This weapon is a sign of intelligence and clever planning," Simon clipped. "I notice *you* don't have one!"

Jenny tensed. She realized that Tom was playing for time, waiting for the right moment to leap for that gun. He really meant to go for a loaded revolver pointed right at him! She shivered. Her body filled with pain.

"You, March," Simon said almost conversationally, "have only yourself to blame for this. You had to come to Florida, stick your nose into Townsend affairs. And, Jenny, had you only chosen to marry a Townsend—any Townsend—the way Grandfather wanted, none of this would have happened. Then the family millions would have remained in the family, and we wouldn't have had to devise this little plan of ours."

"You . . . followed a plan?" Tom asked. "I don't see what it was. Doubt if one existed."

Simon gave a chopping laugh.

"It was too subtle for you, March."

"Since you've got us at gunpoint, how about letting us in on it?" Tom asked, body taut against Jenny. Slowly, his arms loosened and Jenny knew—fearing it—that he was ready to jump Simon when the time came.

If it came.

If Turcotte helped, and please God he would help.

"That way," Tom continued goading, "we'll know what clever things you did that I was too thick to see at the time."

"Or to understand, if you had." Simon nodded at David. "The first move was yours. Tell them."

"I was standing by Romantic Sally's gate that time Jenny got bit," David said. "I could have kept her from going in, but I didn't. I knew either Simon or myself would 'save her,' get her gratitude, make her inclined to trust one of us Townsends, marry one, and so protect all those millions."

"It was the same with the swimming accident," Simon put in proudly. "David held Jenny underwater. I 'rescued' her."

"She began to trust us," added Simon.

"The tack in the dog's foot," David went on. "I put it where she'd step on it."

"But *why?*" gasped Jenny.

"We didn't like March hanging around. It was plain you were attracted to each other. It wouldn't do for you to marry him instead of one of us. So we started by trying to discredit him in your eyes. I loosened the lug on his car wheel for that same purpose. To make him seem inept and careless."

"You didn't!" breathed Jenny.

"Indeed we did," Simon boasted, "and more. The fight at the airport and the attack in the penthouse—I planned those. Paid Perez good cash to stage them. Didn't even approach the other fellow, Max Vernon. He's too square to be bought, too 'honorable.' "

"You thought Jenny would blame all that trouble on me," Tom said. "You thought she'd hold all those things against me and I'd not have a chance with her."

"Precisely. When that didn't work and Jenny wouldn't marry me under any circumstances, David and I really got our heads together. We arranged to pay Perez one thousand dollars to see that you ended up dead, March. He tried to do the job by setting fire to the shed after hitting you with a club."

Now Tom's arms were no longer around Jenny. So unobtrusively had he moved them that she'd been totally unaware. It was only a matter of moments, she knew, before he'd strike.

"I paid Perez his thousand," Simon bragged on, "to keep him on my side in both things—the migrant negotiations and getting rid of you, March. Then we found out you'd made Jenny pregnant, and *still* she wouldn't marry one of us, so—"

"This, tonight, was *my* idea!" David cut in proudly. "I told Simon that Jenny had to die, her ten million had to be divided among us! She made it easy for us by taking a late night swim. Together, we threw her into the Gulf Stream."

"Now do you comprehend, March?" asked Simon. "Do you see that we're forced to kill both of you?"

He stabbed a look at Jenny. "It's your own fault. For losing your head over March. For showing it in every word you spoke, every look you gave him, every motion you made! Getting pregnant by him!"

"He's worth *a hundred* of you!" Jenny cried, her voice still shaky.

"None of that matters now," chortled David. "You're going into the water, both of you, either of your own accord or with a bullet. You too, Turcotte. What we don't need is a witness."

Laughing, he grabbed the wheel of the plunging boat, steadied it somewhat.

"You'll never get away with it," gritted Tom. "You won't be able to explain losing three people."

"Two people," Simon corrected. "The authorities will never know we found Jenny. We'll explain how you saw a flash in the water and, believing it was Jenny, went overboard, Turcotte following. Only, we'll explain, it wasn't Jenny, but a school of sharks. And they got you both. David and I will be inconsolable. The papers and television will be filled with the tragic news of your deaths."

"And Rolf?" cried Jenny, moaning with pain. "What of him?"

"He knows nothing of what's happened," David crowed. "He's innocent. He wouldn't have gone along with us on this, but he'll get a third of your money without ever knowing he has us to thank for it!"

Another wave rolled under the launch, lifting it.

Tom didn't wait.

Even as Simon's gun wavered for the first time, Tom hurtled across and into him. The gun went off in Simon's upflung hand, then flew into the water.

At the instant Tom crashed into Simon, Turcotte threw himself at David. The four of them grappled, staggering and falling from the pitching, plunging motion of the launch.

Simon and Tom, bodies entangled, leaned dangerously close to the edge, then fell overboard. Turcotte and David continued to fight in the launch.

Jenny leaned over the edge, trying to see. Tom and Simon were still fighting. And oh, dear God, it looked as if they were choking each other to death!

She heard a body fall inside the launch. It struck a seat, and she knew that it lay still as the other man, whoever it was, plummeted into the water.

She couldn't bear to look. If it was Turcotte in the boat, then it was all over. Tom, strong as he was, would never be able to fight off both Simon and David. She burned to know, had to know, but couldn't make herself look at the still figure in the boat to see who it was.

It was only when Turcotte, then Tom, hoisted themselves aboard, that she knew. She glanced then—one fleeting look—to make certain for Tom's sake, for his safety.

David. David was in the boat, unconscious.

Then Tom had her in his arms again, his safe and

tender arms. His breath was heaving; her whole upper body rose and fell against his chest.

Turcotte made for the wheel of the launch, tried to control the tossing vessel. At the same time, he was looking at David.

"He's knocked out," he reported. "Not badly hurt." He let go of the wheel, quickly tied David with rope, grabbed the wheel again, fought the current.

"Simon?" Jenny asked, voice small against the surge of the Stream, the noise of Tom's breathing.

"Drowned. Dead. Choked. Gone."

"Who—?"

"I did. Or Turcotte."

"Both of us," Turcotte said. "What's good is that it's done. And I'm alive to bear witness against this other rat."

"We'd have brought his body," Tom said. "But in his case—well, there really was a shark."

Jenny felt herself go limp against Tom, felt herself sink into utter, blessed, peaceful blackness.

The hospital room was bathed in sunlight. An enormous vase of crimson roses stood on the windowsill. Jenny awoke to find a nurse bending over her. That was why she was certain she was in the hospital.

She felt so tired—drained. The pain was gone though, and she could breathe without difficulty.

Off to one side of the big room were people. Weakly she looked over at them, identifying one after another.

Madeline. Rolf. Oliver. Tom.

She held out her arms to Tom, the nurse gave way, and he was there, lifting, holding her against his wide, wonderful chest.

"The doctor just left," he murmured. "You're going to be all right. But we lost the baby, darling."

Jenny nodded, began to weep. Sobs shook her entire body. She was so terribly weak. Still, she had to talk, had to let Tom know how things were, in her heart.

"All my f-fault!" she managed to gasp. "Not you— never you! If—I hadn't been s-so stubborn—so b-blind—"

Her sobs increased as she thought of the terrible wrong she had done this man, the unjust thoughts she'd had of him.

He cradled her with one arm, pressed a finger to her lips with his free hand. "I was the stubborn one," he insisted. "Bossing you around, telling you what to do. With never a hint of tenderness or consideration. Nothing but plain old Missoura bulldozing!"

"It wasn't l-like that!" she gulped tearfully. "You were only f-firm and m-masterful! You should have shaken me until my teeth rattled!"

"Never an honest word of love did I utter!" he reproached himself, holding her gently, yet close to his chest. "Well, you're going to hear it now, and so are these other folks! I love you, Jenny Townsend, love you beyond love, and I will not—I repeat, I will not, even if I'm still bulldozing—live without you!" His intense face went stern, eyes searching into hers. "If only you'll have me! Marry me."

"I will," she whispered, "oh, I will, darling."

She turned her head a bit, gazed into his wonderful eyes. All of tenderness lay there, all of adoration. She drew a quivering breath.

"Jenny Townsend," he said, loud and clear, "I asked you something and you only whispered an answer. I want the others in this room to hear what it was, want to shout it from the rooftops. I love you. I want you to marry me, and fast. Don't be shy, love. We love each other, have from the start. Isn't that true, my darling?"

She couldn't tear her gaze from his. Aware of the others, aware too, that from this moment forward anything that Tom March wanted her to do was what she herself wanted, she nodded. Then, weak though she was, her words came clearly for all to hear. "All true, Tom. I love you, and I'll marry you today, right in the hospital!"

"And you'll live in Missoura as my wife, help me raise a family on the farm?"

"Of course, darling," she said, for all to hear. "And the bigger the family the better!"

He held her to him, stroking her hair, kissing it, and she'd never felt as protected, as safe, had never known that love could be so strong, so complete. She nestled in his arms, wrapped in contentment.

He spoke again, gently. "Darling, you need to know what's happened. Then you can put it behind you, never give it another thought."

She stirred, but only to stay close, close in his arms.

"Simon and David confessed in the boat," he reminded. "You heard all that. Remember, darling?"

She moved her head in a tiny nod. Then, remembering the terror and the pain she'd suffered in the Gulf Stream, in the boat, fresh tears wet her cheeks. Tom stroked them away, kissed one cheek, then the other. He kissed her lips, and the kiss was salty with her tears.

"What will happen now?" she asked.

"The police know all. Turcotte and I have been cleared—the police believe we killed—if we killed—in self-defense. David has been taken into custody, and is being charged with attempted murder."

"W-what will happen to him?"

"Whatever the law decides."

"The money. I want to give it all to Rolf."

"That's kind, Jenny. But I won't—can't—accept it," Rolf said quietly.

"You'll have to keep it, darling," Tom murmured. "It doesn't matter now."

"The migrants . . . they can have it."

"Rolf and I talked in Freeport. Came up with a solution the workers will accept. Vans—campers—some of those sleep as many as eight. They can park at the modern campsites you'll build. Max Vernon is honest and fair and dependable. He'll lead the migrants to see that this is the sensible solution. The Townsend banks will lend the pickers money for the campers—regular mortgages—and wherever they go, they'll have a home. As soon as you're strong, we'll have a meeting to tie up all the loose ends. You can vote for or against."

She could hear the deep and steady pumping of his

heart under her cheek. "I vote 'for,' " she whispered. "It's . . . the perfect solution."

He held her tenderly, safely. "We'll get married right in the hospital," he said gently. "Okay?"

" . . . kay," she croaked as loudly as she could, and glimpsed his homely-beautiful grin as she closed her eyes. She felt herself dropping into blessed sleep, safe in the arms of her man.

THE BEST OF ROMANCE
FROM WARNER BOOKS

NO GENTLE LOVE
by Rebecca Brandewyne   (91-183, $2.50)

She was a beauty, besieged by passion, sailing from Regency England to mysterious Macao on an uncharted voyage to love. She was also unready to accept the love in her heart for the domineering, demanding man whose desire for her was jealous, violent, engulfing, but enduring.

RAKEHELL DYNASTY
by Michael William Scott   (95-201, $2.75)

From the first time he saw the ship in full sail like a winged bird against the sky, Jonanthan Rakehell knew the clipper held his destiny. This is his story of conquering the seas, challenging the world and discovering love in his dream—the clipper. His is the bold, sweeping, passionate story of a great New England shipping family caught up in the winds of change and of the one man who would dare sail his ship to the frightening, beautiful land of China.

HER SHINING SPLENDOR
Valerie Sherwood   (85-487, $2.75)

Lenore and Lorena: their names are so alike, yet their beauties so dissimilar. Yet each is bound to reap the rewards and the troubles of love. Here are the adventures of the exquisite Lenore and her beauteous daughter Lorena, each setting out upon her own odyssey of love, adventure, and fame.